Praise for
by P. J.

"Lush, descriptive writing is the hallmark of P. J. Alderman's novel *Haunting Jordan*."

—DIANE MOTT DAVIDSON

"Blending a small measure of romance and a healthy dose of comedy into the suspenseful plot kept me up all night while I secretly attempted to figure out the 'who-dun-it.' *Haunting Jordan* is a breath of fresh air!"

—*Suspense Magazine*

"A fun read for the paranormal mystery fan, with lots of action and well-drawn characters you will enjoy meeting."

—*New Mystery Reader*

"This book is wonderful. I got so wrapped up in it that I couldn't put it down. Forget doing anything around the house or even going to sleep, I had to know who the murderers were."

—Night Owl Romance

. . . and for her RITA-nominated debut, **A Killing Tide**

"Tense and riveting, Alderman's debut delivers."

—COLLEEN THOMPSON

By P. J. Alderman

Ghost Ship

Haunting Jordan

A Killing Tide

Ghost Ship

A Port Chatham Mystery

P. J. Alderman

BANTAM BOOKS
NEW YORK

A Bantam Books Mass Market Original

Copyright © 2011 by P. J. Alderman

Published in the United States by Bantam Books, an imprint of The Random House Publishing Group, a division of Random House, Inc., New York.

BANTAM BOOKS and the rooster colophon are registered trademarks of Random House, Inc.

978-0-553-59211-5

Cover design: Marietta Anastassatos
Cover illustration: Fernando Juarez

Printed in the United States of America

www.bantamdell.com

2 4 6 8 9 7 5 3 1

To my sister Julie

Ghost Ship

A False Light

HE was a damned fool.

Michael Seavey braced a boot against the taffrail at the stern of the *Henrietta Dale*. As he held a match to his cigar, the hand he cupped around the flame clenched into a fist.

The deck rolled as the clipper ship sliced through swells, leaving washes of luminous phosphorescence in its wake. An invisible salt-laden mist turned his silk cravat uncomfortably damp. Shivering, he tossed the match into the sea and tugged the lapels of his coat closed.

They ran on a broad reach, a chill, penetrating breeze cutting across the stern from the west. He'd chosen the night of the new moon for the *Henrietta Dale*'s maiden voyage, confident the lack of natural light would obscure their presence from Customs revenue cutters. Setting sail out of Victoria, British Columbia, and bound for Port Chatham, Washington, his sloop carried precious cargo. Its spoils would provide him with the necessary currency to once again rule the waterfront.

Yet imprudently, he'd risked it all to save a fifteen-year-old girl who should have meant less than nothing to him.

"Let me live with you," she'd pleaded two days past, standing in his hotel suite in her torn dress, her slender body trembling, her blue eyes awash in tears. "I'd make you happy—you won't regret your decision."

"It would be as if I'd slept with a ghost," he'd replied with atypical gentleness. And God help him, he'd uttered none other than the truth.

His refusal should have signaled an end to their liaison. But ensnared by the knowledge that his own actions had endangered the girl, he'd felt compelled to bring her under his protection. And thus he'd exposed a fatal weakness to his enemies.

He shifted his feet, impatient. What was done could not be undone, no matter the consequences. Had Hattie still been alive, she would've expected no less of him.

The ship heeled hard to port on a gust of wind, its studding sails topping the waves, seawater sluicing off its creaking booms. He grabbed the rail to maintain his balance. Ten feet forward, the ship's captain stood, feet braced wide, a sharp eye trained on the helmsman. Next to the forecastle, the current watch gathered, smoking pipes and talking quietly, their faces reflecting the green glow of the starboard lamp. None seemed concerned by the worsening seas. Michael relaxed once again.

Despite his relative inexperience at sea, he'd insisted on being aboard for the launch of his new business venture. So little interested him these days, yet he'd felt certain the thrill of the crossing—and of outfoxing the Customs agents—would stir his blood.

Even this initial voyage promised to prove quite profitable. The tins of opium concealed in secret compartments would net more than he made in a fortnight "procuring" crews from the logging camps for shipping masters. Rumors of his success would surely put an end to the recent erosion of his reputation.

And thus perhaps put an end to this cursed malaise he couldn't seem to shake.

His jaw clenched, causing him to bite through the cigar's wrapper. Even now, his enemies whispered that he'd gone soft. Utter nonsense, of course; he'd always bested them by whatever means necessary. Failure had never been an option.

It mattered not that he continued to be plagued by the memory of the only woman to have brought him to his knees. A woman dead these three long years. God *damn* her.

"Our current speed, Captain Williams," he snapped.

"Roughly twelve knots, sir." Williams was a short, stout man with a weathered countenance, and his overcoat strained across his barrel chest. "By dead reckoning, our remaining time to Port Chatham should be just over an hour and a half."

Michael watched Williams triangulate their position using the lights of New Dungeness and Point Wilson, then give the order to correct their heading. Experienced yet ruthless, loyal yet greedy, the captain was a resource Michael could exploit if necessary. "And how is she handling?"

"She moves through the water without effort, sir! You did right by her during the restoration." Williams paused long enough in his calculations to scowl. "I've never taken to those damned merchant steamers. Have you never smelled nothing so sweet as this air? Who would want to foul *that* with coal smoke, I ask you?"

"I doubt a steamer's ambience would be palatable to my clientele," Michael agreed wryly. Under the best of circumstances, opium smokers had tender stomachs.

Yet another pungent whiff of the stuff, smelling faintly of roasted peanuts, wafted through the portico of the great cabin he'd converted into a luxurious smoking den. Thank God he had the aroma of his cigar to mask such malodorous fumes. Though he'd been tempted by a great many vices in his lifetime, the heavenly demon held no allure. He smiled briefly. Fortunately, the same could not be said for Port Chatham's social elite, who promised to line his coffers quite nicely through their love affair with the stuff.

His passengers this night were few but nonetheless prestigious: Jesse Canby, the dissolute son of Port Chatham's self-acknowledged society matron Eleanor Canby; a town councilman determined to hide his addiction from his unforgiving electorate; and two eminently bribable, wealthy businessmen. Plus, of course, Michael's beautiful young charge, serving as chef and assisting in the preparation and smoking of the pipes.

The ship abruptly dropped in the water, its forward momentum faltering. Sails flapped, thousands of yards of canvas and rigging slamming in deafening cacophony against the masts.

Michael flinched. "Good Christ, man! Do something about this infernal racket!"

Williams strode swiftly along the port side, hands clasped at his back, peering into the distance. He shook his head. "We're experiencing variable winds, sir. You'd have better luck requesting God to intervene than to ask the impossible of me."

"Then adjust your heading, dammit!" Seavey snapped. "The passengers enjoying the excesses on offer in my dining salon will be ill within minutes."

"And run us upon the rocks? I'm having enough trouble—*dear God!*" Abandoning all manner of poise, Williams raced to the bow. "*Lay aloft and furl fore and main courses!*"

The first mate bellowed orders, and men leapt to, scrambling up masts.

What the devil? Michael straightened, tossing his cigar into the water.

Williams clutched the railing, bending low and staring down. He reared up. "*Let go port anchor!*"

Uneasy, Michael pushed away from the taffrail just as the *Henrietta Dale* gave a tremendous, grinding jolt, slamming him to the deck.

From below, a woman screamed. The crack of the mizzenmast giving way rent the air like a gunshot. Michael glanced skyward as crew fell from yardarms like rag dolls.

Rigging and canvas rained down, obliterating his vision. Cursing, he shoved with both hands, managing to rise to his knees.

He was tossing aside lines and sheets when a massive weight crushed him, turning his world black.

Chapter 1

Dungeness Spit, Admiralty Inlet, Washington
July, present day

CALL me crazy, to use an imprecise term," Jordan Marsh huffed as she trudged down the beach, "but you know when your surgeon cleared you to start physical therapy? I don't think she had in mind a ten-mile forced march through sand."

"Is that a whine I'm detecting in your voice?" Darcy Moran's pace showed no sign of moderating. As she was built like a modern-day Valkyrie with the inseam of a pro basketball player, Jordan had to take three steps to Darcy's two.

They'd planned the hike the night before while comfortably ensconced at their favorite pub, listening to live jazz. Darcy had waxed poetic about the trek along the west side of Dungeness Spit. She'd made it sound as if Jordan would emerge from the experience renewed in both body and spirit.

Five miles in length, the spit—a driftwood-strewn, narrow stretch of windswept sand and intrepid beach flora—hooked away from the northern edge of the Olympic

Peninsula, into the busy shipping lanes of Admiralty Inlet. Their destination was the area's oldest lighthouse, built in 1857. They had the hike to themselves; Jordan hadn't seen another soul since they'd left the parking lot.

The lack of fellow enthusiasts should have been a sign.

"We have just three hours to reach the lighthouse and make the return trip before the tide comes back in," Darcy pointed out as she attacked the beach with militaristic zeal. Unlike Jordan, she'd dressed practically for the day in a silk turtleneck and Gore-Tex jacket, jeans, and rugged hiking boots. "Do you want to crawl over those stacks of logs, or stroll through this nice, soft sand?"

"*Stroll?*"

"Besides," Darcy continued, showing no sign she'd caught Jordan's sarcasm, "I thought you said you wanted to lose a few pounds."

"Well, sure, but I hadn't envisioned losing them all in one day."

Their hike was along a gently sloping beach that—by mile two—had threatened to permanently shorten Jordan's uphill leg. She already had blisters, and her calf muscles were screaming. Since mile three, she'd had a clear vision of tomorrow's front-page newspaper headline:

Port Chatham Resident Rescued from Certain Death

Jordan Marsh, the most recent owner of historic Longren House, was found unconscious this morning on Dungeness Spit. She was said to be suffering from advanced hypothermia.

Neighbors expressed shock, though some privately

admitted she probably deserved to suffer, since she'd been responsible for the recent wounding of their beloved police chief, Darcy Moran . . .

"This is payback, isn't it?" Jordan demanded. "You still blame me. Not, mind you, that I blame you for blaming me—*I* blame me."

Darcy stopped, hands planted on her hips. "You had no way of knowing that the man had violent tendencies. A guy who has that many screws loose—"

"Another phrase reviled by the psychiatric community . . ."

"—whatever. A *narcissistic stalker* can turn on you in the blink of an eye."

"Still, as a psychologist I should've recognized the signs. I didn't, and you paid the price." Jordan doubted many people could claim the distinction—only a few days after arriving in town—of causing the near-mortal shooting of a police chief. One, no less, who had gone out of her way to make Jordan feel welcome, offering both friendship and support.

Darcy heaved a sigh. "Look, I knew the guy was acting weird as hell, but even with all my law enforcement training, I didn't put it together, either. I see no reason why you should shoulder all the blame."

"Hmph." Jordan waved off a pesky black fly suicidally attracted to the fragrance of her shampoo. "So explain to me again why we're out here? We could have hiked North Beach, or taken any number of nice walks closer to town. Locations," she emphasized, "that don't require calling out a medevac helicopter when you collapse at my feet."

Darcy shrugged and continued down the beach. "Chalk it up to having to play the invalid for the last several weeks. I wanted to get out of town, and I like to set challenging personal goals."

"Right." Jordan shook her head and slogged through more sand.

A hundred yards out, a seagull dipped in and out of a layer of fog floating just above the water's surface. They were surrounded by three mountain ranges—the rugged peaks of the Olympics to the southwest, the British Columbia Coastal Range to the north, and to the east, the more gently formed, tree-covered Cascades, over which towered Mount Baker's giant snow-covered cone.

Other than the occasional cry of an eagle perched on a piece of driftwood, the only sound was of the waves lapping soporifically against the sand. Jordan indulged in a moment's fantasy of lying down in the sun and taking a nice, long nap.

Tragically, Darcy's voice intruded. "A hike such as this requires discipline, planning, and timing." She was once again warming to her favorite subject since The Incident: extreme goal-setting plus rigid control of every minute of every day. Jordan figured Darcy would eventually adjust, but it was a toss-up whether Jordan would expire before that blessed day arrived. "Discipline," Darcy continued in a lecturing tone, "that is sadly lacking in your own life."

"Did I mention that I read an article just the other day about the dangers of Americans' obsession with discipline? Europeans focus on living life to the fullest, giving greater priority to such indulgences as relaxation and fine foods and wines. Go figure, but they have longer life spans than we do."

Darcy's only response was a loud snort.

"Besides which," Jordan persisted, "Malachi and I walk every day."

"Yeah, you walk to that French restaurant three blocks over to have breakfast."

"Hey. Don't knock it—that restaurant has *great* espresso and *The New York Times*. Neither of us sees the point in extreme exercise."

"As far as I can tell, that mutt of yours doesn't see the point in anything except a nap in the sun."

Precisely. Smart dog.

As Darcy picked up the pace, Jordan lagged farther behind. "And do not malign Malachi," she said in a raised voice. "He's been a great comfort to me."

The stray dog had adopted her immediately upon her arrival, supporting her during a less-than-smooth transition. Within days, she'd had to deal with a century-old murder, an embittered LAPD detective intent on arresting her for killing her husband, and, well, *other* things. Things she'd given herself permission to deny.

Catching movement out of the corner of her eye, she turned, her footsteps faltering. A few yards offshore, a man rose up from the ocean, wearing a loosely fitted, rubberized gray suit that draped in folds over his rugged build. Seawater poured off him as he sloshed through the waves and onto the beach, removing a metal, helmetlike mask. In his other hand, he held an ornately decorated tin box.

He grinned, revealing crooked teeth. "Nice day for a dive!"

"I guess." Jordan was perplexed. "Isn't the water awfully cold around here, though?"

"Not if you don't stay down long," he replied cheerfully. Nodding politely, he stomped down the beach in his flippers, heading toward the peninsula.

"Hey," Darcy called out, looking irritated as she turned back. "Make more of an effort, will you?"

"I was just . . ." Jordan's gaze slid from the retreating figure of the diver to Darcy, who gave no indication that she'd seen him. "Never mind." Jordan broke into a jog.

"So how's it going with the ghosts?" Darcy asked uncannily as Jordan caught up.

"I don't want to talk about them." Or the fact that seeing them made her question her own sanity.

So far, Jordan hadn't discovered anyone else who could see and converse with *both* communities in Port Chatham—one human, the other spectral. And neither community seemed to be overly concerned that she possessed such "special powers."

"Are Hattie and Charlotte still giving you trouble?"

"Assuming they exist, yes."

That earned her an assessing glance. "I thought we were beyond this. You're regressing."

"I'm *not* regressing," Jordan objected grimly. "I've just given myself permission to deny that they necessarily exist."

"Uh-huh." Darcy shook her head. "You know I'd kill to be in your shoes. It's damn hard to do my job well when I can't see or communicate with half the town's residents."

Jordan did a mental eye roll. Her corporeal friends, whose powers of perception only included a general sense of the ghosts' presence, professed to be extremely envious of Jordan's abilities, not understanding the unique challenge they presented. After all, outside of walking up and rudely poking the person in question to see whether he or she was solid, she had no surefire method of differentiating ghosts from humans.

"It's bad enough that I sleep in a bedroom where a century-old murder occurred," she grumbled. "I didn't sign up for having permanent roommates. I solved Hattie's murder; therefore, it's only reasonable to expect that they all politely vacate the premises."

"'All'?" Darcy looked intrigued. "Have *more* shown up?"

"Just Frank, so far," Jordan replied, referring to the ghost of Frank Lewis, the man who had hanged for Hattie's murder in 1890. "He and Hattie are attempting to *requite* their unrequited, century-old love." Jordan picked her way around a gelatinous substance on the sand that looked like it might be the remains of a jellyfish. "I walk into a room, and they're *cooing* at each other. I turn a corner, and they're in a *clinch*."

Darcy shot her a wary glance. "You haven't been reading romance novels, have you?"

"Not that I couldn't use the escapism right now, but no. 'Clinch' just seems appropriate when describing the mating habits of ghosts."

"So we're talking *spectral sex*?" Darcy grinned. "Cool."

"*Not* cool," Jordan insisted. "What about Charlotte? She's too young and impressionable to be exposed to such things."

"We *are* talking about the ghost who was a prostitute

before she died in the 1890s, right? I suspect Charlotte knows more about sex than you do."

"Well, it's not the 1890s anymore. And I've got a home renovation to manage—I don't have the time to chaperone an impressionable young ghost."

Darcy shook her head and picked up the pace again. "I heard Tom wants to talk to you about the work on the house."

Tom Greeley, one of Port Chatham's amateur historians, specialized in custom paintwork for historic homes. He'd been gracious enough to volunteer to help Jordan come up with a restoration plan for Longren House. After days of crawling around the attic and the basement, he'd left a hastily scribbled note requesting a meeting with her. The note was still lying on the kitchen table, intimidating her.

Okay, so her initial fantasy of slap-on-some-paint-and-new-wallpaper had died a quiet death around the time she'd discovered that the gorgeous wisteria vine on the wall of the library had grown straight through the siding and into the attic. But dammit, she *loved* Longren House. It represented the one truly impulsive decision she'd ever made. Well, maybe not the *only* impulsive decision—that was stretching the truth a bit. But she'd taken one look at the house and fallen head over heels, instantly envisioning the cozy home she'd never had. She'd be damned if she'd let a few repairs ruin that dream.

And frankly, it was easier to hold on to the dream if she didn't know the full extent of the necessary repairs. In fact, she was considering submitting an article to a prestigious psychology journal, describing the underrated benefits of a well-orchestrated strategy of personal denial. Life really was wonderful if one simply refused to acknowledge the impending train wrecks.

"Earth to Jordan? Hello?"

She realized Darcy was still waiting for her response. "Tom probably just wants to talk to me about bidding out the work," she said, hoping for reassurance.

"I doubt it. We can refer you to the right people."

"But—"

"This isn't L.A., it's a small town. For most jobs, there will only be one or two people who do that type of work. We know who you can trust, and who you can't." Darcy stopped abruptly, causing Jordan to plow into her. "Okay. See?" She pointed to a tiny white speck in the distance. "That's New Dungeness Lighthouse."

Jordan righted herself and squinted at the landscape beyond the end of Darcy's finger. "*Clear down there?* We still have *that* far to go?"

"It's only another mile or so. Piece of cake."

Jordan groaned. "We could turn around right now, head back to the pub, and place our order for a truly *sublime* Shiraz." Served up by an equally sublime pub owner, although she was in denial about him as well. "I don't care whether we tour the lighthouse—we could come back another day."

She could've sworn Darcy looked apologetic. "There's a rumor the lighthouse is haunted," Darcy admitted, "and several of us thought you might be able to confirm whether it is."

Jordan narrowed her gaze. "You're using me as some sort of *ghost detector?*"

"Well, yeah. We started talking about it last night after you and Malachi left the pub, and one thing led to another. We've got a pool going on whether you'll see the wife of the original lighthouse keeper, who is rumored to haunt the grounds. The wife, not the lighthouse keeper," Darcy clarified. "After all, you're in a unique position to confirm the veracity of all those ghost stories we've heard over the years—"

"*Oh. My. God.*" Jordan stared past Darcy's shoulder.

"Look," Darcy said, sounding uncomfortable. "If it bothers you that much—"

"No, no!" Jordan tugged on her sleeve to turn her toward the surf. "That's not what I think it is, is it? *Is it?*"

Darcy peered in the direction Jordan pointed. "Son of a bitch!" Jogging over, she knelt next to a black, rubber-encased body floating facedown in the shallows.

When Jordan started to follow, Darcy put up a hand. "Stay back." She felt for a pulse, then turned over the body, pulling back the hood of the dry suit.

Jordan pressed fingers against her mouth. She would have recognized that bleached-blond buzz cut anywhere. "That's . . ."

"Yeah."

Holt Stillwell. Port Chatham's most notorious womanizer, descended from a long line of infamous criminals, not the least of whom was the Pacific Northwest's most ruthless shanghaier of the late nineteenth century, Michael Seavey.

Holt's eyes were closed, and his skin had a weirdly translucent pallor.

He also had a bullet hole in the center of his forehead.

Chapter 2

JORDAN didn't have any experience with dead people, other than from the night she'd had to identify her husband's remains. Her former patients, no matter how damaged when they came to her, had always been alive and kicking.

She couldn't seem to quit looking at Holt's face. Swallowing rapidly, she concentrated hard on not losing her lunch.

"You're not planning to hurl all over the crime scene, are you?" Darcy asked absently as she studied the area around Holt's body.

"Of course not."

Darcy pulled out her cellphone, flipping it open and sweeping it in an arc. "*Dammit!* No signal." Leaning down, she braced her hands on her knees and stared at the sand. "Okay, it looks like the tide has washed away any footprints, so I guess it doesn't really matter. Get over here and help me."

"What're we doing, exactly?" Jordan asked warily.

"We're moving him above the tide line. I can't stand in

forty-degree water, holding a corpse in place until the crime-scene techs get here."

That made sense. Rubbing her palms on her jeans, Jordan edged forward.

With her grappling Holt's bare ankles and Darcy at his shoulders, they managed to drag him out of the shallow surf and up the beach. They stood over the body, catching their breath. Jordan's running shoes were now filled with sand and salt water, and her blisters were stinging big-time.

"The medical examiner is going to kill me for messing with the position of the body," Darcy muttered, as if talking to herself, "but it couldn't be helped."

Holt's torso was propped against a giant log, his head lolling to one side. There was no way Jordan was sitting down on that log to empty out her shoes. And she *really* didn't want to stand there, staring at the nasty little hole in his forehead.

"What do you suppose he was doing way out here?" she asked, to distract herself.

"Good question. As far as I know, Holt wasn't a dive enthusiast. And even if he was, there are far more interesting dives closer to town or off the west side of Vancouver Island."

Jordan raised a brow.

"Old shipwrecks and the like," Darcy elaborated.

"Shouldn't he have been with a dive buddy? Don't divers usually swim in pairs, for safety reasons?"

Darcy shrugged. "It's not like Holt ever played by the rules."

"True, but . . ." Jordan thought about the man she'd seen earlier. Had he been real after all? "Maybe the dive buddy *is* the murderer." Maybe she'd just exchanged pleas-antries with a cold-blooded killer. "Holt could've pissed him off, just like he did everyone else, and the guy lost it."

"And shot him with the handgun he just happened to have in a watertight Baggie stowed inside his dive suit."

"Okay, point taken." Not to mention that if it had been the person Jordan had seen, his suit had lacked such con-veniences as pockets. Did some people make their own dive gear? She didn't know; she'd never been interested in the sport. "So what do we do now? Look for the murder weapon?"

"You've been watching *way* too many *CSI* shows. If you'd just shot a guy and dumped him in the water, what would you do with the gun?"

"Well, assuming I have homicidal tendencies *and* I've thought the crime through before committing it, I guess I would've tossed it as far out into the ocean as I could . . . No, wait." Jordan reconsidered. "Unless I'm familiar with the local currents, I'd be worried the tide would wash the gun back onto the beach. And there's no good place to hide it on this spit; you could bury a gun in the sand, but a good metal detector would find it in a heartbeat. I sup-pose you could toss it into the reeds on the protected side, but to be safe, I'd probably carry it back with me, intend-ing to dispose of it somewhere else."

"Exactly," Darcy confirmed. "We'll get teams out here to comb the driftwood and beach grasses, but I doubt we'll find anything. The gun could be anywhere."

Jordan glanced around. "Where's Holt's gear? You know—oxygen tanks, flippers? You don't suppose some-one *robbed* him, do you?"

"I doubt they killed him for his dive equipment," Darcy replied drily, "though a friend of mine regularly complains about the cost. But you're right—it's odd that he doesn't have any."

"Maybe he was killed somewhere else and then dumped here. Maybe the killer was hoping the tide would carry him out to sea before someone noticed him. After all, normally he could've counted on a fair amount of time elapsing before someone would come along and notice. It's not like anyone in their right mind takes this hike *willingly*."

Darcy gave her an exasperated look. "I shouldn't even be discussing this with you."

"Hey." Hadn't she just solved a murder? A hundred-year-old murder, no less?

Darcy checked for a signal again, then swore. "See if you have cellphone coverage; your carrier is different from mine."

Jordan did as she asked, with the same result, then gazed in both directions. No one in sight, not even the other diver, who seemed to have disappeared. She spread her hands and gave Darcy a shrug.

"Okay." Darcy drew a breath, sounding businesslike, "I need to stay with the body, to protect the integrity of the crime scene as much as possible. So I need you to continue on to the lighthouse."

Of course she did.

"You should be able to pick up coverage there," she added. "Call 911 to report the crime."

Jordan hesitated. With the exception of Darcy, she still didn't feel completely comfortable around cops, given her recent experiences with the LAPD. And she'd be calling to report a murder, which might lead to all kinds of speculation. After all, it had only been in the last week or so that the speculation over her husband's murder had finally died down.

Darcy correctly interpreted her expression. "Relax. I can verify what you tell them—they aren't going to jump to any conclusions about your being out here. And put in a call to Jase—have him come pick you up. He can borrow a power boat and bring it to the landing area on the south side of the lighthouse."

The aforementioned sublime pub owner. Damn. Jordan was finding it hard to remain in denial when her hormones rioted every time he came within twenty feet of her.

The implication of what Darcy had said sank in. "You mean we could have taken a *boat* out here?"

"Sure. But then we wouldn't have found Holt, would we?"

Jordan risked another glance and suddenly found herself with a lump in her throat. "I was going to ask him to bid a portion of the paint job," she admitted. "You know, to be fair."

Darcy nodded, and they were silent for a long moment.

"Will you be all right here by yourself?" Jordan asked, noting the lines of strain on the other woman's face.

"I'm tired but fine." She grimaced. "I'd just hoped to leave this type of crime behind when I moved from Minneapolis."

"I could come back and wait with you," Jordan offered. "Not necessary."

"How about I call one of your deputies to come out, then?"

Darcy shook her head. "The local police will respond

to the 911, and I'll have to wrestle them for jurisdiction before I can involve anyone from my force in the investigation."

"*You* want the case?" Jordan was surprised.

"Damn right I do. Whoever killed Holt may live in Port Chatham."

Jordan didn't like the sound of *that*—she preferred any local murders remain in a different century. "Who do you think might have done it?"

"No clue yet. But a good place to start would be any of the women Holt bedded within the last several years. They all walked away mad enough to kill."

* * *

SINCE Jordan was eager to put as much distance as possible between herself and the crime scene, the last mile of the hike went by quickly, wet, sore feet notwithstanding. And Darcy had been right—the minute Jordan reached the edge of the lighthouse grounds, bars popped up on her cellphone. She placed calls, then sat down at a picnic table in the sun, trying not to think about Darcy's wait in much less pleasant circumstances.

The grounds at the end of the spit were landscaped simply—just grass and a two-rail, painted wooden fence that separated the buildings from the surrounding tide flats. The lightstation—a single-story, rectangular building with a pitched roof—stood to one side, its lamp perched atop a circular white brick tower with a conical red metal roof. Across the grass on the other side of the fenced area was the keeper's quarters, a Cape Cod–style bungalow with a covered porch, square, divided-light windows, and shutters. The buildings were painted white to match, with green trim and red metal roofs. Despite their century and a half of exposure to harsh elements, they were well kept. Darcy had explained that a nonprofit association used volunteer lightkeepers to maintain the site, now that the Coast Guard had been forced to slash its budget for lighthouse personnel.

An osprey flew overhead, hunting for its next meal in the tide pools beyond the fence. Other waterfowl Jordan didn't recognize perched on driftwood or floated in the water just offshore. A few people—smart enough to have traveled by boat, she surmised, since she hadn't seen them before now—wandered in and out of the lightstation. If the cameras they held were any indication, they were tourists, not ghosts. A slender woman wearing a loose cotton smock, wooden gardening clogs, and a floppy straw hat was planting daisies and snapdragons along the foundation in front of the keeper's quarters. The scene was quaint and peaceful . . . as long as Jordan didn't factor in Holt's body lying on the beach less than a mile away.

She raised her face to the warm rays and willed herself to think about something—anything—else. With so many recent stressful events in her life, she found herself savoring those short stretches of time when she could close her eyes and feel at peace.

Until a year ago, her days had been . . . well, predictable. She'd had a thriving therapy practice in L.A., based on the tenets of Rational Therapy. Her husband—she'd believed—had been in love with her. But that life had disintegrated into a media frenzy surrounding her very public divorce and Ryland's murder. Though she hadn't admitted as much to Darcy, her reluctance to take on big challenges or set goals was really an attempt to remain calm and centered while she struggled to adjust to her new life.

From a psychological standpoint, figuring out what made a person reach the point of committing murder was fascinating, in a somewhat morbid way. She knew people killed for all kinds of reasons. Her own stalker, for instance, had killed on the spur of the moment, out of an irrational need to eliminate his perceived competition. What had Holt done to cause his assailant to reach such a breaking point? Or had the person simply been mentally unbalanced, and Holt had done nothing to incite the violence?

She hadn't known Holt all that well, except by reputation as a womanizer. Her only real contact with him had been to ask him for access to his family papers, which had included the personal diaries of Michael Seavey, the 1890s shanghaier, who had been at the top of her list of suspects when she'd investigated Hattie's murder.

Though Holt had professed indifference to what she'd discovered about his ancestor, she'd always thought he'd secretly cared a great deal. She suspected a good portion of his "bad boy" reputation had been based on an attempt to live down to the low expectations of the locals, who considered Stilwells to be at best societal misfits, at worst hardened criminals.

Jordan had heard that in recent weeks, Holt had been working on a job at the historic Cosmopolitan Hotel in downtown Port Chatham, which had at one time been owned by Michael Seavey. Rumor had it that the basement of the hotel still had a door leading to the underground tunnels used by the shanghaiers back in the day to hold recalcitrant sailors. Had Holt bid on the job partially because of some sense of connection to his past?

He hadn't been around the pub much lately, which she'd simply chalked up to long work hours. However, she now had to wonder whether he'd been taking trips out here for dives. And if so, why? She found it difficult to believe that he was diving for historic artifacts on sunken wrecks. Even less credible was the idea that he was diving because he enjoyed watching the fish. As far as she knew, the only hobby Holt enjoyed was bedding women—a different one every night.

Jordan squinted at the distant horizon, holding a hand up to shade her eyes. A black speck had appeared, slowly growing in size. Some kind of commercial fishing trawler, by the looks of it. But as she watched, the speck gradually became separate sticks—masts, she realized. A beautiful old sailing ship rose up, coming toward her, almost as if it had emerged from the sea. Logically, she knew it only looked that way because of the curvature of the earth, but still, it was a wonderfully romantic sight.

The ship had three masts, each supporting rows of squared-off sails that appeared to be completely unfurled. It was running before the wind, moving silently through the water, small white waves curling back from its cutwater. The closer the ship came to shore, the more stunning it appeared to be, its bowsprit rising and falling with the swells. Jordan could just make out the carving of a woman whose dress flowed back in soft folds, molding to her feminine figure.

"Gorgeous, isn't she?"

"Hmm?" Jordan turned her head toward the voice.

The gardener stood beside the picnic table. She lifted a hand to point at the ship.

"Oh! Yes." Jordan smiled. "I hear there's quite an active wooden boat society in this area, dedicated to refurbishing old ships."

The woman hesitated. "I suppose that's true, yes." When Jordan gave her a questioning glance, she shrugged. "I don't get to town much."

"That's understandable. If I lived out here, I wouldn't want to leave, either. It's an arduous hike."

"Oh, I'd take a boat," the gardener replied matter-of-factly. "Nevertheless, I find it difficult to leave."

Jordan turned back in the direction of the ship, which was very close now. The wisps of fog in its path near the water's surface dispersed, making the air around the ship seem brighter. "It must be quite expensive to maintain a ship of that size. Are you familiar with this one?"

The woman pursed her lips. "I believe she was originally built in the mid-1800s and used as a passenger ship between China and the West Coast. For a short time until the steamers came along, clipper ships were the fastest vessels on the ocean. They had wonderfully plush accommodations for their passengers."

"You seem to know a lot about them," Jordan noted, curious.

"Yes, it's an interest of mine. The ship ran aground not far from here in 1893," the woman continued. "Most of the crew and passengers died in the wreck."

"How tragic." Jordan winced at the vision of such a

beautiful ship breaking up in the surf, then paused, con-fused. "But she couldn't have been *completely* destroyed if someone restored her, right?"

"No, I guess not," the woman murmured, her gaze dis-tant.

The ship really was coming quite close to shore, almost bearing down on them. "She's not going to repeat history, is she?" Jordan asked worriedly.

The woman gave her an odd look. "She'll turn at the last minute, running along the tip of the spit. I've seen her do this dozens of times. It's beautiful to watch."

The ship did indeed change course and sail past to the north. It was so close that Jordan could hear the clanking of its rigging and the swish of water as it cut through the waves. Someone out of sight, perhaps one of the crew, was singing a song. Jordan caught a phrase here and there in a deep, lilting baritone, but she didn't recognize the tune. It must have been the misty air, or perhaps the angle, but she couldn't quite make out the name painted on the stern. "Do you know what she's called?"

"She was renamed the *Henrietta Dale* by her new owner in 1893." The woman drew on her gardening gloves and began to turn away. "Supposedly, he had her completely rebuilt for the purpose of making trips between here and Canada. Not that he ever had the chance."

"Why's that?"

"She ran aground the night of her maiden voyage." When she looked back over her shoulder, the woman's ex-pression had become grim. "Some say she was deliberately lured onto the rocks."

Chapter 3

ANOTHER hour passed. Jordan soaked up the sun, hoping to offset the chill that had settled deep inside her after learning the story of the *Henrietta Dale*. She'd heard that drowning was a particularly horrible way to die.

There had to have been numerous local shipwrecks over the past 150 years. After all, the area had thriving ports that had harbored substantial criminal activity. And the local waters were known for their dangerous currents, dense fog, and unpredictable weather. But how many of the ships that had gone down had been deliberately sunk? It was a terrible thought.

She watched Coast Guard lifeboats arrive and anchor offshore from Darcy's crime scene. A helicopter hovered for a time. Jordan could just make out the tiny shapes of a number of law-enforcement types working the area, probably gathering evidence and preparing Holt's body for transport to the morgue. At least, that's what she assumed from her limited knowledge of crime-scene processing. Even from where she sat, she could see that the waves were breaking farther up the beach—the techs had to be racing against time.

"Hey."

Jordan looked back over her shoulder. Jase strolled toward her, Malachi at his side. Spying her, the huge dog broke into a lumbering gallop, leaving Jase to follow at a more leisurely pace.

She braced for Malachi's greeting, but he still managed to almost knock her off the picnic bench. A mix of several large breeds, Malachi embodied the classic adorable mutt, complete with shaggy fur and soulful brown eyes. Adorable, that is, until Jordan remembered the dent he put in her food budget by wolfing down several cans of organic dog food each day.

She wrapped her arms around his neck and gave him a hug, receiving a thorough slobbering in return. "You're not supposed to be out here, fella. If they find you, they might haul you off to doggie jail."

"He looked so lonely on your front porch that I didn't have the heart to leave him behind," Jase explained, coming to a stop in front of her. "Did you know he loves boat rides?"

"I haven't had the opportunity to take him out yet." After telling Malachi to stay inside the fence and away from the nesting grounds in the off-limits areas, she rose stiffly, wincing as a chorus of aches and pains made their presence known. Sitting that long without stretching had been a mistake.

Jase cocked his head, silently studying her, his blue eyes reflecting concern. As always when she was around him, Jordan experienced a confusing mix of strong attraction laced with caution. Attraction, because Jase was the sexiest man she'd come across in a very long time. Caution, because between adjustments to her divorce and Ryland's murder, she knew she had no business contemplating a new relationship with anyone.

Ruggedly attractive with a lean build, Jase had a friendly, deceptively laid-back manner that hid a razor-sharp mind and gentle wit. He was also an accomplished jazz piano player—a strong point in his favor. But he came with the baggage of a high-profile celebrity past—a point *not* in his favor. Given her recent experience of being front-page fodder in connection to her deceased husband's sexcapades with Hollywood starlets, Jordan was wary of anyone who had been touted as a celebrity by the press.

"You've had a stressful day," Jase observed.

She gave him a weak smile. "An understatement." She took a couple of steps then stopped, grimacing.

He reached out to grip her elbow. "You okay?"

"Just blisters."

"Ah."

"I'm worried about Darcy. She wasn't looking all that great when I left. I don't think she should be taking on this much, this soon."

"Darcy's tough—she'll be okay." He stared down the beach at the distant crime scene, his expression pensive. "Holt's death is already all over town. This kind of thing doesn't happen very often around here, even if it is an accidental death."

Jordan realized she hadn't been clear when she spoke with Jase earlier on the phone. "Holt's death wasn't accidental—he was murdered."

Jase's head whipped around. "You sure?"

She nodded. "I saw the bullet hole . . ." She paused to swallow. "I don't know how Darcy deals with this type of thing."

"When you've seen as many crime scenes as she has, you grow a pretty thick hide."

"I suppose." Jordan didn't think her hide would ever be that thick. "Were you frequently exposed to crime scenes? You know—before?"

Jase had been a sought-after criminal-defense attorney. To be fair, his skills had come in handy when she'd had the LAPD breathing down her neck—only his legal maneuvering had kept her out of jail.

"Yeah, I've seen my share of corpses," he replied, "and I don't care to repeat the experience. You found Holt?"

"Floating in the water just off the beach," she confirmed. "Someone . . . shot him in the forehead."

"Execution style, then." Jase was silent for a moment. "It's not like we have any professional hit men hanging around town. And it's odd that Holt was all the way out here—I've never known him to take an interest in hiking."

"He wasn't hiking—he had on a dive suit."

Jase frowned. "That *really* doesn't make sense—Holt was deathly afraid of the water."

"Maybe he was trying to manage his phobia and took diving lessons as a way of conquering his fears."

"Maybe. Doesn't sound like Holt, though." Jase watched Malachi chase a seagull. "Someone could have dumped his body out here after murdering him at a location closer to town, to confuse the authorities."

"That's what I suggested to Darcy, but that still doesn't explain why he was diving."

"No, it doesn't, does it?"

The gull was having no trouble eluding capture, but that didn't deter the dog. Jordan kept an eye out for anyone who looked as if he was upset by the dog's presence near the off-limits area.

"Well, Darcy will sort through it all, I'm sure," Jase finally said.

"She thinks whoever killed Holt probably lives in Port Chatham. That maybe it's one of the women he dated."

Jase appeared to consider the idea, then shook his head slowly. "Shooting someone isn't a typical MO for a woman—it isn't personal enough. Now, bashing in his skull or poisoning him? *That* I could buy."

"But you think it's possible his murderer lives in our town."

"Makes sense, doesn't it?"

Jordan shuddered.

Jase noticed and held out his hand. "C'mon, let's get you back to the pub." One corner of his mouth quirked up. "After hiking with Darcy, it's always best to imbibe."

"Why didn't you warn me?" Jordan grumbled as they turned toward the inner harbor. "Oh, wait—I get it. The pool. You placed a bet, didn't you?"

The quirk became a grin. "You know about that?"

"Darcy came clean somewhere around mile four."

They walked across the grass toward the boat landing on the far side of the lighthouse. Most tourists had already departed, and the gardener she'd talked to earlier was nowhere to be seen. A sleek blue-and-white cabin cruiser rocked gently in the water. Jordan whistled for Malachi.

"I had an interesting chat earlier with the gardener about the ship that ran aground not far from here in the 1890s," she told Jase as they waited for the dog.

"Yeah?" Jase's tone was suspiciously casual. "About what time was that?"

"Around three. Why?"

"We bet on the time of the sighting as well as the possibility of the sighting."

Her gaze narrowed. "The only person I talked to was the *gardener*, and everyone else I saw was a tourist. The subject of the shipwreck came up because the *Henrietta Dale* sailed by. The gardener seemed to believe that the ship had been deliberately lured onto the rocks back in 1893."

Jase nodded equably. "I've heard the story. If you're interested, you should ask Bob MacDonough to tell you what he knows. He's the current president of the Port Chatham Wooden Boat Society, and he's very knowledgeable about all the old wrecks in the area. He drops by the pub most nights, though he's pretty busy right now. The historic tall ships are starting to show up in port for the upcoming Wooden Boat Festival."

"Whoever refurbished the *Henrietta Dale* has done a beautiful job."

"You'll have to ask Bob about that—he knows pretty much everyone who owns and works on the sailing ships." Jase paused while Jordan whistled a second time for the dog. "I believe the *Henrietta Dale*'s logbook is on display in the lightstation—did the gardener mention it?"

"No, she didn't. I'd love to see it, actually." Jordan

debated going into the lighthouse, then quickly abandoned the idea. No way was she climbing all those steps, not given the current damage to her feet. "Do you suppose they have a copy of the logbook in town at the Wooden Boat Society?"

"If not, I'll bring you back out." Jase gave her a curious look. "Why are you so interested?"

Jordan shrugged. "Old shipwrecks are always fascinating, aren't they? And this ship is particularly beautiful."

Malachi finally came galloping toward them, giving them a happy canine grin. "It's about time," Jordan told him. "I don't think I've ever seen you expend that much energy."

That earned her The Look, Malachi's patented expression combining equal parts personal affront and derision. She and Jase lifted him on board, then climbed in after him.

Malachi flopped down at her feet. Jase went below. He returned with a first-aid kit and a pair of thick wool socks. "While I get us under way, why don't you use the shower in the head to rinse the saltwater off your blisters?"

Minutes later, she climbed back up the stairs, her feet warmer, cleaner, and stinging less. Standing behind Jase in the wheelhouse, she gazed back at the lighthouse grounds as the cruiser picked up speed, water rushing under its hull. Jase steered toward the distant headlands, and a chill breeze grew in strength, buffeting her hard enough that she had to widen her stance. She pulled her denim jacket closed, hugging herself.

The Olympic Mountains had taken on a pink glow against the setting sun. The beach blurred, then disappeared altogether in the gathering mist. Darcy was still out there documenting the crime scene, which would probably take several more hours. Though Jordan knew she was used to murder investigations, she didn't envy her the task.

Jordan also didn't envy her the task of discovering who in their small, friendly town hated Holt Stilwell enough to point a gun at his head and, without remorse, pull the trigger.

* * *

THE sun had dropped below the horizon by the time they returned the cabin cruiser to its berth in Port Chatham Harbor. Lights had blinked on in the downtown historic buildings, and the bluff running between the waterfront business district and the residential areas on the hills above was bathed in dark shadows.

They climbed the steep grade in Jase's truck, driving through block after block of quaint, painstakingly refurbished Victorians surrounded by lovingly tended gardens. Views of the fading sunset over Discovery Bay, and of distant islands across midnight-blue water, greeted them as they drove up the street.

When Jordan had moved to town a few weeks ago, she'd been stunned by the contrast between the sleepy tourist town of present day and the stories of its rough-and-tumble past. At one time, Port Chatham had been the second-largest seaport on the West Coast, its waterfront rife with crime. But over the years, the town had evolved into a charming seaside village best known for its

historic buildings and its jazz and wooden boat festivals.
Modern-day murder simply didn't fit with Jordan's mental picture of her adopted town—at least, not in contemporary times. It was unsettling to think that someone,
possibly living in a Victorian not far from her own, might
be a murderer.

As they turned down a side street one block over from
her house, Jordan noticed a number of residents out enjoying the fair weather, sitting in their porch swings, sipping wine, or strolling through the neighborhood. A
woman in her thirties whom Jordan had yet to meet was
washing her car in her driveway. Halfway down the block,
a man wearing elegant black evening clothes and a top hat
pulled his horse-drawn phaeton over to the curb as they
passed, touching a finger to the brim of his hat and nodding to her. Just a few yards beyond, a teenage boy on a
skateboard almost ran through a couple strolling down
the sidewalk in ankle-length capes and walking boots.
The man hastily tugged his wife aside, giving the young-
ster an irritated glance.

Jordan huffed out an exasperated breath.

"What?" Jase asked as he turned the corner onto the
main thoroughfare running through the upper part of
town.

"It would be a lot easier if vintage clothing wasn't all
the rage right now."

He gave her a perplexed look, then clued in. "I can see
where that might make things a bit difficult," he allowed,
tongue in cheek.

"Oh, shut up," she grumbled. "I mean, unless someone

is sporting a pierced earring or dreadlocks, how am I supposed to *know*?"

"Actually, dreadlocks have been worn since ancient times, so they aren't a good indicator."

Jordan just shook her head.

"I'm not running anyone down, am I?" he asked, looking worried about what he couldn't see.

"I'll let you know."

He slowed as they neared her street. "Pub or home?"

She considered. If she went home, she'd avoid having to talk about Holt. But she hadn't gotten around to grocery shopping this week, and Jase had a killer wine selection. "Pub," she decided.

"You need to stop by the house for dry shoes?"

"Not unless you mind me wandering around in socks. Thanks for coming out to fetch me, by the way."

He shot her a look that clearly said it hadn't been a hardship. "I enjoy being out on the water now and again." He pulled the truck into the parking lot behind All That Jazz, his pub that was located in the small, gentrified business district at the crest of the hill. "Want to help mix drinks this evening?"

"You *do* realize the last person for whom I mixed a dry martini never stepped foot back in my house, right?"

"You sure the martini was the reason?"

"Humor. Ha."

He reached over to tug on a lock of her hair, his blue eyes twinkling. "Relax. The job mostly entails pulling pints of beer, pouring the occasional shot of hard liquor, and washing glasses. I can help you with anything exotic."

"Okay by me," she said, opening her door. "But if you lose customers, it's your fault."

She roused Malachi, who had settled in for a snooze on the backseat of the king cab. Once he realized where they were, he scrambled to his feet and pushed his way out the passenger door. Organic hamburger patties, cooked medium-rare by Kathleen, the pub's cranky chef, had become the nightly treat.

Jase offered to carry Jordan inside, but she refused—there was no way she trusted her hormones to behave while being held in his arms. Instead, she picked her way gingerly across the gravel parking lot.

He held open the rear door to the pub, his amusement plain. She hadn't fooled him in the least.

They walked down the back hall past the kitchen. The pub was housed in a building that was a historic landmark in its own right. Jase had done a marvelous job of restoring the distressed brick walls and huge timber beams that crisscrossed the arched brick ceiling. A local stone artisan had used rugged slabs of granite to build a freestanding fireplace, which Jase kept lit with a cheerful fire most evenings. Oak tables with captain's chairs created casual groupings throughout the spacious room, while more private leather booths lined one wall. An old-fashioned bar, built of ornately carved mahogany, stretched the length of the opposite wall.

For Jordan, the pub had already become a home away from home, where she could count on finding friendly conversation, live jazz most evenings, and excellent food. The fact that dogs were welcome was also a plus.

The room was already crowded, and since the majority

of the patrons appeared to be drinking, Jordan decided that they were most likely still on this side of the veil. Jase took her jacket and hung it along with his own on the coat tree in the entrance.

Jase's full-time bartender, Bill, a slender man with a long silver ponytail who was rumored to have once been a Wall Street broker, moved from table to table, taking drink orders. Though Bill remained somewhat distant with Jordan, she'd felt nothing but affection for him since he'd shown up at her house with his chain saw to help remove the wisteria vine from her attic. As far as she was concerned, Bill walked on water.

As Jase sorted through a stack of drink orders, Jordan surreptitiously studied the people sitting on barstools.

"How many people do you see sitting at the bar?" she asked in a low voice.

"Eleven. How many do *you* see?"

She released a breath. "The same."

Jase raised his voice. "Yo, Bob?" A big-boned, sandy-haired man sitting at one of the tables near the fireplace cocked his head in their direction. "Jordan has some questions for you."

Bob pushed away from the table and walked up to the bar. He was well over six feet tall, yet his hands and feet still looked too large for the rest of his body. And with his shambling gait, it was a miracle he didn't trip and fall on his face. He gave Jordan a friendly grin as he slid onto the stool across from her.

"Jordan Marsh, the lady who sees and talks to ghosts." He stuck out a huge paw to engulf her hand, then shook it so vigorously Jordan feared for the health of her shoulder socket. "*Real* pleased to meet you. You should come down to the wharf sometime—I'll take you on a personal tour of our haunted ships."

"You have haunted *ships?*" She took the drink list Jase held out, idly wondering what ships' captains looked like in ghostly form.

"Hell yes we do. It only stands to reason that a lot of the older boats in the harbor would have a past skipper or two hanging around, right?"

"Right." She shook her head as she drew the first pint. "Something to look forward to."

Foam overflowed, spilling down the side of the glass and over her hand. She poured it down the sink drain.

"Tip the glass like this." Jase moved in close, showing her how to run the beer gently down the side, minimizing head. He handed the full pint to her, then told Bob, "She saw the gardener around three this afternoon."

"Damn." At Bob's response, a collective groan rose from around the room and money started changing hands.

"She was just a *gardener,*" Jordan said firmly. "The lighthouse association has volunteer keepers out there every week."

"Nice try, but the original lightkeeper's wife was a gardener." Tom Greeley wandered over, beer in hand, and snagged a stool two down from Bob. "That means Jase wins, lucky dog."

"Juvenile, very juvenile." Jordan gave them a chiding look. "Even if she was who you say, what if I *hadn't* seen her?"

"Then Kathleen would have won." Tom grinned, slouching comfortably with his elbows on the bar. "She's a nonbeliever, so she bet against the rest of us."

"Smart woman," Jordan muttered.

"We've all been talking about Holt," Tom said, sobering. "You found him?"

"Yeah." Jordan gathered clean glasses.

"You seem to be a magnet for dead bodies," Bob noted. At her cool stare, he held up both hands. "Hey—just saying."

She related what she knew so far. While Holt's death was widely known, everyone was shocked by the news that he'd been murdered. "Is it true what Jase told me, that Holt didn't like the water?" she asked Tom, who had probably known him the best since they'd been competitors in the same business, custom house painting.

"Yeah," Tom replied, clearly shaken. "Holt had a bad experience as a kid, almost drowning. Ever since, he hasn't been interested in getting anywhere near a body of water larger than a bathtub."

"Well, he must have gotten over his fears, because we found him in a dive suit."

"What about dive gear?" Jase asked.

Jordan shook her head. "I pointed out to Darcy that even if he'd been diving in shallow water, he should've at least had *some* gear on him."

"Not if someone killed him on a boat, then dumped him in the water," Bob said.

"Good point. Maybe Darcy can tell us more when she gets here." Jordan suddenly realized how hungry she was. "Food."

"I'll put an order in with Kathleen." Jase headed toward the kitchen, maneuvering past Malachi, who was stretched out and snoring, taking up all the floor space where they needed to work.

"So." Bob placed his forearms on the bar. "Jase said you had some questions for me?"

"Yeah, about the wreck of the *Henrietta Dale.* I understand she ran aground on Dungeness Spit in 1893, and that it's rumored she was purposely lured onto the rocks."

"Yup." He handed her his empty pint and pointed to the tap he preferred. "According to my great-great-grandfather's papers—he was the master ship's carpenter who handled all the renovations—Michael Seavey purchased the *Henrietta Dale* from a San Francisco shipping company in 1893 and had her refurbished. He hired a crew and set sail out of Victoria. She never made it to Port Chatham—she ran off course and grounded on the west side of the spit, killing most on board."

"*Seavey* was the owner?" Jordan digested that bit of news while she drew his beer. "Interesting coincidence, given that he was Holt's ancestor."

"No kidding. History repeating itself and all that." Bob took a long draw from his new pint. "The lightkeeper and his wife tried to help the few survivors."

"Was the weather bad the night of the wreck?"

"Not that I know of. And that spit is way off the route they should have taken. Seavey didn't hire fools; his captain had a good reputation. Which is why folks thought he had to have been lured onto the rocks."

Jordan ran hot water into the sink, added detergent, then dumped in a tray of empties to soak. "How does one go about luring a ship off course?"

"Back then, a ship captain would've used the lights of

Point Wilson—that's the lighthouse right here in town—and New Dungeness to triangulate his ship's position. Once he had a position and his speed, he could then use maps to set a heading. If someone purposely changed the location of the light on Dungeness Spit—say, by disabling the lightstation and then putting a bright lantern somewhere farther down the beach—the captain would have triangulated their position incorrectly, adjusted the ship's course, and then run aground."

"She's a clipper ship, right?" Jordan asked as she handed Bill a tray of drinks to deliver.

"And a real beauty, according to the articles in the newspapers back then," Bob confirmed. "Clipper ships had a huge sail area, which made them very fast for the day. If the captain calculated their position incorrectly, by the time he'd realized his mistake, there would've been no stopping her—the crew couldn't have gotten the sails down in time."

"So who would have done that?" Jordan asked, intrigued.

Bob shrugged. "My guess? Maybe a business competitor. A lot of folks wouldn't have minded if Seavey disappeared off the waterfront."

Jase returned with plates for her and Malachi, who miraculously woke up from his coma the moment Jase placed the food under his nose.

Jordan set her own plate of grilled sturgeon and sautéed greens where she could take bites while mixing the next round of drinks. She picked up a drink slip. "What in the world is a Mexican Martini?"

"Tequila, Cointreau, lime juice, and sweet and sour . . ."

Her eyes must have glazed over, because Jase took the slip away from her.

"Seavey's partner was also a real piece of work," Tom was saying. "He had a history of violence. I wouldn't put it past him to have tried to cut Seavey out of their business."

Bob looked as if he wanted to disagree, but the front door opened, snagging their attention, and Darcy entered. Acknowledging Jordan's wave, she came over and took the stool between Bob and Tom.

She gave Jordan a wary look. "You're *bartending?*"

"I was properly warned," Jase said.

"And still you proceeded." Darcy shook her head. Her clothes were streaked with sand and mud. She leaned both elbows on the counter.

"You look like hell," Jordan said, worried.

"Nice to know I look exactly like I feel," she retorted wryly.

"How'd you get here so fast?"

"The Coast Guard guys gave me a lift back to my SUV in the helicopter. We lost the light, and no one thought to bring battery-operated floods. It was pointless to continue, so the plan is to go back out tomorrow morning."

"Were you able to wrangle jurisdiction?" Jordan placed a pint of microbrew in front of her.

"Yeah." Darcy took a large gulp and closed her eyes for a moment.

"Anything you can tell us?" Tom asked.

"Not much. Holt was probably murdered late last night—the ME said he'd been in the water less than twenty-four hours. It'll be a couple of days before I get the autopsy report." She reached for a napkin as Jase set down her dinner. "Come to think of it, I didn't see Holt in here last night. Did you?" she asked Jase.

"Not that I remember. But Holt always paid with a credit card, so if he was here, I'd have the slip for his meal and drinks." Jase wiped down the bar with a cloth. "You saw what a zoo it was in here last night—he could've escaped my notice easily."

Darcy swallowed a bite of sturgeon, then turned to the others. "Did you guys see him?"

"I wasn't here last night," Bob replied, and Tom shook his head.

"I'll ask around and check the receipts," Jase assured Darcy. "Do you have detectives tracing his last movements?"

"Yep. Hopefully, they'll find something useful."

Tom leaned toward Darcy. "What's this about you finding him in a dive suit and without gear? You know he hated the ocean, right?"

"That was my understanding. The only explanation that makes sense is that he was dumped off a boat, but I have no idea why he was diving in the first place. Or where, for that matter. He could've been killed anywhere out on the water, then brought to that location." She grimaced. "Which means, of course, that we're probably processing only the dump site, not the primary crime scene. We'll have to keep looking, based on what we find Holt was up to."

Jordan told Darcy about the nineteenth-century shipwreck and Seavey's ownership of the *Henrietta Dale*. "Don't you think that's an odd coincidence, given that Seavey and Holt were related?"

Darcy's shrug was indifferent. "Maybe. Then again, it could just be that—a coincidence."

"Do you think Holt might have been diving for artifacts off the old shipwreck?"

"Seems unlikely that there would be any *other* reason Holt was diving in that location," Tom pointed out.

"Then again," Jordan thought it through out loud, "when I was looking at Seavey in relation to Hattie's murder, Holt professed to be uninterested in any of his ancestors."

"Maybe he hoped he'd find something of value," Tom said. "Holt was always looking for ways to make an extra buck or three. And there's been a rumor floating around lately that he underbid the hotel job and was losing money."

Darcy pushed away her half-eaten dinner, then leaned forward so that she could address a woman with dishwater-blond hair, dressed in work clothes and boots, sitting three stools down. Jordan remembered serving her a whiskey, neat. "Hey, Sally? Do you happen to know who Holt was dating in recent weeks?"

The woman scowled. "It's just like you cops to think that some woman did it, right? Blame the victim, that's what you always do."

"Sally . . ." Darcy warned.

Sally abruptly stood, digging a hand into her pocket. "Holt hated women. Not the other way around."

"Why do you say that?" Jordan asked, curious because she had suspected the same.

Sally dismissed her question with a cool look. "I'm not interested in psychoanalyzing the son of a bitch." She glanced at the tab Jase had handed her, then tossed a couple of twenties onto the bar. "All I know is, whoever did Holt in, I hope they get away with it. In fact, I'll hold a damn block party in their honor."

Jordan watched her stalk out, stunned. She opened her mouth to ask Darcy more about her, but stopped when she got a good look at her friend's face. She was alarmingly pale, her eyes dull with pain. Her movements, when she picked up her beer mug to take a sip, were sluggish.

"I'm dead on my feet," Jordan told Jase, cocking her head slightly in Darcy's direction, silently telegraphing her concern. "You okay with me heading out?"

"Go ahead," he told her. "Bill and I can manage."

"Can you give me a lift?" she asked Darcy.

"Sure. I need to be up early, anyway."

"All right if I come by in the morning to chat about the work on the house?" Tom asked Jordan.

Damn. She sighed, then nodded.

"I'd like to drop by your offices at the wharf tomorrow, if that's okay with you," she told Bob. "Ask more questions about the *Henrietta Dale*."

She could have sworn he hesitated before shooting her a grin. "Caught your fancy, has she?"

"She's a beautiful ship," Jordan admitted.

Bob's smile slid a little. "Pardon?"

"I said, she's a gorgeous ship. Whoever refurbished her did a wonderful job. I'd love to take a tour of her."

Bob exchanged a look with Tom.

"What?" Jordan demanded.

"The *Henrietta Dale* broke up in the surf that night in 1893," Bob carefully explained, "which is why so many people died. There's no way anyone could have refurbished her."

"That can't be right." Jordan frowned. "Unless the gardener was mistaken, she identified the ship by that name."

"You saw the *gardener?*" Darcy asked, perking up.

"You owe me twenty bucks," Jase informed her. "Three o'clock, on the nose."

"Crap." Darcy pulled out the bill and slapped it onto the bar. "Jordan, the gardener was living out there at the time of the wreck. So I'd believe her if she said it was the *Henrietta Dale.*"

"Well, I couldn't have seen a ship that no longer exists." Jordan wondered if Darcy was so tired she was no longer lucid.

"Oh, now, that's not necessarily true..." Bob murmured.

"Where did you see the ship?" Tom asked.

"She sailed toward the spit, then at the last minute, turned and went to the north past the lighthouse." Jordan's exasperation with them was growing.

He nodded sagely. "That makes sense, since that's roughly where she went down. The course she would've taken if she hadn't run aground—in other words, if she'd succeeded in turning and avoiding the rocks—is exactly as you described."

Jordan stared at them, chilled.

Tom merely grinned, then turned to address the room at large. "Hey, folks? Looks like we've got ourselves the first confirmed sighting of a Pacific Northwest ghost ship."

Amid widespread applause and cheers, Darcy told Jordan, "*Seriously* cool. Your powers are expanding."

Chapter 4

JORDAN gripped the edge of the bar sink. "You mean to tell me that instead of just the occasional ghost here and there, I'm now seeing entire ghost *ships*?"

"Looks like," Bob replied cheerfully. "What's the problem? It's not as if sightings like yours haven't been fairly common—just not so much in these waters."

"Why is she out there?"

"She's probably repeating her voyage at the time of the shipwreck."

Jordan conjured up an image of what she'd seen. "So your supposition is that the *ghost* of a wrecked ship forever sails the waters, running the same course over and over, but as a spectral . . . *whatever*, gets to avoid running onto the rocks?"

"Depends on the ghost ship. Some are seen sailing the waters successfully, righting the old wrong; others are doomed to forever repeat their captain's mistakes."

Jordan concentrated on what was becoming her favorite pastime—breathing.

"Ever heard of the *Flying Dutchman?* Or the *Mary Celeste?*" Tom asked her. "There've been stacks of books written about famous phantom ships down through history. Trust me, you're in good company."

She rolled her eyes. "Yeah, the 'good' company of the whack jobs who write those kinds of books."

"'Whack jobs' being, of course, another term reviled by the psychiatric community?" Darcy wondered out loud.

Jordan shot her a dirty look.

"At least it doesn't sound as if the ship had it in for you—some of them can be pretty malevolent," Bob said.

"Gee, that's nice to know." Jordan seized the bottle of Cuervo Gold from Jase, poured herself a shot, chugged it, then started coughing.

"Careful there." Jase pounded a fist between her shoulder blades. "What, exactly, did you see?"

"An old-fashioned sailing ship, dammit!" she croaked, then paused. "Okay, maybe I didn't see a lot of crew, but I heard them singing. And the light was a little weird, but I'm sure that was just because of the fog, right? You can't convince me she wasn't *real.*"

Everyone looked amused.

Jordan turned back to Bob. "All kinds of tall ships are supposedly sailing into port right now, because of the Wooden Boat Festival, right? *Rationally speaking,* it could've been one of those."

"Actually, only a few have shown up so far—we're over a month out from the festival. And a lot of the boats that enter the festival are small craft."

"Okay, okay." She paced back and forth in the six

square feet of space she had behind the bar. "Wait—we've established that the gardener saw the ship, too."

"Which stands to reason, since she's the ghost of one of the rescue party that night back in 1893," Tom said.

"*If* she's a ghost," Jordan corrected him stubbornly. "And why the hell do you think it makes sense that a *ghost* would see a *ghost ship?*"

"Why do ghosts see other ghosts?" Jase asked, maddeningly logical.

Jordan glared.

"Plus," Tom said, "even if I go with your theory that the gardener isn't a ghost—which I don't, by the way—a lot of the sightings of phantom ships throughout history have been by more than one person, sometimes entire *groups* of people."

Jordan resumed her pacing. "I suppose it's possible I have a brain tumor." She halted. "Yes, that's it! I really *am* imagining all of this. There are all kinds of weird stories about people believing in entire alternate universes because of pressure on parts of their brains from a growing malignant brain tumor. Now *that* works for me."

"If a tumor was to blame, what you see would have no correlation to actual historical events," Darcy pointed out pragmatically.

"She's right," Jase said. "You see things, *then* you do the research and find out they existed."

But Jordan refused to concede the point. "Maybe I'm overhearing a few historically accurate tidbits, then my tumor embellishes what I heard, then I do the research."

"You can't *seriously* tell me you would prefer to have a

brain tumor rather than see ghosts and ghost ships." Darcy said it carefully.

"A girl *can* dream."

Darcy shook her head. "Sarcasm."

"You aren't alone in this, you know," Bob assured Jordan. "There have been dozens of sightings of ghost ships."

"But why me?"

They all looked at her as if the answer was obvious.

"I meant, why me, why *now*? If there have been dozens of these sightings, why hasn't anyone else sighted *this* ship over the years?"

"Maybe you're supposed to investigate what happened that night?" Tom speculated.

"No, wait—she *does* have a point," Jase said. "The timing of the sighting appears to be unexplained. How would any spectral entities know that she'd be hiking today, or that she'd put two and two together, for that matter?"

"Oh, I don't know," Darcy mused. "I'd assume that along with Jordan's powers comes some kind of *connection* with the spectral entities, such that they'd know what she was up to and when it would make sense to try to influence her."

"You guys *do* know how insane you sound?" Jordan fumed.

"But why *now*?" Jase asked, obviously considering her question rhetorical. "Do you suppose we're coming up on the anniversary of the shipwreck?" He turned to Bob. "Do you know the exact date?"

"Sometime in August of ninety-three, I think. I'd have to look it up. And I don't think it has anything to do with the upcoming boat festival, since nothing like this has happened in prior years."

"Jordan wasn't in town in prior years, though."

"Hmm. Valid point." Bob rubbed his chin. "At any rate, I'm not sure the sighting is supposed to mean anything other than what it was. Such sightings have occurred throughout history, but they didn't translate into some kind of cry for help from a different dimension."

"Still," Tom said, "it makes sense that she should look into the shipwreck."

"I can assure you I feel absolutely no desire to do so," Jordan replied grimly.

"There was never any conclusive evidence as to whether the *Henrietta Dale* was deliberately lured onto the rocks," Tom continued as if she'd never spoken. "If Jordan researches the incident, maybe she can find some tidbit that provides proof one way or the other, thus giving the ship some peace of mind."

Jordan groaned and buried her face in her hands.

"I can bring you some books to read as a starting point," he offered.

"If you darken my doorstep with any books on the subject, I will take Darcy's gun and shoot you between the eyes."

"Are you all right?" Jase asked.

"I need to go home." *And climb into bed and pull the covers over my head. Denial, that's the ticket.*

"You can't leave now—we want to hear every detail," Bob protested.

"Giant wooden ship. Lots of masts and sails. Singing

crew," Jordan ticked off on her fingers. "What else do you need to know?"

"Well, for starters, we need to carefully document your sighting—the exact longitude and latitude of the ship, time of day, atmospheric conditions, and so on. Experts who track this kind of thing will want a full accounting for their records."

"It might also be a good idea for you to work with a sketch artist," Tom added, receiving an eager nod of agreement from Bob. "You can generate a sketch from your memory of what you saw. Then we could compare it to the specifications for the *Henrietta Dale,* to see how accurate the sighting was."

"I can put you in touch with the sketch artist the police department uses on occasion," Darcy offered. "She's very good."

Jordan looked at her.

"Or not," Darcy said.

"No, that's an *excellent* idea." Bob grabbed a bar napkin and pulled a pen from his shirt pocket to start making notes. "I've got calls to make. Jordan, we need your eyewitness account recorded right away, so that it's as accurate as possible."

"That's it!" Jordan muttered. "I'm out of here. Darcy, I'll drive—you're too tired. Keys. Malachi! Let's go." When Bob started to protest, she held up a hand. "I'll come by your offices tomorrow." She crooked the fingers of her extended hand at Darcy for the keys.

Darcy opened her mouth as if to say something— probably, Jordan thought darkly, some pithy observation about who was in the worst shape and therefore who should be driving—but then wisely seemed to think better of it. Without a word, she handed over the keys to her SUV.

Jase placed a hand on Jordan's shoulder. His expression was solemn, but his blue eyes held a definite twinkle. "Want me to carry you out to the truck so that you can retrieve your shoes?"

* * *

IT took less than a half hour to drive Darcy home, talk her into taking her pain medication, and make certain she was alert enough to get ready for bed on her own. Jordan then pulled on her damp, salt-encrusted running shoes, and she and Malachi walked the two blocks to Longren House in the dark.

As they turned the corner on her block, Malachi growled low in his throat. Jordan slowed, laying a hand on his collar. She studied the surrounding shadows, wondering what had set the dog off.

Nothing looked out of place in the yards on either side of her house. Amanda, the landscaper she'd involuntarily adopted, had probably already retired to her tent in the backyard, having long since quit for the day. Jordan recognized Amanda's handiwork in the careful pruning and temporary supports for the wisteria, which would eventually climb a new iron trellis along the library wall. She halted in her tracks, peering more closely at the support structure. Was that . . . *scaffolding*? Maybe that was what had spooked Malachi—it was certainly enough to spook *her*.

The moon and stars had come out, providing enough illumination that Jordan could make out the lines of her house's nineteenth-century Queen Anne architecture. Though relatively small in terms of square footage, her home was a glorious example of the ornate, wacky home designs of that era. A covered porch ran the length of the front, curving around the corners and decorated with gingerbread-style carved balusters. The turret off her master bedroom rose into the night sky above her, its darkened antique glass windows shining in the moonlight. A hall light glowed softly through the beveled glass of the front door. Someone had left lights burning in the kitchen and the library.

Jordan loved how the house looked at night, when darkness obscured the peeling paint and missing siding. Her first priority had been to hire a carpenter to repair and hang the old porch swing, whose use was essential in helping her cling to her dream of a warm, cozy home.

Malachi growled again, straining against her grip on his collar, and, increasingly uneasy, she studied the house more carefully. The gallon of wood brightener she'd bought the day before at the local hardware store still sat on the porch where she'd left it. Nothing seemed out of place.

Something flew past the library window, *inside*. She stared, wondering if her imagination was running away from her. A smoky, amorphous shape flew past again, this time in the opposite direction. It was followed by several airborne books. She heard a faint crash in the general direction of the antique table and wing-back chair.

Malachi pulled out of her grip, barking, and leapt onto

the porch. She followed, easing open the front door and cautiously entering the hall. The sound of crashing objects in the library intensified. Crossing to the arched doorway, she peeked inside.

Books she had meticulously dusted and shelved in alphabetical order in the ceiling-to-floor bookcases now lay in heaps on the floor. Ornately framed pictures of dour Longren ancestors hung askew. The wing-back chair was overturned. Plants in the conservatory had toppled, their soil spilled onto the red and white Aubusson rug.

Hattie and Charlotte huddled together behind the massive oak desk, holding onto each other. As usual, the sisters wore elaborate examples of the gowns of the time. Charlotte's was the more fashionable of the two, made up of yards of shimmering dark blue muslin and sporting a small bustle, a tiny waist almost certainly created by a tightly laced corset, and a rather revealing bustline. Hattie, who believed more in comfort and in not damaging her internal organs, wore a simple shirtwaist-style teal bodice with a high, lacy neck, tucked into a straight black skirt that fell to her ankles. Both women's expressions were wary, their materializations weaker than normal.

Two other ghosts flew around the room at dizzying speed, engaging in fisticuffs. One landed a punch, the other exploding in a puff of particles. The air across the room shimmered as he reappeared, and they circled each other once again. At ceiling height.

Malachi took one look and fled to the back of the house.

Jordan recognized one of the ghosts as Frank Lewis, Hattie's handsome, brawny lover from the 1890s, whom Jordan had posthumously cleared of any involvement in

Hattie's murder. The other ghost, however, Jordan had never seen before.

For a brief moment, she considered quietly backing out and returning to the pub. Someone would surely offer her and Malachi a bed for the night. Or there was always the porch swing. Maybe the ghosts would be gone by morning. Then again, her house might be *rubble* by morning.

"Oh!" Hattie spied her. "Thank goodness you're here!" she breathed, wringing her hands. "I haven't been able to make them stop."

"Do something!" Charlotte cried, fading in and out spastically.

"*Hey!*" Jordan tried to get the men's attention, but they ignored her.

A lamp bit the dust as Frank exploded, then rematerialized on top of the leaded glass shade, shattering it.

Jordan put two fingers to her mouth and whistled loud enough to raise the dead.

The ghost she didn't recognize halted in a hover not far from her, clapping his hands over his ears. "Good Christ, woman! Cease that infernal racket! Have you no sense of decorum?"

She scowled. "Who the hell are you?"

Frank lingered not far away, his expression still murderous. Jordan shot him a stern look, just in case he was considering landing another punch.

The other ghost dropped to floor level, straightening his cravat and black swallowtail coat. "Must you swear like a sailor as well?"

"'Hell' is perfectly acceptable as part of modern-day speech," Jordan retorted. "Who are you?"

He executed a mocking bow from the waist. "Michael Seavey, at your service."

She gaped. "The *shanghaier?*"

"Please, madam." He looked offended. "I merely supplied a much-needed commodity."

Oh, no. No, no, no. This was bad. Having ghosts around who had been hardened criminals in their former lives was *very bad.* Light-headed, she reached out to brace a hand against a bookshelf.

Seavey withdrew a cigar from an inside breast pocket. He ran it under his nose, sniffing appreciatively before preparing to light it.

"This is a no-smoking establishment," she said faintly. When he looked confused, she clarified. "I don't allow anyone to smoke in my house."

"Then we shouldn't have a problem," he replied smoothly, holding the flame to the tip of the cigar and drawing to create an even burn. He eyed the tip of the cigar critically, seemingly satisfied. "For unless I'm mistaken, this house belongs to Hattie."

"Michael . . ." Hattie began hesitantly, sending Jordan an apologetic glance.

"You are, in fact, quite mistaken," Jordan said, recovering enough to walk over and set the wing-back chair upright. "I bought the house last month."

"Nonsense." Seavey ignored her request. "You may currently have squatter's rights, but the house remains Hattie's."

"*I beg your pardon?*" Jordan shoved an armload of books

onto a shelf, then turned to face him, waving at the cloud of smoke. "Put that out, dammit."

"You're the only human who can see and smell the smoke," he said, amused. "Except, interestingly, for the odd interloper in my hotel suite. If I blow smoke right in their faces, they seem to get a whiff."

"You have your own place here in town?"

He inclined his head. "I maintain a suite of rooms at the Cosmopolitan Hotel, of course."

"Then you could go back there, right?"

"You're being uncommonly rude," Charlotte admonished Jordan.

"Now, Charlotte," Hattie reproved. "I think Jordan is taking all this quite well."

"That's only because after the day I've had, nothing could faze me," Jordan muttered.

"Pardon?"

"Never mind."

Seavey blew smoke in Jordan's face, and she waved her hands more frantically. "Dammit! You're putting me at risk for secondhand smoke."

He looked exasperated. "You humans persist in talking in riddles. What the devil is 'secondhand smoke'?"

"Your smoking can cause cancer in the other people in the room. Now *please*, do as I say, or I'll take that cigar away from you and dispose of it myself." It was an empty threat—she doubted she could put out a spectral cigar.

"Michael," Hattie said quietly. "If you would be so kind . . ."

Seavey shrugged, giving Hattie a surprisingly tender

look. "Very well, my dear." He made a production of disposing of the cigar in an ashtray.

Jordan folded her arms. "Okay. Now would someone please tell me what is going on here?"

"It's quite simple, really." Seavey flicked ash from his sleeve. "I've come to ask for Hattie's hand in marriage. And this *cretin*"—he gestured in Frank's direction—"seems to think he has a prior claim."

"Oh, dear," Hattie murmured.

"How *romantic*," Charlotte sighed, clasping both hands over her heart.

Chapter 5

I may not deserve Hattie, but I will never stand for her belonging to the likes of you," Frank growled to Seavey.

"At least *I* avenged her death, Lewis," Seavey replied calmly.

"I was hanged, man! I had no choice in the matter."

"How *thrilling*," Charlotte gushed, "to have two such charming suitors fighting over you."

Jordan held back a snort. Only someone so young could hold such an unrealistic view. Then again, what constituted "realistic" when one was standing in a room with four ghosts, contemplating the marriage of two of them?

She had to admit, if she were forced to choose between the two men, she would find it a tough call. Rawboned and dressed like a nineteenth-century dockworker, Frank Lewis was nevertheless handsome, highly educated, and ethical, though at times admittedly moody, bordering on downright surly. But Michael Seavey embodied the very essence of a stylishly attired, charming sociopath, not unlike her deceased husband and just the type of man she found irresistible.

In a terrifyingly, psychologically unhealthy sort of way.

"You're so lucky!" Charlotte told Hattie.

Hattie looked pained.

"Are ghosts even allowed to marry?" Jordan asked the room at large. She was ignored.

She needed to check into a hotel. No, she needed to quietly slip out of town. She'd take Malachi, of course—she couldn't leave him behind. But really, a new town sounded like just the ticket. Her friend Carol would probably agree to prescribe a nice sedative to help her deal with her grief over losing Longren House . . .

Seavey harrumphed. "If you had been a better man," he informed Frank, "you would've escaped from jail and solved the crime properly. You are correct—you *don't* deserve her. *I* would never have shown such weakness or passivity."

Frank visibly flinched; the shanghaier had hit a nerve. "If you knew I didn't murder Hattie, it was your responsibility to speak up. Yet you did nothing."

"Good God, man, I'm not dull-witted!" Seavey looked amused. "Why would I help a known union sympathizer escape from jail? You would've continued to wreak havoc upon my business interests."

Charlotte clapped her hands together, though they made no sound. "I can't wait to plan the wedding! We can have it right here in the front parlor!" She hesitated, then frowned at Jordan. "You must work *harder* on the renovation. Everything must be *perfect.*"

"You son of a bitch!" Frank snarled, gliding toward Seavey, who turned to face him, widening his stance, his hands falling loosely to his sides.

Jordan gave another sharp whistle. "*Stop!*" She glared at the two men. "There will be *no more fighting* on the premises. We will solve this like *civilized human beings.*" She paused, then waved a hand. "Whatever."

She really was way too tired to deal with any of them. And she *really* wanted a hot soak in her claw-foot tub, then eight solid hours in her nice, soft bed. Turning to Hattie, she ordered, "Choose one and tell the other to get lost."

Seavey hissed, and Hattie looked horrified. "I couldn't possibly!"

Frank's head swiveled toward Hattie. "You would actually consider his suit?" His expression was incredulous.

Hattie wrung her hands.

"Michael is a *wonderful* man," Charlotte said loyally, shooting Frank a disgruntled glare. "Most people don't understand that about him, but he truly cares."

Seavey looked gratified.

Jordan closed her eyes, pinching the bridge of her nose. "Remember our discussion a few weeks ago about the number of people this man murdered during his lifetime?" she asked Charlotte. "I'm with Frank—I think the choice is obvious." She gave Hattie a chiding look. "I'm surprised you even need to give it a moment's thought."

"But—" Hattie began, only to be interrupted by Charlotte's shriek of outrage.

"Michael is a *good* man! Why, just before he died, he—"

"That would be when someone deliberately lured his

ship onto the rocks, correct?" Jordan drove her point home as she picked up pieces of the lampshade and dropped them into an ashtray. "It seems to me someone wanted him dead. And probably for good reason."

"Nonsense," Seavey replied. "They lured the *Henrietta Dale* onto the rocks because they wanted to eliminate a competitor, nothing more. It was merely my bad luck to go down with the ship."

Frank snorted. "You mean, someone finally had the good sense to rid the waterfront of its worst nemesis. I'm sure you deserved whatever happened to you."

"'Worst nemesis,'" Seavey murmured, looking quite pleased. "I like that."

Hattie looked confused. "But Michael, you *didn't* go down with the ship."

He gave her a tender yet patronizing look. "I'm sorry, my dear; that's precisely what happened. If it makes my death any more palatable, rest assured that I felt no pain."

"No, no!" She roiled the newspapers strewn across the desktop, then zinged one at Jordan, who barely managed to react fast enough to snag it out of the air. "Jordan, if you would be so kind as to read the article halfway down the front page?"

Reluctantly curious, Jordan searched until she found the news story Hattie referred to, then skimmed through the text:

Escalating Lawless and Licentious Activities on the Waterfront

August 7—Further proof of the disintegration of the social fabric of our beloved Port Chatham society was evidenced by the recent murder of the ruthless shanghaier, one Michael Seavey, whose body was found by this paper's reporter early this morning, floating in the waters under Union Wharf, the victim of an execution-style slaying . . .

Jordan raised her head to frown at Seavey.

"See?" Hattie gave an affirming nod, then addressed Seavey. "The article states that your body was found floating under Union Wharf. You'd been *shot*."

"Yellow journalism." Seavey waved his hand. "We both know Eleanor Canby told her reporters to write whatever suited her purposes, which fluctuated from one day to the next. The woman despised me."

"No, Hattie's right," Jordan said slowly, reading further. "The article is quite detailed—you were found under the wharf at dawn, wearing the evening clothes you'd been seen in the night before." She lifted her gaze. "Someone shot you in the back."

Everyone looked horrified with the exception of Frank, who nodded matter-of-factly, saying, "Any one of your known associates would have been capable of it."

"A common enough occurrence in those days, even if untrue in my case," Seavey agreed.

"Actually, it seems to be common in your family," Jordan informed him. "I found the body of your great-great-nephew this afternoon. He'd been shot as well."

"How horrible!" Hattie exclaimed.

"How *unseemly*," Charlotte countered. "Women shouldn't be exposed to such things. If you'd been here at the house, concentrating on restoring our home, ensuring that it will be ready for the *hundreds* of guests that will attend the wedding—"

"What the devil are you talking about?" Seavey demanded of Jordan. "I don't have any descendants."

"Yes, you do," Jordan replied, ignoring Charlotte's tirade. "I'd have to go back through your papers, then trace the family genealogy, but you definitely have descendants."

"*You're reading my personal papers?* Woman, have you no sense of decency?"

"If you didn't want them read, why did you write them?" Jordan retorted, exasperated. She drew in a deep breath. "Look, can we get back on topic here?"

Everyone stared at her as if she'd spoken in tongues. "Can we return to the matter at hand?" she paraphrased.

"An excellent idea," Seavey concurred. "We should discuss Hattie's and my forthcoming nuptials."

Out of the corner of her eye, Jordan saw Frank puff up threateningly. Hurriedly, she intervened. "Actually, we were discussing the report of your murder. Though for the life of me, I don't remember how we got on that topic, either."

"I wasn't murdered. The last thing I remember was the shipwreck. How could I have gotten from there to dead under the wharf?" Seavey shook his head. "No. I'm certain the article must've been fabricated."

Hattie moved over next to Jordan and laid a hand on her arm. Jordan's arm tingled as if she'd picked up a charge, not unlike static electricity. "I don't suppose you could look into the matter and make a determination for us?"

"*What?* No, no . . ."

"She's hardly capable—you would do better to ask a man," Seavey pointed out.

"*Hey*," Jordan snapped. "This is the twenty-first century. That kind of thinking went out of fashion a long time ago."

His shrug was one of indifference. "Nevertheless, I admit to being unconcerned about the entire affair. Who cares how I died?"

"Your murder shouldn't go unsolved." Hattie's comment earned her a hard look from Frank.

"Was there a follow-up article providing details of the murder investigation?" Jordan asked.

"I don't know." Hattie turned to Frank with a beseeching expression.

He quickly held up both hands. "Forgive me," he said, his tone cool, "but I have no interest in looking into the murder of the man who allowed me to hang for a crime he knew I didn't commit."

"I think it's a great idea to ask Jordan to solve Michael's murder," Charlotte piped up, ignoring Jordan's quelling glance. "After all, she solved Hattie's."

Frank waved a hand dismissively. "She was rather inept, though she managed to stumble upon the solution."

"But she *did* solve it, did she not?" Charlotte pressed him before Jordan could form a retort. "Without her, you never would've known who framed you for my sister's murder. So I think we should give Jordan a chance to help us solve Michael's murder."

All eyes turned toward her.

A Mexican Martini had never sounded better.

* * *

TWENTY minutes later, Jordan settled with a sigh into steaming, lavender-scented water in her claw-foot bathtub. Vanilla candles perfumed the air, casting flickering shadows on the mahogany wainscoting that surrounded the tub. Soft classical music played in the background. She'd turned out the lights so that the cracks in the tile floor weren't as noticeable. Malachi had his muzzle propped on the rounded edge of the tub, content to let her rub his ears.

Sheer bliss.

She'd managed to convince the four ghosts to table all further discussion of marriage and mayhem until morning. Even Seavey had grudgingly agreed to leave for the night, though Jordan suspected his equanimity wouldn't hold for long.

"No spectral wedding will be held in this house," she reassured Malachi. Since the dog's arrival on her doorstep, she'd gotten into the habit of discussing all important issues with him. His advice was usually far more pragmatic than that of the humans with whom she'd become acquainted.

"Rooooooo," he agreed now.

"And there's no way I'm investigating Seavey's murder."

"Raaaooow."

"After all, he's a sociopath. It's not like he deserves to know who killed him. And who knows what he'd do if he found out? He could go after someone's descendant, out of pure spite. I could end up responsible for some poor innocent person's death."

Malachi made the supreme effort to lean over and lick her cheek in agreement, then sank back down.

"Precisely."

Jordan scrunched around in the tub, trying to get her neck positioned more comfortably against the rim. A folded towel hovered in her peripheral vision. With a scowl, she grabbed it and wedged it behind her neck.

"We need to establish some house rules," she complained. "I deserve privacy in my own bathroom."

Hattie floated toward the opposite end of the bathtub. Malachi whined.

Jordan felt like doing the same. "I'm not interested in hearing anything you have to say at the moment," she told Hattie. "I've had a long, stressful day, and all I want is a relaxing soak, then bed."

Hattie wrung her hands.

"Quit that."

"It's just . . ." Hattie hesitated. "I thought Seavey had murdered me, you see. I've maligned his good name all these decades—"

"He doesn't have a good name."

"Michael *isn't* a bad man. He simply did what he had to, to survive. Just as I did after my husband died."

Jordan sighed. "I'll grant you that Seavey probably isn't truly evil in the tradition of Jack the Ripper, but he isn't exactly a model citizen, either. And it's *not* the same. You intended to run your husband's shipping business ethically, siding with Frank's union to provide better treatment of sailors. You were *murdered* because you only wanted the best for Charlotte. Seavey, on the other hand, murdered for financial gain. And let's not forget he was *blackmailing* you into his bed, for Christ's sake, as a condition for helping you get Charlotte back. Those are *not* the actions of an honorable man."

"But he avenged my murder," Hattie pointed out.

Jordan gave up and stood, wrapping a bath towel around herself and blowing out the candles. "That doesn't cancel out his other criminal activities." She shooed Hattie out the door.

The ghost trailed her down the hall and into the bedroom. "I'm merely asking you to look into the circumstances surrounding his death. Maybe he's right—maybe Eleanor *did* publish lies to support her editorial position. But I owe him the courtesy of finding the truth."

"Michael Seavey was the bane of your existence until you died—how can you possibly believe that you owe him anything?"

"Couldn't you just look into the shipwreck and see if there were any survivors?" Hattie pleaded. "You were so good at understanding the motivations of the people I knew back then, and of understanding who might have been capable of murdering me. Wouldn't this be similar?"

"What is this? Good ghost, bad ghost?" Jordan grumbled. At Hattie's confused look, she said, "Never mind."

Drying the ends of her hair with the towel, she explained impatiently, "First of all, I'm not interested in functioning as an amateur detective for all the ghosts in this town." She paused, shuddering at the implications of what she'd just said. "And second, in this case, *everyone* probably wanted Seavey dead—he had so many enemies I wouldn't even know where to start."

She rummaged through a drawer, looking for the cotton T-shirt Jase had given her as a belated house-warming present and she'd converted into a nightshirt. The one that stated across the front, in large block letters, REALITY IS JUST A STATE OF MIND.

Hattie wrinkled her nose. "I don't understand this modern practice of painting comments on your night-wear," she said. "Or of wearing something to bed that should be worn during the day. Last week, your nightshirt said something that sounded like a local football team. Don't you have a proper nightgown?"

"They get too tangled—they're a hassle," Jordan replied, turning back the down comforter on her bed. "Didn't you have any slogans back in the 1800s?"

Hattie looked confused.

"You know, like something the president might have said that became a common phrase people used to explain how they felt or how something worked in the world?"

"Maybe," she replied, but her expression said she doubted it.

"Well, there you go." Jordan glanced toward the hall. "Where's Charlotte?"

"Downstairs practicing her telekinesis powers, using them to straighten up the library."

The relevant word in this instance being "practice." Jordan closed her eyes. She'd think about it tomorrow, she reminded herself.

Hattie continued to hover just inside the door.

Jordan sighed. "All right, I'll take a trip out to the historical society tomorrow to see if there are any other newspaper articles about Seavey's murder or survivors of the shipwreck. If there aren't, that's the end of it."

Hattie sagged with relief.

Of course, the historical society was still closed for remodeling, which meant Jordan would have to ask Darcy to meet her there and let her in. Not a good plan, given how buried Darcy would be with Holt's murder investigation. And hadn't she mentioned something about going back out to the crime scene tomorrow?

Alternatively, Jordan could break into the building. Again. Breaking the law was becoming habitual for her—during her last visit she'd stolen materials from the archives, then broken in to return them while Darcy was in the hospital.

"In the meantime," she told Hattie sternly, "I expect you to resolve this marriage issue. I'm not keen on having either man in this house."

Hattie made several reassuring noises that Jordan knew better than to believe signaled the end to *that* discussion, then faded away, leaving her in peace.

Malachi slipped into the bedroom and jumped onto the bed, settling in. Jordan climbed in right after him, fighting for her half of the comforter. She was about to turn out the bedside lamp when she saw Michael Seavey's personal papers, still stacked where she'd left them on her nightstand. She'd been procrastinating about returning them to Holt, not looking forward to having to fend off his inevitable advances. And didn't *that* make her feel guilty, in light of today's events? She and Hattie were certainly a pair. First thing tomorrow, she'd take the papers to the local mail shop and copy them, then drive them out to Holt's house. His family would want to know that she returned them, since they would be part of Holt's estate.

She leaned against the headboard, still too worked up to fall asleep. Perhaps if she read Seavey's papers she wouldn't lie in the dark and think about the *other thing* she'd seen that afternoon. Or maybe she'd find information that would indicate the thing she'd seen wasn't the *Henrietta Dale*, thus proving the gardener wrong.

Surely, if Seavey had owned a clipper ship, he'd have written about it. And if so, he also would've detailed his plans for the ship. It seemed unlikely that he would've gone into any kind of shipping business, given his established shanghaing practices. And no one had mentioned to her that Seavey had taken over Longren Shipping after Hattie's murder. Jordan couldn't come up with any reason why he would've needed to expand his interests in that direction. So if he *had* purchased the clipper ship, why? And who might have tried to run it aground? And what, if anything, did the shipwreck have to do with his murder? Or Holt's, for that matter?

She grabbed a couple of pillows and punched them into submission, shoving them behind her, then leaned back. Reaching for the papers, she flipped through a stack of yellowed, handwritten notes until she came to a sheaf of pages dated 1893.

Before she had a chance to search for a mention of the *Henrietta Dale*, a diary entry from the month before Seavey's death caught her eye:

July 8, 1893: I found much in the events of this evening to be cause for increased concern. Garrett grows ever bolder, taking unwise risks, even flaunting our successes in front of the Customs agents . . .

Jordan looked up from the page long enough to adjust the light from the bedside lamp, then settled in to read.

Lost Nerve

July 8, 1893
(one month earlier)

MICHAEL propped a shoulder against the back wall of Mayor Payton's luxuriously appointed parlor, sipping after-dinner port from Baccarat crystal and listening to the evening's guest performer, Payton's unmarried sister. A quiet mouse of a woman dressed in a dull green gown that did nothing for her sallow coloring or plump figure, she'd been seated next to Michael during dinner. She moved effortlessly between Bach, Schumann, and more contemporary ragtime songs, displaying a far better command of the pianoforte than she had of polite dinner conversation.

Michael's fellow dinner guests, polished in deportment yet woefully uneducated in the fine arts, ignored Miss Payton's stunning musical talent in favor of consuming large amounts of the admittedly excellent Duoro port the mayor imported for his frequent fund-raisers. Drowning out the music with chatter, the guests bemoaned the cool, wet summer weather that had ruined the Independence Day fireworks display; worried aloud about their risky investments in the proposed railroad between Port Chatham and Portland, Oregon; and vociferously predicted the demise of the local shipping industry. The latter was based on the increased business that lately had gone to that "upstart" port town of "heretics and hedonists," Seattle.

Michael found it all intolerably boring. Savoring another sip of the port, he wondered whether he could manage a glance at his pocket watch without appearing rude. And whether, if he found enough time had passed, he could slip away without drawing unwanted attention.

Loud laughter erupted from the opposite corner of the room, causing Miss Payton to falter in her otherwise flawless execution of a Bach cantabile. More than one set of eyes averted as Jesse Canby staggered then fell onto a velvet settee. His silk cravat wine-stained and askew, his legs splayed, he raised his head to lock gazes with his mother, Eleanor, who stood rigid with embarrassment. Jesse's eyes were feverishly bright, his laughter uncaring as the effort to hold his head up became too much.

As owner of the *Port Chatham Weekly Gazette*, Eleanor Canby held sway over the opinions of the town's social elite. She'd made it clear that Jesse, an unrepentant alcoholic who had taken an unhealthy interest in the waterfront's opium-smoking parlors, not to mention its brothels, was no longer welcome in her home. And recently, she'd become ever more strident in her stand on her editorial page, railing against the evils of such licentiousness. Indeed, given the potential for offending Eleanor, Michael was surprised that Payton had allowed Jesse to attend this evening's event.

Then again, when one craved the heavenly demon, all else took a backseat. Jesse was quietly supplying the good mayor with contraband, thus minimizing the risk that someone would witness Payton's visit to a known opium den.

Michael was careful to keep his expression bland, not allowing his amusement to show. Payton was in a delicate position: he couldn't slight Eleanor without suffering political repercussions, yet neither could he publicly snub his supplier. Nevertheless, Eleanor possessed a keen intelligence—it wouldn't take long for her to piece together the reason for Jesse's presence tonight.

The irony was that half the guests this evening, including Jesse, were Michael's regular customers. The new pastime of Port Chatham's social elite was a visit to one's favorite Chinese "laundry," taking a walk on the wild side of the waterfront. And Michael's goal was to ensure they could engage in their illicit activities with a minimum of risk, in the company of like-minded friends. Once his plans were complete, his customers would no longer feel compelled to sneak through the back door at a laundry; instead, they would recline in splendor served by Michael's charming chefs, smoking chandu opium of the highest quality, smuggled in weekly from Canada.

Oddly enough, his customers seemed to relish taking the risk of inviting him into their homes. They constantly plied him with invitations to attend the season's most prestigious gatherings, be they dinners organized to belay the tedium of the cold, cloudy summer, or political fundraisers meant to line the coffers of the mayor and his cronies.

Michael wanted nothing more than to hole up in his hotel suite. He remained haunted by the thought that Hattie would walk into a hostess's parlor, or that Hattie was seated at the other end of the dinner table, just out of sight. Though it had been three years since her death, he continued to be plagued by imagined glimpses of her among the crowds on the waterfront boardwalks, and by his memories of her gracing the elegant homes of her neighbors.

The persistence of those memories infuriated him.

Miss Payton brought the Bach piece to an end, pausing to shuffle music scores before launching into her next song. Michael set his glass on the tray of a passing housemaid, then slipped out the French doors to the garden.

Pausing on the steps leading down to a brick patio surrounded by sodden plants, he stood under the dripping eaves, gazing into the damp darkness. As was so often true this dreary summer, a steady, misting rain fell from a heavy sky, soaking all it touched. His forthcoming rendezvous on the north side of town promised to be an uncomfortable one.

The door behind him opened, spilling light onto the wet bricks, and he turned, thinking to see a fellow guest as intent on escaping the smoke-filled room as he. To his surprise and displeasure, Eleanor Canby stepped out.

"Mr. Seavey." She nodded stiffly. "A moment of your time, if you please."

Michael managed a formal bow. "As you wish, Mrs. Canby."

He had never forgiven her for her treatment of Hattie in the days before her death. As editor-in-chief of Port

Chatham's only newspaper, Eleanor had long ago established herself as the town's moral compass. She had denounced Hattie's attempts to manage her husband's shipping business after his death at sea, claiming such work didn't suit a woman of high social standing. Eleanor's public condemnation had undermined any chance Hattie might have had of saving the business, thus removing her only means of financial survival.

Michael also suspected that the disintegration of Longren Shipping within mere weeks of Hattie's murder had been no coincidence. Eleanor had powerful business allies, many of whom would have been gleeful at the prospect of taking over the shipping contracts. He had it on good word that Charlotte, left with no means by which to support herself, was now under the tutelage of Mona Starr, the madam of Port Chatham's most notorious brothel, the Green Light.

"I thought it only fair to warn you, Mr. Seavey." Eleanor's stentorian voice pulled him from his thoughts. "I plan to run an editorial this coming week decrying the increased use of opium by this town's citizens. I am not unaware of your involvement in that business, of course."

Michael raised both brows, feigning amusement. "My *dear* Eleanor. I have no idea to what you refer."

Her lips thinned. "Come now, Mr. Seavey. We all know how you've replaced the income you lost from the demise of Longren Shipping. It's no secret that Sam Garrett smuggles in contraband under your protection."

"Sheer speculation."

"Nevertheless." She smoothed the skirts of her midnight-blue silk evening gown with hands encrusted with jewels. "My editorial will condemn the purchase and use of the disgusting drug. Though few speak out on the matter, I find the drug's long-term effects on smokers distressing."

She was referring, of course, to the continued deterioration of Jesse's health in the face of her efforts to curb his voracious appetites. She'd even gone so far as to engage the services of a local physician, Willoughby, to treat Jesse for alcohol addiction. Unfortunately, the good doctor's prescription of regularly administered doses of laudanum was no doubt the cause of Jesse's newfound craving for opiates.

Though Michael was unsympathetic with regard to Eleanor's plight, even he could see that she grew more desperate with each passing week. Jesse's self-destructive tendencies betrayed her failures as a mother, and such knowledge surely ate away at her. The boy had a sensitive, artistic temperament; her rigid parenting had contributed greatly to his gradual withdrawal from those around him. Unfortunately, Eleanor's despair might lead her to launch a public campaign that could become a rather large thorn in Michael's side.

"I trust you won't be naming names in your editorial," he told her dispassionately. "That would be exceedingly unwise, Eleanor."

Her spine straightened. "Do not believe, Mr. Seavey, that because you are an investor in my newspaper, you will be immune to condemnation in print. If I decide you are the cause of the moral decay of Port Chatham's citizenry, I will not hold back."

"I can only hope to attain such lofty status," he replied

wryly. "Watch your step, Eleanor. As a businessman, I never operate without contingent plans. Most in this town know not to cross me."

"You *threaten* me?"

"Not at all," Michael replied. "I'm simply making the point that ownership of the local newspaper might be an interesting addition to my business holdings."

For the first time, he glimpsed pure rage in her eyes. Evidently, control of an editorial page trumped the well-being of her only child.

Across the garden, Michael's bodyguard, Remy, stepped out of the shadows, reminding him why he'd slipped away from the evening's social obligations. "Quite frankly, though," he continued, keeping his tone light as he pulled on his kidskin gloves, "I doubt your newspaper campaign against the heavenly demon will have much effect—it isn't as if the stuff is illegal. Most folks consider it a harmless bit of play to try to outwit the Customs officers and evade paying the import duties."

"They'll soon change their minds when I educate them on the drug's deleterious health effects," Eleanor snapped, "not to mention the precious tax dollars that are being lost."

He shrugged. "I care not what people put in their bodies—'tis a free country, after all. And for the moment, our town suffers little from funds lost to shrinking revenues."

"People must be saved from their own poor judgment, Mr. Seavey!"

"As you saved Jesse from himself?" he asked softly.

"You go too far, sir! I intend to push for the eventual outlawing of all forms of opium, just as I've already done with those who introduced the wretched drug to our shores!"

She referred, of course, to the Chinese Exclusion Act that had been passed by Congress, placing a moratorium on the immigration of Chinese. The supposed argument had been a concern for the jobs they held in the gold fields, but Michael had always suspected that racial prejudice was the stronger motivation. And though the authorities had announced their intention to be vigilant, he doubted the law was enforceable—the West Coast had thousands of miles of remote inlets and beaches, any of which could be used for a night landing of unwanted immigrants.

Remy appeared more anxious with each passing moment. Michael donned his top hat. "As much as I would love to continue our debate, Eleanor, I must take leave of your excellent company. A prior engagement, you understand."

"Of a clandestine nature, I presume, Mr. Seavey?" Eleanor's voice was laced with disapproval.

"You may presume to your heart's content—I only hold the power to stop you from putting those presumptions into print."

"Stay away from my son, Mr. Seavey."

He didn't respond, instead bowing his head politely. "I bid you a pleasant evening, madam."

* * *

REMY waited at the entrance to the back alley, shifting from one foot to the other, holding open the door to the coach. "Trouble at North Beach, Boss."

Michael sighed. His new business partner was proving to be more of an inconvenience than he was worth. Climbing into the coach, he took a seat across from Remy, pounding on the ceiling with his fist. Max, his second enforcer, whistled to the horses, then snapped the reins. The coach lurched forward.

The trip was swift—Payton's residence was less than a mile from the hill above North Beach. Short in distance yet a world apart, the land abutting North Beach was inhabited by the poor Chinese farmers whose produce graced the elegant dining tables of Port Chatham.

Max pulled the horses to a halt at the top of a pasture that fell steeply away to the bluffs running along the beach. Remy opened the door, and Michael stepped down from the carriage. To his left halfway down the slope stood the black silhouette of a barn. Just before the water's edge, a huge old maple tree spread its branches, barely discernible through the light rain that fell. He saw shadows floating across the ground, low against the barn's east foundation. Chinese, no doubt, smuggled in along with their contraband from Victoria. His partner did indeed grow increasingly reckless.

As Michael strode quickly through the pasture, the rain clinging to the tall grass immediately soaked through his boots. Spying the silhouettes of three men standing next to the tree, he veered in that direction.

At his approach, Sam Garrett dropped the butt of a cigarette and ground it out with his boot. The two men at his back were as brawny in build as Garrett, and as heavily muscled. Michael had discovered Garrett working the fire crew aboard a steamship and, impressed with the man's quick wit and strong physique, had made an offer Garrett couldn't refuse: an illicit partnership in his growing smuggling business. It appeared, however, that Michael had exercised faulty judgment that day.

As had been the case on many days of late.

He shook off the thought, his gaze sharpening on a faint movement under a large limb of the maple. Peering into the gloom, he was able to make out the kicking feet of a man strung up to one of the lower branches.

"I didn't know we'd taken on the business of lynching the Chinese, Garrett," he said calmly, holding his anger in check. "Pray explain yourself."

Garrett shrugged, folding massive arms across his chest. "The Customs agents came a bit too close, so I stashed the shipment on the beach earlier. When I returned to retrieve it just now, it was gone. That Lok fella there, he supposedly gardens this piece of land—I saw him lurking about earlier. I don't tolerate theft."

"Nor do I." The victim's kicks had become feebler. "However, nor do I want the authorities targeting us as part of a murder investigation."

"Hell, his own kind didn't even try to save him—that tells you he's guilty as sin." Garrett spit into the tall grass, then shrugged. "Let him swing awhile longer, then we'll see what he has to say."

Michael nodded to Remy and Max. "Cut him down."

"What're you about?" Garrett's expression was incredulous. "Every Chinaman in town will hear of this. You've undercut my authority, damn you!"

"Would those be the Chinese you smuggled in this

evening, or the ones already living upon our fair soil?" Michael asked mildly.

Garrett swore. As one of his thugs made a move to intervene, Michael held up a hand. "Call your men off, *now*."

Garrett hesitated, then grudgingly gave an order to have his men stand down. "You'll regret this, Seavey."

"I'd regret even more visits from the new police chief—the man is a bit too eager to prove his worth to our town council."

Michael watched dispassionately as his bodyguards untied Lok's hands and set him free. The man staggered, hands at his throat, then disappeared into the shadows.

"A few more minutes, and I'd have had the information I needed to retrieve our shipment," Garrett complained.

Michael seriously doubted the man had purloined the drugs, though that did leave a question as to who *had*. "A few more minutes, and you would've had a body to dispose of," he retorted. "Dead men don't talk."

Garrett's laughter echoed harshly through the hushed night. "I didn't believe the rumors about how you'd lost your nerve, but now I've got the hard evidence of it."

Michael reached up to turn the collar of his coat higher—the rain fell more steadily now, running down the back of his neck to soak his shirt. He wanted nothing more than for this meeting to end—he had no patience for explaining himself to others. "You purposely taunt the revenue agents, Garrett, making no effort to disguise your weekly trips. Already, they pay more attention to our shipments than before. If anyone is the fool this night, it is you."

"And what?" Garrett asked, amused. "You think to

outrun Customs when your little ship is finally sea-worthy? Everyone knows steamers are the only vessels fast enough to beat the revenue cutters."

So Garrett had heard about his project to refurbish a clipper ship that had been pulled out of service by its shipping company. 'Twas a pity; Michael had hoped to keep the new business venture a secret from Garrett, since he planned to cut him out of the proceeds.

"I don't intend to outrun Customs, merely to *outfox* them," he explained with more tolerance than he felt. "Pray tell, Garrett, what does every steamer trafficking in contraband do when the Customs boats approach? They run up sails, to make the agents believe they are a sailing ship, because everyone knows sailing ships don't carry contraband. What better way to sail right past the authorities than with a luxury clipper ship? And even if the agents come aboard, no passenger will admit to their activities belowdecks." He shrugged. "Besides, I merely plan to provide my passengers with luxurious accommodations in which to indulge their tastes, not traffic the drug," he lied.

"I've saddled myself with a business partner who clings to old methods," Garrett scoffed. "Your judgment is faulty at best. And, I suspect, compromised by your inability to forget the past."

Michael froze. "If that's your belief, you are welcome to strike out on your own," he replied, his tone arctic.

"With what funds? You've cost me my stake by letting Lok go."

"On the contrary—you've cost us *both* our stakes this night through your own recklessness, which I will not tolerate. What happened to the original shipment is of little consequence. Find a way to provide recompense, and soon, or face the consequences."

Garrett's expression was contemptuous. "If you flinch at the sight of a Celestial swinging from a limb, I doubt you have the stomach to take me on."

"You have seventy-two hours."

Michael jerked his head at Remy and Max, then turned to leave. With his bodyguards flanking him, walking backward with sharp eyes trained on Garrett's men, Michael returned to the carriage.

As the carriage wound its way down to the waterfront, his mood remained pensive. Regardless of the reasons he'd given Garrett, he wondered if the man had been right in his assessment. When it came to murder, Michael had never been squeamish. And yet tonight, if he hadn't intervened—indeed if he'd let Lok die—he knew he wouldn't have slept for days.

Chapter 6

THE next morning, Jordan lay in bed, scowling at the water spot on her bedroom ceiling. Tom was no doubt anxious to tell her all about it, to explain how it was a symptom of a malevolent type of impossible-to-find leak in the roof that would dog her to her grave.

Roof leaks, she'd read, could start anywhere. Rain could seep through in one spot—perhaps because of a relatively innocent cracked or broken roof tile—then travel along the roofline forever, finally soaking through where one least expected. The old water spot on her ceiling was probably just such a beast. She suspected Tom had a long, detailed list of such beasts. She was doomed.

And if the events of yesterday were any indication, her strategy of denial had also taken a severe hit. Not that it wasn't salvageable, but still. It was hard to ignore an object as imposing as a ghost ship with thousands of yards of sails and rigging, tons of decking, and multiple masts resembling giant, old-growth trees. An object large enough *and* fast enough to mow her down, squashing her like a gnat.

By comparison, planning a wedding for the ghost of an opium-smuggling sociopath was starting to look like a cakewalk.

She tossed the covers aside, climbing stiffly from bed. After a halfhearted attempt to look presentable in case any ghosts were lingering about, she hobbled on sore joints and aching muscles to the upstairs landing, pausing for a moment to enjoy the early morning peace and quiet.

At this time of the day, the house felt settled, peaceful, and . . . well, welcoming. Though it had been vacant for a number of years before she'd moved in, it held an indefinable quality that made her believe—in some woo-woo sort of way—that it had been waiting for her. Ridiculous, but she suspected that all old houses, saturated as they were with the memories of a century or more of personal history, gave off that vibe. Old houses talked as well—via the creaks in their worn floorboards, the distant rumble of their ancient furnaces, the echoes of footsteps as one walked down hallways over hardwood floors that had long ago given up their tight fit.

In the air above her, sparkling dust motes caught updrafts in the fractured rays of sun that shone through windows high over the stairwell. Someone's handprint marred the light film that had settled on the shiny mahogany railing since she'd polished it a few days ago. The pale, robin's-egg-blue runner still showed bits of bark here and there—the remaining evidence of sections of wisteria vine having been hauled down from the attic and out through the front door. She *really* needed to unpack her vacuum and clean up the debris rapidly accumulating on every stair riser and in every room corner.

Malachi yawned, ending with a whine that urged her to quit woolgathering. She started down the stairs, and he followed, so sluggish that he tripped, hitting the back of her knees and causing them to buckle. But for her death grip on the railing, they both would've tumbled and landed in a heap at the bottom. Shaking her head, she motioned for him to precede her.

She crossed the foyer and stood in the library's arched doorway, assessing the damage from the prior night's events. As far as she could tell, Charlotte's telekinetic attempts at straightening had created *more* havoc, not less. Admittedly, a few books had been placed back on shelves, but they were upside down and out of order. Pictures still hung askew, plant pots still lay on their sides.

From the beginning, the library had been her favorite room and one of the reasons she'd lost all rational thought, writing an obscenely large check for the house. Ceiling-to-floor, glass-fronted bookcases lined the walls, stuffed with books on every subject and published in every decade from the 1800s to present day. The far end of the room included a cozy conservatory with French doors, and when she opened them on nice days, she was drenched with fragrance from flowering bushes and vines that had managed to survive decades of neglect.

In the last few weeks, her attempts to clean and organize the house had primarily centered on this room, as if she subconsciously understood that turning it into a cozy, comfortable escape was a huge step toward turning Longren House into a true home. She'd dusted, scrubbed, and polished woodwork, and spent days organizing and shelving stack after stack of books. But after last night's debacle, she wasn't certain she could still see the fruits of her labors.

She walked through the room, opening the French doors to let in fresh air. The doors banged against something, then swung back into her. She put up her hands instinctively to protect her face, then leaned outside to see what they'd hit, which turned out to be the steel supports of the scaffolding she'd caught a glimpse of the night before. Making a mental note to inquire about it, she adjusted the doors to partway open, then got to work.

Not knowing where to start, she knelt next to a toppled plant, scooping soil back into its pot. Her mind drifted back to what she'd read the night before. Evidently, Michael Seavey had become heavily involved in smuggling opium around the time of his murder in 1893. The guys at the pub thought whoever had lured the *Henrietta Dale* onto the rocks might've been a business competitor. But given Seavey's misgivings about his partner Sam Garrett, it seemed more likely *he* was the culprit, not a competitor.

She'd have to ask Tom to educate her with regard to opium smuggling in the 1800s. Who had been the players? How prevalent had smuggling been along the Northwest coast? When she drove out to the historical society later today, she should look for the editorial Eleanor Canby had supposedly written in the *Port Chatham Weekly Gazette*. Given the dates on Seavey's papers, the editorial should have been published well before his murder—in Jordan's estimation, at least several weeks.

As she walked over to a bookshelf to straighten its contents, she noticed Malachi sitting just inside the library door, holding his leash in his mouth, his expression disgruntled. She'd altered their usual morning routine of a walk over to the restaurant, and in his opinion, for no good reason. When she made eye contact with him, he heaved a martyred sigh.

"Don't give me any grief," she warned, using a dust cloth to wipe down a leather-bound copy of *War of the Worlds*, then wedging it at the end of a shelf holding *Acts of Malice* by Perri O'Shaughnessy and *Promised Land* by Robert B. Parker. "This is therapeutic."

"What's therapeutic?"

She glanced over her shoulder to see Jase standing on the steps outside the French doors. He ducked under the scaffolding and waved the latte he held—probably freshly made in the kitchen of his Arts and Crafts–vintage cottage just down the block. He wore one of his trademark dark blue Henleys, sleeves pushed up to his elbows, and well-worn jeans sporting frayed cuffs and a rip above one knee. With a day's growth of beard shadowing his jaw, he had her thinking of things she'd avoided for the last year during her divorce.

"Alphabetizing the books," she answered, focusing on his question and ignoring her X-rated thoughts. Giving a brief prayer of thanks that she'd thought to pull on jeans and comb her hair into submission, she motioned for him to enter and accepted the latte. "Organizing them gives me a feeling of control over my environment."

He studied the shelves. "Wouldn't it make more sense to group books by subject?"

Jordan shrugged, taking a sip. Whatever complaints she had about Jase—and they were becoming increasingly difficult to remember—she couldn't fault his coffee. The man was dead serious about his java—he even imported special beans from a microroaster in Portland.

"What're you doing out and about so early?" she asked. "You couldn't have had more than a few hours of sleep."

"Bill closed for me." He leaned down to rub Malachi's ears. The dog gurgled appreciatively around the leash. "I wanted to check on you, make sure you're okay. You looked like you felt pressured to investigate the shipwreck, and I wanted you to know that hadn't been our intent. Our discussion was more in the way of a healthy debate."

"Uh-huh." She rolled her eyes and went back to shelving. "I took Darcy home, then came back and went to bed myself, though I did read through a few of Michael Seavey's personal papers." She didn't mention the mess that had greeted her in the library.

Jase smiled. "Figured you could find something in Seavey's papers that would refute Bob's assertions, proving that the ship you saw was real?"

"Okay, yes. What I discovered, though, was that Seavey and his business partner were smuggling opium from Canada. Evidently, Seavey planned to use the *Henrietta Dale* for that purpose. He also intended to cut his business partner out of the deal."

"I didn't know opium was illegal then."

"It wasn't—they were smuggling it past the Customs agents to get around paying import duties, thus probably keeping more of the profits for themselves."

She stepped back to judge whether the row of books she'd just straightened was aesthetically appealing, deciding they would look better if several were stacked on their sides. "Given what Seavey probably had on board the *Henrietta Dale* the night of the shipwreck, if his business partner—a man named Garrett—knew of Seavey's plans to cut him out of the take, it makes sense he would've been behind luring the ship onto the rocks. It also follows that Holt might've thought there was something valuable enough to salvage."

Jase gave her a frown. "I don't want you going anywhere near Holt's murder investigation."

She stopped shelving books to give him a quizzical look. It wasn't like Jase to ever give orders—he'd been nothing but supportive while allowing her to find her own way through the morass of events that had blindsided her since her move to town.

"This isn't the equivalent of researching Hattie's murder," he warned now. "Someone in *this* time period, someone—in all likelihood, in *this* town—committed murder. That means he has a lot to lose if you start poking around."

"I'm aware of that. But all I'm doing is trying to figure out if the *Henrietta Dale* really did run aground anywhere near where we found Holt, and whether it's connected to his possibly diving in that area. You have to admit, the coincidences are piling up. Holt was working in the hotel originally owned by Michael Seavey." *A hotel still haunted by his ghost.* "And you said yourself it didn't make any sense that Holt was diving—he must have had one hell of a reason to overcome his fear of the water. If I can just establish a connection, it would help Darcy—"

"What you're doing is dangerous," Jase interrupted, his tone unusually blunt. "*Anything* you do to give the murderer the impression you are trying to find out what happened to Holt gives him a reason to come after you."

Jordan was so taken aback she couldn't form a response. Until now, issuing orders hadn't seemed to be in Jase's DNA.

Tom chose that moment to arrive, ducking through the French doors, carrying coffee in one hand and a sheaf of papers in the other. He took one look at their faces and halted in his tracks. "You two want me to go back out, wait until one of you gives me the all-clear signal, then return?"

After a tense silence, Jase blew out a breath, his expression discomfited, as if he realized just how dictatorial he'd sounded.

"Are those your notes for the restoration plan?" Jordan asked Tom, pasting a welcoming smile on her face.

"Yeah." He glanced at the nearest shelf of books, which were still in a jumble. "Wasn't this room all straightened up yesterday?"

Jordan sighed. She started to explain, but Tom frowned and leaned closer to read the bindings. "Are your books *alphabetized?*"

"It helps me find what I'm looking for more easily, and I like the sense of order."

"But wouldn't it be more practical to organize them by subject, so you can browse?"

Jase coughed.

"How about I fix us some breakfast," Jordan said grimly. She turned to Jase. "Are you sitting in on this meeting?"

Jase nodded. "Tom thought it might be helpful if I was here."

"A restoration on this scale can be a bit overwhelming, when viewed at the planning level," Tom explained.

"In comparison to dealing with ghost ships, I think we're good," Jordan said wryly.

Both men looked skeptical.

"You lived in a condominium down in L.A., right? One that you bought already completely finished?" Jase asked.

"Of course." Jordan had never liked the place. Ryland had bought it as a wedding present, and she'd never had the heart to tell him she found its modern architecture cold and impersonal.

"And you never redecorated it or remodeled any part of it, right?" Jase continued.

"Right. So?"

"So there's a certain amount of . . . chaos that accompanies any house renovation."

She shrugged, stuffing the dust cloth onto a shelf where it would be handy later on. "It'll be fine—I'll just make a plan to keep the restoration well under control."

"Right." Jase's expression was bland. "Where's that stack of books I had you buy when we were at the hardware store? Have you read the one on old-house restoration?"

"I haven't had time."

"Which book is that?" Tom asked.

"The one that explains the difference between historical restoration and remodeling."

"Oh. Yeah, good—that one gives a person a clear idea of the types of decisions she will face. It also explains the best process to use when renovating an old home—how to assess the work, draw up a plan, and so on."

"If she continues to clean and organize while she reads

the book, she'll become intimate with all of the rooms, while at the same time avoid damaging them," Jase pointed out.

"Great idea," Tom agreed.

"So I'm being reduced to a maid in my own home," Jordan concluded. "Keep it up, and there'll be no breakfast for either of you."

"I'm fairly certain even the book advises that you start with cleaning each room." Tom was fighting a grin. "But for the sake of my stomach, I'm willing to strike a compromise."

"What's with the scaffolding?" she asked him.

"Makes it easier to deal with the repairs to the siding and the underlying structure. You've got some dry rot here and there that will have to be taken care of before we can construct the iron trellis."

Not knowing what dry rot was or wanting to think too deeply about it, Jordan quickly alphabetized the pile of books she held, then led the way down the hall to the kitchen at the back of the house.

* * *

THOUGH its cracked, yellowed linoleum and warped countertops bespoke a misguided remodel, the kitchen was spacious and had a homey feel to it. Hints of the original design could still be found in the mahogany wainscoting and in the glass-fronted cabinets that graced the butler's pantry. A huge, white porcelain sink stood against the back wall, next to an ancient refrigerator that made strange sounds and did its best to keep Jordan's electric bill well into the stratosphere. She'd also discovered boxes full of antique kitchenwares in the attic—chromolithograph tins for coffee, tea, and sugar; yellowware crocks and bowls; and wooden utensils. Once she fixed the room up, she was certain it would become one of her favorites.

Both men sat down at the well-worn pine table that took up most of the center of the room. Pulling out a carton of fresh farm eggs she'd bought at the Saturday market, she rummaged in the cabinet next to the stove for a porcelain mixing bowl.

"Scrambled eggs and toast okay?" she asked, plunking the items on the counter next to the ancient gas stove.

"We're pathetically easy," Jase replied, leaning back and stretching his legs under the table.

"I read a few pages of Seavey's personal papers last night," she told Tom while she cracked eggs and beat them with a whisk. "I didn't make it far before conking out, but it appears as if Seavey knew his business partner was going to cause him trouble. He wrote about an incident in which the partner tried to hang a Chinese vegetable farmer. Seavey intervened on the farmer's behalf."

"I seem to remember reading something about that in newspapers from that time." Tom took a sip of his coffee. "The partner accused the vegetable farmer of making off with a shipment of opium, right?"

"Yeah. It's pretty clear from what I read that Seavey and his partner were smuggling in opium on a regular basis." She added milk to the eggs, then reached into the fridge for fresh herbs and a plate of organic butter from the local dairy. Using a spatula, she cut a small wedge of butter and dropped it into her cast-iron skillet to melt.

"Seavey talked about the Chinese as if they were illegal immigrants, but my memory of the nineteenth century on the West Coast is that the Chinese were laborers."

"They were," Tom confirmed. "They came into the country around the middle of the century to work in the mines during the California Gold Rush. But that was before the passage of the Chinese Exclusion Act. Not one of our country's finest hours."

She glanced over her shoulder, one eyebrow raised, then used kitchen scissors to snip fines herbes into the eggs.

"Congress passed the law in 1882," Jase explained. "It gave lawmakers the ability to suspend immigration. The original intent was to exclude Chinese immigrants from working in mines, taking jobs away from Americans, but the restrictions were gradually expanded to include Chinese living in cities. One senator called it nothing less than legalized discrimination."

"So by 1893 when Seavey died," Tom added, "there was a thriving business in smuggling Chinese immigrants out of Canada—where they could enter legally—and onto our shores. If you read the local papers from that time, you'll see numerous accounts of the authorities rounding up Chinese and returning them to Canada."

Jordan shivered as she poured the eggs into the skillet, then got busy slicing a loaf of artisan bread. "Pretty grim."

"Definitely not cool for a nation that prides itself on its support of human rights," Jase agreed.

"That explains the comment Seavey made in his papers that he wouldn't have anything to do with transporting Chinese immigrants. He was concerned his business partner was combining human trafficking with the smuggling of opium." She reached for plates and cutlery, handing them to Tom.

"The two crimes were miles apart in severity," he pointed out as he laid the plates on the table. "Opium smuggling occurred simply to avoid paying duties, thereby increasing one's already substantial profits from the sale of the stuff. Smuggling immigrants, though—now *that* was a federal offense. Seavey seemed to stick with highly profitable businesses in which the authorities tended to turn a blind eye, like the shanghaiing. Everyone knew it took place, but the ships needed crews, so no one really cared except the union reps. In the case of opium, no one cared except the Customs officials—at least, to begin with."

"The common denominator being," Jordan pointed out wryly, "that no one seemed to care much about upholding the law."

"Well, you're definitely right about that." Tom sat back down, eyeing her curiously. "So why *were* you reading Seavey's papers last night?"

She stirred the eggs while she debated whether to admit that Hattie wanted her to look into Seavey's murder. *And* whether to let on that the number of ghosts hanging out around the place continued to increase. Of course, said ghosts were conspicuously absent this morning, without explanation, which always made her more nervous than when they were present. She never knew quite what to think when they disappeared.

Pulling the skillet off the stove, she served the eggs. On the one hand, if she admitted she was looking into Seavey's murder, she could avoid the type of discussion she and Jase had been having when Tom arrived. Then again,

Seavey's murder really wasn't her only motivation to go poking around in the past. She didn't like lying, even by omission, to her friends.

"Just curious, that's all," she prevaricated, silently rationalizing that she'd explain later. "I was hoping to find a mention of the *Henrietta Dale*." Grabbing toast from the toaster oven and putting it onto a plate, she sat in a rickety chair across from the two men. "I figured that if Seavey purchased a clipper ship and was using it for business purposes, he'd have mentioned it. According to the gardener I talked to yesterday on Dungeness Spit, the ship ran aground during her maiden voyage. I also wondered what Seavey had intended to use her for, which I found out—smuggling opium. But I had hoped he would mention the shipwreck."

Though come to think of it, she realized, a forkful of eggs stalling midair, Seavey couldn't have written about it if he had been aboard and died that night, as he insisted.

Jase was frowning at her again. "You *do* realize that if you interfere in Darcy's investigation, she'll come down on you like a ton of bricks. Right?"

Who knew the man was such a pit bull? Jordan sighed. Maybe she *should* mention Seavey's ghost. It might distract Jase from his current goal, which seemed to be acting dictatorial.

"I'm just following up because of the coincidences," she reminded him. "I know you two don't think Holt would've been diving out there, but we found him in the same approximate location as where the ship ran aground. If Seavey was using the ship for smuggling, it stands to reason that Holt might've been curious enough to see if he could locate the shipwreck."

Jase shook his head. "There's no connection unless Holt knew about the shipwreck, and you had Seavey's papers, which, by the way, wouldn't even have mentioned the shipwreck if Seavey died that night. You said yourself that Holt had no interest in reading them, and even if he had, he wouldn't have found anything. So I don't see how he could have known to go diving in that location."

Dammit, he was right. She got up to open a can of dog food for Malachi, who viewed it with disdain, then went back to staring intently at the toast on her plate. He'd become addicted to the freshly churned butter she bought.

She returned to the table, brooding while she fed her toast to Malachi. Okay, maybe it *was* just a coincidence that Holt had been found in that location. Unless . . . another thought occurred to her. "Didn't you say Holt was working at the Cosmopolitan Hotel?" she asked Tom.

"Yeah." Tom swallowed a bite of toast. "He won the bid to repaint the top three floors—the new owner is doing some upgrades. That means Holt would have been working in the suites from which Seavey ran his businesses, back in the 1890s. Seavey bought the hotel from the person who originally built it, then added onto it substantially. He also knocked an entrance from the basement of the hotel into the network of underground tunnels running under the waterfront that were used for smuggling and shanghaiing."

"So it stands to reason that Holt could've run across some old business papers, then got curious," she concluded.

Jase's expression was skeptical. "We're talking Holt, here—he rarely showed interest in anything other than custom paint blending and hitting on women in All That Jazz. If he came across old papers, he would've chucked them into the trash."

"It can't hurt to drop by and have a chat with the owner," she insisted.

"Just be careful how far you take this," Jase warned. "Even if you do find a connection, it may not relate to Darcy's investigation. If Holt *was* diving for sunken treasure, I can guarantee he wouldn't have told anyone about it. Therefore, I still don't see how it could be relevant to his murder."

Jordan opened her mouth to argue further, sorely tempted to point out how thickheaded he was being, but she was interrupted by the back door swinging open. Amanda entered, bleary-eyed and sporting bed hair, a coffee mug dangling from the limp fingers of one hand. Dressed in torn jeans, layered tank tops, and high-top running shoes, even just out of bed, the lithe blonde managed to ooze a girl-next-door sexy appeal. Jordan considered snarling.

Amanda halted, blinking at them. "Oh. Um, morning."

"Hey." Tom smiled fondly at her. Jordan had observed that he functioned somewhat as a mentor, since the two frequently ended up working on the same homes.

Though her parents lived right next door, Amanda had pitched her tent in Jordan's backyard the first day she'd shown up to work, claiming that she had to live with a garden 24/7 in order to tune in to its "vibes." Jordan had long since ceded kitchen rights to her, including the use of the espresso machine.

"Pull up a chair," Jordan offered, "and have some breakfast."

The young woman accepted a plate of eggs from her with a sleepy smile, giving Jase a limp "high five" before sitting down. "You talked to Jordan about the plan yet?" she asked Tom.

"We were getting to that."

"It's important that she's fully on board, since we'll be counting on her to provide critical information." Amanda shoved eggs into her mouth.

"I'm sure you both know more than I do," Jordan pointed out.

"Oh, we don't mean about the restoration work itself," Amanda assured her. "You don't have a clue about *that*." Jordan debated whether to be insulted as Amanda continued. "We need you to talk to the ghosts. You know, ask them about the original design of the house and the gardens. Our goal is a completely integrated, historically accurate restoration."

Tom held up a hand. "Why don't you let me explain everything to Jordan before we go there?"

Jase obviously agreed. "You don't even know if Jordan wants to stick with the original design of the house, *or* if she's interested in applying for historic landmark status. That's a headache all on its own, not to mention whether the original design of the house is livable, in terms of modern conveniences."

Amanda looked mutinous. "But—"

"It's not as if Jordan likes to go without her comforts," Tom interrupted.

"Hey," Jordan said. She *was* insulted.

"We're not saying there's anything wrong with wanting to be comfortable," Jase hastily assured her. "I upgraded both the kitchen and bathrooms in my house when I restored it. I wasn't interested in living without a dishwasher, among other things."

"But we need her to talk to the ghosts, so that we have *all* the information," Amanda insisted. "This is an exciting opportunity for all of us, having the original inhabitants of a haunted house available for interviews during the restoration."

Jordan tried to wrap her mind around that comment and failed. She settled for saying, "I can't bring the ghosts into the process until I have a vision of what I intend to do." Standing, she removed plates and stacked them in the sink. "Tom, did you bring your papers with you from the library?"

"Yep." He pointed.

The sheaf of papers sitting in the middle of the table looked thick and intimidating. Jordan blew out a breath. "So. Who wants more espresso?"

* * *

THREE hours later, Jordan drove out to the Port Chatham Historical Society research building, weaving around horse-drawn carriages and old-fashioned bicycles. If any cops were on traffic duty, they probably thought she was careening wildly down the road under the influence. But it wasn't as if she had any choice in the matter—she couldn't drive *through* people, even if they weren't of this world.

Halfway into Tom's recitation of the many repairs needed to Longren House, she'd started hyperventilating over the projected costs. Apparently the diagonal crack running the length of the bay window in the parlor was a "compression shear crack of moderate size," a *not so bad* problem *yet*, while the cracks in the plaster behind the bookcases in the library were possibly the result of ground settlement, a *worse* problem, and *troubling*. Tom had then talked about finding no "pyramid" failures in the exposed portions of the foundation in the basement, maybe a *good* sign, but quickly segued into a discourse on water being the "adversary" they had to decisively rout from the entire structure.

About the time he anthropomorphized a structural defect in the staircase—describing it as relentless in its attempts to undermine the second and third floors of the house—she'd called a halt. After shooing everyone out, she'd straightened up the rest of the mess in the library, agreed to let Malachi take her for a walk, then shoved him into the Prius for the trip out to the Historical Society research facility.

Her favorite route from home to the south side of town where the facility was located was admittedly circuitous. Instead of heading straight south through her neighborhood along the main drag, she turned east, driving down the hill to the waterfront. This route gave her sweeping views of Admiralty Inlet and Port Chatham Bay, where she could observe the ferries and other marine traffic. The harbor was filled with sailing ships of all kinds—even an old-fashioned steamer or two with their huge smokestacks and paddle wheels.

In the past, she'd taken for granted that the beautiful old ships she always saw anchored throughout the bay were actually *there*. Now, of course, she had to wonder, which really put a dent in the pleasure of simply observing. Did ghost ships—if those were what she was actually seeing—simply hang out in the harbor? Was the ghost of every wrecked ship from over the centuries still lurking about? If she walked into a historic bar down on the waterfront, would she find a higher ratio of ghosts to patrons than in All That Jazz, because of the number of spectral sailors living along the waterfront?

She braked at a red light downtown, scowling at the two ladies attired in ankle-length day dresses with parasols, jaywalking half a block up. Dammit, this simply wouldn't do—she couldn't spend all her time speculating about the ramifications of what she saw versus what everyone else saw. And more to the point, she refused to lose the simple pleasure of enjoying the scenery on her outings. There had to be some way to control this crap. She had enough challenges in her *real* life.

The light switched green and she turned onto the main drag heading out of downtown. Challenges, for instance, such as money, which was beginning to loom large, particularly after talking to Tom that morning. She supposed she'd have to consider starting up a new therapy practice earlier than she'd originally intended. Though the insurance settlement she'd received from her husband's murder would tide her over for now, the repairs would make a serious dent in those funds.

Her plan had been to take at least a year's sabbatical from therapy work, and frankly, she wasn't even convinced in light of recent events that she should return to a practice at all. Given that she hadn't had a clue that her charming sociopath of a husband had been bedding his patients for years—she wasn't exactly confident of her skills in her chosen profession.

Granted, when she'd mentioned her concerns to her good friend Carol, a fellow professional, Carol had pooh-poohed them. She'd pointed out that no one does a good job of sorting through events affecting her own life, and that Jordan's recent failures had no correlation to her effectiveness as a therapist. But Jordan wasn't convinced. And because she'd lost her confidence, she knew she'd second-guess every decision she made in a therapy session, which wasn't fair to her patients.

In addition, her discipline had been Rational Therapy. *No one*, at this point, would describe her life as anything remotely resembling *rational*. She turned into the Historical Society's parking lot. No, she really didn't believe she should be taking on patients—at least, not until she could come to grips with her own problems. If anything, her original plan for a one-year sabbatical should be extended.

Maybe Jase would let her waitress for tips. "That should give me just enough money to pay for your dog food," she said out loud to Malachi.

"Rooooo . . . ooow." He yawned, then inched forward to lick the side of her face.

Spying a construction worker in overalls coming out of the building, she cracked the windows, then hopped out of the car, poking her head back in just long enough to tell Malachi, "I promise I'll only be a half hour or so."

Malachi heaved a sigh, his expression skeptical yet resigned, and lay down.

She jogged across the lot, Seavey's papers tucked under one arm, catching the man just as he was locking up. She stuck out a hand, saying cheerfully, "Hi! I'm Jordan."

He shook. "Travis, ma'am." He looked to be in his thirties, and his overalls were covered with smears of something white and gunky. He was frowning at her.

"Any chance you'd let me inside the building for a bit?" she asked. "I need to check the newspaper archives for information on a murder that occurred in the nineteenth century."

His face cleared. "Hey, you're that ghost lady, right? What? Are you investigating again or something?"

"Or something," she replied vaguely. "I won't be long, I promise."

He hesitated, scratching his head, transferring some of the white goo in the process. "I'm not really supposed to let anyone else in."

She pasted a reassuring expression on her face, hoping she looked trustworthy.

He gave a small shrug. "I guess it doesn't matter all that much. I figure you'd just get one of your ghosts to go through the wall and unlock the door from the inside, right?"

As if she could get any of "her ghosts" to do *anything* she wanted. "Right."

"And it *would* be kinda cool to help you solve an old murder, I guess."

"Absolutely."

He unlocked the door but kept his arm across the door-jamb, blocking her from entering. "Just don't touch the walls, okay? The Sheetrock mud is still wet, and I don't want to be sanding your handprints out of it."

"Scout's honor," she promised. "I can lock up after myself if you're leaving for the day."

"Nah." He stepped back to let her through. "I'm headed to the lumber company to pick up some extra mud. I was gonna stop for some lunch, but I'll be back in an hour or so."

She beamed at him. "Perfect."

Inside, she was hit with a mildly chemical odor that tickled her nose. She hastily headed downstairs to the basement, where the Society's archived collections were temporarily being stored during the remodel. The two elderly docents, Nora and Delia Hapley, were still on vacation in the south of France, happily avoiding the mess of the remodel. Little did they know how many times Jordan had illegally accessed their historical papers. She suspected there would be hell to pay when they found out.

She was pleased to find that the overhead lights had been turned back on—an improvement since the last time she'd visited, huddling in the dark and using her penlight to read. From memory, Jordan quickly found the stacks that contained binders of newspapers from the 1890s. Before she'd left the house, she'd checked the date of the story about Seavey's murder, which made it easy to narrow down which binder to pull from the shelves. Her best guess was that the shipwreck had to have occurred either immediately before that article was printed, or within a few days of it. And the shipwreck would have been big news—there should be several articles about it.

Sitting down at a small desk on the back wall, she set Seavey's papers, which she'd brought as another point of reference, aside for the moment. She opened the binder and started carefully lifting out stacks of brittle yellowed newsprint, scanning for dates and headlines. As luck would have it, she found what she was looking for in the first set of papers, spying the following banner headline, stretching across the front page:

Tragedy Strikes in Local Waters: Scores Perish as *Henrietta Dale* Founders on Dungeness Spit

August 5—Captain Nathaniel Williams, commander of the ill-fated clipper ship the *Henrietta Dale*, stood beside this reporter late last night on the west edge of Dungeness Spit, tears pouring down his ruddy cheeks as he watched the ship disintegrate, having fallen victim to powerful waves. "I've never skippered a finer ship," he cried. "It breaks my heart to watch her die."

While en route from Victoria, British Columbia, the ship mysteriously ran aground south of the New Dungeness Lighthouse. As of this reporter's deadline, many of the crew and passengers on board have perished, though the lightkeeper, with the help of his wife, has been able to pull a few blessed souls from the icy surf.

Rescue personnel from neighboring towns—

including our own Port Chatham—tried in vain to help those injured in the sudden grounding, but the precarious nature of the ship in shifting sands was a danger to all those who valiantly attempted to save lives.

Captain Williams removed his wool cap in a gesture of respect as the beautiful ship met her final death throes, her masts crashing into the surf, her hull breaking into pieces. "She was the pinnacle of my life's work," he said, visibly distraught. "I'll never skipper another like her."

Though few in number, the injured will be transported to Port Chatham to be treated at local infirmaries. Relatives of crew members and passengers can inquire as to the status of their loved ones at the Port Chatham Police Station.

Jordan set the newspaper aside, leaning back in the wooden chair she'd pulled up to the small desk. So there *had* been survivors. That meant there must be a list of victims in a subsequent article, as well as stories from survivors that would give her an idea of how many survived and who they might have been. It was possible she'd even run across a mention of Michael Seavey, either listed among the dead or noted as transported to the local infirmary.

She sorted through the rest of the stacks of newsprint, frustrated when she found nothing other than the article Hattie had shown her mentioning Seavey's murder. As with many historical collections, not all issues of the old newspaper had been preserved—there were gaps in the coverage, *big* gaps. She had a few more issues at home, but the chances were slim she'd find what she needed there.

Dammit! Scrubbing her hands over her face, she thought about what she knew so far, which was precious little: The ship *had* run aground, and it was possible that Michael Seavey had survived the wreck. She'd found no mention, though, of the ship being deliberately lured off course.

If Seavey *had* survived, why didn't he remember? And why weren't there more articles about Seavey's murder? Did the lack of stories about a formal murder investigation support his contention that Eleanor had planted the article for some reason? Surely even the murders of known criminals had been investigated in the nineteenth century. And such an investigation wouldn't have been ignored by the newspaper, if only for the purpose of underlining Eleanor's unyielding editorial stance regarding the evils of such activities.

Then again, Jordan supposed it didn't matter *how* Seavey had died, necessarily. Because if the ship had been lured onto the rocks, someone had most likely intended to murder him. In fact, whoever that person was may have realized Seavey had survived and come back to finish the job. If she could find evidence that someone had deliberately wrecked the ship, then either way, she had a murder to solve.

She pulled herself up short. *If* she decided to solve it. As far as she was concerned, she'd found her answer, that she really was—alarmingly—seeing a ghost ship. The article was clear: The *Henrietta Dale* had broken up in the surf off Dungeness Spit that night over one hundred years ago. So Bob was correct; there was no way anyone could have refurbished the vessel.

Jordan let her mind slide away from that scary little fact and focused on murder instead. Seavey didn't seem to care how he had died. But Hattie *did*. And dammit, if she were in Hattie's place, she would feel a similar level of guilt. Hadn't she wanted to solve her own husband's murder, even after he'd slept around on her, dragged her name through the papers, and battled her for more than his fair share of the assets in the divorce? Admittedly, Ryland had turned out to be a major jerk, but he hadn't deserved to die. And although Jordan had been implicated, her main motivation had been to find out who killed the man she'd once loved.

In Seavey's case, there was no question that he had a violent past, but he'd cared enough for Hattie to avenge her murder, and he hadn't deserved to be falsely accused. Even if Hattie eventually chose not to marry him, she would feel better if she at least helped find out what had happened to him. So Jordan had no problem empathizing with Hattie's point of view. Unfortunately.

She felt like banging her head against the nearest brick wall. Besides Seavey, who had been on board the *Henrietta Dale* that night? Obviously, the crew and its captain; Bob had said that Seavey had hired a captain known to be extremely competent. Had that captain been hired locally? If so, it was possible the captain had written a memoir. After all, he would want to defend his actions that night, in case anyone wondered about his culpability.

She stood and walked over to the stacks, hunting for collections that were perhaps from famous Port Chatham maritime families. If she could piece together the details of the events surrounding the *Henrietta Dale*, then research the laws and cultural mores of the time regarding the importation and use of opium, perhaps she'd start to have a sense of Michael Seavey's life in the weeks before his death.

Hunting through folders and binders for more than a half hour, she was about to give up when she found a small packet of papers written by Captain Nathaniel Williams. Opening it, she discovered a sheaf of badly frayed, handwritten pages, presumably from a personal diary, carefully encased in plastic covers. She flipped through them, looking for dates, but most of the entries didn't have any. There was no telling whether the pages documenting the shipwreck had survived—she'd have to go through what was there to determine if the collection contained any information of use.

Tucking the folder under one arm, she headed back to the small reading table, stopping on her way to snag the binder of newspapers from the weeks before the shipwreck. According to Seavey's personal papers, Eleanor's editorial campaign began around then. If Jordan could find the editorial mentioned by Seavey, it might give some clues as to who had been smuggling opium into Port Chatham then, and who might have had a reason to want Seavey out of the way. Then, using Seavey's and the captain's papers, she might be able to put the rest of the picture together.

Sitting down, she stacked her reading materials to one side and started sorting through newspaper issues. Minutes later, she had Eleanor's editorial in hand.

Guarded Secrets

Union Wharf
July 10, 1893

**Contraband Floods Our Shores, Ripping
at the Very Fabric of Our Beloved
Port Chatham Society**

Opium is a drug many of us may have originally viewed as imbued with a mysterious and sinister beauty, capable of opening the doors to a never-before envisioned, dreamlike paradise. Now it threatens to destroy the very society we depend on as stalwart citizens. Not only does our community lose precious tax dollars from the frequently condoned practice of smuggling this contraband past revenue agents, but the drug itself, addictive in the most horrific sense, slowly and relentlessly destroys its users.

Businessmen well known to all in our town think nothing of increasing their profits through their illicit dealings in this drug. And community leaders turn a blind eye, enamored themselves with the perilous effects of smoking the drug, shielded from view in their own parlors. But as a society, we must stand up to the evil purveyors of this diabolical substance, declaring its import and use outlawed. We must impose stiff fines and jail sentences on those who would flaunt their wares, luring our children into their malodorous smoking dens of iniquity, turning those we love into emaciated, melancholy ghosts who can no longer contribute meaningfully to our town's prosperity.

We must fight valiantly against the invasion of this devil drug, just as we fought against the invasion of those who introduced the drug to our shores. Let this letter be a warning that this newspaper—indeed, this voice of moral constancy for our community—will not stand mute while local businessmen continue to corrupt and ruin the lives of our citizens.

Standing in the early-morning light on the waterfront docks, Michael Seavey tossed the paper back to Remy. "Dispose of it," he snapped. "The woman is unhinged, clearly misguided in her beliefs."

"She grows more dangerous by the day," the burly bodyguard cautioned.

"To date, she has made no accusations against specific individuals." Michael slapped his gloves against his pants leg. "Nevertheless, I want to know the minute you hear of any other planned actions on her part."

Remy's expression turned sharklike. "You want me to send a message, Boss? I could pay a visit to one of her reporters—"

"No." Michael hesitated. "Not yet. I'll let you know."

Dismissing his bodyguard, Michael stood for a moment, regaining his temper and gazing up at the clipper ship he'd recently purchased. After a lengthy stay at the docks in Port Blakely, during which portions of its deck and hold had been completely rebuilt, he'd had it moved to Union Wharf for the finishing touches to the passenger suites. He'd already spent more than he'd intended to refurbish the vessel, but he was pleased with the result. By the time he was finished, he'd own the fastest ship sailing the local waters.

For his passengers, he'd provide the plushest accommodations, the finest opium, the most ornately designed smoking pipes. Just this week, he'd received a shipment of cloisonné enamel boxes and hand-carved jade smoking pipes from the Orient. Yes, overall, his plans had been executed quite smoothly.

A problem remained, however, that he now needed to rectify: Garrett had somehow managed to discover what he was up to. In the event that his partner was foolish enough—or cunning enough—to expose Michael's plans to the authorities, further precautions were required.

From somewhere belowdecks, Michael could hear the sounds of someone wielding a hammer. "Ahoy! You there!" he shouted.

After a moment, a grizzled head popped over the railing.

"You'd be Grady MacDonough?"

"Yessir. Master ship's carpenter, sir!"

"Come dockside, and bring the plans with you. We have much to discuss."

Michael lit a cigar while he waited. The wharf bustled with activity. Sailors emerged from boardinghouses and brothels, stretching and squinting into the sun, eyes

unaccustomed to the bright light after a night of de-
bauchery. Tradesmen, dressed in neatly pressed suits,
opened shops for the day's business. Dockworkers unloaded cargo from flatbed wagons drawn by draft horses
that pawed the wooden boards underneath their hooves,
impatient to move on.

Gazing back toward his hotel, he caught sight of Jesse
Canby, walking arm in arm along the boardwalk with a
young woman who looked vaguely familiar. He frowned.
Devil take it, he couldn't place her . . . ah, that was it: Hattie Longren's sister, the lovely young Charlotte.

As always, with thoughts of Hattie came the familiar
rush of grief, followed swiftly by a surge of rage. Avenging
her murder had done nothing to ease his distress. He
should have been able to cast her forever from his mind,
but all attempts to do so had failed. Damn and blast!
What *ailed* him?

His gaze sharpened as Charlotte laughed gaily at
something Jesse Canby had leaned down to murmur into
her ear. It seemed the young Charlotte chose to spend her
time with lost souls. In the case of Canby, she would be
wise to remain more detached.

Eleanor Canby suddenly emerged from the crowds on
the boardwalk, taking hold of Jesse's arm. Charlotte
stepped away, her expression guarded. Though Michael
couldn't hear what Eleanor was saying, it was clear that
the older woman spoke with some urgency to Jesse, who
shook his head vehemently. He jerked his arm from
Eleanor's grasp, then turned his back on her, holding his
hand out to Charlotte. After a wary glance at Eleanor, she

took Jesse's hand, and the pair walked away, leaving Eleanor standing on the boardwalk, shoulders rigid.

MacDonough appeared from down below, bringing Michael's attention back to the matter at hand. The carpenter scrambled down the rope ladder hung over the side of the ship, a thick roll of plans tucked under one arm.

Michael took them and spread them out, studying them intently. MacDonough waited, shifting from one foot to the other, his expression anxious.

"You've begun work on the great cabin, I see."

"Yessir. We're ready to install the mirrors and trim."

"I will expect your very best work for this space. The wall panels should be rosewood, and here"—Michael pointed—"I want you to install a skylight to provide natural light for those who remain in the cabin during the voyage." He glanced up. "Perhaps you can find an artisan who can provide a work of leaded glass to frame into the skylight? Nothing with color, mind you—I want clear glass to allow the maximum light to shine through."

The carpenter looked thoughtful for a moment, then nodded. "I've a friend in the trade whom I think might be just right for the commission."

"I expect a fair return for my money, but buy me the best, do you understand?"

"Understood."

"Good." Michael used his index finger to indicate a particular section of the drawings. "I think it would be best to install a coach roof here over the poop deck, to protect passengers from the harsher weather elements. Something rather whimsical yet tasteful, perhaps with a carved fascia?" He flipped a page to review the details for the stateroom furnishings. "And the settees in all the cabins must be upholstered in the finest velvet. My guests will recline in splendor, not in squalor on filthy bunk beds, as they would in the local opium dens."

"Of course, sir."

Michael turned his attention back to the great cabin, carefully keeping his tone casual. "I'd like secret compartments—double walls, if you will—built into the outside hull, accessible here and here." Again, he pointed on the plans. "There must be no indication that the walls are hollow in these locations—perhaps you can hang decorative mirrors that conceal some kind of invisible doors?"

MacDonough rubbed his chin with a hand sporting chipped and blackened fingernails. "I think it can be done, sir."

"Don't *think*, man," Michael snarled. "Just do it."

The carpenter flinched, then cleared his throat. "Double-wall construction will add weight, which will drag on the speed of the ship," he warned.

"Then find a way to compensate for that added weight elsewhere. I will not tolerate any sluggishness." Michael pinned him with his coldest stare. "You alone will work on these compartments, do you understand? Not a word of this to *anyone*. If rumors of the existence of the secret compartments spread, I will know exactly who was the source."

"No, sir." MacDonough paled. "I mean, yes, sir."

Michael straightened and rolled up the plans. "You'll be meeting the original deadline, I assume?"

"No problem, sir."

"Excellent." Michael's attention was drawn by the approach of footsteps on the dock.

Mona Starr walked toward them, stopping a few feet away. An imposing woman of middle age, she dressed modestly yet expensively in forest green muslin, carrying a matching silk parasol. Her face was artfully made up, cleverly disguising the ravages of her profession. He inclined his head. "Miss Starr. You've picked a fine day to be out for a walk."

"Yes indeed, Mr. Seavey."

Though Mona Starr was the proprietor of Port Chatham's most successful house of ill repute, Michael held only admiration for her. Her girls were treated fairly and given excellent medical care. In addition, Mona was a generous benefactor to the town, donating substantial funds to numerous community projects.

Not, of course, he thought wryly, that Mona's generosity didn't pay her back tenfold. Local authorities rarely targeted the Green Light.

She lifted her gaze to admire the ship that towered over them. "She's beautiful. I trust you're happy with your renovations?"

"Yes, quite happy. I was just discussing the final appointments with the ship's carpenter. She'll be ready for her maiden voyage within weeks."

"Jesse Canby tells me you plan to offer accommodations for passengers of, shall we say, a particular persuasion."

"My accommodations will be elegant as well as discreet," Michael allowed. "I saw Jesse just a bit ago, out walking with Charlotte Walker."

A slight frown marred Mona's features. "Hattie Longren's younger sister, yes. I fear she isn't taking seriously my advice to steer clear of Jesse."

"Canby is slowly destroying himself," Michael acknowledged. "Yet he still possesses the charm and wit to turn a young girl's head. I'd hate to see her dragged down with him."

"As would I," Mona agreed. "Charlotte is well loved by a number of my regular customers; she can have a long and successful career, should she learn to curb her impulsiveness. I fear her sister's death weighs heavily on her, creating a sadness deep within that she fights against."

"In that respect, she is in good company," Seavey murmured, causing Mona to give him a sharp look. He shook off the thought, continuing. "I felt I should mention the liaison between the two, in case you weren't aware of it. I suspect Canby doesn't have long now before his decline becomes impossible to conceal. I'd hate for Charlotte to become unnecessarily attached, only to lose yet one more dear friend."

Mona nodded. "I will see what I can do to persuade her that her friendship comes with certain risks. Unfortunately, barring Jesse from my establishment is probably not wise, but I will do what I can to influence the situation." She appeared to study her parasol, then gave Michael a thoughtful frown.

"Pray, speak your mind, madam," he urged.

Michael was aware that Mona had steered well clear of him in the past, considering him extremely dangerous. In the days leading up to Hattie's murder, when she and Mona had become reluctant allies of a sort, trying to influence events taking place on the waterfront, Mona had even gone so far as to warn Hattie to beware of Michael. Mona's harsh opinion of him had eased, however, once Charlotte had gone to work at the Green Light and revealed Michael's role in the events surrounding Hattie's murder and ensuing investigation.

Mona continued to hesitate, studying him warily. Michael waited, in no hurry to influence her. People believed of him what they would—he'd never found it profitable to attempt to change their minds.

All around them, the noise of the busy wharf ebbed and flowed as dockworkers unloaded ships and placed cargo on wagons. Street vendors hawked their wares to sailors coming ashore; saloons opened their doors in preparation for serving rotgut whiskey to those who couldn't afford anything better. Whores strolled along the docks in their finery, hoping to relieve the watermen of their wages.

"Very well." Mona finally nodded, seeming to have reached the conclusion that it was safe to confide in him. "I hesitate to insert myself into your business affairs, but I feel you should know that your man Garrett has recently taken an increased interest in Charlotte. And though all my customers comment on her improving talents in the bedroom, as well as her sweetness and willingness to please, I suspect there's more to Garrett's interest than meets the eye."

Michael frowned. Surely Garrett had no knowledge of Charlotte's family connections to Hattie. Or of the potential leverage he could apply, given Michael's attachment to Hattie at one time. "I will look into the matter," he said at last. "Thank you for bringing it to my attention."

Mona inclined her head, her elaborately coiffed auburn hair shining handsomely in the sunlight. "I suspect we both understand well the advantages of keeping the other informed. There are those who would be pleased to see either of us fail."

Though her warning was necessarily oblique, he took it to heart. He executed a slight bow. "Pray enjoy the remainder of your outing, Miss Starr. I am glad to have had the pleasure of your company."

Her pale blue eyes warmed a bit. "Yes, indeed, Mr. Seavey. I intend to do just that."

As he watched her walk away, Remy appeared silently at his side.

"Inspector Yardley of Customs awaits you in your hotel suite, Boss. He has a matter of some urgency he wishes to discuss."

The sound of a throat clearing came from behind them. "Sir?"

Michael turned back, impatient. MacDonough stood a few yards away, looking nervous. "What is it, man?"

"I'll be needing a name, sir."

"Pardon?"

"A name. For the ship, sir? Unless you'd be wanting to keep the old name, but most owners replace it with one of their own choice, a name that means something special to them . . ." MacDonough's voice trailed off as Seavey scowled, staring out across the bay.

After a long moment, he replied, feeling as if the words had been wrenched from him, "Henrietta Dale."

"A fine name, sir! Would it be belonging to someone I might've met?"

"No," Seavey replied coldly. "It belongs to someone long dead."

"I'm sorry to hear that, sir."

"Yes, so am I."

* * *

IT took Michael only minutes to cross the wharf and walk the block to his hotel. The building was two stories high, and he'd added an annex that allowed for separation of the luxury rooms used by well-heeled guests from the wing of dormitory-style rooms used to accommodate sailors. A balcony ran the length of the second story, and the name of the hotel was attached in large painted wooden letters to the railing. His hotel was easily the most imposing structure along that part of the water-front, just as he'd intended.

Though it was early in the day, he glimpsed a few sailors already partaking of spirits in his bar, while his wealthier guests reclined on comfortable settees in the adjacent hotel lobby, drinking coffee and reading the *Port Chatham Weekly Gazette*. No doubt perusing Eleanor's editorial, Michael thought, and nodding their heads in agreement. Hypocrites, the lot of them.

He quickly climbed the back steps, accessing his suite of rooms through the rear hallway and taking a few minutes to freshen up before entering the sitting room where Yardley waited.

A tall man with a grim expression and a huge handle-bar mustache, Yardley was fond of using his size to intimidate others. The Customs inspector's job was to collect import duties and taxes on incoming cargo, and he had at his disposal a fleet of revenue cutters crewed by agents who had the authority to board and inspect any ship in local waters. Yardley had even become so bold as to insist that his agents travel on board the ships for the shorter runs between local ports.

Still attired in his uniform of wool pants and a double-breasted coat sporting two rows of gold buttons, Yardley must have come directly from being on duty. He held his narrow-brimmed hat with its gold Customs insignia in one hand at his side as he paced. Spying Michael, he halted.

Michael approached, gesturing at the brocade furniture gracing his suite. "Pray be seated, Inspector."

"I prefer to stand." Yardley's tone was pleasant, yet Michael thought he detected a hint of grimness.

"May I offer you refreshment?" he asked, taking a seat in a handsome wing-back chair and propping a boot on one knee.

"No." Yardley must have realized how rude he sounded, for he added, "Thank you." He returned to his perusal of Michael's plush furnishings and expensive artwork, his expression disapproving.

Michael waited him out.

Yardley swung around abruptly. "Last night, my men retrieved the bodies of several Chinese from the local waters. What do you know of this?"

"I'm sorry to hear of it," Michael replied, not revealing the alarm he felt. "I'm afraid I am of no help, however—I was at the mayor's soiree for the evening."

"My men were patrolling an area just off North Beach."

Yardley's tone was impatient. "According to the police, a Chinaman by the name of Lok lodged a complaint this morning, claiming Sam Garrett attempted to hang him last night in that same location. Lok also stated that another man, one fitting your description, was responsible for saving his life."

Michael gave a silent curse. No good would come of this; Garrett would be hunting the man to permanently silence him. One would've thought Lok had the sense to remain silent about the affair.

He shrugged, maintaining an air of indifference. "The man must be mistaken—I know of no such incident. If I had, I would have reported it."

"Do you deny that your man Garrett was out there last night, then?"

Michael feigned astonishment. "Come now, Inspector. Sam Garrett is not 'my man,' as you put it. I take no interest in his whereabouts—indeed, I rarely have any dealings with him at all. Therefore, how could I possibly confirm or deny?"

Yardley snorted. "You don't expect me to swallow that story, do you, Seavey?"

"I don't really care whether you do or not. It is the truth, however."

Yardley clenched his hands at his sides, the only indication that he was less than composed. He evidently decided to take a less confrontational approach, however, for he said in a more equable tone, "As you may know, we're experiencing an increase in these types of incidents. Because of the Chinese Exclusion Act, the Chinese are desperate to find a way to our shores by whatever means.

Unfortunately, they sometimes book passage with ships' captains who are less than candid about the risks associated with the crossing. Many of these captains feel justified in tossing them overboard, should one of our cutters approach, given the steep fines they would face upon discovery."

"It seems a great risk indeed," Michael agreed serenely, "to book passage with someone who thinks your life is expendable at the merest provocation. However, I fail to understand why you've come to me to discuss these incidents. I have no history of—indeed, no inclination to ever consider—trafficking in humans. I can assure you, I hold a man's life to be far more valuable than that."

Yardley merely raised an eyebrow. "Your reputation says otherwise."

"Yes, well." Michael waved a hand impatiently. "A man can't spend his time trying to live down the foolish rumors that circulate about him along the waterfront. I conduct my affairs privately, discreetly, and to the benefit of all those involved. I certainly do not barter in human lives."

"This man Lok," Yardley said, abruptly changing the subject. "He claims you saved him from certain death last night. Do you categorically deny it?"

"I wouldn't think such a crime would fall under your jurisdiction, Inspector."

"It would if it had anything to do with illegal smuggling—either of drugs *or* humans."

Close scrutiny by the authorities would be most unwelcome. It was imperative that he stop this line of inquiry immediately. "The man appears to be delusional on this account," he lied without compunction. "I was at the mayor's home until quite late. Any number of his guests can vouch for my presence throughout the evening. Payton's sister, whose name escapes me at the moment, played an exceptional Bach cantabile. And I do admit to indulging in the fine port on offer. I was hardly in any shape to be gallivanting about on North Beach." He paused, then shook his head. "Perhaps this man—Lok, you said?—suffered some disorientation because of the alleged attempt on his life."

"Perhaps," Yardley allowed, studying Michael silently for a long moment. "I suspect it's also quite possible, however, that you guard your secrets closely." He placed his hat on his head, turned to leave, then turned back. "I trust that if you hear of anything that might help us solve the drowning of the Chinese, you'll contact me at once?"

"On that, Inspector," Michael felt comfortable replying, "you can rely."

Chapter 7

THE sound of the construction worker's footsteps over-head roused Jordan from her reading. Glancing at her watch, she was astonished to learn that more than two hours had passed, and immediately felt a pang of guilt about Malachi. She contemplated the various papers she'd gotten only halfway through, then—without a qualm—stuffed the pages from Captain Williams's diary inside her jacket and headed upstairs.

Travis paused in the act of smearing grayish-white stuff vertically down a wall seam with a metal trowel. "Find what you were looking for?"

"Not entirely," she admitted. "I seem to have more questions than when I started."

He went back to his scraping, the tool scritching against the wallboard. "That's usually the way of things, now isn't it? Some days even this Sheetrock mud refuses to give up its mysteries." He leaned down to scoop up more of the glop. "You found the section of the archives we had to temporarily relocate to the other side of the basement, right?"

She turned back from the front door. "You did what?"

"Let me show you." Dropping the trowel into a tray, he led the way back downstairs and to a darkened corner of the basement. There, binders full of newspapers, photos, and books had been stacked on a wooden shelf. "We needed the room for the display cases we moved down from upstairs. We were afraid we'd crack the glass, then have to pay for them." He looked apologetic. "I probably shoulda told you about this right away, huh?"

"No problem." She peered at the handwritten labels, her excitement building as she spied several from July and August 1893.

"I'll just head back upstairs then?" he asked after a moment.

"Hmm?" She refocused. "Oh, sure." She shot him a distracted smile. "Thanks."

Selecting a binder from August, she balanced it on top of the stack of papers in her arms and hauled everything back over to the small table where she'd been reading. Flipping through the binder's contents, she quickly found a second issue of the *Port Chatham Weekly Gazette* displaying a banner headline about the wreck of the *Henrietta Dale.*

Survivor Describes Final Moments of Terror and Despair Aboard the Ill-Fated *Henrietta Dale*

August 8—"The moment I felt that awful grindin' jolt, I knew we were doomed. It's a miracle any of us survived," First Mate Dan Jensen told this reporter just hours after the heroic rescue. "We were goin' full bore on a broad reach, sails extended, when we hit the spit. 'Tweren't no chance to slow 'er down."

As related in this paper's previous issue, the *Henrietta Dale,* owned by Michael Seavey, a businessman well known on Port Chatham's waterfront, ran aground on the west side of Dungeness Spit late in the evening of August 5. Locals did their best to help rescue survivors, though by the time they arrived, the beautiful clipper ship was already mortally damaged by high waves and was a danger to those on shore.

According to what this intrepid reporter has been able to discover, the *Henrietta Dale,* recently refurbished by Seavey, was on her maiden voyage from Victoria, British Columbia. Along with the crew of the ship, passengers included several Port Chatham residents as well as the son of this paper's owner and editor-in-chief, Eleanor Canby. Jesse Canby is believed to have perished when he was crushed by the collapse of the mizzenmast, which caused the deck to cave in, damaging the great cabin below. An unofficial accounting of the victims can be obtained by their loved ones from the Port Chatham Police Department.

Rescue workers were able by valiant measures to help six souls extricate themselves from the terrible wreckage. All suffered from severe injuries and were transported to medical clinics in Port Chatham. Among the survivors were three of the *Henrietta Dale*'s crew, including Captain Nathaniel Williams and the first mate quoted above. A young girl, Martha

Smith, and Michael Seavey were also among the wounded.

Though rumors abound regarding the purpose of the doomed ship's voyage and of nefarious attempts to lure her off course, this reporter has not yet been able to determine the cause of the lethal grounding. A formal inquiry into the matter will no doubt be held, at which time the *Gazette* will provide for its readers full coverage of the proceedings. It is essential that, in these modern times, we continue to monitor the safety and well-being of those among us who choose to travel our treacherous waterways.

Yes! Seavey was listed among the survivors.

After scribbling the names of the survivors on a crumpled bank deposit slip she found in her pocket, Jordan returned the newspaper to its binder. So Jesse Canby had been on board the *Henrietta Dale* that night. And he had perished. Could that be the reason behind Seavey's comment that Eleanor had despised him?

Replacing the binder on the shelf, Jordan gathered her papers and headed back upstairs. She thanked Travis and went outside to let an outraged Malachi out of the car. He sniffed the grass at the edge of the lot while she mentally reviewed what she'd learned. Although Eleanor Canby had railed in her editorial against the demon opium, her writing style had more to do with ranting than providing useful facts. Not one opium smuggler had been mentioned by name. Which meant Jordan had no idea who Seavey's competitors were, and therefore no idea who might have lured the *Henrietta Dale* onto the spit. Then again, if she assumed Seavey was telling the truth in his own papers, wouldn't his business partner have had motive?

The real surprise she'd uncovered in her reading was that Charlotte probably knew even more about Michael Seavey than she'd let on. If Charlotte had been close to Jesse Canby, and if Jesse had been purchasing opium from Seavey, then it stood to reason that she might also have been around Seavey during the weeks before his death.

Until now, Jordan had purposely avoided asking Charlotte about her life in the years following her sister Hattie's murder in 1890. She was afraid of raising issues that would be too painful for the young ghost to discuss. In less than a year, Charlotte had gone from a carefree, pampered teenager to losing her parents in a carriage accident in Boston, then traveling out West to live with her older sister here in Port Chatham. Even worse, within months of her arrival, Hattie had been murdered, leaving Charlotte destitute and in the employ of a notorious madam. The psychological trauma from such events could cause irreparable damage to a strong person for life, and, well, Charlotte simply wasn't that strong.

Perhaps, given the lengthy passage of time, there was a way to gently question Charlotte about what she knew. Whistling for Malachi, Jordan decided that she should proceed cautiously. Regardless of the teenage ghost's antics, she'd become fond of Charlotte and didn't want to be the cause of her becoming even more fragile.

Jordan helped Malachi into the Prius's cramped hatchback area, then drove downtown. The night before, she'd promised Bob MacDonough she would stop by the Wooden Boat Society's headquarters at Point Hudson to provide more details about her sighting of the ghost ship. And after what she'd learned in the last two hours, she had a few questions of her own.

Her stomach growled, reminding her that it had been a long time since breakfast, so she stopped at a natural food cooperative to grab an energy bar and some dog biscuits for Malachi. As she drove down the main drag, she munched on the bar, getting crumbs all over her sweater. Glancing down from the steering wheel to brush off the crumbs, she came within inches of running through a black carriage carrying a beautifully dressed woman holding a black Battenburg lace parasol. The horse shied, almost flipping the carriage. Jordan jerked the wheel to the right, craning her neck to assure herself the lady and the horse were okay.

And then had to slam on the brakes to avoid hitting the car in front of her.

Malachi plowed into the back of her seat, slamming her into the steering wheel. She held her breath, but the airbag didn't deploy.

"Raaaoomph!" Malachi scrambled to right himself, giving her a baleful look that said he thought the entire affair was her fault. She supposed it was. Easing her foot off the brake pedal, she edged the car forward once again, catching one last glimpse of the black lace parasol in her rearview mirror.

Once in the downtown area, traffic became congested, slowing her down. Tourists—both spectral and human— were out in force. Service trucks and horse-drawn flatbed wagons clogged the street. She crawled past block after block of majestic, Victorian-style buildings that housed apartments, offices, and boutiques. Impatiently drumming her fingers on the steering wheel, she noticed faded white block lettering on the balcony railing of a two-story clapboard building facing the waterfront: Cosmopolitan H--el. On impulse, she pulled out of her lane and whipped down the side street, parking across from the hotel's entrance.

Telling an impatient Malachi to stay, she jogged across the street. Inside the hotel, she discovered a small, tastefully appointed lobby with high, stenciled ceilings and massive wood columns. Plush carpet muffled her footsteps. Groupings of overstuffed, comfortable-looking furniture were cleverly placed about the room for optimum privacy. Under a leaded-glass window, a sturdy Arts and Crafts library table offered an assortment of baskets containing mouthwatering pastries and thermoses filled with gourmet coffee blends.

Across the room stood an ornate oak conference table that held a telephone, a leather-bound guest register, and stacks of papers. A short, trim man with a receding hairline, dressed in dark wool slacks and a crisp white Oxford shirt, sat at the table. He glanced up from the pages he was reading, gazing at her through expensive, rimless eyeglasses, his expression briefly impatient.

"May I help you?" he asked in a clipped East Coast accent. He pasted a smile on his face.

Jordan walked over and offered her hand, introducing herself. "Are you the owner?"

"Yes," he replied, not volunteering his name. "I really don't have time right now for solicitations. I'm terribly slammed, so . . ."

She was momentarily speechless—she wasn't often mistaken for a salesperson. "Um, sorry, didn't mean to give the wrong impression. I live up the hill in Longren House, and I'm researching a historic event that may have a connection to your hotel."

"*Boutique* hotel," he corrected her. "Please refer to my establishment that way in any future conversations. It's important to distinguish oneself from the chains these days, so that people understand we provide a much higher quality of service and more pleasant experience for the traveler."

Right. "I understand a shanghaier from the nineteenth century, Michael Seavey, used to own this building?"

He relaxed slightly. "Yes, indeed. His ghost haunts the penthouse suite even to this day. It's quite the draw for tourists visiting our region."

"Really?" She wondered if he'd made that up as a promotional gimmick, or if he could actually sense Seavey's presence. "Would you mind if I viewed that suite of rooms?"

"I'm afraid that's impossible—they're currently under renovation. In fact, that's why I'm so far behind in my work. The individual handling the renovation is suddenly indisposed, and I must find someone to replace him." The owner scowled, straightening the sheaf of papers he held and setting them down so that they were perfectly aligned on the desk. "Although I certainly sympathize with the man's plight, it has simply *ruined* my schedule. I may have to turn away customers because of this disaster!"

It was on the tip of her tongue to point out that Holt probably viewed his murder as representing more than a scheduling inconvenience, but she managed to say instead, "I don't mind a little plaster dust. I was actually hoping to speak with any workers who might still be up there. If you're too busy to accompany me to the penthouse, I'd be glad to go up on my own."

"Out of the question!" Though the owner was still seated, he somehow managed to look down his nose. "I can't have you interrupting what little work is still being accomplished."

"I promise I won't take up too much of their time," she assured him. "One question, and then I'm gone."

"What is it, exactly, that you wish to know?"

"I'm hoping that the workers might tell me whether Holt Stilwell found any old papers during the renovation. Perhaps something left behind by Michael Seavey—"

"Absolutely not!" The owner jumped to his feet, his face flushing an unbecoming shade of puce. "If any historic documents had been found, those documents would be the property of the hotel. You have no right to them *whatsoever!*"

"No, no," she backpedaled. "I wouldn't try to claim them or anything. I just want to take a look at them. You see, I'm researching the circumstances surrounding Michael Seavey's death in 1893—"

"*No!*" He rushed around the desk, pointing a trembling finger at the front door. "I want you to leave, immediately!"

She gaped at him and backed up a few steps. "Have I offended you in some way, Mr. . . . ?"

"You have no right to be here! If you don't leave, *right this minute,* I'll call the authorities!"

"Whoa. Okay." She danced back a few more steps, hands raised. "No problem. I'm leaving."

"Get out!" he shouted, advancing on her.

She turned and ran out the front door, noting the curious stares from the few guests who were seated in the lobby.

"And don't come back!" he screeched from inside the lobby.

Outside, she walked a few yards toward the bay, then stopped, thoroughly shaken by the encounter.

"Your apparent lack of social skills continues to be a detriment, I see."

The deep baritone came from behind her. Michael Seavey appeared from the shadows, looking amused. He must have witnessed her argument with the owner.

"That man needs his meds adjusted," she grumbled.

"Pardon?"

"Never mind."

"He's an obnoxious little creature, is he not? I quite enjoy making his life difficult at every opportunity."

Jordan glanced around to make certain no one was observing their conversation. She was still unused to appearing to others as if she were talking to herself. "What's that guy's problem? Do you know?"

Seavey shrugged, his shoulders moving under the expensive slate-gray fabric of his coat. "I confess I have no idea," he replied.

Today he wore a beautifully tailored suit over a pale gray silk shirt, a snowy white handkerchief tucked into his breast pocket, a black top hat, and black leather walking boots. In deference to her, he'd removed his top hat and held it in one hand. She had to admit, he was certainly the most stylishly dressed ghost she'd come across.

"I don't spend my time worrying about the man," Seavey continued. "If he becomes too intrusive, I'll find a way to be rid of him."

His mildly disapproving gaze traveled over the jeans and cotton sweater she'd thrown on earlier in her haste to leave the house. "I had thought perhaps the outfit you wore last evening was an aberration, but you seem to delight in wearing mannish clothing. My deceased wife wore such garments on occasion, but for good reason: It's quite difficult to wield a bullwhip wearing silk skirts. You, however, have no such excuse."

She planted her hands on her hips. "This is perfectly acceptable attire for a woman of this century—just look around you. I'm sure you've seen worse on the guests staying in your suite of rooms."

He waved a hand. "Cretins, the lot of them." He frowned, considering. "Admittedly, modern clothing leaves little to the imagination, but truthfully, I haven't yet decided whether I believe it to be an improvement. After all, to view a woman's lush form through the thin fabrics of my day—say, perhaps, a woman gracing my private rooms wearing a chemise of the finest muslin—"

"Too much information," Jordan interrupted. "Let's not go there."

He dipped his head. "As you wish. I merely meant to acquaint you with a stairway at the back of the building. I suspect you can slip past the manager unnoticed. But if you prefer not to . . ."

Jordan realized he'd taken her literally. "That's not

what I meant, but . . ." She contemplated his suggestion, sorely tempted to slip up that stairway. The prospect of being discovered and dealing with the police, however, was unappealing. "Is anyone up there right now?"

"Two workers are repairing the plaster walls and painting the ceiling. Though I suppose it is only to be expected that the rooms would need refurbishment at some point, I don't approve of the decoration scheme that absurd man has chosen. I can only hope they don't do anything to ruin the ambience of the Turkish motif."

"Remember your great-great-nephew? The one I told you was murdered a couple of nights ago? He was in charge of the renovation of your suite. He was, according to those in the business, extremely good at historically accurate renovations. I don't think you have to worry—"

"That loudmouthed, uncouth, sorry excuse for a gentleman was *related* to me?" Seavey interrupted, rising to his full height and glaring down at her. "*I think not, madam!*"

"Yes, he was." She fisted her hands on her hips. "How can you act so offended? Weren't you a hardened criminal in your time?"

He sniffed. "I may have—allegedly—engaged in certain illegal acts, but I assure you, I was never *crass* in my dealings with the fairer sex."

Well, he had her there—she couldn't exactly defend Holt's treatment of women. Better to change the subject. "I found some old newspaper articles this afternoon about the wreck of the *Henrietta Dale*. You were listed among the survivors."

He looked unimpressed. "I believe I indicated I thought such articles were fabricated."

"I find it hard to agree with you that the articles about the shipwreck would be fabricated. What's the last thing you remember from that night?"

"The ship hit the spit and knocked me off my feet. Then the rigging fell on me." He paused, then shook his head. "After that—nothing."

"Is it possible that you were knocked out, but then were rescued and taken unconscious to Port Chatham?"

"Anything is possible, madam. But the fact that I don't remember waking up and finding myself in a different location lends far more credibility to my contention that such articles are erroneous."

"Not necessarily. You could've been murdered while you were still unconscious," she argued.

He shrugged. "Perhaps. I confess, I don't see that it matters."

"Did Eleanor Canby blame you for the death of her son?" At Seavey's look of confusion, she explained. "Jesse died that night."

"Ah. I hadn't realized."

Of course—he wouldn't have known. "Why didn't you ask about survivors after you came back as a ghost?"

His impatience was beginning to show. "The matter simply wasn't of interest to me. And I didn't 'come back,' as you put it, for a number of years. It's not a simple process."

"So you must have had other reasons for telling me last night that Eleanor despised you," Jordan persisted.

Another shrug, this one accompanied by a sideways glance. "Eleanor disapproved of me on general principle— I didn't measure up to her high moral standards. She was an uptight, rigid individual, who in my opinion caused more harm than good through her endless prose-lytizing."

After having read Eleanor's editorials, Jordan wasn't certain she disagreed. She glanced up at the second floor of the old hotel, her thoughts returning to the present. "By any chance, did you keep business papers in a safe or some other secret compartment in your hotel suite when you were alive? Anything that Holt might have found while renovating your rooms?"

Seavey's eyes shifted. "I don't pretend to follow every activity of the humans who come and go from my estab-lishment."

"But you don't deny that you had such papers," she pressed.

He studied her for a long moment, gently tapping the brim of his top hat against one leg. "Even if something of the nature you describe were to exist," he said finally, "I wouldn't admit to it. Surely you can see that I wouldn't want information regarding my past activities to under-mine my courtship of Hattie. She wouldn't—in many cases—necessarily approve."

"I think you'll find that Hattie is more flexible in her outlook these days than she might have been in the past."

He shook his head. "Indeed, I doubt that." A calculat-ing gleam flickered his pale gray eyes. "It's possible we might come to a mutually advantageous arrangement, one that would allow me to exchange information in return for, shall we say, certain favors."

"What do you have in mind?" Jordan asked warily.

"Merely that I might indeed have knowledge of docu-ments that I kept in my private rooms. If I were to reveal the location of those documents—should they exist—in return I would have your promise that you won't show them to Hattie or talk to her about them." When Jordan started to object, he held up a hand. "Further, that you would refrain from voicing any negative opinions you might hold as to my worthiness as a suitor."

"You're asking me to advocate that Hattie marry *you?*"

"Certainly not," he snapped. "I don't need a woman to present my case; I'm perfectly capable of convincing Hattie myself. The task should be simple—the union would obviously be mutually beneficial. I would merely ask that you don't actively *dissuade* her. After all, you might even discover certain facts indicating my character isn't as impoverished as you might currently believe."

"I doubt it," Jordan retorted wryly. "And as a counselor, I'm not in the habit of withholding advice that might result in a person making a decision that could cause her to align herself with someone of dubious ethics."

He snorted. "You exaggerate, madam. I'm merely a businessman who employed tactics—and sometimes, I admit, the judicious use of violence—that might be less than palatable to the fairer sex, though quite necessary in the day."

Jordan eyed him curiously. "Why *do* you want to marry Hattie?"

An emotion flashed through his eyes, gone so swiftly she couldn't get a handle on it. "I don't see that my reasons are any of your concern."

"You're in love with her," she realized suddenly. Why hadn't she seen it before now? He had, after all, avenged Hattie's death. Now she knew why. One mystery solved.

His expression, however, turned to one of contempt. "Love is an utterly childish notion. Hattie and I are simply well suited to each other."

"Uh-huh." Jordan wasn't buying it. Seavey had all the hallmarks of a person deep in denial concerning his true feelings toward Hattie. Then again, most criminals weren't real big on analyzing their feelings or motivations.

She folded her arms. "So let me get this straight: You're asking me to stay out of your way while you court Hattie, in return for information concerning the whereabouts of business papers that Holt might have discovered in your suite of rooms during the course of a remodel. Correct?"

He looked relieved. "Precisely."

"No."

He started. "I beg your pardon?"

"No," she repeated flatly. "If I conclude that you aren't a worthy suitor, I will say so." She paused, realizing how crazy it was to comment in this day and age on someone's worthiness as a suitor. "Hattie wants me to solve your murder, out of some misguided sense of guilt over the way she's maligned your character for the last century. Go figure. But if I can help her feel less guilty by discovering how you died, then I will. In addition, I will also let her know that you were helpful during my investigation into your death."

He stared at her broodingly, a muscle ticking in his jaw. "Very well, I agree to your stipulations." His nod was abrupt. "I admit that I have found this Holt you refer to, to be brutish in the extreme. Because of that, I've ensured I was away at various social commitments much of the time he labored in my suite. Therefore, it's possible the man could've found a ledger and other files."

"So you're admitting to their existence?"

"Hypothetically, papers of that nature existed, ones that might have documented certain shipments and payments of . . . shall we say . . . *contraband*. At the time, it would have made sense to keep them concealed in a false compartment in my sitting room wall. Therefore, also hypothetically, the documents could have been discovered as part of the recent repairs to the plaster in that room."

Jordan felt a surge of excitement. So Holt *would* have had access to information about the *Henrietta Dale*. And he might have been curious enough to check it out. "And did your documents mention what the *Henrietta Dale* would have been carrying as 'cargo' the night she ran aground?"

Seavey fiddled with the cuff of his silk shirt before answering. "It's possible such information existed in my ledger of accounts."

She barely managed to restrain herself from pumping her fist in the air. The workers would probably know what Holt had done with the ledger and files. With any luck, the papers might still be in the suite.

Glancing back toward the entrance to the hotel lobby, she couldn't see the owner lurking about. If he called the cops on her, so be it. She turned back to Seavey. "Show me those stairs you mentioned."

She followed him as he floated across a small gravel lot around to the back of the building. He stopped by a set of rusty iron stairs, bowed, and swept a hand upward to indicate that she should precede him. She eyed the steps critically, wondering how safe they were.

"I assure you they are quite solid."

She continued to hesitate. "How would you know? It's not like you weigh anything."

"Good Christ, woman! Try not to be so obstreperous! I've seen the workers use them time and again."

"Oh. Right." She started up the stairs, then turned back to see if he was following. His gaze lifted to her face, and not particularly quickly. "Were you just checking out my *butt?*" she demanded, incredulous.

He merely looked amused. "I'd have to be dead, crossed over, and have lost all powers of perception—which I assure you I have not—to fail to notice a pleasing female form."

"Your ogling being a benefit of the modern clothing you insist is in such poor taste?" she said drily.

"Of course. I'm a discerning man, and I might prefer that you show off your assets in a manner that leaves more to the imagination, thus providing an air of alluring mystery. But I am not stupid."

Shaking her head, she continued up the stairs.

* * *

Less than a half hour later, she and Malachi were on their way to Point Hudson east and slightly north of the downtown waterfront district. She had more information, though not the documents she'd hoped for. Holt's workers had been quite talkative, answering all her questions as well as those prompted by the ghost lurking at her side.

Holt had found Seavey's ledger and files approximately a week ago. Apparently, he'd become excited after reading about the *Henrietta Dale* but had acted secretive about the details of what he'd learned. The next day, he'd left work early on the excuse that he had a scuba diving lesson. Every day after that, he'd disappeared by midafternoon, indifferent in the face of the owner's complaints that he was slacking off. When Jordan had asked what Holt had done with the original documents, though, no one could tell her. And a hasty search of the suite turned up nothing.

She needed to verify that the location of the shipwreck matched where she'd found Holt's body. If she could nail down that detail, none of the skeptics in the pub could ignore the strong possibility that Holt had been murdered because of his interest in salvaging the *Henrietta Dale*. But who had told Holt about the shipwreck in the first place? He couldn't have found out about it from Seavey's papers, and neither of his workers had known about it. He must have mentioned the *Henrietta Dale* to someone who told him about the 1893 shipwreck. But who? Was the history of the shipwreck well known around town?

She parked in front of the Wooden Boat Society at Point Hudson. Each time Jordan had glanced at the marina on her trips downtown, she'd been intrigued by the quaint, bungalow-style building that sat adjacent to the docks. She'd assumed it housed some type of business associated with the marina. In fact, it was the home of a society dedicated to restoring and building wooden boats—evidently one of only a few such societies in the United States.

Out on the inlet, a sailboat, its spinnaker taking advantage of the breeze rippling the water, came within feet of an anchored tall ship. Jordan took a moment to study the tableau stretched out before her.

Now that she thought about it, she realized she had an unconscious expectation that objects from another dimension would at least be a little faded, sort of like the sepia-toned prints one saw in history books. But everything, real *and* spectral, appeared to her in full Technicolor. Some of the ships might have a slight variation in the quality of the air surrounding them, but that was the only difference she could detect. And with so many refurbished historic ships sailing the local waters, she couldn't count on the design of the boat as a reliable clue. Though of course there *was* the fact that the real ones could sail right through the unreal ones.

Shaking her head, she walked up the sidewalk to the front door. Inside, she found the space divided in half, the right side organized into a small shop offering books on wooden boat building, souvenirs, and marine maps of the area's waters. The left contained a library jam-packed with crowded bookshelves and a beat-up but sturdy-looking oak desk.

From behind the desk, Bob glanced up from the book he was reading, grinning when he spied her. "Couldn't help yourself, could you? Hey, I got hold of the guy who wrote one of the more respected books on phantom ship sightings. He wants to interview you over the phone."

"I can't wait."

Her sarcasm seemed to sail right over his head. "And I've got the sketch artist lined up. If you agree, I'll have her come to the pub tonight to see if she can draw something reasonably accurate."

Jordan knew if she refused, she'd be hounded until she agreed. "Go for it," she said, resigned.

He looked pleased. "In that case, I'd like to talk to you about giving a short speech during the Wooden Boat Festival. It'd be a real crowd pleaser, if you could just describe what you saw, then let me talk about the original shipwreck and the questionable circumstances around the grounding."

Jordan frowned. "Oh, well, I don't know—"

"Something real casual. You don't have to prepare a speech or anything," he quickly assured her. "Just show up and chat with folks. You'd be surprised at the number of people who have refurbished old ships, who also believe their ships are haunted. They'll eat this stuff up."

"I'll think about it," she promised him, then changed the subject. "I verified that in all likelihood Holt really was diving for salvage. He found documents while he was renovating the hotel suite that mentioned the cargo of the *Henrietta Dale*. There was opium concealed in her hull. And your ancestor was the one who built the secret compartments."

"You mean old Grady MacDonough?" Bob frowned. "That can't be right, or I would have known about it."

"I'm fairly certain—Michael Seavey said as much in his personal papers."

"If you can trust that Seavey wrote the truth. The man was a criminal."

"It should be easy enough to verify. Did your great-

great-grandfather leave behind any kind of papers or diary?"

Bob leaned back, linking his hands behind his head, regarding her thoughtfully. "Unfortunately, no. I have only the stories passed down through family members. But it's always been *the* legend everyone in the family talks about—the fact that Grady MacDonough was the ship's carpenter on the famous clipper ship that ran aground on her maiden voyage. According to family members, the old guy took it really hard. He'd given almost a year of his life working on that ship. I suspect he was as fond of it as its owner was—maybe even more so. Trust me, there's never been any mention of secret compartments."

She didn't point out that family legends tended to be glamorized and edited as they passed through each generation. "If I can pinpoint the exact location of the shipwreck, I might be able to convince Darcy that Holt's murder had something to do with his dives."

"Hmm." Bob swiveled around in his desk chair to stare at the crammed bookshelf behind him. Standing, he pulled a thin brown leather volume with a cracked binding from between two larger books on the topmost shelf.

He thumbed through it. "This is a replica of Lloyd's of London's list of all shipwrecks for the nineteenth century."

"They tracked shipwrecks clear out here?" Jordan asked, surprised.

"Yeah. They were the major insurer of ships and their cargoes back then. And they kept an official record of all shipwrecks, worldwide." He paused to skim down one page, then flipped to the next. "Okay, here we go."

He placed the book, open to that page, on the desk so

that they could both look at it. "According to Lloyd's, the *Henrietta Dale* ran aground on August 5, 1893." He pointed with his finger. "Here are the coordinates for the shipwreck."

Jordan frowned. "Did Holt ever talk to you about the *Henrietta Dale*'s wreckage or ask you for these coordinates?"

"Nope."

Damn. "Did he have any other way of finding them?"

"Something close to the same coordinates would have been noted by the captain in the ship's logbook. The only copy, though, is out at the lighthouse."

"But Holt could have taken the coordinates and used them with some kind of GPS device to locate the wreckage, correct?"

"Sure. All smart cellphones have GPS tracking these days. He wouldn't have needed any special equipment."

She reached for a notepad on the desk, tore off a sheet, and used Bob's pen to write down the coordinates. "How do I go about figuring out if these coordinates match the location where we found Holt's body?"

"I've got just the thing." Bob rummaged through a jumble of rolled-up charts propped in the corner behind the desk. "Ha! Here it is . . ." He pulled off the rubber bands and unrolled a navigational chart, using a stapler and an antique brass sextant to keep the chart spread open. Leaning over, he plotted the coordinates on the chart, pointing to a location just off the edge of the west side of the spit. "Definitely in the ballpark," he concluded. "Sand shifts over time, so we can't expect an exact match, but that spit tends to shift in one direction each winter, then back during the other seasons. I'd say you found Holt within a few hundred yards of the old coordinates."

Bob cocked his head at her. "So are you serious about looking into the shipwreck? Trying to verify that she was lured onto the rocks?"

Jordan shrugged. "Not certain yet. I'm looking into the murder of Michael Seavey, her owner. I ran across a newspaper article in my library dated from right around the time of the shipwreck. It mentioned that Seavey had been found shot dead, floating under Union Wharf. Which doesn't jibe with the assumption that he went down with his ship."

"I didn't realize anyone thought that."

It occurred to her that the only person who *did* think that was his ghost. "I'd heard a rumor to that effect," she answered vaguely. "I went out to the Historical Society this afternoon and checked for more articles around July and August 1893, to see if I could find a list of victims or survivors from the shipwreck. I found two articles about the *Henrietta Dale* running aground, plus a list of six survivors—the captain, three crew members, Seavey, and a woman." She paused. "Lloyd's didn't list survivors in their records, did they? It would be nice to corroborate the locally generated list."

"Sometimes, but their lists were notoriously incomplete, as you might imagine," Bob replied. He pulled the book out from under the marine map and checked. "Nope—nothing." He returned it to the shelf. "So how are you going to go about figuring out if Holt had the coordinates of the shipwreck?"

She thought about it, then sighed. "I can always ask the gardener. She might have seen him out at the lighthouse."

Bob gave her a slight smile. "Well, damn. Why didn't I think of that?"

* * *

MINUTES later, she was back on the road and headed for Holt's house on the south side of town. If she remembered correctly, he lived ten minutes outside of the city limits in an area of modest homes on larger, partially wooded lots. According to Darcy, the area was more reasonably priced in comparison to other Port Chatham real estate because of its being located downwind from the local paper pulp mill. Jordan had caught a whiff of the fumes a few times as she drove around town, and they reminded her of rather potent rotten eggs. Darcy assured her that after living in town for a while, she'd become used to the odor, but Jordan wasn't yet convinced.

A few weeks ago, when she'd needed answers to solve Hattie's murder, Jase had driven her out to Holt's house so that she could ask about family papers. Holt had let them rummage through the boxes in his attic—a grim task, given the state of his housekeeping—to find what she needed. With any luck, she could still remember that trip well enough to find his house.

After a couple of wrong turns and subsequent backtracking, she spied the driveway to his run-down rambler among the trees and turned in. Holt's pickup was absent, probably still parked wherever he'd left it the night of his murder, but a dark-colored sedan sat in the driveway.

Good. As she'd hoped, one of Holt's relatives was at the house, probably packing up the dead man's belongings. She'd just drop off the papers with a quick explanation, advise the person to have them assessed by the Historical Society or an archivist to determine their value, then be on her way. And if she happened to see what looked like Seavey's ledger and files sitting around in plain sight, she might take a peek at them ... If they weren't in the hotel suite, Holt had to have done *something* with them. The question was, what?

She pulled alongside the sedan and turned off the Prius. Grabbing the packet of original documents, she climbed out of the car, letting Malachi out for a romp in the adjacent woods. Since her last visit, Holt hadn't seen fit to fix any of the house's maintenance problems—the roof was still covered with moss and tree detritus, the cement steps leading to the porch were still cracked. The front door was closed—a feat, since it was warped from moisture. She couldn't hear any sounds coming from inside. Climbing the three uneven cement steps, she gingerly crossed rotten porch boards, looking for a doorbell. Finding none, she rapped on the door.

No one responded.

Frowning, she jumped off the porch and climbed through the shrubbery along the foundation to peer in the living room window, but she couldn't see anyone.

Well, damn. She couldn't very well leave the papers propped up against the front door in the hope that someone would eventually find them. They were historical documents, and as such, precious and fragile. Too much humidity, which the Pacific Northwest had in abundance, would ruin the old pages within hours.

She walked back up the steps and tried the front door-knob. It turned freely; the door swung inward. Putting her hand on it, she called, "Anyone home? Hello?"

Silence.

The living room looked even messier than the last time she'd seen it, and that was saying something. Shaking her head, she shoved the door open and was crossing the threshold when it slammed back into her. Thinking the wind had somehow caught it, she put up a hand to keep it from hitting her in the face.

The door kept coming, and she realized someone had to be pushing it from behind.

"Hey!" she said crankily, shoving back with her shoulder. "What—"

The door flew open and a figure wearing a dark hoodie rushed right at her, slamming into her with both hands. In an instant, she and the documents were airborne, flying backward. She landed hard on her back, sliding down the cement steps. The back of her skull connected with something equally immovable.

The intruder leapt over her, landing in the gravel walkway behind her. She heard the sound of running footsteps, then the roar of a car engine and Malachi's frantic barking.

Chapter 8

THE jerk—whoever he was—had knocked the breath out of her.

Malachi whined and licked her face. "It's okay, boy. I'm all right," she whispered, trying to drag air into her lungs.

She lay without moving, listening for any sound that someone might still be lurking. After a couple of minutes, she realized that if he had been, Malachi would still be going crazy. "Did you scare him off, boy?"

"Raaaaooo."

"Good. I hope you also took a very big chunk out of him."

He growled his agreement, then anxiously nudged her with his nose.

It took her a moment to figure out that most of her skewed perspective came not from brain damage, but from the fact that she was lying almost upside down, angled down the steps. She reached into her jeans pocket for her cellphone and held it up to her face so that she could punch buttons on the display.

"Where are you?" she asked when Darcy answered.

"Just coming up to Holt's place with the crime-scene technicians."

"How convenient." The phone went silent long enough that Jordan wondered if she'd lost the connection. Then she heard the crunch of gravel as vehicles turned into the driveway.

"Do I want to know?" Darcy asked finally.

"Probably not. Did a dark sedan come flying past you just now?"

"No, why?"

Malachi started barking directly above Jordan's head. "Arrrgh!" Jordan dropped the phone and clapped her hands over her ears. She couldn't decide which hurt worse, the loud noise or the movement caused by touching her skull.

A car door slammed, unhurried footsteps crunched the gravel, then Darcy knelt by her head. Upside down, they gazed at each other. "Am I to assume you aren't in this position on purpose?" Darcy asked tartly.

"Someone was inside the house," Jordan explained. She managed to scrunch around, rolling sideways down the steps.

Darcy gripped her under her arms and hauled her to her feet, then helped her brush dirt and leaves off her clothes. "I'm guessing whoever it was, wasn't thrilled to see you. What the hell are you doing here?"

"Returning the family documents. You know, Seavey's papers that I borrowed from Holt and never got back to him? They're part of the estate, and I thought Holt's relatives would want them right away." Jordan winced as she gingerly felt the back of her skull, her hand encountering something wet and sticky.

Darcy brushed her fingers aside and looked for herself. "Yuck. A smashed slug"—she pulled it out of Jordan's hair—"a scratch and a nice goose egg. Most of the sticky stuff is blood. Head wounds bleed a lot, but it's already stopped. You'll live," she pronounced. She waved the crime-scene techs inside, then turned back to Jordan. "Holt doesn't *have* any relatives in the area. In fact, we haven't been able to locate any at all yet. Did you get a good look at your assailant?"

Jordan shook her head, then instantly regretted it. "He shoved me backward down the steps, then drove away in the car." She frowned. "I must have hit my head when I fell."

"What did the car look like?"

"Dark. A sedan. I don't know what kind."

"Color? License plate number?" When she drew a blank, Darcy looked disgusted. "You mean you can't tell me *anything* about it, other than it was dark?"

"Well it's not like I drove up thinking, 'Hey, that looks like a villain's car, so I'm going to write down the license number and commit its description to memory,'" she grumbled. "It was either blue or black, maybe midsized, and it might have had four doors."

Taking a careful step into the grass, she tried to bend over to pick up some of Seavey's papers that had landed there, but her head wasn't having any of it. She must have hit it fairly hard.

Darcy made a rude noise and started picking up papers and handing them to her. "Unbelievable. Holt Stilwell was just murdered, and you thought it was safe to come waltzing out to his house all by yourself?"

"I do not *waltz*. I told you, I figured his relatives might be here." Jordan flipped pages this way and that, trying to arrange them into some semblance of order. "You know, packing up his stuff, figuring out what he had that would be part of his estate. I didn't feel right hanging onto family papers, and I had no idea there weren't any other Stilwells around. How could I?"

"You still should have thought before coming out here alone," Darcy retorted, holding out more crumpled pages. "What if the person you ran into was the murderer?"

"It's the middle of the day. And Holt was murdered miles from here," Jordan reasoned.

"You don't know that for certain."

"Besides, what kind of murderer—or burglar—breaks into a house in broad daylight, leaving his car parked in plain sight in the driveway?"

"Hmmph."

"Honestly, it never occurred to me that I would be in danger. I planned to drop off the papers, then head home. If someone had answered the door when I knocked, I wouldn't have even tried to go inside."

"So you can't describe the car *or* your assailant. What about general height and build? Clothing? Even a fleeting impression?"

"If I go by how strong he was, since he pushed me hard enough to make me fly backward, whoever it was participates regularly in pro wrestling."

"Right." Darcy said it sourly.

Jordan stopped straightening pages and squeezed her

eyes shut, trying to conjure up an image of who she'd seen. "A few inches taller than me, so maybe just under six feet? He was moving fast, and I didn't have any contact with his body, just his hands, which seemed big but not overly so."

"He pushed you?"

"Yeah."

"We'll get one of the techs to use UV light on you to see if they can raise the beginning of any bruises. You may have handprints on you."

"That sounds slightly kinky."

Darcy rolled her eyes. "Okay, what else? Clothes? Hair? Coloring?"

"Jeans and a hoodie—black, I think. I couldn't see either hair or coloring, though I remember a pale glimpse of his face."

"So we've got an assailant of unknown build and weight, average height, unknown coloring, and wearing a hoodie and jeans. Just great." Darcy shook her head. "Real helpful."

Jordan had a thought. "Check Malachi—I heard him barking right after I fell; he might have gotten in a bite. And if he did, there might be bits of fabric, or even DNA, caught between his teeth, right?"

Darcy yelled for a technician. It took him several minutes to convince Malachi to let a stranger look inside his mouth. Nothing.

Jordan fed him a treat for the indignity he had to suffer, then cocked her head in the direction of the house. She could see the other crime-scene techs inside, processing the living room. "So do you think my attacker was burglarizing the place?"

Darcy shrugged. "I don't know if we'll be able to tell. It was always a filthy mess; now, it's just messier."

"Actually, I was here fairly recently—I might remember a few items."

"Are your prints in the system? Did Drake ever fingerprint you during the investigation down in California?" Darcy asked, referring to the LAPD detective who'd been convinced Jordan was guilty of her husband's murder.

"No, why?"

"Because if I let you inside, I'll need to take your prints for elimination purposes. I don't necessarily have to put them in the system, but there's always a chance they'd end up there. Are you okay with that?"

Jordan shrugged. "Sure. I touched the handle and the front panel of the door, so you probably should take my prints anyway."

"Just be careful not to touch anything unnecessarily, okay?"

Together, they climbed the front steps and walked into the living room. Furniture had been tossed, tables overturned. But a flat-panel television still hung on the wall over the fireplace, which was filled with empty beer cans and looked as if it hadn't been used in decades.

Jordan nodded in the direction of the television. "I'd say that's a pretty good indication that the person's motive wasn't robbery. Aren't those worth over a thousand?"

"Yeah," Darcy replied, studying the room. "Look around—was it this messy the last time you were here?"

Jordan frowned. "No. There were a few pizza boxes piled up on the coffee table with some empty beer bottles, and of course there was dust everywhere, but this mess looks more ... *methodical*. Like someone went through the room and flipped every cushion, moved every picture, opened every drawer. And it looks like he was in a real hurry, since nothing was properly replaced."

"Yeah, I agree." Darcy was silent while she looked the room over a second time. "Or else, he didn't care if he straightened up behind himself."

Jordan glanced around, hoping to spy the papers Holt had lifted from the hotel. She caught Darcy watching her with one eyebrow raised. Avoiding her gaze, Jordan headed for the bedroom and its adjacent bathroom.

The bed was unmade, the sheets half pulled off. The closet doors stood ajar, hanging clothes shoved to one end of the rack. No papers on the nightstand, either.

Toiletries sat haphazardly on the bathroom counter, along with substances Jordan didn't want to examine too closely, and the medicine cabinet door hung open. The toilet seat was up and smelled of urine. Struck by a thought, she headed over to look inside the closet to confirm her suspicions. "It doesn't look like a woman has been living here, right? No clothes in the closet except a man's, no women's shampoo, makeup, et cetera, in the bathroom."

"Maybe he always went to her house," Darcy suggested. "Women typically like to spend the night at their place, not at a guy's."

She was right. Jordan had gotten as far as thinking about the *possibility* of spending the night with Jase, but she'd always been stopped—at least, partially—by the lack of privacy at her home. And whenever she thought about going to his place instead, she hadn't been ready to take a step that big. It seemed somehow like more of a commitment, and she was betting any woman who was picking up subliminally on Holt's lack of respect would have instinctively felt the same way.

"Well, whoever came through here, he was looking for something," she concluded.

"I wonder what?" Darcy mused, still studying the room.

Jordan had an idea or two, but she figured it would be better to mention them after she'd poured a couple of glasses of wine down Darcy's throat at the pub. "So if it wasn't a burglar and it wasn't an ex-girlfriend picking up her belongings, . . ."

"It was probably the same person who murdered Holt," Darcy confirmed bluntly, finishing Jordan's thought.

How pleasant—she'd probably just been assaulted by a killer. It was a good thing Malachi had been with her to scare him off. From now on, the dog could have as much organic food as he wanted.

* * *

AFTER making a plan with Darcy to meet later at the pub, Jordan dropped by home to see if she could catch up with Charlotte. She needed to ask her some questions about her relationship with Jesse Canby. Now that Jordan had thought about it, she was fairly certain Charlotte had started to say something the night before about what Michael Seavey had been up to in 1893.

Parking at the curb in front of Longren House, she let Malachi out of the back of the Prius and crossed the front lawn to climb the porch steps. Inside the door, a tall vase crammed with a jumble of long-stemmed, red roses sat on a small side table. Roses? She searched her brain. Jase, perhaps? It certainly didn't seem like something he'd do out of the blue, but what girl didn't go all instantly mushy at the sight of red roses? Feeling a thrill of pleasure at the unexpected gift, Jordan crossed the entry and leaned over to sniff them while she looked for the florist's card. Petals dropped onto the table in a shower; evidently the flowers had been bruised during transport by a careless delivery person.

"The roses are from Michael," Hattie said from behind her. "Wasn't it a nice gesture?"

Jordan stopped hunting for the card, noting Hattie's blush. Okay, so *not* from Jase, but from a ghost. That explained the slight damage and messy arrangement. She straightened some of the stems, allowing herself a moment to swallow her disappointment.

"You don't happen to know which florist he ripped off, do you?" she asked, trying not to sound cranky. "So that I can go by and pay them for the flowers?"

"Ripped off?"

Jordan rephrased. "Which florist he stole the roses from."

"It's the thought that counts," Hattie said loyally.

"For the shop owner trying to run a profitable business, not so much." Jordan paused, making a connection from her reading earlier. "Do you have a middle name?"

"Why, yes," Hattie replied, looking perplexed by the question. "Dale."

"Flowers!" Charlotte floated down the hallway from the kitchen. "Oh, Hattie!"

Frank appeared in the library doorway. "The man has hidden motives." His expression was grim.

"Oh, I don't think this one is very hidden," Jordan replied before Hattie could protest.

"Certainly not!" Charlotte agreed. "He really loves Hattie!"

Frank folded his arms. "I have no doubt Seavey wants more from Hattie than her affections. He must suspect she still has assets he can get hold of, or that perhaps she can provide him a certain social legitimacy with others in our community." He shrugged. "Sending flowers is a brazen attempt to manipulate her affections."

Wishing to avoid another ghostly squabble, Jordan headed down the hall to the kitchen. "You might want to rethink that strategy," she hinted at him as she passed. "Women love flowers."

Frank merely snorted.

She heard simultaneous gasps from behind her and turned back. Hattie and Charlotte were clutching each other, their mouths agape, their expressions full of fear. "What?" she asked them.

"Your clothing is torn, and smeared with dirt and debris," Hattie said faintly.

"And your hair has *blood* in it!" Charlotte cried. She circled the stairwell twice at ceiling height, then vanished in a puff of particles.

Hattie sighed. "She faints at the sight of gore." Her expression remained troubled. "What happened to you?"

"Nothing much." Jordan continued down the hall to the kitchen, dropping into the chair at the table. After a minute or two, she'd get those aspirin tablets she badly needed, she promised herself. "Someone shoved me down some cement steps and I hit my head."

"What did you do to provoke him?" Frank leaned a shoulder against the kitchen door.

Jordan narrowed her gaze. "Nothing. Someone was inside Holt Stilwell's house when I arrived. Obviously, they didn't want to be caught in there, or they wouldn't have attacked me." She reached up to touch the lump on the back of her head. It hadn't gotten any smaller.

"Hmm." Frank's expression remained skeptical.

In her peripheral vision, the teakettle landed askew on a stove burner, which turned on by itself. A coffee mug fell from the cupboard above onto the counter beside the stove, herbs pouring into it. Within seconds—much faster than normal, which had Jordan wondering about the damage to her fuse box—the teakettle whistled, then floated over to the cup, pouring steaming water into it. The cup then landed in front of Jordan, almost tipping over. She leaned back warily as hot water splattered across the table.

Charlotte's image rematerialized beside her. "The tea will ease your headache," she said, her eyes brimming with tears. "I can't believe someone attacked you! How horrible. You must have been terrified!"

Jordan was touched by her concern. "Not so much terrified as pissed off," she admitted, then added in a soothing tone, "I'm fine, really, Charlotte. I wasn't hurt."

"You could have been *killed!*"

Frank rolled his eyes. Which didn't come off quite like

when a human did it—his eyes sort of rolled around in the sockets like marbles. It was not an attractive sight.

Hattie wafted down into one of the chairs across from Jordan. "It's all *right*, Charlotte. As you can see, she's unharmed."

Jordan took a sip of the hot tea and hurriedly spit it back into the cup. "*Gah!* Unharmed until *now*! What the *hell* did you put in this?"

"It's willow bark tea, which will ease your aches and pains from the fall," Charlotte replied. Her expression stern, she pointed at the cup. "Now don't be such a child—drink every drop. It's *good* for you."

Jordan stood and walked over to the sink, dumping out the tea despite Charlotte's outraged shriek. Pulling an aspirin bottle out of the cupboard, she showed it to Charlotte. "*This* is the same thing—they now make it in tablets, so you can swallow them without having to actually taste it. Trust me, it's a vast improvement." She filled a glass with water and downed the tablets, then refilled the kettle to put it back on the burner and make herself a more palatable cup of Earl Grey.

"I do appreciate that you tried to help," she added gently, turning back to lean against the edge of the counter while the water heated. "Charlotte, you started to mention something about Michael Seavey last night, but I interrupted you. Did you know him back then?"

Charlotte fidgeted, her hands gripping the skirts of her pale blue silk gown tightly enough to cause wrinkles. "The Green Light was right around the corner from his hotel. Therefore, I frequently ran into him. And some of my 'clients' would tell me about Michael, of course. He was quite famous along the waterfront." She sent an apologetic glance to Hattie. "Michael was a good man in many ways. He always treated me kindly."

Hattie's eyes grew round. "Do you mean to tell me that he . . . *visited* you at the Green Light?"

"Oh, goodness no!" Charlotte assured her hastily. "I just meant that I would run into him from time to time out walking, and he always treated me with great respect." Her expression darkened. "Unlike that business partner of his."

The teakettle shrieked, and Jordan removed it from the stove, rummaging for a tea bag. "Did Sam Garrett ever hurt you?" she asked Charlotte carefully.

Charlotte's face immediately closed up. "Not so much," she replied vaguely, twisting a blond ringlet of hair with her fingers. "I just didn't like having him as a customer."

"Did you know Michael Seavey was smuggling opium?" Jordan asked.

Charlotte became agitated, circling the room, the swishing of her skirts audible. "I won't talk ill of Michael!" she cried.

She swooped down on the stack of papers Tom had left behind, scooting them across the table toward Jordan. "And what's the meaning of *this*?" she asked angrily. "Surely you won't let those people who have been hanging about make *this* many alterations to Longren House!"

"I haven't decided yet," Jordan prevaricated, not objecting to the change of subject, "but I promise that when I do, I'll consult with you and Hattie first."

Charlotte looked mollified.

"Though we might want to revisit your attempts to doctor the home inspection report," Jordan added mildly. "Did you really think to keep the full extent of the necessary repairs from me? How do you expect me to come up with the money for everything that needs to be done to preserve your home?"

"You could go back to work," Charlotte replied. "Many respectable women of our time, such as Eleanor Canby's niece Celeste, were in the trades." Charlotte's expression turned dreamy. "Celeste ran the most wonderful millinery shop . . ."

"I doubt Jordan would make very much money, since she doesn't seem to be very good at her prior trade and has few skills," Frank pointed out. While they'd been talking, he'd come into the room to study Tom's list. "And repairs such as these will be quite expensive."

"I made very good money in L.A., I'll have you know," Jordan retorted. "I helped numerous people improve their lives."

"You could use the money in the wall safe to pay for the repairs," Hattie suggested.

Jordan's head swiveled around. "*What*? What money?"

"Ah." Frank looked smug. "So *that's* what Seavey is after. I thought as much."

"Nonsense," Hattie protested. "Michael had no way of knowing about it."

"You don't know that for certain," Frank replied. "And if Seavey had any inkling that it was there, I'd wager he's been trying to get hold of it ever since."

"What are you talking about?" Jordan was bewildered. "What wall safe? I haven't found anything of the sort in this house."

"That's because it's been concealed behind a bookcase since I came back as a ghost," Hattie replied. "I didn't want any of those questionable owners in past decades to get hold of the money. They would have used it to tear down walls and build on rooms of dubious architectural integrity. Why, they would have used it to *destroy* Longren House!"

Jordan held up a hand. "Hold on—let me get this straight. Are you telling me there's a hidden safe in this house that contains all kinds of money?"

Everyone looked at Hattie, including Charlotte, who looked as surprised as Jordan.

"Yes," Hattie replied serenely. "It's in the library. Come—I'll show you."

Jordan grabbed her cup of tea and they all trooped down the hallway and into the library. Hattie floated around behind the oak desk and pointed to a bookcase covering the wall that, on closer inspection, *did* seem to be of slightly different design than the other bookcases in the room. Frank moved over to it, inspecting it more carefully.

"When I was alive," Hattie explained, "my husband, Charles, kept a wall safe there for his business papers. After his death, I discovered a large amount of cash in it, possibly ill-gotten gains from smuggling, although I was never able to prove it. I was forced to use some of the money to free Charlotte from her kidnappers, but the rest was still in the safe at the time of my death. Therefore I made certain, once I was able to come back to earth, that our housekeeper, Sara, returned to the house and hired workers to conceal the safe behind a built-in bookcase."

"*Wait a minute*," Jordan said, excitement chasing chills down her spine. "Do you mean to tell me that someone else, *someone human besides me*, has been able to see you?"

Hattie frowned at her. "Well, of course. Though admittedly, there have only been a few of you over the years. Fortunately, Sara was one." Her expression turned sad. "I like to think I was able to console her a bit—she was devastated by Charlotte's and my deaths."

Jordan waved that aside. "All *right*. Maybe I'm *not* crazy; maybe I can find others whom I can at least talk to about all this—"

"Oh, I doubt others exist *today*. And really," Hattie sniffed, "I'd think you'd be much more interested in the money."

Scrutinizing the bookcase, Frank faded through it, then reappeared. "There's definitely something back there," he told Jordan. "But you'll need to have one of your workers dismantle the bookcase to get to it. You don't want to unduly damage the plaster."

Jordan remembered her tea and took a sip before it got too cold. "How much money is in there?" she asked Hattie out of curiosity.

"About forty thousand dollars, I think."

Jordan spewed the tea all over the Aubusson rug. "Are you *kidding* me?"

"Kidding you . . . oh, you mean would I say it in jest? Whyever would I do that?" Hattie asked seriously, not understanding the colloquialism. "Unless someone was able to remove the money before I returned, that's what should be in there."

"This is wonderful!" Charlotte cried. "We can use it to pay for your wedding."

Chapter 9

AFTER taking a shower and downing several more aspirin tablets, Jordan stopped in at the neighborhood florist's to pay for Hattie's roses. The owner seemed more thrilled by the prospect of being robbed by a ghost than by Jordan's offer to reimburse her for the loss.

By the time Jordan arrived at All That Jazz, Darcy was already holding a table. As Jordan crossed the room, she gave Jase a questioning look, wondering if he needed help behind the bar, but he shook his head. Relieved that she would have some downtime, she headed for Darcy's table, but ended up detouring to check in with Tom, who was sitting at a nearby table with two men she'd never met before. Both wore paint-streaked overalls, though, so she surmised that they worked with him.

"Any chance you can drop by the house tomorrow morning to help me dismantle a bookcase?" she asked Tom when she was within hearing.

He raised both eyebrows but refrained from asking outright. "What time?"

"Tenish? That gives me time to take Malachi out for breakfast."

"I'll be there."

The pub was crowded for a Wednesday night, and several of the patrons weren't drinking. Absently noting a number of ghosts dressed in old-fashioned work clothes, Jordan pulled out the chair across from Darcy and sank into it. An unshaven man two tables away caught her eye. While she was puzzling out why he looked familiar to her, he looked her way, locking gazes with her. He smiled, his expression more cocksure than friendly. Then he stood and left. She frowned, still not placing him, and gave up, shrugging the feeling away.

Malachi made the rounds, greeting everyone he knew with a lick, holding up his paw for a shake, then took up his favorite position on the floor by her feet. Not for the first time, Jordan wondered why the big dog didn't seem to be wary of the ghosts in the pub, while at home, he frequently disappeared when they were around. Perhaps it had more to do with the level of tension in the house, versus the relatively low-key buzz from the ghosts in the pub, who were typically on hand to socialize and listen to the live jazz. Whatever the reason, she found it reassuring that he could see them.

"Looks like we've got four distinct sets of unidentified fingerprints at Holt's house," Darcy said by way of greeting. "Your fingerprints were all over the attic."

"That would be from when I hunted through the boxes to find Michael Seavey's papers, about three weeks ago." Jordan propped her running shoes on the extra chair. "So three sets that are unidentified."

Darcy nodded. "You *did* notice that there are mice up in that attic? Lots of them? Everywhere?"

"Yeah."

"Okay, then. So much for worrying whether you contracted hantavirus." Darcy shook her head, taking a sip from her glass of wine.

When officially off duty, Darcy typically exchanged her work clothes for outfits that were more flattering to her tall, slender build. This evening, she had on a jazzy red, form-fitting, ribbed cotton sweater with a high collar, low-rider black jeans, and black leather boots—as usual, effortlessly pulling off far more style than Jordan would manage in her entire lifetime. It hadn't escaped her notice that whenever Darcy entered a room, more than one man's gaze followed her, showing appreciation and interest.

"We've pretty much wrapped up work at Holt's house and on the beach," Darcy said, looking more relaxed and less tired than the night before. "No murder weapon, no dive gear. Anywhere. And nothing at Holt's house that indicates a struggle, though it would be hard to tell in all the mess."

"So maybe he was killed on a boat and dumped?"

"Who the hell knows? I have no identified crime scene and a complete lack of evidence, so I don't even know how to start speculating."

"Can the medical examiner tell if Holt fought with anyone?"

Darcy raised an eyebrow.

"What?" Jordan spread her hands. "Half the population knows to ask that question. The only shows on television these days are reality and crime."

"Preliminary findings indicate no sign of a struggle. My guess is Holt knew his killer, who walked up to him and put a bullet through his brain. Or who gave him a lift in a boat, blew his brains out, and dumped him overboard. The gun was a .22, which explains the lack of an exit wound—the bullet bounced around inside, turning his brains to mush." Darcy must have noticed Jordan's expression. "Sorry—I forget sometimes that I'm talking to a civilian."

Jase dropped off a glass of wine for Jordan on his way to the piano. Evidently he would be providing the entertainment this evening. She took a bracing sip.

"It would be nice to know who Holt's most recent girlfriend was," Darcy mused out loud. "But so far, I can't find anyone who knows or at least is willing to tell me."

The wine selection for that evening was a crisp, dry Merlot, which Jordan thought went down just fine. "So what's the deal with Sally? She sounded angry enough to do a little B&E. Did she and Holt date?"

"Nope, Holt dated her sister, who committed suicide not long afterward."

The next sip of wine almost went down Jordan's windpipe. "Jesus." She hated the thought of anyone committing suicide. In her opinion, suicides represented a failure by the therapy community to intervene before it was too late. "Dammit, wasn't *anyone* paying attention?"

"Evidently not. Everyone knew the sister had problems—a history of drugs, in and out of institutions, and so on. But she'd been relatively stable for a year or so when Holt got hold of her."

"You said Holt treated women badly, but I had no idea."

"Actually, though Sally told me she blamed Holt, I

never completely bought her reasoning," Darcy replied. "I suspect his treatment of the sister might have contributed but wasn't the primary cause. Melissa—I think that was her name—was always unstable, and the family had limited funds to pay for her care. Sally did what she could, but the treatments never stuck. Melissa would take her meds for a while, then fall off the wagon."

"And Holt sensed a vulnerability and exploited it," Jordan concluded bluntly. "Or was too oblivious to understand her fragile state."

"Yep."

"If I were in Sally's shoes, I can't say for certain that I wouldn't have reacted the same way about Holt's death," Jordan admitted. "She's got to believe that if not for him, her sister might still be alive. That's strong motive."

"I'm checking into her alibi," Darcy agreed.

Jase ran his fingers lightly over the piano's keys, then launched into a mellow, familiar tune. It took Jordan a few minutes to place it. "Body and Soul." She gave him a quiet look, but he merely smiled. Lazily.

"Why don't you put all of us out of our misery and jump the poor man's bones?" Darcy asked, observant as ever.

"No privacy, for one thing. I'm not big on exhibitionism, and the ghosts are around all the time."

"I'm betting if you knocked on his door, he wouldn't leave you standing on the porch."

"Remember that discussion we had earlier about how a woman prefers to have the man stay over at her house, not go to his? Besides, according to my Four Point Plan for Personal Renewal, I'm still eleven and a half months away from allowing myself to make any kind of new relationship commitment—six for grieving, six more for looking but not touching," she reminded Darcy. She was referring to the personal renewal plan her friends called the FPP that she'd implemented to help herself recover from the upheavals in her life.

"Give me a moment to bang my head on the table." Darcy's tone was sarcastic. "That plan was a total non-starter. You're way too impulsive to ever stick to something so rigid."

"I beg your pardon?"

"Did you or did you not write a check on the spot for a house that you'd barely seen? Shut down your practice in L.A. and move up here basically on a whim?" Darcy shook her head. "All I'm saying is that you need to loosen up. Have some sex—it's a terrific stress reducer."

"People who live in glass houses," Jordan pointed out. "When was the last time you took some hot guy up on his offer?"

"Dating the chief of police tends to warp your expectations for the relationship. You, however, have no excuse."

"Murdered husband? Several life changes that hit high up on the Richter stress scale? Any of this ringing a bell?"

Darcy made a chickenlike clucking noise.

Jordan's retort was delayed by Kathleen suddenly appearing at their table, radiating a grim intensity.

According to Jase, his cranky chef had once been a fighter pilot in the military. She now managed an organic garden of herbs and greens behind the pub with ruthless efficiency, using its produce to create the mouthwatering meals she intimidated pub patrons into eating. One didn't

182 • P. J. ALDERMAN

try to order from Kathleen—one simply agreed to eat what she served.

"Yes," Jordan agreed, and Darcy nodded.

Kathleen left without a word.

Jordan returned to the possible cause of the break-in, avoiding further discussion of her romantic life. Or lack thereof. "So maybe someone knew Holt was diving for salvage and decided to break into his house, to see if he came up with anything of value. Maybe the burglar knew *what* Holt was diving for."

"We don't know Holt was doing any such thing," Darcy reminded her.

"No, but it's looking pretty likely that he was." Jordan filled Darcy in on what she'd learned talking to the workers at the hotel, and also that she and Bob had pinpointed the coordinates of the shipwreck, which basically matched where they'd found Holt. "Those workers said Holt had been taking diving lessons."

"So what part of 'don't mess with my investigation' don't you understand?" Darcy asked.

"I was actually looking into something else, but since I was at the Historical Society and the hotel, I decided to see if I could discover anything that would help you out."

"Right," Darcy said drily. "Wait—what *were* you doing at the Historical Society? And no, don't tell me how you got inside. I don't recommend that you confess to me when you commit felonies."

"A worker let me in," Jordan replied in a virtuous tone. She didn't volunteer that she'd filched more historical documents. "I was looking for information about the *Henrietta Dale*. I figured that the shipwreck had to be big news at the time, and that there'd be a number of stories about it. I was also looking for information about Michael Seavey's murder."

Darcy looked confused. "The shanghaier? Why?"

"Hattie wants me to find out who killed him, because he's courting her. And by the way, I think Seavey's murder might relate to your murder investigation."

"*Whoa.*" Darcy held up a hand. "Did you just say that Michael Seavey is *courting* Hattie? She has *two* lovers? Has Seavey's ghost been at your house?"

Jordan sighed. "Yes, yes, and yes. Michael Seavey has decided to come back from . . . *wherever* . . . and hang out part of the time at my house. He lives in the upper floors of the Cosmopolitan Hotel, but he visits my house to court Hattie. Seavey thinks he perished on the *Henrietta Dale*, but Hattie found an old newspaper article . . ."

"Boil it down," Darcy ordered impatiently.

Jordan gave her a silent look, then continued. ". . . claiming that Seavey had been murdered. And Seavey left behind business papers. They were hidden in the rooms Holt was remodeling, identifying the cargo on board the *Henrietta Dale* the night she ran aground. So Holt was after the sunken loot, and someone probably killed him for it," she concluded. She was pleased she'd been able to articulate it so clearly.

"Shit." Darcy scowled. "Setting aside for the moment that the number of ghosts in your house continues to multiply, and ignoring the fact that one of them could actually be rather dangerous to have lurking about, let me just be perfectly clear: I don't think Holt's murder has anything to do with the past. I believe the fact that we found him where we did *may be*, at best, an indication that he'd developed an interest in that old shipwreck. His murderer could easily have decided to take advantage of a remote location, nothing more. You have absolutely *no* proof that anyone in present day could have had a motive to kill Holt over a salvage operation that likely doesn't include anything of real value."

"What about the stash of opium? That's got to be valuable. And we don't know what else might have been on board the *Henrietta Dale*. Seavey went to great expense to have secret compartments built into the hull."

"The opium is a plant-based product that would have lost its potency a long time ago, not to mention gotten waterlogged, in all likelihood. Do you actually *know* what else was on board the ship that night? Did you find the business papers?" Darcy stopped abruptly. "I get it—that's what you were looking for at Holt's house. The papers. I *knew* you were searching for something." She glowered at Jordan. "You are a real pain in the butt, you know that?"

"Seavey showed me where the papers had been hidden in his hotel suite," Jordan explained. She decided not to mention the obnoxious owner and her foray into illegal trespass. "I also talked to one of Holt's employees, who told me he'd found the papers, then signed up for diving lessons." She drank the last of her wine, then leaned back in her chair, folding her arms. "I'm not just making this up, you know. Holt really was diving for whatever was on the ship at the time she went down."

Which made her wonder, come to think of it, who the guy was that she'd seen on the beach during their hike. At the time, she'd thought he was a ghost and discounted his presence. He'd been diving, and he'd had some kind of decorated tin in his hand. After all, Darcy hadn't even noticed him. But maybe he was the murderer after all.

Darcy waved a hand in front of her face. "Hello? You flew away there for a minute."

Jordan hesitated; then she shrugged. "Just thinking, is all." Until she was certain of what she'd seen, she wasn't going to mention it.

"Fine," Darcy said, "but let me repeat: I'm not interested in some old shipwreck, even if that's why Holt was in a dry suit. This murder took place in present day, and it most likely has something to do with events in *Holt's* life that don't relate in any way to Michael Seavey and the nineteenth century. I'm focusing on who in recent months—including old girlfriends or disgruntled business associates—would have wanted him dead."

Her last statement caught Jordan's attention. "Disgruntled business associates?"

"Holt's fired a few workers over the years who subsequently let it be known they thought they'd been treated badly."

"Anyone I know?"

"Down, girl. I haven't gotten far enough in my search to identify specific individuals yet. I've been busy with the various crime scenes and running down your elusive assailant. And people don't go around just announcing that they were fired from jobs. Besides, running any names past you that I might come up with is of very little value. Even if I introduce you to each person, it's not like you have a lot of experience counseling murderers and delving into their psyches. You wouldn't immediately recognize a homicidal tendency in someone you met."

"Valid point." Witness her stalker, who Jordan had thought was completely nonviolent. When it came to wielding a gun, he'd been quite casual about it. He'd probably been equally casual when he'd cut the brake lines on Ryland's Beemer. Jordan shuddered.

"What?" Darcy asked, watching Jordan's face closely. "What do you know?"

"Nothing, really," she answered truthfully.

"Look, go ahead and investigate Seavey's murder if you like, but stay out of the current-day investigation. I don't want you to get hurt."

Jordan nodded. "As much as I can, I will."

Darcy looked unhappy with her answer. "Are you worried about Seavey being in your house?"

"Not really," Jordan said. "As sociopaths go, Seavey's a fairly harmless one. And besides, he's mostly focused on Hattie, not me."

Darcy grinned. "A spectral wedding, huh? *This* should be interesting."

Jordan leaned forward, suddenly remembering the biggest news of the day. "So get this: Hattie had her maid from the 1890s, a woman named Sara, return to the house a few years after their deaths to hire workers to build a bookcase behind the desk in the library."

Darcy raised both brows. "And this is important because?"

"Think about it," Jordan said impatiently. "That means another human could see Hattie. *I'm not alone.*"

"Why did Hattie want the bookcase built?"

"What? Oh, to hide a wall safe that contains about forty thousand dollars, supposedly."

"Shit!" Darcy hastily glanced around, then leaned over the table. "Keep your voice down, unless you want to be burglarized, too." She paused. "Forty thousand dollars? Are you certain?"

"You're missing the point here," Jordan said, exasperated.

"I repeat—*forty thousand dollars?*"

Jordan sighed. "That's what Hattie claims, though it's entirely probable someone in the intervening years found the cash. Tom's going to help me remove the bookcase tomorrow morning, but I'm skeptical the money will still be there." Bill had noticed their empty wineglasses and dropped off refills. Jordan smiled her thanks, then continued. "You know, I *could* go back out to the lighthouse and talk to the gardener about who survived the shipwreck that night in 1893. I found a list today at the Historical Society, but it would be helpful to ask her about the details of the rescue. And also I could find out if Holt ever went out there to look at the *Henrietta Dale*'s logbook."

"So you're ready to admit that the gardener is probably a ghost?" Darcy asked with a grin.

"Treat me nicely if you'd like me to make the trip out and ask her if anyone from present day who might be associated with your investigation has been lurking about."

"Hell yes, what an excellent idea. I can see myself explaining that one in court. 'My hearsay testimony, Your Honor, comes from a civilian unrelated to the case, who told the story to me after talking to a ghost who can't be called as a witness.'"

"Geez, never mind."

A young, slim woman approached their table, wearing a Victorian-style purple velvet dress, complete with a fitted short cape, and a felted, beaded beret. She carried a large, leather portfolio under one arm.

Jordan sat up straight in her chair, suddenly uneasy. Up to now, she'd never been openly approached by any of the ghosts in the pub.

"Hey, Susan," Darcy greeted her.

"Hey, yourself." The young woman smiled at Darcy.

Jordan gave Darcy a sideways glance, reassessing. "You can see her?"

"Of course."

"Jordan Marsh?" the young woman asked, turning to her. "Bob MacDonough sent me. He couldn't be here tonight, but he said you want me to sketch some sort of ship you saw?"

"Oh, right." Jordan noted Darcy's amusement and felt foolish. She shook the young woman's slender, fine-boned hand. "Nice to meet you, Susan."

"We'd better get to work, then. I have a portrait sitting in an hour. If that's all right with you?"

"Absolutely."

Jordan gave the woman a few moments to get settled, then started describing what she'd seen. Susan's pencil moved rapidly over a sketch pad until Kathleen reappeared with their dinners.

She glanced at the sketch Susan was working on. "Why are you having her draw a tall ship?" she asked as she placed the warm plates of food in front of Darcy and Jordan.

"It's a sketch of the ghost ship Jordan saw yesterday off Dungeness Spit," Darcy explained.

Kathleen glared. "The crap I have to put up with in my diners." She turned on the heels of her sensible loafers and stalked away.

Jordan shook her head and dug into Kathleen's seasonal greens and polenta.

Susan showed her the incomplete sketch—it was a surprisingly accurate likeness of what she'd seen. "The masts were taller, with more rows of square sails, here and here," Jordan told her, pointing. "And she had this pointy piece of wood on her bow—"

"A bowsprit?" Susan asked, her hand flying across the page.

"I guess, and about twenty feet long, I think . . ."

The front door burst open, and Jordan turned her head in midchew. The owner from the Cosmopolitan Hotel stood in the entry, his eyes scouring the room, obviously looking for someone. Jordan slid down in her chair.

Spying her, he pointed at her, bellowing, "*You!*" He advanced on them, his strides as long as he could make them, given that his legs were shorter than hers.

Jordan tensed, gripping the arms of her chair.

Conversation in the pub ceased as patrons moved out of his way, warily tracking his progress. Susan grabbed her sketchbook and stood, backing away from the table. Out of the corner of Jordan's eye, she saw Jase leap up from the piano and plow right through several ghosts, headed in her direction.

Darcy rose and blocked the hotel owner's path, but the man planted a hand on her chest and shoved her out of the way.

"Burglar!" he screeched as he reached Jordan. He grabbed her by the upper arms and hauled her onto her feet. *"Arrest this woman!"*

"Hey!" Jordan yanked futilely, wriggling to dislodge his painful grip. He yanked back, hard, pulling her off-balance, and she stumbled into his chest.

Malachi came snarling out of a dead sleep and launched, his big, angry body glancing off the man and crashing into the next table. Mugs toppled, splattering beer in every direction. The hotel owner skidded on the wet floor, pulling Jordan down with him.

Darcy clamped a hand on his shoulder. "Let go of her, Walters. *Now.*"

Malachi scrambled to his feet, and sank his teeth into Walters's thigh, ripping the fabric of his wool slacks.

"Get your dog off me!" Walters shrieked.

Jase waded in, and with a swift upward movement, broke Walters's grip on Jordan, stepping between the two of them. Darcy twisted Walters's arms behind him, using her other hand to grip his shirt collar.

Walters howled in pain.

"Malachi, leave!" Jordan commanded, and he loosened his grip, backing away a few steps to place himself at Jordan's side, growling.

"You've got two minutes to explain yourself, pal," Jase said in the iciest tone she'd ever heard from him, "before I kick you out of here on your stupid ass."

She stood on her tiptoes and glared over Jase's shoulder. "Yeah. What he said."

Chapter 10

"That *bitch* trespassed in my hotel after I expressly *forbade* her to do so." Walters's face was white with fury. "She stole valuable historic documents!"

"Whoa, wait a minute." Jordan was confused. "What are you talking about? I didn't steal anything."

"You're way out of line, Walters," Jase said. "No one manhandles a woman in my pub. And if you lay a hand on Jordan again, no matter where—"

"But you *did* trespass?" Darcy interrupted. She was glaring at Jordan.

"Sort of . . ."

"See!" Walters said triumphantly. "I told you so. *Arrest* her! And let go of me, dammit! *I'm* not the criminal, here. *She* is."

Darcy released him, and he staggered backward, scowling at all of them and rubbing his arm. She pinched her nose. "You really can't go around breaking and entering in the name of historical research," she told Jordan.

"All I wanted to do was chat with the workers for five

minutes and find out if Holt had run across anything interesting," Jordan explained. "And I asked permission first."

"Which I denied," Walters spit. He turned back to Darcy. "She stole the papers, I'm telling you! I *know* she did. I demand that you arrest her—I want to swear out a complaint."

"Do you have any witnesses who saw her trespass?" Darcy asked him.

"Yes."

Darcy muttered something under her breath. Then she sighed again. "Look, Clive . . ."

Jordan started to snicker—his name fit him *really* well. Darcy shot her a hard look, and she struggled, somewhat unsuccessfully, to swallow the sound.

"The way I see it," the police chief continued, "Jordan could swear out a complaint against you for assault, with the whole pub as witnesses."

"*What?* That's preposterous. *She's* the one who stole from me. You ask her if she has those papers."

"I didn't steal anything," Jordan repeated. "All I did was ask the workers if Holt had found any papers. Which, by the way, he did. We looked for them, because I was going to—I admit—glance through them. But I had no intention of taking them from your hotel." At least, she told herself, she *probably* wouldn't have. "We didn't find papers anywhere in the suite, and I have no idea where they are."

"I don't believe you! You—"

"Well, I'm inclined to," Darcy interposed firmly, "because I witnessed her looking for the same papers just a few hours ago in a different location. If she had them, she wouldn't have been looking for them, now would she?"

"She would if she wanted you to think she hadn't stolen them," he argued. "What kind of a law-enforcement officer are you? *Totally* incompetent?"

"Oh, for . . . I didn't steal your damn papers!" Jordan snapped. "Have you sought the advice of a professional therapist regarding your extreme paranoia? Because you really need to, you know—" The rest of what she'd planned to say was stifled by Jase clapping his hand over her mouth.

"*Not* helpful," he said quietly in her ear.

"You're accusing me of being unbalanced?" Walters demanded. Now his face had turned beet red.

Jordan gave Darcy a look that said she wasn't touching that one.

Darcy held out both hands palms up as if she was weighing something. "Assault versus simple trespass," she said to Walters. "Felony versus misdemeanor. Do you really want to go there?"

Walters fumed, saying nothing.

Jase's shoulders subtly relaxed. "I suggest you leave quietly, before I have you forcibly removed."

"I can see I'm not being taken seriously." He glared at Jordan. "I had no idea you had the law in your pocket."

"Watch it," Darcy warned. "You don't want to go there, either. I take my job very seriously. If one of your witnesses will swear out a statement saying that they saw Jordan remove historic documents from your hotel, then you have the proof you need to ask me to arrest her for theft. Otherwise, quit wasting my time."

"Leave," Jase repeated quietly. "Now."

Malachi growled for good measure, baring his teeth.

Walters harrumphed, then stalked to the exit. "This isn't over," he threatened in a loud voice, looking at Jordan. He stabbed a shaking finger at her. "And stay away from my hotel, do you hear me?"

"Believe me," Jordan told him fervently, "*not* a problem."

He slammed out the door. The room was silent for a moment, then patrons slowly turned away and began talking quietly among themselves.

Susan sidled past her. "I'll, um, just give this sketch to Bob MacDonough, okay?"

"Sure," Jordan said. "Sorry about the commotion."

She nodded without comment and fled.

Jordan dropped into her chair, hugging Malachi.

"Are you completely out of your mind?" Darcy demanded in a low tone. "Clive Walters is a known trouble-maker. Half the people who have worked for him can attest to his temper tantrums. He's been in my office numerous times, trying to swear out complaints against the people he's fired—almost no one in this town will work for him. *And you thought it was smart to sneak around after he told you not to?*"

"I may have experienced a slight lapse in judgment," Jordan admitted.

"You think?" Darcy sat down across from her. "Listen, you *really* need to back off. Next time I might not have any choice but to arrest you. If he hadn't manhandled you, we'd be down at the station right now, swearing out a warrant."

"You're right," Jordan agreed, realizing how much the encounter had shaken her up. "It won't happen again."

"Yes, it will," Jase said. "You won't stop."

"Hey," she protested, surprised.

He gave her a disgusted look. "What? I've already talked to you about this, and so has Darcy. But it didn't deter you, did it?"

"I honestly didn't think—"

He rolled right over her. "What if that jerk had discovered you in the hotel? He might have beaten you up, or worse. For that matter, what if he murdered Holt? You could have been confronted by a killer." He turned to Darcy. "Does Walters have any weapons registered in his name?"

"Not that I know of, but it's easy enough to buy an illegal one. We've got any number of survivalist-militia-type enclaves just outside of town. Those folks would be glad to help him put his hands on a weapon."

"Do you really consider him a suspect?" Jordan asked Darcy.

"I hadn't until now," Darcy answered. "I have to wonder what's got him so hot and bothered about those papers, but it's not like they're worth all that much. I've seen people murder for fifty bucks, but in my opinion, this is just Clive being Clive."

Jordan thought about it and agreed with her assessment. The guy was paranoid but that didn't mean he was also a killer. Most paranoids didn't escalate to murder. "Those papers are nothing more than a ledger of accounts showing the cargo of the *Henrietta Dale* the night she ran aground. The ledger itself can't be worth more than a few thousand at auction. Certainly not enough to go postal over." An idea occurred to her. "Just in case, can you search his hotel, to see if the murder weapon turns up?"

"Not without probable cause," Jase said. "And she doesn't have it."

Darcy snorted. "Hell, given your questionable behavior over the last twenty-four hours, Jordan, I've got a better chance of obtaining a search warrant for Longren House than I do for the Cosmopolitan Hotel." She rubbed the back of her neck, looking tired. "I'll go talk to Walters tomorrow after he's calmed down a bit. Maybe we'll get lucky and he won't have an alibi for the time of Holt's murder."

"You'd better hope those papers turn up," Jase told Jordan. "He'll be on a mission to prove you stole them until they do."

* * *

JORDAN stayed long enough to finish her meal, which was now cold, then left for home. The sun had set, and a sharp breeze was coming out of the south off the water. The neighborhood was quiet; most people were already inside for the evening. Yards were bathed in deepening twilight; lights shone through windows here and there, providing extra illumination as she walked the few blocks between the pub and Longren House. Her footsteps echoed on the pavement as she made her way down the street.

The house was silent and dark when she entered; evidently everyone had left for the day. No ghosts made their presence known. Still unsettled by Walters's accusations, Jordan flipped on the hall light and wandered back to the kitchen. She pulled a can of dog food from the cupboard, putting its contents on a plate for Malachi.

"Seriously cool defense of me back there, pal," she told him, running a hand down his back.

He looked up from his food, wagging his tail.

"That guy is certifiable," she said.

"Roooo."

"You've got to wonder what's so damn important about those papers that he would make such a stink," she said thoughtfully. "And even more to the point, where the hell *are* they? I don't have them. And they don't seem to be in Holt's house."

Evidently Malachi didn't share her curiosity, because he didn't respond. Instead, he focused on eating his food.

Jase and Darcy were both clearly cranky with her over her meddling. And so far, in one day, she'd managed to get herself shoved down a flight of steps *and* manhandled. And she knew little more than when the day had started. She had to admit, her detecting skills were pretty abysmal.

Restless, she wandered over to the stove to put on a kettle for tea. Finding a clean mug, she dropped a bag of chamomile into it, thinking it would help her get a solid night's sleep, then sat at the kitchen table to wait for the water to boil.

Earlier, she'd dropped the jumbled stack of Seavey's personal papers there, meaning to go through them when she had the chance and arrange them by date. They sat where she'd left them, still needing to be carefully reorganized and placed in some kind of protective, acid-free cardboard box, if she could find one. Obviously, even though Holt hadn't cared if the papers continued to deteriorate, walking around with them in their current, exposed state wasn't exactly good for them. Several pages now had grass stains and dirt smudges, and some of the ink had smeared where it had come into contact with the moisture on the grass.

The kettle whistled, and she got up to fix her tea. Mug in hand, she walked back over to the table, focusing on Seavey's blurred longhand script on the topmost page. Sam Garrett's name caught her eye. Carrying her tea in one hand and the papers in her other, Jordan headed upstairs to her bedroom.

Deadly Force

MICHAEL was still drinking his last cup of coffee, newspaper in hand, when he heard footsteps approach in the hall outside his suite. A fist pounded on the door of the sitting room where he took his breakfast each morning, a jarring intrusion in the peace and quiet of his routine. He frowned; his men knew better than to interrupt him at this hour.

Ever since he'd pulled himself out of the gutters of New York City, he'd made a point of taking time each day to appreciate the luxuries he was now able to afford. As part of the renovation he'd undertaken after purchasing the Cosmopolitan, he'd converted his sitting room into the style of the Turkish smoking room. Rich, golden, inlaid mahogany panels lined the walls, topped by warm white friezes sculpted in a Middle Eastern motif. Heavy maroon brocade curtains hung from the tall windows, gathered with twisted cords at frequent intervals and puddling on the hardwood floor, framed lace sheers hand-sewn in intricate patterns. Eastern rugs in swirls of dark colors graced the floor. When he relaxed in this room, he was able to temporarily push away the harsher realities of his workdays, and sometimes even the lingering grief.

The knock came again, this time more insistent. He folded the paper and laid it beside the remains of his breakfast, impatiently commanding, "Enter."

Sam Garrett opened the door, dressed in soiled work clothes and boots, a heavy canvas sailor's sea bag slung over his shoulder. He waited, his expression sardonic, for Remy to let him pass on Michael's nod, then walked over and dumped the sea bag on the dining table, causing the fine china dishes to clatter. He tossed the key to the bag's brass bar lock to Michael.

"Delivered as promised." His tone was insolent. Without waiting for an invitation, he took a seat across the table, his soiled clothes probably leaving stains on the fine silk fabric.

After calmly pressing a napkin to his lips, Michael stood and fitted the key into the padlock, then removed the bar, opening the bag to peer inside. Watertight tins filled the sea bag to overflowing. He broke the wax seal on one to open it and examine the individual balls of brown-colored opium within.

"I trust that you made certain the quality meets my usual high standards," he said.

"Of course," Garrett scoffed. "I can lay my hands on as much as you can sell to your wealthy clients."

Satisfied, Michael closed the bag and motioned to Remy. "The usual amount to Jesse Canby," he told his bodyguard. "And prepare the rest of the deliveries, making certain you exercise the appropriate amount of caution, arriving at the servants' entrances."

"Sure, Boss."

Michael returned to his seat, unhurriedly taking a sip of coffee. "I assume you weren't foolish enough to rely on smuggling Chinese immigrants to fund this purchase," he said to Garrett.

"What do you care?" Garrett challenged. "You got your shipment. It should be of no concern to you how I acquired it."

"On the contrary," Michael replied, keeping his tone mild. "The authorities are quite vigilant with respect to human trafficking."

Garrett shrugged. "You worry too much, old man. I can easily elude the Customs agents. I was able to do so the other night, and will continue to do so in the future."

Michael had to work to unclench his jaw. He found Garrett overly confident; such smugness in a business associate was a harbinger of unacceptably reckless behavior. "When Inspector Yardley sees fit to question me about the drowning of several Chinese, whose bodies were found just off North Beach, your activities are of the greatest concern to me. I'm not interested in attracting that kind of scrutiny. I fear you have knowledge of this incident?"

Garrett shrugged. "Yardley and his men came a little too close the other night—I did what I had to do. The Chinese were a liability."

Michael stiffened. "Good Christ, man! Have you lost your senses? You've just admitted to murder."

"Bull. I dumped them off the boat within sight of the

beach. It's not my fault that some of 'em didn't know how to swim."

"So you tossed the Chinese overboard, then stashed the opium on the beach, which resulted in its theft? Then you attempted to hang Lok. I can hardly comprehend the stupidity of your actions."

Garrett's eyes went flat. "Lok was on the beach. He either stole the drugs or saw who did. I was within my rights to question him."

"By doing so, you've brought the authorities down on your head. Lok took his story to the police, implicating both of us. Yardley has already questioned me about the incident. I can't rely on a business partner who is constantly in danger of being arrested for his ill-conceived actions."

Garrett reached across the table to pick up a half-eaten piece of toast from Michael's breakfast plate, biting into it. "You whine like a little boy, Seavey."

From the corner of his eye, Michael saw Remy start forward. He gave him a slight hand signal to remain where he was for now. "No doubt Lok was on the beach because he was trying to help his countrymen come ashore. And he would have been a fool to admit as much to the authorities. But he could achieve a similar end by claiming that you attempted to kill him, could he not? The greater the scrutiny by Yardley, the greater the chance that we will be put out of business."

Garrett swallowed the rest of the toast, then said, "Yardley is harmless. He can be controlled. After all, he doesn't want his own secrets to come out."

"Think, man! Do you really believe the operation Yardley has going, selling small amounts of confiscated contraband on the side, is valuable enough to bribe him to keep his mouth shut about *murder?*"

"Of course not," Garrett retorted. "But he's expanded far beyond the simple failure to report a few pounds of opium to the evidence locker. My sources in Victoria say Yardley's been setting up his own suppliers, making plans to go into business for himself. With his fleet of revenue cutters, and with no one monitoring his agents' trips in and out of Canada, he's in the perfect position to import large quantities of opium without being detected."

Michael leaned back in his chair, surprised. His men had heard nothing of these rumors. Yet if Garrett was correct, this was bad news indeed. Yardley stood to become a major competitor in the opium trade, driving the price so low that the risk to import the stuff would no longer be worth the rewards gained.

Even Michael had to admit, Yardley had put together a deucedly clever scheme. The Customs inspector had the authority to stop any vessel and confiscate whatever contraband he found. While at the same time, his revenue agents could move their own shipments without fear of detection.

"I see you have fully comprehended the situation." Garrett looked satisfied with Michael's reaction. "I now suspect Yardley is behind the theft of the shipment two nights ago. The man needs to be stopped before he puts us all out of business."

"No," Michael said abruptly. "This situation calls for

finesse. And I refuse to be a party to any violence perpetrated against an officer of the law. I have no wish to hang for a capital offense." Garrett didn't reply, merely watching him with a slight smile, which Michael ignored. "I will have a quiet word with Mayor Payton, suggesting that he might wish to investigate possible corruption in the Customs Service."

He took a moment to drink more coffee before changing the subject. "I understand you've been spending a goodly amount of time lately at the Green Light."

Garrett gave Michael a wolfish grin. "Now why would that news be of interest to you, Seavey?"

"Any activity you engage in that draws attention concerns me."

"A man's got to relax from long, stressful days out on the water. The Green Light provides an excellent service for the price."

"I have no quarrel with that," Seavey replied. "However, you'd do well to spread your largesse among a number of the soiled doves, rather than concentrate on just one. An established pattern raises attention and leaves you open to being blackmailed, should you find yourself with a loose tongue one evening, admitting more than is wise."

Garrett crossed his arms. "The soiled dove I'm most fond of, however, exhibits such a fresh innocence that I find it quite satisfying to teach her the harsher realities she can expect to encounter in her profession. And she seems to have very little tolerance for pain, which I might find most useful in the future." His eyes gleamed. "I understand you might even know of the chit, Seavey. She goes by the name of Charlotte."

"I know of her," Michael admitted softly. "Nevertheless, do not be so foolish as to think you could use her to gain any leverage with me. I've never lifted a hand to help a soiled dove, and I never will."

•

Chapter 11

JORDAN came out of a deep sleep only hours later to the feeling of cold liquid running down her cheeks and onto the pillow. She heard loud hissing overlaid by Malachi's anxious whine. Something rolled off the bed, thunking onto the area rug on the floor.

Someone had thrown her leftover tea in her face.

She reared up, swiping at the liquid. "What the—"

"Sshhhhh!" Someone whispered next to her ear.

Heart pounding, she leapt from bed and ran for the door. Malachi did his best to tangle his paws with her feet.

"Be quiet!" Hattie said, next to her. "He'll hear you!"

Something zipped over Jordan's head, and she heard Charlotte screech, "Call the fuzz, call the fuzz!"

Jordan skidded to a halt, grabbing Malachi's collar and shushing him. "Who's 'he'?" she whispered blindly, shaking.

"Someone is in the library," Hattie said quietly. "Frank wanted to get rid of him, but I said we should wake you first."

"Nice outfit," Frank remarked, his tone sardonic.

Jordan whispered to Malachi to *stay*, then snatched up her sweats to pull on over her tank top and underwear. She tiptoed over to the bedroom door, then stuck her head into the hall, listening.

After a moment, she heard it—screeching on wood, as if someone was opening drawers in the library desk. There was a distinct thump, then low swearing. Whoever it was, he had probably walked into the wing-back chair.

She eased back into the bedroom, moving away from the door.

"Do something," Frank demanded. "Now is not the time to be cowardly."

"Now isn't the time to foolishly confront an intruder who might be armed, either," she retorted, sotto voce. Charlotte was still flying about the room, screeching. "Get control of Charlotte before she knocks something over," she told Hattie.

"I *heard* that," Charlotte hissed. "The prior owner left a baseball bat in my room. Go get it and hit the thief over the head."

"I am in agreement," Frank said. "If you wait for the police to arrive, it will most certainly be too late."

"I was dropped from the softball team in college because of my low batting average," Jordan retorted. "I'm sticking with calling the fuzz."

Moving silently to her nightstand, she picked up her cellphone and hit speed dial. When Darcy answered, she whispered, "There's someone in the house."

"Where?" Darcy said, sounding instantly more alert.

"In the library, I think."

"I'm on my way," she said, making rustling sounds in the background. "Jordan, do *not* go down there. Lock your bedroom door and wedge a chair under the doorknob, then get inside your closet and lock it. Wait there until I come get you."

"But what about the ghosts? I can't leave them to the mercy of whoever's down there."

"Yes, you can. They're already dead—they can fend for themselves. Put Malachi in the closet with you, and don't let him bark." Jordan heard her car door slam. "Don't hang up. I'm there in three minutes."

Jordan crept over to the door to close it, heard shuffling, then heard the front door crash against something. "Is that you?" she breathed into the phone.

"No, I'm still a block away. Christ! You're giving me a heart attack. Close the damn door and get in the closet!"

"He left," Frank reported, floating back into the room.

Hattie zipped out into the hall, hovering for a second. "Yes, he's gone," she confirmed.

"Darcy, the ghosts say he's left," Jordan relayed in a normal tone. "Dammit!" She flipped on the hall light and stomped down the stairs, Malachi and the ghosts trailing behind her. "If he stole something valuable, it's really going to piss me off."

"*Don't* go downstairs until I get there," Darcy ordered. "I'm turning the corner."

"Too late," Jordan said. She walked through the front door, which had been left standing wide open, just as Darcy pulled up to the curb. She met Darcy on the porch.

"I goddamn *hate* civilians—you don't take orders worth

shit." Darcy moved past her, gun drawn. "Stay out here while I check things out," she ordered.

After a moment, she reappeared, holstering her gun. "The house is clear."

"We already said that," Charlotte pointed out, flying around Darcy's head. "And you *told* her we said that. Doesn't she listen?"

"Not real well," Jordan replied.

"What?" Darcy asked, frowning.

"Never mind."

"Since you willfully disobeyed my orders, did you at least catch a glimpse of the perp?"

"No." Jordan went back inside, flipping light switches. She walked into the library, her jaw dropping. Books had been thrown about, lamps and chairs upended. Pictures pulled off the walls and dumped on the floor, their frames broken. Again.

She scrubbed her face and sighed. "I had just realphabetized those books."

Malachi circled the room sniffing suspiciously and growling low in his throat, then sank down on the Aubusson rug, his expression watchful.

They heard footsteps on the front porch and Darcy whirled around, her gun raised. Jase came through the door, halting when he saw her weapon. His hair was mussed and his shirt unbuttoned, as if he'd hurriedly pulled his clothes on. "What's going on? Is everyone okay?"

Darcy shook her head and holstered her gun. "Join the party."

"We had an intruder, but he's gone," Jordan told him.

Jase looked around with a grim expression while Darcy

carefully studied the room. "Anything missing?" she asked Jordan.

"I don't think so." Jordan walked over to set the wing-back chair upright. Again. "You know, this day *seriously* needs to be rewound. Two assaults and a burglary within twelve hours. That's got to be some kind of Guinness world record."

"*Two* assaults?" Jase queried. "I only know about one."

"Long story," Jordan muttered.

"Where's that wall safe you were talking about earlier?" Darcy asked her. "Obviously, someone overheard our conversation in the pub."

"What wall safe?" Jase asked.

"I'll explain later," Jordan told him. "Behind that bookcase. Since the bookcase is intact, they didn't find the safe. Right, Hattie?"

"Yes, of course."

"The ghosts are here with us?" Darcy asked.

"Sure. Where else would they be?"

"Indeed," Frank retorted. "She can hardly expect us to vanish, given the events of the evening. It's not as if we bother the humans who can't detect us."

"So what are they saying?" Darcy glanced around the room, as if she might catch a glimpse of something.

"That the safe is fine," Jordan lied.

Keeping a wary eye on Jase and Darcy, Frank went over to inspect the bookcase more closely. "No sign of damage," he reported.

"This may be about the papers Walters thinks Jordan stole," Jase said. "The obvious next step was to break in here and see if you were lying about having taken them."

"Maybe." Darcy looked skeptical. "But the most likely scenario is that someone was after the money in the safe, heard you moving about upstairs, Jordan, and decided to hightail it before I arrived."

"'Hightail it?'" Hattie repeated. "What does that mean?"

Frank snorted. "If you and your friends would confine your vocabulary to what can be found in the *Oxford English Dictionary*, we wouldn't continually be in need of elucidation."

Jordan sighed. "I'll explain later."

"I don't need you to explain a thing to me," Darcy told Jordan, exasperated.

"That's not—"

"The money is the strongest motive for whatever happened here," Darcy continued. "And it's not like people don't know you and I are friends, or that I live a few blocks from here. Any planned theft would be risky, in terms of my response time if you called me. If I were the burglar, I'd be nervous as hell that you'd wake up while I was here. Therefore, why take the risk for a few old papers?"

"*What money?*" Jase asked in a cranky tone.

Jordan rubbed the bridge of her nose. She needed 180 proof alcohol. In large quantities.

Darcy walked past her into the hall to examine the front door. She straightened, nodding. "Just as I suspected—the door's been jimmied. You'll need to get someone out to repair it." She cocked her head at Jordan. "Why is your hair all wet?"

"Er . . ." Jordan said.

"Tell them we woke you up!" Charlotte urged. "We *saved* you!"

"Did you see who it was?" Jordan asked Charlotte.

"It was too dark," Hattie pointed out.

"Do you mean to tell me you can't see in the *dark?*" Jordan asked.

"Of course not. Why would you think we could?"

"Oh, maybe because you're ghosts?" Jordan replied sarcastically, and Darcy snickered behind her. From the corner of her eye, she saw Jase crack a smile for the first time since he'd arrived.

"As ghosts, we aren't all-powerful," Frank retorted. "Mostly, we have the same powers of deduction and senses that a human has, plus a few extras."

"Oh, well, *that* explains it."

"At least you're sarcastic with everyone," Darcy said. "I'd hate to think you reserve it just for us."

Jordan ignored that. "So what *did* you see?" she asked the ghosts.

"He had some small kind of light he was holding, like a directed candle, but the flame didn't flicker," Frank said.

"A flashlight," Jordan explained. "Probably a small penlight." At Frank's perplexed look, she added, "Too complicated."

He shrugged, accepting her answer. "I caught a glimpse of a mask, as well. Not just over the eyes and nose—bigger, as if he'd pulled it over his head."

"Like a ski mask," Jordan concluded.

"I have no idea what that is," Frank replied.

"His clothing was dark, and he wore a hood over his head," Charlotte contributed.

"Sounds like the same person who attacked me at Holt's house," Jordan deduced as she propped a fallen portrait against a bookcase, then set a toppled plant upright. Again.

"Wait, don't tell me: dark hoodie and jeans, right?" Darcy asked.

"Close enough," Jordan replied, inspecting the plant more closely. The poor thing—it had almost no soil left in the pot.

"You were also attacked at Holt's house?" Jase asked grimly.

"I'll explain—"

"—later," Jase finished for her. "Got it." He shook his head and started picking up books, replacing them on their shelves.

"Aren't you going to dust for prints or something?" she asked Darcy.

"I'll send someone around to dust the door and the desk in the morning," Darcy replied. "But it's not like you want fingerprint powder all over those rare books. And it would take forever to try to locate a fingerprint on them."

"So that's it?" Jordan asked.

"Yeah." Darcy yawned. "I'm going back to bed. Your intruder is gone, whoever he was. I doubt he'll be back tonight, but you seem to have a good warning system in place. If anything happens, call me."

Jordan followed her outside. "Well, thanks for coming over."

"That's the job." She nodded her head toward the house. "Get some sleep, and we'll talk again in the morning. If I were you, I'd make it a top priority to see if that cash is still around, and if it is, get it into a safe-deposit box at the bank. We can let the story float around town that you've found it and removed it from the house. That should discourage any more nighttime visitors."

"*If* that's what he was after," Jordan said.

"It's a safe bet. Those papers Clive Walters claims were stolen are worth only a fraction of the forty thousand Hattie says is in that wall safe."

"Yeah, but Charlotte and Frank described the intruder as looking like the person I saw at Holt's this afternoon."

"Yesterday afternoon," Darcy corrected mildly. "It's way past midnight." She stretched, then stood for a moment, checking out the neighborhood. "Seems quiet enough. I'm out of here."

Jordan watched her drive away, then came back inside. Jase, who had followed them out and listened quietly to their exchange, stayed where he was. "I'll bunk down here tonight. Just in case."

"Bunk down on what?" she asked, grabbing the first excuse that came to mind. She wasn't sure she was ready to deal with a sleepover. "My furniture is piled in the second-floor parlor. There's only the wing-back chair in the library, or the desk chair, and you can't sleep sitting up all night. Besides, the ghosts will alert me if anyone tries to break in again."

"Yes, you can count on us to remain vigilant," Hattie assured her.

"*Hattie!*" Charlotte hissed. "If he stays here, they might end up making passionate love! We should leave, so that he feels compelled to protect her!"

"Whoa," Jordan protested. "I don't need ghosts playing ma—" She glanced at Jase, who had his arms folded across his chest and one eyebrow raised, listening with amusement to her side of the conversation. Swallowing the word "matchmaker," she sent Charlotte a scorching glance.

"I'll be fine," she told Jase.

He studied her for a moment in silence, then gripped her shoulders with warm hands and leaned in to place a light kiss on her forehead. She felt tingles all the way down to her toes. In the background, Frank snorted.

"I'll get out of your hair, then," Jase told her. "Pleasant dreams." Jogging down the front steps, he disappeared into the night.

"Huh." Jordan stared after him. "He didn't even put up a fight."

"You know *nothing* about attracting men." Charlotte hovered in the entry. "If you had acted as if you were indisposed with a fit of the vapors, he would have remained by your side throughout the night."

"Indeed," Hattie agreed, "he seemed to be looking for any excuse to do so."

"This is a conversation I wish to avoid," Frank said.

Jordan shook her head. Then she shooed all of them back inside, closing the door. "Go back to your portals, or wherever you go at night to sleep."

"Well!" Charlotte sniffed. "You are singularly *ungrateful* for our assistance this evening."

"Thank you," Jordan told them belatedly. "Really." She made another shooing motion. "Now go away."

She turned her back on them and stood in the doorway of the library, staring glumly at the mess. There was no way she was alphabetizing those books a third time. And since Tom would be tearing out the bookcase within a few hours, she could deal with the rest of the damage in the morning.

Before turning out the lights, however, she walked over to the desk and rummaged for a piece of paper and a felt pen. In large, thick block letters, she wrote: I DON'T HAVE THE PAPERS. She found some masking tape and attached the note to the front door. Then she took the small hall table and wedged it under the doorknob.

Satisfied, she and Malachi traipsed back upstairs to get whatever sleep they could before the sun rose.

Chapter 12

JORDAN woke up to a deafening, rumbling roar resembling a jet engine on bad fuel. Shooting straight up before she had fully comprehended the noise, she stared at her room from wide-open, unfocused eyes. The bed vibrated beneath her as the noise continued. Rising and lowering in volume and pitch, it was sometimes a whine, sometimes a deep, grinding sound.

Grabbing her sweats, she ran out into the hall and in the direction of the noise, which seemed to be coming from inside the second-floor parlor. That room was packed to the ceiling, but between boxes and pieces of stacked furniture, she thought she glimpsed sunlight. *Where there was no window.*

Hopping about on one foot, she tugged on her sweats, slapping a palm against the wall when her balance became precarious. She then headed for the stairs, taking them two at a time. Where the hell were the ghosts? How could they let something like this happen?

Yanking open the front door, she ran out, trying to

pinpoint the location of the noise, tripped over something solid, and was airborne. Strong arms grabbed her before her face pancaked against the porch decking.

"Morning," a deep voice rumbled from beneath her, barely discernible over the god-awful grinding roar.

Her eyes locked with Jase's sleepy, amused gaze. He lay in a sleeping bag positioned crosswise in front of the door.

Scrambling off his lap, she demanded, "What are you doing here?"

He seemed to accept her retreat with equanimity, running a hand along his unshaven jaw. "Figured I'd camp out on your porch, just to make certain no one came back to bother you last night." He pointed at the hand-lettered sign taped on the door above him. "I was probably more of a deterrent than *that*."

She reached over him and ripped the paper off the beveled glass. "You slept *outside*?"

He shrugged, yawning. "It's summer—I was fine. Actually, this makes a nice sleeping porch during fair weather. The birds woke me up at dawn, serenading from your maple tree. It's a nice change of pace."

The grinding noise started up again, reminding her of why she'd tripped over him in the first place. "Shit! Don't move," she commanded. "This conversation isn't finished."

"Yes, ma'am."

She jogged down the steps and around the side of the house. Tom stood high on the scaffolding, wielding a huge tool that had a long blade made of sharp, menacing teeth. Below him, Amanda was organizing a pile of debris, moving it onto the patio. A second pile of what looked to be dusty, broken pieces of lumber lay nearby on the grass. The air smelled faintly of a peculiarly sharp, musty mold.

The tool was shaking the entire house as it cut. *Through her wall.*

Tom spied Jordan. "Good morning!" he shouted over the whine, his expression businesslike. People didn't act calm and businesslike while they destroyed a historic house, right? "Thought I'd get an early start on this," he added.

"What are you doing?" she shouted.

He turned off the machine halfway through her question, causing her words to echo throughout the neighborhood in the sudden silence. "You've got dry rot in through here." Setting the monster down, he dropped to sit with his legs hanging over the scaffolding, his arms propped on the metal supports as he smiled at her. "We can't let it go any further without replacing the framing, or it will continue to travel through the structure, eventually causing the wall to collapse. And of course if it should reach the floor joists, that could weaken the supports for the second floor—"

"Stop! No caffeine."

His smile turned to a grin. "You offering some up?"

"Maybe. I thought I was going to bid out this work."

"You can bid a large portion of it," Tom replied, "but this couldn't wait. It's never a good idea to wait when it comes to dry rot."

That sounded ominous, but she decided not to ask for clarification. "What *is* that thing?" She pointed at the tool.

"It's a sawsall." Amanda swung around, her ponytail hitting her cheek, her expression surprised. "Haven't you ever seen one?"

"Oddly enough, outside of my life experience up to now."

"Really." Amanda pursed her lips.

"Its real name is 'reciprocating saw,'" Tom elaborated. "Kind of a cross between a Skilsaw and a chainsaw. Very handy for sawing in places other tools can't get to. And it cuts right through nails, roofing, lumber, and the like."

"Should I use it to remove the bookcase?"

His easygoing expression turned to alarm. "No! I mean, sawsalls can do a lot of damage if used by someone who doesn't have much experience." At her frown, he added hastily, "They really shouldn't be used for delicate work like dismantling a bookcase made of quality finish wood."

Jordan stepped back and craned her neck, looking at the large hole above the French doors that gaped almost to the roof. "So how big will that be once you're finished?"

"Not sure yet," he answered cheerfully. "Dry rot always travels farther than you would expect, so I'm finding more rotten supports than I originally thought I would. It's probably moved down through the first floor on this side of the house."

Of course it had. Honestly, she was quite proud of her composure.

"The boards look just fine to me," she said, studying the wall structure he'd uncovered where he'd removed the siding. "Are you sure?"

"Believe me, once you've smelled dry rot, there's no mistaking the odor," he assured her. "If I took a screwdriver and tried to ram it through any of these two-by-sixes, it'd push straight through with almost no effort."

"I'm kinda surprised, given that this wall had the

weight of the wisteria on it, that it's still upright," Amanda added.

Jordan instantly envisioned a house of extremely old, dusty toothpicks. And she'd been sleeping *on the second floor*.

Her thoughts must have been reflected on her face. "Whoa," Tom said hastily. "The rot is just right in through here, nowhere else that I've been able to find. The house is basically solid; don't worry."

"Right," Jordan said faintly. "I'll just go away now and leave you to it. If anyone asks me, I'll deny that I saw anything."

He chuckled. "I'll be down in a bit to see about that bookcase, but I wanted to get this handled first."

"You do that," she said, backing away.

* * *

JASE was still inside his sleeping bag on the front porch, sitting upright, his back propped against the wooden panel at the base of the front door. Malachi lay beside him on his back, all four paws in the air, and Jase was rubbing his stomach.

The sleeping bag had pooled at Jase's waist, revealing a nicely muscled chest with just the right amount of dark, soft-looking chest hair that arrowed down . . . She jerked her gaze up to his face and scowled. "I thought I told you last night I didn't need you to stay."

He shrugged. "A little extra insurance never hurts, particularly after the day you had yesterday. I don't like the coincidence of you being attacked twice in one day, then a burglar last night." One side of his mouth quirked. "I didn't mind playing knight in shining armor for one night."

She felt a pang of guilt at her ingratitude. And then a pang of irritation: She didn't *need* a knight in shining armor.

"All right, thanks," she said. "Actually, I don't think I thanked you for coming over last night . . ."

"I saw your lights go on from down the block, then Darcy pull up," he replied. "I was worried. And I'm willing to admit that I don't like the thought of you being in danger. I wish you'd drop this one. Just let Darcy do her job."

"I've backed off," she assured him. "Believe me, I don't like being attacked. I've got bruises that are going to keep me sore and aching for days." She felt the back of her head. The bump was smaller this morning, but still there.

His gaze sharpened. "You hit your head?"

"I fell down the steps at Holt's yesterday. Or, rather, I was shoved, and I hit my head on the cement stoop. I'm fine, though." She quickly explained why she'd been out at Holt's, ignoring that he didn't seem any more convinced than Darcy had by the soundness of her reasoning.

Jordan's gaze dropped south again, to that nice-looking chest. She gave brief thought to the FPP, then consigned it to the dust bin. "How far does that"—she waggled her index finger up and down at the portion of his anatomy she was trying so hard not to look at—"state of undress go?"

His frown turned into a sexy smile. "Want to find out?" he asked, his voice deeper than normal.

Far too tempted, she folded her arms and cocked her head. "You've decided to get sneaky, haven't you?"

"Gotta make use of all that legal background."

She closed her eyes momentarily. "How about I fix us a couple of espressos?" she asked brightly. She gestured in the direction of the other side of the house. "I'll just, er, use the back door . . ."

She retreated to the sound of his soft laugh.

So much for her plans for a peaceful, solitary breakfast at her favorite French restaurant.

* * *

JASE came into the kitchen, dressed in jeans and a T-shirt with his feet still bare, as she was grinding the coffee beans. Leaning against the counter, he folded his arms and watched her work. It was starting to feel natural— and comfortable—to have him there.

"Who sent you red roses?" he asked casually.

She gave him a sideways glance as she tamped coffee grounds into the Gruppo. "They weren't for me."

He waited, his expression expectant.

"They were for Hattie," she explained reluctantly. "The ghost of Michael Seavey stole them from the shop a few blocks away. He's courting her."

"Really?" Jase grinned. "I like it. The man may have been a shanghaier, but from everything you've told me about him, he had class."

Jordan rolled her eyes, then poured water into the reservoir.

The racket outside started up again, causing her to wince. "That's worse than a chainsaw, in my opinion. I hope I don't get complaints from the neighbors."

"He won't be at it long. You can tear down an entire

house with a sawsall in less than a day. The only reason it's taking him this long is that they're probably stopping to remove any salvageable siding. Reproducing historically accurate siding can cost an arm and a leg. It's worth the labor to remove and refurbish the original shingles."

She was still stuck back on his remark about destroying an entire house, shuddering at the thought.

"So what's this about a safe and some money?" Jase asked.

"What? Oh." She told him the story Hattie had related to her. "So we'll see. I doubt the money is still there."

"Hmm." Jase reached over her for espresso cups. "I wonder why Hattie didn't make certain Charlotte knew of it. Didn't Charlotte end up working in a brothel after her sister died? That kind of money would have been enough to support Charlotte well into adulthood, as well as provide a dowry for a husband."

"I wondered about that myself," Jordan admitted. "The answer Hattie gave me has more to do with how one 'comes back' as a ghost than anything else. If I understood the convoluted explanation I was trying hard not to examine too closely"—Jase grinned again, and she ignored him—"it takes a while to learn the skills you need to return in spectral form. By the time Hattie, er, reappeared, Charlotte was already dead. As was Michael Seavey."

Jase nodded as if that made sense. "So you have the combination to the safe?"

She finished making a shot of espresso and stared at him in consternation. "Well, shit."

He chuckled. "You'd better conjure up Hattie between now and when Tom removes that bookcase, unless you don't mind destroying the safe. And they can be pretty hard to break into without an acetylene torch."

"Good point." She handed Jase his cup of espresso, then turned back to make one for herself. Malachi wandered in, yawning, and while more water heated, she fed the dog breakfast. "I wonder if Hattie even remembers the safe combination. After all, she hasn't had an occasion to use it in well over a hundred years." She frowned. "And where the hell are they this morning, anyway?"

"Who, and how many, are you talking about?"

"Just the ones who live here—Hattie, Frank, and Charlotte. Michael Seavey lives at the Cosmopolitan and has only visited once." She paused. "That is, that I know of."

Tom came through the back door, and she realized that it was blessedly silent once more. He walked around to sit in a chair at the table, a small cloud of sawdust puffing off his clothes. Gratefully accepting the espresso she'd made for herself, he reported, "Turns out the dry rot isn't quite as bad as I'd feared." He paused to take an appreciative sip. "It stops just above the French doors in the library, and it didn't spread too far on either side."

"How can rot be dry?" she wondered out loud, tamping more coffee grounds.

"It's a fungal disease that invades lumber, among other things," Tom explained. "The wood remains relatively dry as the fungi invade the fibers, causing the wood to become brittle and crumbly. But moisture has to be present for it to occur."

"Yuck." She decided to avoid that side of the house for

the next few weeks. Months, maybe. "Can you get the wall rebuilt today?"

He nodded. "I've got a call in to Bill; he's a whiz at framing, and he doesn't mind the odd job on top of his bartending. Everyone else is already booked for the summer. But it's much easier to frame when you've got two people," he explained. "We'll put up construction plastic for tonight, which will keep everything in the upper parlor from being exposed to the night air. I'll come back tomorrow and reinstall the siding."

"If you need help, I can give you a half day tomorrow," Jase offered.

"I'll take you up on that," Tom replied. "The more, the merrier."

Jordan cocked her head. "I'm confused—I thought you were a painter. Explain to me why I'm not calling a carpenter?"

"I *am* a painter," he replied, "but I've done a lot of this type of work. When you work on old houses, you pretty much become a jack of all trades. Most of the really skilled carpenters I know are all working jobs right now; you don't ever want to use one who doesn't know what he's doing. And that dry rot really can't wait."

"Don't worry," Jase assured her. "We know what we're doing."

"Do you think we need to put off trying to get into the wall safe?" she asked. "It's not as high a priority."

"Not a good plan," Jase replied, "in case the money *is* what the burglar is after. The sooner we figure out whether it exists—and if it does, put the rumor out that you've removed it from the house—the better I'll sleep at night."

"Did something happen last night?" Tom asked.

"Break-in," Jordan replied. "Someone ransacked the library."

"That's solves the alphabetizing issue," Jase told Tom.

Jordan slanted them a look.

"We were concerned," Tom allowed, grinning.

"Keep it up," she warned.

"Did the burglar get anything?"

"No." She thought more about the framing project. "I'm a bit uneasy about how you all are always volunteering to help on the house. I don't know how I'll ever pay you back."

"Don't sweat it," Tom said with a shrug. "Around here, everyone pitches in when needed. And the time will come when you can return the favor. Until then," he added with a grin, "the entertainment value for us is real high. You have no idea how much we appreciate that."

"If you're feeling indebted, I need another bartender tonight," Jase added.

"Sure." Since their cups were empty, she went back to pulling espresso shots.

"I asked a couple of workers last night at the pub about the hotel job Holt was working on." Tom settled back in his chair.

"You're referring to those guys I saw you seated with?"

"Yeah. They said Holt definitely was losing money. According to the rumors on the street, Clive Walters was complaining that Holt's work was substandard and asking him to redo a lot of it."

Jase shifted, frowning. "That doesn't sound like Holt."

"Yeah, there's no way Holt would have done a sloppy job," Tom agreed. "In all the years I've known him, the only complaint I ever heard was that he took too long, because he was such a perfectionist. I never had a qualm recommending him for a job that I didn't have the time to take on. So something's rotten about that story. Crazy Clive is up to no good."

Darcy popped her head into the kitchen.

"Hey," Jase said.

"Hey, yourself." She turned to Jordan. "Did you know there's a giant hole in the side of your house?"

"Dry rot," Tom offered.

"Ouch." Darcy winced. "My sympathies. All right if I have the lab tech dust the desk and front door for prints before any more sawdust settles on everything?" she asked Jordan.

"Go for it." *Sawdust?* She hadn't even thought about sawdust. And she didn't *want* to think about it, either. "Either of you need caffeine?"

"Do you even have to ask?" Darcy headed back down the hallway and out of sight.

Jordan spooned beans into the grinder and hit the button. At this rate, she'd need to stop by the deli this afternoon and buy more of their special blend. Running out of coffee beans was never an option.

Darcy reappeared, apparently having put the tech to work. After taking an espresso back down the hall to him, she sat down at the table with Tom.

"Did you talk to Crazy Clive yet and ask him about his alibi?" Jordan asked her.

"'Crazy Clive'?" Darcy raised an eyebrow.

Jordan flushed. "Tom's nickname, not mine. Though I have to admit—in a momentarily unprofessional lapse of judgment, that is—the name fits. The man really needs to chill." She leaned against the counter next to Jase. "We were just talking about him," she explained to Darcy, then told her about the rumors regarding the hotel job.

"I've got a meeting set up with him this afternoon," Darcy said. "So Holt was losing money, huh? And Walters was claiming he was doing substandard work? Not, mind you, that it's all that unusual for Clive Walters to be at cross-purposes with his employees. But I wonder what was really going on there." Her gaze shifted to Jase. "Did you check through your receipts for the night Holt was murdered?"

"Yeah. Holt didn't charge any drinks that night, so I doubt he was at the pub. I asked Bill, and he couldn't remember seeing him, either. I also looked at the receipts for the previous two nights—nada, which is highly unusual for Holt. I can count on one hand the number of nights this year he hasn't shown up for a beer and to hit on a woman. Have your men been able to piece together where he was that night?"

Darcy shook her head. "So far, all we know is that he stopped by a dive shop downtown to pick up full oxygen tanks around six in the evening. The owner said he asked Holt where he was planning to dive, and Holt clammed up and wouldn't say. So then he tried to chat up Holt about the local shipwrecks that folks like to explore, and he got what he called a cold, 'mind your own business'-type reaction."

"Holt wouldn't tell his workers at the hotel, either," Jordan said. "So Holt didn't want anyone to know where he was diving. Which leads to the question, how did the murderer know where he'd be?"

"The murderer was the dive buddy?" Tom suggested.

"Darcy and I wondered that the first day when we found his body," Jordan admitted, thinking once again about the man she'd seen. But she was becoming more convinced she'd seen a ghost, not a human. She turned to Darcy. "Is there any evidence he *had* a dive buddy?"

"Not according to the dive shop owner. He even lectured Holt on the subject, but Holt didn't seem interested in hearing about how unsafe it was to dive alone. The shop owner chalked it up to stupid first-timer mistakes and Holt's willingness to break the rules."

"Uh-uh." Jordan shook her head. "I think it had more to do with Holt not wanting anyone to know what he was up to."

"Well, *someone* knew where he was that night," Darcy grumbled. "He didn't shoot himself in the head, or we would have found stippling around the wound. And it's not like he could have hidden the gun after he killed himself."

"So still no murder weapon?" Tom asked.

"No, dammit."

"What about his truck?" Jordan asked. "Have you found it yet?" They all looked at her as if her "powers" had expanded to include prescience. "*What?* It wasn't parked in his driveway yesterday, so it was kind of obvious that he must have left it parked somewhere else the night of his murder."

"We found it parked on a side street not far from the Hudson Point marina. A homeowner reported it after it had sat in front of his house for a few days and no one moved it. We've gone over it, but nothing unusual is showing up. No forensics other than what you'd expect."

"No business ledger or files of any kind?" Jordan asked hopefully.

"Nope."

"Damn."

"So whatever boat Holt used to get out to Dungeness Spit was moored at the marina," Jase concluded. "And since you didn't find it anchored nearby, the boat probably belongs to whoever killed Holt."

"Possibly. I've got my men looking over the boats as we speak, but we can't board without a search warrant. So unless they find something suspicious in plain sight, we'll have to figure out who killed Holt first, then execute search warrants on his house and any other vehicles or boats registered in his name."

"What about the ballistics?" Jase asked. "And the fact that Holt was shot execution-style? That tells me the shooter was probably a man, and professional. I've heard of professionals using silenced .22s."

"The ballistics report came back this morning—no match to anything in the criminal databases. So whoever our shooter is, he's not in the system."

"It's possible that he hasn't been caught yet," Jase pointed out.

"Yeah, but I think Holt knew his shooter, and that the bullet-in-the-forehead thing is misleading. An amateur can take aim and fire, hitting in that location simply out of sheer luck."

"What's the ME say about angle of entry?"

"What's that?" Jordan asked.

"Determines height of the shooter," Jase briefly explained.

"Nothing, yet," Darcy answered him. "The autopsy report isn't back."

"Do you intend to ask Crazy Clive whether he owns a .22?" Jordan asked.

"Yeah, but he isn't known for being cooperative, so we'll see if he deigns to give me an answer. The man is paranoid as hell—it never occurs to him to simply tell the truth."

"People who suffer from severe paranoia read all kinds of meaning into other people's statements that isn't there," Jordan said. "He probably counters every question you ask with a question, the purpose of which is to figure out your hidden agenda, right?"

"Yep." Darcy gave a silent nod to the lab tech, who had appeared in the kitchen doorway. She stood and stretched. "I've got to go. You coming by the pub tonight?" she asked Jordan.

"Bartending," Jordan replied. "But I want to hear all about this meeting with Crazy Clive. That's what constitutes entertainment for us therapists."

"As long as he doesn't decide on a repeat performance," Jase warned.

"Not to worry," Darcy said. "If he darkens the pub's doorstep, I'll shoot him. Nobody messes with my downtime two nights in a row."

* * *

AFTER Darcy left, they reconvened in the library. While Tom and Jase examined the bookcase and determined the best way to dismantle it without causing damage, Jordan cleaned up more of the mess the burglar had made. Tom set to work with a drill and hand carpentry tools, and after observing for a few minutes, Jase wandered over to help her reshelve books.

"Humor me and summarize what happened yesterday," he said. "I'd like to see if anything pops out at me."

She described her trip to the Historical Society, the articles she found, then her visits to the Cosmopolitan and Bob MacDonough at the Wooden Boat Society headquarters. She also told him about her conversations with the ghost of Michael Seavey and agreeing to take on the investigation of his murder in 1893. "He was on the *Henrietta Dale* the night she went down," she said, handing over a stack of books. "He believes he died in the shipwreck, but the old newspaper articles list him as a survivor."

"Have you been able to figure out who his competitors would have been back then?"

"So far, I have two names—Sam Garrett, who was his business partner in the opium smuggling and, according to Seavey's personal papers, a growing problem, and the Customs inspector back then, a man by the name of Yardley. Seavey and Garrett were convinced that Yardley was running his own smuggling business on the side. So Yardley might not have appreciated the competition." She remembered something else. "This was interesting:

Bob's great-great-grandfather was the one who built the secret compartments into the hull of the *Henrietta Dale*, where the opium was hidden. I don't think Bob believed me, actually—he sounded a bit put out when I mentioned it."

Tom had been listening to their conversation while he removed shelves and set them on the floor. "Sounds like Bob," he remarked. "How'd you find out about the secret compartments?"

"Seavey wrote about his plans for the *Henrietta Dale*. He's got an entry in his papers discussing his trip down to the docks to direct Grady MacDonough to construct the secret compartments. MacDonough was concerned that the extra weight would slow down the ship." She rehung an ancestral portrait with Jase's help. "I don't see what the big deal is, really. So Bob's ancestor helped someone smuggle contraband. Sounds to me like something that would be entertaining to tell your houseguests."

"Actually, I'll bet it frosted Bob big time," Jase said.

She gave him a questioning look, but Tom was the one to explain. "Bob takes his role at the society real seriously. His reputation in the community is a big deal to him. The fact that he descends from a line of famous ship's carpenters is something he's quite proud of."

"A bit *too* proud," Jase replied.

Jordan remembered another tidbit she'd read. "And get this: Charlotte and Jesse Canby knew each other back then. Seavey was worried about her association with a man who was slowly succumbing to his opium addiction. So was the owner of the brothel where Charlotte worked, Mona Starr."

"Remind me who Jesse Canby was?" Jase asked.

She explained about Eleanor Canby, the ownership of the newspaper, and Jesse's addiction.

"I remember now. And weren't Mona and Hattie briefly friends right before Hattie was murdered?" Jase asked.

"Yes," Jordan replied. "Mona tried to help her get Charlotte back from the kidnappers."

"Pretty interesting stuff you're digging up," Tom said. "I didn't know half of it, and I've read fairly extensively about that time period."

"Which reminds me," Jordan said. "I've been meaning to ask if you knew of any other major players in the opium smuggling back then."

Tom frowned as he used a crowbar, leveraged against a block of wood that protected the plaster, to gently pry a section of the bookcase away from the wall. "Well, obviously, you know two of them—Seavey and Garrett. And I knew about the rumors surrounding the Customs Service. I'm pretty certain there were some Asian players—folks who ran 'laundries' on the waterfront. I read a newspaper article from that period about a huge sale of opium to one of the people who owned the most prosperous opium den. Why do you ask?"

"Just curious." Jordan picked up another painting and replaced it on the wall. "Seavey stopped his partner from hanging a Chinese farmer—I think I mentioned that to you. There was some question as to what the man was doing on the beach that night when Garrett brought the contraband ashore. Garrett initially thought he stole the shipment, but Seavey believed otherwise."

"I suppose he could have sold it to one of the opium den owners, so it's possible," Tom mused. "But why take the risk? Seavey and Garrett were known to be scary dudes you didn't ever want to cross."

"What strikes me about everything you've turned up so far is that your investigation—even just into the murder of Michael Seavey—is potentially putting you in harm's way," Jase said. "You go out to Holt's house to return papers and look for the ones you claim he might have removed from the hotel, and someone attacks you because he doesn't want you to know he was there. You visit the Cosmopolitan and get assaulted by Walters after the fact. And then last night, someone breaks into your home."

"The attack at Holt's could have been just pure bad luck," Jordan pointed out. "If I'd been a few minutes later, my attacker might have been gone. He wasn't necessarily there for any reason related to what I've been investigating."

Tom pulled the last board off the wall, setting it aside. Jordan stared at the small wall safe he had uncovered, stunned. "I don't believe it! Hattie was right—it really is there."

"Of course I'm right," Hattie said from beside her. Jordan, who was becoming more used to the ghosts' sudden appearances, didn't even jump. "Did you think I had lied to you? I kept track over the years—none of the other owners ever thought to look behind there, thank goodness."

She noted that Hattie still wore her nightdress and had her hair tied with pieces of fabric. She also wore a scowl on her face. "It's very hard to get any beauty sleep around here with all the noise," the ghost complained. "We were up fashionably late, and etiquette dictates that you don't allow visitors on the premises before a more respectable hour."

"We were eager to see what's in the safe," Jordan explained apologetically, avoiding mention of the hole in the parlor wall.

Tom and Jase looked at the space beside Jordan, their expressions curious. "So we have company?" Jase asked Jordan.

"*He's* the company," Charlotte sniffed as she materialized on Hattie's other side. In no better state of dress than her sister, she peered sleepily at Jordan. "I trust the hole in the upstairs parlor wall is necessary, and that you will have it fixed prior to the wedding," she said archly.

Damn. "Of course," Jordan said, hoping that was true. Truthfully, she hoped the wedding would simply cease to be an issue, and the sooner, the better. She shuddered to think about the logistics of such an affair. The house would have to be fixed up as much as possible, but no humans could attend or, rather, it didn't make any sense for them to attend.

"Would you happen to remember the combination to the safe after all these years?" she asked Hattie.

"Ten to the right, twenty-three to the left with an extra revolution, then six to the right," Hattie replied promptly. "I memorized it."

Jordan rubbed damp hands on her cotton sweats, then walked over to the safe. She raised her hand to the old dial, then hesitated. "You know," she said, turning back to the ghosts, "this really isn't my money—it belongs to you."

"We want you to have it for the renovations," Hattie insisted.

"Halt right there," Frank ordered as he materialized. "If you open that safe, you are exposing yourself to great risk. Seavey will go to any lengths to get his hands on that much cash."

Hattie gave Frank a cool look. "Michael has no use for the money, nor would he steal it from me. You are mistaken in that regard." She turned back to Jordan. "We want you to have it. You can put it to good use, making Longren House into a comfortable home for yourself."

"I think it should be used for the wedding," Charlotte insisted stubbornly. "It's extremely important to ensure that the ceremony and reception are lavish, as befits Hattie's station in society prior to her death. We simply must not *scrimp* on the preparations."

"I really don't feel comfortable accepting a forty-thousand-dollar gift," Jordan repeated. "From anyone."

"Nonsense," Hattie said. "You should feel perfectly comfortable accepting the money."

"Do you have any idea what's going on?" Tom asked Jase. Both men had been watching Jordan intently.

"I'm getting the gist. I think."

"We're discussing who gets the money," Jordan explained to them. "Frankly, until we have that issue decided, I don't want to open the safe. Once the money is real to us, making any kind of ethical decision regarding it becomes much harder."

"Precisely my point," Frank stated. "When faced with the reality of that amount of cash, Seavey simply would *not* be able to help himself."

"You don't know Michael at all!" Charlotte cried. "He's a wonderful man!"

"Now, Charlotte . . ." Hattie began.

"Pragmatically speaking," Jase pointed out, talking over Hattie because he couldn't hear her, "your discussion is moot if the money isn't there."

"He doesn't know what he's talking about," Hattie scoffed. "The money exists. I removed only a small portion the night I paid the ransom to Seavey for the return of Charlotte. The rest has remained untouched all these years."

"Please, Jordan!" Charlotte cried. "Open the safe."

"I beg you to reconsider," Frank importuned, earning a wrathful glance from Hattie. "If Seavey finds out about that money, no one will be secure in this house."

"Oh, for . . ." Jordan threw up her hands. "If the money is in there, it's yours to do with as you wish. Agreed?"

"And I will wish that you use it for the renovation," Hattie replied, refusing to budge.

Using the combination Hattie had recited, Jordan spun the dial. With an audible *click*, the safe door swung open in her hand. Everyone crowded around, peering inside.

Hattie gasped.

The safe was empty.

* * *

"I don't understand." Hattie paced the library, wringing her hands. "I was so certain it would still be there. Whatever could have happened to it?"

Now that the excitement was over, Jase had left to deal

with suppliers at the pub, and Tom had returned to the framing, accompanied by Malachi, who seemed to want no part of any further discussion with the ghosts.

"Was the safe combination written down anywhere?" Jordan asked. "Could someone have had access to it and found the money before you came back as a ghost?"

"No. Before I had Sara hire the carpenter, I asked her to open the safe and verify that the money was in there."

"When was that?"

"Well, let's see." Hattie turned to Charlotte. "You died in 1895, correct?"

Charlotte bit her lip and nodded.

"So that would make it the winter of 1896 that I contacted Sara with my plan." Hattie gave Charlotte a look filled with sadness. "You see, I had planned to make the money available for you. But by the time I was able to return, you were already lost to us all."

Charlotte hugged her. "It's all right. Mona took good care of me for as long as she could. I was young and reckless and . . . We all knew back then that prostitutes had short life spans. It was only a matter of time."

"So the money was in the safe after Charlotte's death," Jordan repeated, bringing them back to the subject at hand. "Was the house vacant in the winter of 1896?"

"Yes," Hattie replied. "It wasn't sold at auction until a year after that."

"Who knew of the money besides you?"

"No one except Frank, and he only knew of the recorded income; he never saw the actual cash," Hattie said. She looked in Frank's direction. "Frank knew that my late husband, Charles, had been engaging in illegal smuggling on his ships. We reviewed a list of payments Charles had recorded in a small ledger. But I never told Frank about the cash. And regardless, he was dead by then."

"So Sara knew, and Frank, but he was gone," Jordan concluded.

"I trust that Sara would not have taken it." Hattie paced a bit, obviously lost in thought. She halted. "Mona Starr knew that I had access to enough cash to pay for Frank's medical bills and for the ransom for Charlotte. She could have deduced from that, possibly, that there might be money hidden somewhere in Longren House."

"Mona would *never* have stolen the money!" Charlotte protested. "Why, she had no need—she was very rich."

"That's true," Hattie admitted. "I would have to agree with Charlotte. Mona had no reason to come looking for the money, and I would be stunned to discover that she engaged in that kind of theft. If so, I greatly misread her character."

"The truth is that anyone could have taken the money at any time over the intervening years," Jordan said glumly. "I doubt we'll ever know."

"But we kept an eye on all the owners," Charlotte insisted.

"Every minute of every day, for over a hundred years?" Jordan asked. "That's impossible. Anyone could have hired a locksmith, or a safecracker, for that matter, to open it. Who knows? Perhaps they even sensed, on some instinctive level, that they had to hide their activities from whoever was haunting their home. There's nothing we can do about it—the money's gone."

Hattie nodded dejectedly. "Nevertheless, I had hoped that I had the solution to your financial troubles."

242 · P. J. ALDERMAN

"I'll figure something out," Jordan assured her. She paused, then carefully asked, "Charlotte, did you know of Seavey's murder? And of Jesse's death on board the *Henrietta Dale?*"

Charlotte gave Hattie a nervous glance.

"Whatever you have to say," Hattie assured her, "I won't judge you harshly."

Charlotte shook her head. "It's more that I worry you'll judge *Michael* harshly, and he doesn't deserve it, truly he doesn't. He saved me, you know. And Jesse—*dear* Jesse— was the one who managed to get me to Seavey's hotel suite and convince Seavey we needed his protection. After Jesse died in the shipwreck, well . . ." She paused to swipe at a tear. "It was just so hard to continue on, don't you see? Michael was gone, and Jesse, *and* so were you, Hattie. It seemed like all around me, people were dying."

So Garrett had acted as Seavey had feared, Jordan thought. "Why don't you tell us about it?" she said gently.

Charlotte trembled, eyes brimming, and shook her head. "I just *can't!* If you want to know what really happened back then, you need to read Eleanor Canby's memoir. The wretched woman was responsible for so much of what went wrong, you see! And of course she wrote about all of it in that disgusting memoir of hers. She thought she was so virtuous, and yet she destroyed the people who came into contact with her. She ruined you, Hattie!"

Hattie put her arm around Charlotte. "I think that's enough for today," she told Jordan softly, then turned to Charlotte. "Jordan will read Eleanor's memoir, and she can ask Michael to fill in the blanks of what she doesn't know.

What's important is that we find out who murdered Michael, but I doubt we need your help to do that."

"Absolutely," Jordan agreed. "I've got some time between now and this evening's plans, so I can spend some of it reading the memoir, which I brought home yesterday. Charlotte, was there ever a formal investigation into the wreck of the *Henrietta Dale*? I'm asking because it seems there would have been. Do you remember hearing about something like that?"

Charlotte dabbed her eyes with an embroidered handkerchief. "Yes, of course. Mona followed the investigation with great interest and told me all about it. The ship's captain—I can't remember his name . . ."

"Nathaniel Williams," Jordan supplied.

"Yes, that's it. Captain Williams testified that his calculations were accurate that night, that never before in his career had he ever made such a grievous error. He claimed that someone had to have deliberately lured the ship off course."

"Did the lightkeeper testify?"

Charlotte nodded. "The New Dungeness light had been turned off for maintenance. The keeper claimed he had discovered something wrong that needed to be repaired." She wrinkled her nose. "Of course, I didn't pay any attention to the mechanical details of what the man described. But he swore the captain couldn't have used the New Dungeness light in his calculations."

"And yet the captain claimed he triangulated off two lights, is that correct?"

"Yes, exactly."

Frank spoke up. "I have some knowledge of these

things from my time at sea. It seems reasonable to assume that if the captain claimed he used two lights for triangulation, then indeed, a second light was shining that night. I suspect someone with nefarious motives placed a light farther along the shoreline, perhaps even at the base of the bluffs along the headlands."

"Would that have caused the captain to correct his heading enough to run aground in the location of the shipwreck?" Jordan asked him.

"Yes, absolutely," Frank replied. "The strategy has been used by pirates for centuries, and it is relatively foolproof. The real question, in my opinion, is who would have had a reason to do so?"

"Yes, that is the question, isn't it?" Jordan murmured.

* * *

AN hour later, she had taken a shower, grabbed some breakfast, and hauled Eleanor Canby's memoir, along with Seavey's stack of personal papers, out to the front porch. She settled onto the sunny end of the porch swing with Malachi lying underneath.

She had several hours before she'd planned to meet up with Darcy at the pub—a concentrated block of time when she could read, then try to piece together everything she had learned. What with the attacks, missing papers, missing money, and last night's break-in, her brain was a jumble. She needed to make sense of everything before she could help Hattie come to any meaningful conclusions about Seavey's murder. And if she could just keep her mind off the sawing and hammering, she stood a good chance of figuring out what might have happened that deadly night in August 1893.

Balancing a cup of tea precariously on one of the swing's broad arms, she decided to start with—or rather, to finish—reading Michael Seavey's papers, then move on to Eleanor's memoir.

Unacceptable Risk

THOUGH there was a crisp breeze coming off the water, the sun shone on the newly painted decking of the *Henrietta Dale*. Michael stood on the poop deck with his recently hired captain, Nathaniel Williams, and the ship's carpenter, Grady MacDonough. Below them, people streamed across the docks, preparing to board a large passenger steamer bound for San Francisco.

Neck craned, Williams gazed overhead at the rigging, hands clasped at his back, a pleased smile on his weathered face. "A beautiful ship indeed, Mr. Seavey. The sailcloth is of the finest quality! It will be a pleasure to sail her."

"I'm hoping to take her out on her maiden voyage on August 5," Michael replied, gratified by his reaction. The man had years of experience; his judgment was quite sound in these matters. "Do you think you can have crew hired and be ready to sail by that date?"

Williams frowned, as if considering. "Barring a shortage of available experienced sailors, I believe we should be quite ready by then."

"I can procure most for you, though I suspect you'll wish to hire the officers yourself."

"Yes, indeed. I always pick my seconds-in-command quite cautiously. One doesn't need to discover *after* they're at sea that his first mate can't follow orders."

"No, I imagine not," Michael said wryly. Turning to MacDonough, he asked, "I trust the renovations will be complete by then?"

"Yessir! We've only the skylights to install, then I'll be putting the finishing touches on the trim in the great cabin." He hesitated, glancing at Williams before lowering his voice. "That other matter we discussed is taken care of, Mr. Seavey."

"Excellent." Unusually restless, Michael stared out at the water for a moment, lost in thought. Such smooth preparations should have him excited over the upcoming voyage, yet he found himself oddly unmoved. He sighed. "Then I'll leave you gentlemen to your chores."

"Seavey!" The shout came from below.

Michael walked to the taffrail and looked down at the crowded dock. Customs Inspector Yardley stood below, his expression grim, his manner agitated as he paced to and fro the length of the *Henrietta Dale*. "I must speak to you at once, man!"

"Inspector," Michael acknowledged, taking hold of the rope ladder and climbing down. He stepped onto the dock, brushing off a bit of sawdust that clung to his morning coat. "To what do I owe the honor of a second visit in so short a time?"

"Two of my men did not return to port last night as planned," Yardley stated. He returned to his pacing.

"I'm sorry to hear that," Michael replied, not revealing the alarm he felt over the news. "Was the weather inclement? I don't recall."

Yardley slashed a hand through the air. "You know damn well it wasn't!"

Michael raised a brow. "Actually, no, I don't. I was at yet another interminable fund-raiser, this time held by one of our esteemed town councilmen. I spent most of the night indoors."

"My men were again patrolling an area just off North Beach," Yardley stated, seeming not to have heard Michael's explanation. "They didn't return to port at the designated time. I suspect they may have had an altercation with Sam Garrett. Was he scheduled to be at that location last night?"

Michael *tsked*. "I believe we've already had this discussion, Yardley. I am not in business with Sam Garrett, nor do I have any idea where he might have been last night."

"Then you claim to have no information about what may have happened to my men."

Michael chose his words carefully. "Though I'm certainly concerned as you are for their welfare, I know of nothing that would assist you in your efforts to find them."

"I don't believe you."

Michael shrugged, drawing on his cigar.

Yardley's face mottled with rage. "You smug son of a bitch!" he growled softly. "The entire waterfront knows you and Garrett have an agreement with suppliers out of

Victoria to bring in opium. I'll be damned if I'll stand here and let you lie to my face, when two of my men may have been murdered by your partner!"

"Do you have evidence to back up your wild accusations?" Michael asked calmly.

"You know I don't! And unless the bodies of my men wash ashore, I doubt I'll find any."

"Then I believe this conversation is over, Yardley."

Yardley's fists clenched. "If I find out you've had anything to do with my men's deaths, Seavey, by God, I'll—"

"You'll do nothing," Michael interrupted, "unless you want me to reveal your latest side business to your superiors. Do not threaten me, Yardley—you will be the loser in that battle."

Yardley laughed harshly. "Everyone knows you've lost your stomach for violence, Seavey. Your threats are empty."

"If you want to put that rumor to the test, just say the word, and I'll be happy to oblige." He arced his cigar into the water. "I've other business to attend."

Yardley stood for a moment, his harsh breathing audible over the background hum of freight loading on the wharf. Turning on his heel, he stalked away.

Michael looked at Remy, who had appeared silently at his side. "Bring Garrett," he ordered softly. "If the fool resists, employ force."

Chapter 13

A particularly deafening crash brought Jordan out of 1893 and back to the present. Loud swearing ensued, followed by more crashes. Dust floated down from the porch ceiling, and a film of brown stuff settled on the surface of her tea.

Sighing, she got up and took her documents to the kitchen so she could make herself another cup of Earl Grey. While it brewed, she stood next to the counter, reading the sheaf of pages she held in her hand.

Payment in Kind

UNSETTLED by Yardley's accusations, Michael took a few minutes to stroll along the waterfront. If Garrett was responsible for the deaths of two Customs agents, then he'd become an unacceptable liability and must be dealt with accordingly. This, in turn, meant that Michael must be ready to take over the regular shipments of opium so his customers experienced no fluctuations in their supply.

He stopped to watch the activity out on the bay while he considered his options. All was in place and would be ready, his people had just assured him, for the launching of his new enterprise, which would combine luxurious accommodations aboard the *Henrietta Dale* with passage to and from Victoria. All that remained was that he notify his Canadian suppliers that his man Remy would be replacing Garrett.

Passengers aboard the clipper ship could sail in complete comfort, take in a day of sightseeing in the charming town of Victoria if they wished, then return. His cruises would become the talk of the town, a sought-after social event. They would also provide him with the contraband he needed to ensure a steady supply of profits from the distribution and sale of the heavenly demon.

He smiled to himself. Yes, indeed, his plans should provide a lucrative revenue stream. Perhaps he would even enjoy the occasional outing himself. And truly, he no longer needed Sam Garrett.

From the corner of his eye, he noticed Jesse Canby hovering nearby. Turning, he nodded a greeting to him.

The young man was ill-kempt indeed, his expensive clothes falling limply about his emaciated frame, his complexion sallow, his eyes sunken. It appeared that Canby's addiction had progressed even further than Michael had realized. There was good reason for the observation among opium-smoking circles that its addicts resembled melancholy ghosts.

"Canby," he said. "A nice morning, is it not?"

Jesse approached, reaching out a shaking hand to clutch at Michael's jacket sleeve. Several days' growth roughened Canby's cheeks. Michael took a careful step back, breaking the contact.

"I need more opium," Jesse pleaded in a low voice, his eyes taking on a look of desperation. "Do you have any?"

"You know I don't handle the sale of the stuff directly," Michael replied in a lowered voice.

"Then tell me where your man is—I need it as soon as possible."

"This would be for your personal use?"

"Yes."

Michael considered him, silently debating. "You might

want to lay off the stuff, Canby. I suspect it's doing you a great deal of harm."

Canby shook his head bleakly. "What does it matter, one way or the other?"

"It matters a great deal to your family. And frankly, having one's customers die off is bad for business."

The young man's eyes blazed. "Do you want to sell me the drug or not? I can always go to one of the Chinese instead."

Michael studied him for a moment longer, then he shrugged. "You'll find Remy on Union Wharf, I believe. Tell him I sent you."

"Thank you." With an unsteady bow, the young man left, walking rapidly in the direction of the wharf. Michael sighed, turning to continue his walk, only to find himself face-to-face with Eleanor Canby.

She stood rigidly, fists clenched at her sides, her face flushed with anger. "My son buys his drugs from *you?*"

Michael raised an eyebrow. "I don't know what you believe you just overheard, Eleanor, but I can assure you I have no idea what you're talking about."

"Don't lie to me!" she yelled.

Michael quickly took her arm and drew her to a less-crowded portion of the sidewalk, near the entrance to an alley. "Kindly keep your voice down, Eleanor. You are attracting notice."

"I don't care!" she spit. "*You* are the reason my son's health deteriorates daily! Dr. Willoughby and I have him on a strict regimen of prescribed laudanum, hoping to withdraw him from your beastly contraband. And yet amoral purveyors like you continue to supply him!"

"I thought you had washed your hands of Jesse."

"He is my *son*, Seavey."

"Indeed, he is," Michael agreed soothingly. "Nonetheless, since you persist in trying to rid Jesse of an addiction by supplying him with the very drug you are withdrawing, I don't see the reason for concern."

"We are cutting back the dosage slowly and carefully," Eleanor explained impatiently. "Not that it's any business of yours."

"You'd do well to have someone counsel Jesse for his mental condition, if you want to solve his addiction to opium," Michael observed. "The opium is merely a symptom of underlying problems that have been present since adolescence, I suspect."

"How *dare* you suggest that my son is unbalanced," Eleanor hissed, glancing around to ensure that no one could hear her. "My family does *not* suffer from such afflictions. You are merely attempting to absolve yourself from any blame in this matter. I demand that you have no further contact with Jesse, and that you refrain from selling him any drugs."

"My dear Eleanor," Michael sighed. "As to the first, your son is an adult and may socialize with whomever he pleases. Though I don't seek out Jesse's company, I have no control over where he spends his time. And as to the second, I believe we've already established that I have no business dealings in the area we're discussing."

Eleanor's shoulders shook with rage. "Cease to supply my son with drugs, Seavey, or my next editorial will name names. And you and your wretched business partner, Garrett, will have places of honor at the top of my list."

"Such threats could cause the loss of your paper and your coveted position as its editor-in-chief, Eleanor. I advise you to proceed cautiously."

"Do not threaten what you cannot accomplish." Her coarse features were flushed, her eyes burning with fanaticism. "My position as owner and editor of the *Port Chatham Weekly Gazette* is inviolable. Now I bid you a good day, Mr. Seavey."

Frowning, Michael watched her sweep away. The publication of his and Garrett's names was a threat he could no longer ignore. And unfortunately, given Eleanor's level of desperation with regard to her son's health, Michael could no longer count on her exercising any sense of caution.

Perhaps it was time to contact several businessmen with whom he was acquainted and offer to purchase their interest in the newspaper for a sum far greater than current market value.

* * *

MICHAEL had returned to his hotel suite and was sealing with wax on the last of the purchase offers to local businessmen when Remy and Max arrived. Tossing Sam Garrett into the room, they positioned themselves as sentries just inside the door.

Garrett picked himself up from the floor, brushing his clothes. "Really, Seavey, all you had to do was request a meeting—I would've been happy to oblige," he said in a show of unconvincing bravado. "Sending your thugs was a misjudgment on your part."

"The misjudgment is yours, if you had any role in the disappearance of the Customs agents last night," Michael replied. "I warned you to cease such reckless and ill-conceived actions, or there would be consequences."

Garrett swaggered over to sit in the chair across the writing desk from Michael. "And I made it clear you aren't the arbiter of the decisions I make with regard to my side of the business."

"I did not give you leave to sit," Michael said. "You will stand where my men indicated. *Now.*"

Cold rage flared in Garrett's eyes, quickly banked. After a tense moment, he rose to casually move about the room. "The Customs agents were becoming a nuisance, and it was necessary to get rid of them."

Michael slowly drew a breath. For the first time in years, he was deeply worried. The wrath of the authorities over such an incident would not be easily controlled. "You fool. We could both hang for this."

"Not if they don't find the evidence linking us to the crime."

Michael caught the slight smile on Garrett's face, stunned to realize that the emotion behind it was pride. The idiot was pleased with his accomplishments. Perhaps he had even experienced a thrill in the killing of the two officers.

He'd seen the attitude before, of course. Some men, once having killed, actually felt a need to continue. He suspected Garrett was one such beast, and that it hadn't been a difficult decision to take two lives. Further, it was clear he failed to be plagued by any remorse over the murders. Which made him a very dangerous business associate indeed. Michael had no stomach for men of his ilk.

Garrett moved over to study a watercolor that Michael had purchased on a recent trip to the Seattle waterfront, then turned back to give him a sardonic look. "I'd assumed you wouldn't be baring your soul to the authorities regarding this matter. But perhaps I underestimated the depth of your current failures and the effect they've had on your ability to run your businesses."

Michael refused to respond, waiting him out.

Garrett grinned. "I admit, Seavey, I assumed you wouldn't tolerate any interruption in the flow of goods. But I can see now that your newfound—shall we say, hesitancy? Or shall we just name it what it is, cowardice—holds more sway over your business decisions than I had previously thought."

Remy uncrossed his arms and took a step forward, but Michael waved him off. "Enough, Garrett. You may taunt me all you wish, but it is a waste of your breath. We both know you've made a grave error in judgment, from which you have little hope of evading the consequences. However, I have no intention of paying the price of your mistakes. As of this moment, our business association is henceforth dissolved. I have no knowledge of your activities, in the past or present. I will immediately notify our suppliers that you are no longer my representative. Indeed, I will suggest that they will find it far too risky to conduct business with you at all. I suspect they will heed my advice."

"You won't do that," Garrett scoffed. "You have no current method of transporting the drug. And we both know your customers will exhibit no loyalty in the face of the numerous alternatives available to them here in town."

Though Michael had no intention of informing Garrett of the imminent launch of the *Henrietta Dale*, he replied, "On the contrary, my customers find my willingness to provide adequate camouflage for their illicit activities to be quite beneficial. Indeed, they would be relieved to hear I have eliminated what could potentially have become an embarrassment and risk to them, that being even the most tenuous connection with your recent activities."

"We have an arrangement, Seavey." Garrett's tone had turned cool. "Break it, and no one along the waterfront will work with you in the future."

"Oh, I doubt it will be my reputation that suffers," Michael retorted, refusing to acknowledge that there was some truth in Garrett's statement. This business would certainly feed into the rumors already circulating, of that Michael had no doubt. It would be necessary to control the damage. However, he had no choice in the matter— any further association with Garrett was far more dangerous than the nuisance of rebuilding a bit of trust among his business associates. "Regardless," he continued calmly, "you won't be around to hear of any rumors in that regard. I expect you to leave town within the hour and not to return."

Garrett barked out a laugh. "You can't be serious!"

"I assure you, I'm deadly serious," Michael replied. "Leave town within the hour, or my men will assist you. And I guarantee you'll find their 'assistance' less than pleasurable."

"You son of a bitch! I have no intention of leaving

town. Honor our arrangement, or I swear to you, you'll be sorry."

"Get out," Michael said. "You disgust me."

This time, he didn't intervene as Remy and Max took hold of Garrett's arms.

"We had a deal, Seavey!" Garrett shouted as he was dragged from the suite. "Mark my words, you'll pay!"

Chapter 14

Just because the money wasn't in the safe, doesn't mean the burglar wasn't after it," Darcy argued while Jordan pulled beers. "You still have a problem."

Tonight's entertainment was a local jazz band that never failed to draw a large crowd. Jordan hadn't stopped mixing drinks since she'd stepped behind the bar. Fortunately, with Bill taking the drink orders, she didn't have to worry about ghosts ordering drinks they wouldn't consume, because he couldn't see them to ask. That kept the orders down to a manageable level.

"I'm not too worried about someone trying again." She shrugged. "I can always put two notes on the front door tonight: one that says I don't have the money, and the other that says I don't have the papers."

Jase reached around her to snag a bottle of Scotch. "You want me to sleep on your front porch again tonight?"

"Not necessary," Jordan replied. "Try to beat back those chivalrous inclinations."

"You're no fun at all." He gave her a wink, then took a

tray of drinks from her and handed them across the bar to Bill.

Darcy raised a brow, refraining from making a comment.

"So spill," Jordan told Darcy.

Darcy merely snorted. "I talked to eight of Holt's past girlfriends today. All of them have ironclad alibis, and they all were supremely unconcerned about admitting to an officer of the law that they were thrilled someone else had done the job for them. Somewhere in Port Chatham tonight, there's a hell of a party. Several mentioned calling Holt's other old flames and getting together to celebrate his demise."

"So the murderer probably isn't an old flame."

"It's looking less likely," Darcy agreed morosely.

Jordan asked Jase for mixing instructions for a whiskey sour.

"You're kidding, right?" Darcy asked in disbelief.

"I've led a sheltered life. What about Sally's alibi? The sister of the girl Holt dated who committed suicide?" Belatedly, Jordan glanced down the bar and saw Sally looking straight at her. Jordan winced. "Sorry," she told her in a raised voice.

Sally slid off her barstool and walked over. Dressed in jeans, boots, and a flannel shirt, the woman wore a baseball cap stenciled with the name of the local mill where she worked. "Might as well ask me to my face," she told Darcy, her tone belligerent, "because I certainly wanted the son of a bitch dead. I've been positively giddy ever since I heard someone popped him."

"So where were you the night Holt died?" Darcy asked.

"At home, alone, watching television." Sally drank the rest of the shot of tequila she was carrying, then set it on the bar for a refill. "And no, I didn't call anyone, and I didn't go out to buy anything, so no one can vouch for me." She paused. "I suppose you could check with my Internet provider, since I was on email at some point."

Darcy sighed. "I don't suppose you have any idea who ransacked Holt's place yesterday?"

Sally shook her head. "I was out there, but the place was in its usual shape—filthy, not ransacked."

"When were you out there?" Jordan asked.

"Around midafternoon. I went inside long enough to retrieve something of mine. Why?"

"You really shouldn't tell me that you entered Holt's house without permission," Darcy grumbled. "Why is it that everyone in this town thinks they can commit felonies at will? And that I'll look the other way when they do?"

"Hey." Sally glared. "That asshole wouldn't give back a locket Melissa left there last year. It's a family heirloom, and one of the few items of Melissa's that I have left. I wanted it back, and I was damn well going to get it."

"Did you see anyone else when you were there?" Jordan asked, handing her the tequila shot. "Someone driving a dark, midsize sedan?"

Sally knocked it back, then shook her head. "Nope. The place was deserted. Look, all I wanted was the locket, okay? And yeah, I didn't have any qualms about breaking and entering to get it, but the front door was unlocked in any case." She looked at Darcy. "Are you going to arrest me?"

"I should, just to make a point," Darcy said. "Otherwise, at the rate I'm going, the town will be completely lawless within a year or two."

"So you weren't the person who shoved me down the stairs?" Jordan asked Sally as she pulled two microbrews for the crowd at the closest table.

"Of course not." The surprise on Sally's face looked genuine. "Why on earth would I do that? Those stairs are cement—you could've been hurt."

"Probably accounts for one of the set of fingerprints you lifted, anyway," Jordan told Darcy. "I still think the person who pushed me was a sumo wrestler."

Sally smirked. "Slammed you back real good, did he?" She turned to Darcy. "Are you any closer to finding Holt's killer?"

"The investigation is still in its initial stages, so no, no suspects as of yet."

"Good." Sally looked satisfied.

"You willing to come down to the station to be fingerprinted? Just so I can rule you out?" Darcy asked sardonically.

"Bite me," the other woman replied, then left to go chat with some folks who were seated at the far end of the bar.

Darcy watched until she sat down, then pulled a Baggie out of her jacket pocket, picking up the shot glass by its rim and dropping it inside.

"Sneaky," Jordan said.

Darcy shrugged. "Whatever it takes."

Kathleen delivered burgers to them without a word. The beef was grilled to perfection, served on what appeared to be homemade whole-grain buns, and garnished with fresh tomato slices and homemade coleslaw. The potatoes were roasted organic fingerlings that Kathleen grew in her garden, and they gave off a heady aroma of garlic and Parmesan.

Jordan paused from mixing drinks long enough to take a huge bite of the burger, closing her eyes in ecstasy. "Holy God. I need to make this a permanent job. Screw the tips, as long as the meals are free."

Darcy nodded, her mouth full. "Easy come, easy go on the money in the safe. But withdrawal of Kathleen's cooking? *Not* an option."

Jase, who was passing by, leaned across the bar to murmur in Jordan's ear, "The perks are *very* good." He winked, then headed over to deliver drinks to the band.

"I'll just bet they are," Darcy replied drily.

"So we know Sally's visit probably accounts for one of the sets of fingerprints. That leaves two," Jordan mused, ignoring them both.

"And one of the three matches the prints we got off your front door," Darcy informed her.

Jordan raised both eyebrows. "Really? So that means whoever broke into Holt's house is the same person who was in my library."

"Yes, which I consider *not* to be a good sign," the police chief replied. "You could be in real danger from someone, and that someone really could be the murderer. I can't compel people like Sally to give me their prints, unless I want to start acting like a jerk. She did admit to entering Holt's house. If the door really was unlocked, then I would be on thin ice except that she left the shot glass in plain sight."

"Does that mean I need to carry my empty beer mug out of here and throw it away where you can't find it?" They both turned to see Bob wedge his lanky body between Darcy and the patron on the next barstool. He towered over them, grinning affably, and held out his hands. "Cuff me, Chief. I confess, I dropped by Holt's yesterday to pick up a roll of marine charts he'd borrowed from me."

Darcy shot him a dirty look. "So you *also* admit to going into Holt's house without permission?"

"Hey!" he protested. "The door was unlocked. And we both know that everything in Holt's house will go through state-level probate, unless you turn up a distant relative, and it will take *forever* to get anything back. Major hassle. I just wanted to retrieve the charts; I use them all the time."

Darcy swiveled on her barstool and addressed the room at large. "If there's anyone here who *didn't* trespass and break into Holt's house after the murder, please raise your hands."

The ghosts looked confused by the question; only a few human hands went up.

"Jesus Christ," Darcy said. "I might as well call in a paddy wagon."

"Well hell, Chief," a man at a nearby table spoke up, "Holt had my compressor and paint sprayer. Those are expensive items. And the door *was* unlocked."

"Yeah," someone else agreed. "And he had my nail gun."

"He was strapped for cash and borrowing stuff all over town," a third explained.

"I'm amazed you didn't find dozens of unidentified prints," Jordan observed.

"Nah. Most of our stuff was in his toolshed," the third man replied.

"I walked right in and grabbed the sprayer out of the living room," the first said. "I don't remember touching anything except the doorknob, and I was wearing my work gloves."

Jordan remained confused regarding one issue. "I thought you said you didn't talk to Holt about what he was up to," she said to Bob. "He had your marine charts?"

"I didn't talk to him," Bob replied. He pointed to a tap, and she drew a beer for him, sliding it across the bar, which he made a show of handling with only his fingertips. "He dropped by a couple of weeks ago and asked if he could borrow some marine charts. People around here borrow my charts all the time, just to look at them, or to pinpoint a location based on reading some mystery novel set in this area."

"Okay," Darcy told Jordan, turning around, "so that's two out of three sets of prints. Maybe. Barring that they might belong to any one of the several *hundred* lawbreakers in this town, that leaves us with one other person."

"With respect to the fingerprints showing up in both locations, I can't think of any reason for Sally to break into my house," Jordan mused. "So I vote for door number three, whoever is behind it."

"Any ideas?" Darcy asked Bob.

"Nope. I didn't see a soul."

"Whoever it was, they attacked Jordan."

He looked concerned. "Hey, I'm real sorry. That had to have been, what? Right after you left the marina?"

"Yes," Jordan replied.

"Are you all right?" he asked her.

"Sore but fine."

"So you're up to talking to that historian on the phone tomorrow? He'd like to set up a conference call for around nine in the morning, if that's okay." He set down his beer mug to reach into his jacket pocket and pull out a folded sheet of paper. "This is the schedule of events for the Wooden Boat Festival. I've penciled in your talk at the society headquarters for end of the second afternoon, if that's okay."

Jordan took the paper from him, frowning. "Actually, I've given it more thought, and I'm still not sure I'd feel comfortable talking to anyone about seeing the ghost ship, much less a crowd of people."

Darcy raised her brows at Jordan.

"But I've already publicized your seminar; you can't back out now," Bob protested. "The Wooden Boat Festival is the biggest event Port Chatham puts on; folks will be really disappointed if you don't show."

"*Seminar?* Bob, I never committed to do the talk; I just said I'd think about it." Jordan was irritated. She'd been very clear that she'd get back to him with a decision one way or the other.

"Let's start with the telephone interview tomorrow," he said in a placating tone that only served to irritate her further. "If you're okay with how that goes, then you can give the seminar. Deal?"

"I'll do the interview, then decide," she said firmly. "So you have no clue who else might have wanted something inside Holt's house? How well do you know Clive Walters?"

"That guy who owns the Cosmopolitan? I've had a few dealings with him. He wants to advertise in some of my mailings, to pick up bookings during the festival. Tried to get me to let him advertise for free. Said that unless people could find hotel rooms, they wouldn't attend the festival, so I owed him some free space."

"Cheeky," Darcy observed, "but that's Clive for you."

Bob rolled his eyes. "Like I would fall for his bullshit reasoning. The society is always strapped for cash—we don't give away *anything* for free. And we're a major source of revenue for the town's merchants. If anything, I should *raise* my ad rates." He cocked his head at Jordan. "Why are you asking about Walters?"

"I just wondered if you knew whether he owned a .22," she replied. "We got into a scuffle. He thinks I stole historical documents from his hotel. I wondered if he'd fought with Holt, possibly."

"Not a clue," Bob replied.

"He appears to have an alibi for the time of Holt's death, anyway," Darcy put in. "He claims he was hosting a winetasting at the hotel that evening. If so, there's no way he could have hosted the event, then taken a boat ride all the way out to the spit to dump a body. Not according to the official time of death from the ME's report, that is."

"Well, damn." Jordan stared at Darcy in dismay. "There goes your best suspect."

"Maybe." Darcy looked unconvinced. "I'm digging deeper, trying to verify his story with the guests at the winetasting. But his motive is weak. Why kill over a small remodel job? Still, he says he owns a boat that he moors at the marina. Correct?" she asked Bob.

He shrugged. "I don't have anything to do with renting out the slips, but I've seen him around. It's possible he let someone else take the boat out."

"Maybe," Darcy said again.

Kathleen appeared silently at Jordan's side for a second time that night. Jordan picked up her empty plate to hand it to her, thinking she'd come to retrieve their dishes, but got a glare for her effort.

"I don't bus the dishes, for Christ's sake," the chef growled. "Come with me. *Right now.*"

"Me?" Jordan asked.

"You see me talking to anyone else?" she snapped.

"If I'm not back in fifteen minutes," Jordan told Darcy, "come find me."

"I'll send out a search party," Darcy responded cheerfully.

"*Not* funny," Kathleen said.

Curious, Jordan followed the cook down the back hallway, stopping at the doorway to her kitchen. Kathleen kept walking, turning when she realized Jordan wasn't behind her.

Jordan started to explain, "I know you don't like people in your kitchen—"

"Get in here, *right now.*"

"Okay, sure, right," Jordan muttered, edging inside.

A large man dressed in loose work clothes leaned against the counter along the back wall next to the stove, his muscular arms crossed. His dark expressionless eyes tracked her as she closed half the distance between them before she stopped out of an innate sense of caution. He looked familiar, but she couldn't place him.

"You deal with this guy, then get him the hell out of my kitchen," Kathleen ordered. "I have work to do."

"Do I know you?" Jordan asked him, puzzled. The light dawned. "Weren't you sitting at one of the tables in the pub last night?"

"Yeah." The man straightened, and she realized uneasily just how imposing he was. He flashed her a humorless grin, exposing crooked teeth. "You want answers about the wreck of the *Henrietta Dale* and Seavey's murder, and I want to set the record straight."

She eyed him nervously. "And you would be?"

"Sam Garrett."

* * *

JORDAN rounded on Kathleen. "You can see *ghosts*!"

"I don't believe in ghosts," Kathleen grumbled.

"Denial," Jordan said. "Believe me, I can empathize. But you can see *him*, right?"

"Of course she can see me," Garrett answered for her. "Are you daft, woman? How do you think she knew to come find you?"

Kathleen pointed the long-bladed chef's knife she was using to chop garlic at both of them. "Deal with him and then leave. I have work to do."

Jordan folded her arms. "This discussion isn't over, you know," she told her.

"You want to ever eat my food again?"

Well, shit.

"I thought so." Kathleen went back to chopping garlic.

"Ignore the fool woman!" Garrett interrupted, clearly impatient. "We have much to discuss."

It finally dawned on Jordan that she was talking to a cold-blooded killer. If he decided to attack her, she really had no defense against him.

She edged toward the door, then was in the process of realizing she couldn't leave Kathleen alone with a murderer when he made a *tsk*ing sound that halted her in her tracks. "I wouldn't advise trying to run."

Kathleen slammed an iron skillet onto the stove, glaring at her. "If you *rabbit* before handling him, I will bury my meat cleaver between your shoulder blades. He's *your* problem."

Jordan sent up a silent prayer that Jase would come back to the kitchen with dinner orders, but she wasn't hopeful—even Malachi was sound asleep behind the bar, oblivious to the danger she was in. Surreptitiously, she glanced at the knife racks above Kathleen's workstation.

"Those knives can't hurt me," Garrett said, amused.

Her fear must have then shown on her face, because he sighed. "I currently have no plan to kill you. I simply want to set the record straight."

Jordan swallowed and waved a shaky hand. "By all means," she told him, trying to sound courageous, "proceed."

"You consider me a suspect in Michael Seavey's murder, do you not?" he demanded.

Did she dare say yes? "In truth," she allowed, "I hadn't yet reached any conclusions."

"Quit prevaricating!" he snapped, and she jumped a foot.

"Um, what I do know is that you and Michael Seavey were at odds, that you had committed several m-murders . . ." She swallowed. "And that people back then were generally afraid of you." *Versus now, when they have good reason to be flat-out terrified.*

Her answer seemed to mollify him. "Precisely. However, I did not murder Seavey."

"Were you responsible for the grounding of the *Henrietta Dale*?"

A smug look crossed his face. "Of course. It was ridiculously easy."

"How did you do it? Set a lantern farther down the beach? After disabling the one in the lighthouse?"

"The manner in which I caused the grounding of the *Henrietta Dale* is neither here nor there."

"Well, you had to have done something similar to what I describe. Otherwise, the captain wouldn't have made such a grave error in his calculations," she insisted.

He looked amused. "You may believe what you wish."

Exasperated, she pushed him. "So your intention was to murder Michael Seavey?"

"On the contrary. My intention was to *ruin* the bastard by sinking his ship. The fact that he ended up dead because of . . . my actions . . ." Garrett seemed to stumble over the words, then shrugged. "Let's just say that I wasn't unduly concerned about the possibility. Although it would have been more gratifying to watch him experience the humiliation of a total loss of power and influence."

"From what I've been told—"

"—You mean, from what you've *seen*?" he corrected her with a sly grin.

Jordan heard Kathleen snort. She pressed on. "I *read* about the shipwreck in the *Port Chatham Weekly Gazette*. The *Henrietta Dale* broke up in the surf that night, so I'd say you succeeded, if that was truly your goal. You also caused the deaths of dozens of people."

"Their deaths couldn't be helped," Garrett replied, his tone hardening. "No one treats me the way Seavey did and gets away with it."

Jordan shuddered. "So you returned to Port Chatham and finished the job, killing him there."

He hissed angrily, and she backed up several steps. "You haven't been *listening*. I came here to tell you that I had *nothing* to do with the man's murder! Though I would like to take credit for it, certain . . . events, shall we say, immediately after the sinking of the *Henrietta Dale* made it impossible for me to return to Port Chatham."

"Do you know who *did* murder him?"

"I couldn't, could I? I wasn't present. I only care that you understand *I* didn't murder the man."

"Okay, fine. Message received."

"I didn't send a message! I stood here and told you the truth of it!"

"Let me rephrase that," she said hastily. "I meant I now understand that you didn't murder Seavey." She glanced in Kathleen's direction, but the cook had something sizzling in her iron skillet and was pointedly ignoring them. "So you can go now?" she asked Garrett hopefully.

He sent her a chiding glance that had her contemplating whether she could reach the door into the back hallway before he could nab her, or whatever it was a ghost could do to her. Folding his arms across his massive chest, he said, "I have information that I am willing to barter in return for your promise that you will announce I had nothing to do with Seavey's death."

"But don't most sociopaths like to have kills attributed to them that they didn't do?" she asked curiously. Not that she had a clue, really. And what the hell was she doing, asking such questions? After all, reminding a murderer that he got off on the act of murder was sort of like poking a crazed bull with a sharp stick.

"'Sociopaths'?" He thought that over, then nodded. "The term is pleasing. What I wish to impress upon you, however, is that an altercation with Michael Seavey at the moment would be enervating, and these days, I wish to expend my energies on other pursuits."

Honest to God, she *really* didn't want to know.

"Therefore, it's imperative he understand that I wasn't the one to murder him." Garrett's dark eyes were coldly assessing. "Do we have an arrangement?"

"Yes." After all, it wasn't as if she was going to say *no* and risk further pissing him off.

"Excellent." Reaching into the pocket of his wool coat, he did something to cause a small, ornately decorated tin to fly out and float in the air between them. Jordan immediately recognized it from the day at the beach. "I believe *this* is what you have been seeking," he said, zinging it at her.

She grabbed it out of the air, turning it over and examining it closely. It was actually quite beautiful, the lid etched in swirling scrolls of an Oriental design, their colors faded with time and exposure to the elements. "You're the diver I saw on the beach that day," she exclaimed.

"Yes."

"I didn't make the connection; you look different out of a dive suit." She tried to open the box, but it didn't budge—it was probably rusted shut.

"It's sealed with beeswax, to keep the contents dry," he explained. "Each 'package' contains a quantity of chandu opium, molded into small cakes, portions of which are placed in a pipe to be smoked. The cakes were wrapped in waxed paper." His expression was derisive. "Seavey was determined to provide his customers with the highest quality opium, packaged in a pleasing manner. He went to great expense to have the opium cakes brought in from the Orient, then repackaged in a more pleasing way. Really, it's not as if his customers would have known the difference if he'd substituted less expensive product after the first puff or two."

What he was saying was consistent with what Jordan knew of Michael Seavey—the man placed a high value on presentation and style. She doubted he would have stood for increasing his profits through a lowering of the quality of the drug. "So you've been retrieving these from the shipwreck?" she asked.

His gaze slid away. "Of course not. What earthly use would I have of them? Besides, over time, with exposure to the elements, the stuff would obviously have deteriorated to the point of being worthless."

Not in the eyes of collectors, who would pay dearly to own a small piece of West Coast history, she realized. She thought back to her first encounter with him and was still confused on one point. "But I saw you bring one of these tins out of the water, didn't I?"

"I was *attempting* to give you a hint, so that you would think to look into what type of salvage operation was occurring. I know now that you are frequently too oblivious to notice such things." He waved a hand at the tin. "That is one your friend brought up. He inadvertently dropped it on the beach."

A tendril of excitement raced down her spine. "So these tins are what Holt was salvaging from the wreck!"

"Yes." Garrett scowled. "Unbeknownst to me, Seavey had built secret, reinforced compartments into the hull for the purposes of transporting opium. A portion of the ship's hull, along with some of those compartments, apparently survived intact and lies on the ocean floor just off the spit. The human—"

"Holt Stilwell," she supplied.

"By Christ, woman! I care not a whit about the man's name! Will you cease to be so *difficult*?"

Her face must have blanched, because he sighed and then continued. "*Stilwell* discovered the undamaged portion of the hull on his initial dive. Then he came back on subsequent days to retrieve a number of the tins."

"Interesting." To her knowledge, nothing of the sort had been found in either Holt's house or his truck. If it had, Darcy certainly would have told her. "You don't happen to know what he did with them, do you?"

"In that regard, I have no interest in helping you," Garrett replied. "It's not as if I followed the man around town between his dives. I just happened to be on hand, curious about what he was up to, when he was near the shipwreck. The fool was going to sell them in some kind of auction. He called it a name that doesn't match any auction house I'm familiar with . . ."

"eBay, perhaps?"

"Yes, that's it."

"How do you know this?"

"Because I was right there, listening when he told his plans to the person who brought him out to the beach in his boat. Stilwell described that his intent was to hold a press conference, then open bidding on the tins."

"What guy? Holt wasn't diving with anyone else. At least, we haven't been able to locate anyone—"

"The other person wasn't a diver," Garrett corrected her, looking impatient again. "But the person *was* quite angry with Stilwell. I presume that's why Stilwell was murdered. I've never understood the reason to murder in circumstances such as those, when torture or a sound beating, at a minimum, can be far more effective—"

"Wait," Jordan interrupted, excited. "Do you mean to tell me you saw Holt get shot?"

Kathleen stopped what she was doing and looked up.

Garrett shrugged. "Not that it's of any import, but yes, I witnessed the entire affair."

Chapter 15

You have *got* to be kidding me," Darcy groused. "There's an eyewitness to Holt's murder, and it's a *ghost?*"

"Yes."

"And he refused to tell you who did it." Darcy's expression was one of utter disbelief.

"Yep."

The jazz band was on break before its last set of the evening. Customers who didn't count themselves among the diehards had called it quits and left for home. Taking advantage of the momentary lull, Darcy, Jordan, and several of the men had retreated to a table on the far side of the room to discuss the latest development. Microbrew beer was flowing freely.

Darcy had moved into full rant mode. "I don't fucking believe this! It's not as if I can arrest a ghost as a material witness and compel him to testify."

"He said he wouldn't reveal facts that might implicate someone he felt the need to protect," Jordan explained.

"Actually, he acted oddly, given that he's a sociopath. Sociopaths have no conscience."

"This case is *so* in the crapper."

"Who would a sociopath feel the need to protect?" Bob asked. "Another sociopath?"

"Maybe," Jordan replied, unconvinced.

"No other dead bodies floating around that we know of," Tom pointed out.

"What I'm having trouble wrapping my mind around," Jase said, looking grimly at Jordan as he placed a full pitcher on the table and took a seat, "is that you were conversing with the ghost of a murderous drug runner in my kitchen. Did it ever occur to either you or Kathleen that you were in mortal danger from this guy?"

"Of course," Jordan replied. "But what were we supposed to do? It's not like I can control the movements of the ghosts in this town any more than Darcy can successfully arrest one. They can do pretty much whatever they want."

"You could've run like hell."

"I considered it," Jordan admitted. "But he made it clear that I'd never get away. And call me crazy, but I definitely had the sense it was far better to humor him than to anger him."

"Jase is right, though—the trend *is* worrisome," Darcy said. "In the beginning, the ghosts with whom you came in contact were relatively benign. There's been an escalation toward more dangerous ones since then, starting with the ghost of Michael Seavey."

Jordan frowned. "I don't think Michael Seavey is very dangerous. Not really."

"He's not exactly the local choirboy, either," Jase retorted, standing to gather empties from the next table.

Darcy looked thoughtful. "Do *you* know what Garrett meant when he said he felt the need to protect someone?"

"No." Jordan scrubbed her face with both hands. The adrenaline was starting to wear off, leaving her feeling like she'd been flattened by a truck. "I got the impression that at least partially, Garrett just didn't care. Bob could be on the right track: Thinking from the perspective of a sociopath, you would feel a kinship to others like you. So he could just be protecting the identity of a fellow criminal. But I got the strong sense that it was more than that— that whoever had murdered Holt was someone for whom Garrett felt a sense of obligation."

Darcy leaned her elbows on the table, pressing her fingers against closed eyes. "I'm now officially suicidal."

"And it turns out I was right about the two murders being related," Jordan continued. "Holt was salvaging the opium tins from the hull of the *Henrietta Dale*. His plans to reveal what he'd found and to auction off the tins were a threat to someone in present day."

"That's nice," Darcy said.

"The question is, who? And what kind of threat?"

"Uh-huh." Darcy hadn't moved.

"This is progress," Jordan insisted. "We now know Holt's girlfriends didn't do him in."

"I don't see how you can rule out Sally, though," Bob argued. "Didn't Holt date her sister, the one who committed suicide? That's a hell of a motive."

"Have you been able to determine if she has an alibi?" Jordan asked Darcy.

"No. Not unless we can nail down when she was on email that evening. We had to subpoena her Internet service provider, who declined to be nice and hand over her usage records. Subpoenas take time."

"Well regardless, you should be thrilled to narrow the field of potential suspects," Jordan said to Darcy. "What's your problem?"

She opened her eyes to glare at Jordan. "Well, gee. I've got a ghost for the only witness to a murder. That means I have no proof that will stand up in court, and no real evidence so far. And we haven't *narrowed* the field of suspects, we've eliminated *most* of them."

"What about Crazy Clive?" Tom asked.

"He has an alibi," Jordan replied, then looked at Darcy. "Unless you haven't been able to verify it?"

"I'm still trying to get hold of some of the guests at the winetasting." Darcy straightened on a sigh. "Even if you could get Garrett the Ghost to tell us who shot Holt, we'd have to figure out a way to trap the killer into confessing. Which usually gives the defense lawyer the chance to scream entrapment when the case comes to trial."

"Garrett won't talk," Jordan said with certainty. She paused, thinking back over their conversation. "I'm convinced he was lying about something, as well. I just can't figure out what."

"Don't even *think* about getting close enough to him to ask," Jase growled, approaching with a loaded tray.

"I won't," Jordan hurriedly agreed. "Though as I pointed out, I don't control the movements of the ghosts."

"You can at least make an effort to avoid those locations where you think you might run into him," Jase insisted.

"He came to *me*, sought me out in the pub," Jordan pointed out. "He was here last night as well, sitting at one of the tables. So unless I avoid the pub, it's going to be hard to keep out of his way." She shook her head. "My suggestion is that we try to figure out what connects Sam Garrett with someone in this town, and then go from there."

Jase clearly didn't like her answer. "Okay," he replied, his tone reluctant, "so what type of connection would a man like Garrett want to keep secret?"

"The obvious one is some kind of honor among murderers," Bob said. "Like honor among thieves."

"Maybe," Darcy answered, her expression skeptical. "But from what I've read about sociopaths, they're usually only motivated to hide the kills of a copycat killer, because they believe their own work is so admirable and consider the copycat a form of flattery. And Holt was shot point-blank, a technique he would consider amateurish and uninspired."

"Okay, how about those missing tins of opium?" Tom asked. "They would be considered collectibles and fetch a nice price at auction. Holt was right about that. Maybe the killer has Holt's cache and wants to sell them to private collectors."

"So perhaps what Holt was doing wasn't so much a threat as an opportunity for someone to cash in on those tins?" Jase asked. "Makes sense to me."

"But why would *Garrett* care about that?" Jordan asked. "According to what he told me, he sank the *Henrietta Dale* to get back at Seavey, not because of the opium. In fact, I'm fairly certain from what he said that he didn't even know about the secret compartments in the hull until recently. So I doubt he would care if someone in present day was out to make money off the salvage."

"Maybe Garrett has some kind of personal connection to the murderer," Jase mused. "A relative, perhaps? Even murderers have family."

"No one like that has popped up in any of my research," Bob pointed out.

"Mine, either," Tom said. "I'm fairly familiar with the descendants of the founding families—at least, those who still live in the area, and no one pops onto my radar." He looked at Jordan. "Have you seen any mention of what happened to Garrett in Seavey's papers?"

"No, but let me hunt around," Jordan replied. "I'm not done reading Eleanor Canby's memoirs, or with going through the newspapers from the period surrounding the shipwreck. It's also possible Charlotte might know something—Garrett was a Green Light client back then."

"See if you can find any marriage announcements, births, or obituaries," Darcy suggested.

"Good idea," Jordan agreed, reaching over to add her empty glass to Jase's tray.

The band members were filing back onto the stage, tuning their instruments.

"Time to get back to work." Jase stood, placing a hand on Jordan's shoulder. "You're done for the night—Bill and I can handle it from here."

"Come on. I'll give you and Malachi a lift home," Darcy added. "Who knows? Maybe I'll get lucky, and the murderer will be standing on your front porch, waiting to confess."

* * *

DARCY dropped off Jordan and Malachi a few minutes later, after an uneventful ride through quiet streets. At that time of night, most of both communities were at home in bed or in their portals, so Jordan could worry less about witnessing the debacle of Darcy unknowingly driving through someone.

Jordan climbed the front steps and opened the door to discover yet another vase of red roses in the hallway.

Dammit. "Hattie!" she yelled.

"No need to raise your voice beyond what is considered a polite tone," Hattie replied from the entry to the library. "Yelling is extremely unladylike."

Jordan ignored that. "You've *got* to convince Seavey to quit filching flowers from the florist. I'm going broke cleaning up after him."

"I assure you, though I claim responsibility for the original bouquet, I had no hand in the delivery of these," Michael Seavey said from behind her. "I wouldn't be so crass as to send duplicate gifts to a beautiful woman. Each trinket or gesture during courtship should impart a unique, artfully constructed message, designed to communicate the seriousness of the suit. This evening, Hattie and I have been sharing a book of poetry."

From somewhere in the depths of the library, Jordan heard Frank growl.

"No fistfights this evening," she warned in a raised voice. "I'm beat, and I have reading to do." She paused. "So who *are* the flowers from?"

"Since the card is addressed to you," Hattie pointed out

in an arch tone, "I have no way of ascertaining that, do I? I'm not in the habit of reading someone's private missives."

"I'll wager they're from your handsome beau!" Charlotte gushed from somewhere overhead. "Hattie, we should expect him to offer for her hand within the fortnight. Do you realize the import of this new development? We must plan for a double wedding! How *romantic!*"

"Don't even think about it," Jordan warned grimly. "In modern times, men don't 'offer' for a woman's hand."

"Well, I find that to be simply outrageous," Charlotte sniffed. "Some conventions should withstand the test of time."

"Yeah, and obviously, that one didn't." Curious, Jordan walked over to examine the flowers. A card was nestled in the leaves. She plucked it out and removed it from its envelope. There was no message, just a boldly scrawled "J."

She replaced the card and, smiling, leaned over to sniff the fragrant flowers.

"I believe you may be correct regarding the source, Charlotte." Seavey sounded amused. "Of course, the man got the idea from me, which indicates an appalling lack of imagination."

"He was merely making certain I didn't feel left out," Jordan said. "It was a kind, thoughtful gesture." And charmingly sneaky.

"I fail to see why women lose all sense of reason over a handful of hothouse flowers," Frank said, his tone disdainful. "You are, as a sex, such disgustingly sentimental creatures."

Seavey sighed and raised his gaze to the ceiling. "Given

your attitude, Lewis, is it any wonder that Hattie prefers me over you?"

"Michael," Hattie admonished. "As you are perfectly well aware, I haven't made a decision yet. Please do not taunt your competition."

"Regardless of your attempts to manipulate her emotions, Seavey, I feel confident that Hattie will see through you." Frank remained stubbornly focused on his opponent. "She has, after all, an outstanding mind and admirable ethics."

"Thank you, Frank," Hattie replied softly. "You are a good man."

"Enough," Jordan ordered. "I'm way too tired to referee this evening. I'm fixing a cup of tea and then heading up to bed with my stack of reading."

"What, precisely, are you reading?" Seavey asked.

Already halfway down the hall to the kitchen, Jordan slowed and looked over her shoulder. "Your personal papers. I'm looking for information about Sam Garrett. I talked to him earlier this evening, and—"

Charlotte gasped and flew to Hattie's side, clutching her arm. "Garrett is *here*?"

"He is an extremely dangerous man," Seavey admonished Jordan. "I strongly suggest that you have nothing to do with him."

"Believe me," she said fervently, "I never want to cross paths with him again. But I need to know more about him."

"Your investigation into this man could put you, as well as the rest of us, at extreme risk," Hattie warned. "I beg of you to drop whatever line of inquiry you are pursuing."

"You *do* want me to solve Michael's murder, don't you?" At Hattie's grudging nod, Jordan added, "Then I need answers."

Charlotte started sobbing uncontrollably. "If Garrett comes near me again, I simply won't survive! I can't bear to see him!"

Jordan looked at her, perplexed. "What do you mean, 'again'? Has he been coming around Longren House?"

"She means before," Seavey explained quietly. He moved to place a hand on Charlotte's shoulder. "My dear, if Garrett approaches you, you need only to summon me, and I will endeavor to protect you as I did in the past."

"What are you talking about?" Jordan asked, bewildered.

"Yes, I would like to know the answer to that question myself," Hattie said firmly. "Charlotte, did Garrett harm you in some way? And if so, why is this the first time I'm hearing of it?"

Charlotte looked at Seavey with pleading eyes.

He sighed. "Very well, I shall explain. It is probably best that it all come to light. Perhaps we should adjourn to the kitchen, where we can be more comfortable while I relate this sordid little tale."

Unintended Consequences

Cosmopolitan Hotel
August 3, 1893

MICHAEL was awakened by his bodyguard in the early morning hours and informed that unexpected guests awaited him in his sitting room.

Remy's expression was solemn. "It's young Mr. Canby, Boss, accompanied by an injured young lady."

"Please make them comfortable, Remy. I will join them momentarily." He paused while pulling on his silk dressing gown. "How badly is the young woman hurt?"

"She's unconscious, Boss. Someone beat her up bad." Remy hesitated, then leaned closer, lowering his voice. "I believe she's a soiled dove. One of Mona Starr's girls?"

"Never mind that," Seavey replied, knotting the tie of the dressing gown, then sitting down to don the calfskin slippers his bodyguard produced. "Summon Dr. Willoughby immediately."

"Yes, Boss."

"And Remy—remain at Willoughby's and accompany him back to the hotel. I don't trust the man to respond to my summons without the threat of persuasion. Take care, however, not to injure him—we will need his skills intact this evening."

His bodyguard nodded, then withdrew silently.

Opening the sitting room door, Michael stopped at the sight that greeted him. Jesse Canby knelt by Michael's maroon velvet settee, stroking the bruised forehead of Charlotte Walker, who lay unmoving, eyes closed. Her complexion was pale, her gown ripped. Michael thought he could see evidence of some blood spatter on her sleeve.

He closed his eyes briefly. Dear God! As he'd feared, he'd gravely miscalculated.

"Seavey!" Jesse stood to execute an unsteady bow. "I didn't know where else to turn."

"This is the work of Sam Garrett?" Michael asked grimly.

"Yes." Jesse wrung his hands." "I was in the next room when I heard Charlotte's screams. S'truth, I tried to stop him!"

"Where was Mona's bodyguard?" Michael asked.

"As soon as Charlotte began screaming, one of the girls ran to fetch him. It took three of us to pull Garrett into the hall. He was in an uncontrollable rage—we were hardly a match for him."

"Few would be," Michael said, trying to sooth the agitated young man.

He knelt beside the girl, studying her injuries. His gut tightened. Even with the bruises, her resemblance to Hattie was strong enough to bring forth a familiar rush of grief. He took a moment to steel himself, then continued his perusal.

Charlotte's breathing appeared to be even, though

shallow, as if she was in pain. Broken ribs, perhaps? No doubt at least badly bruised. Garrett had managed to land several blows about her face, even blackening one eye. Even more troubling, Michael suspected the worst of the damage had been inflicted where no one would see the bruises unless they removed her clothing.

He stood and lifted a soft wool throw from the back of the settee, gently covering her with it.

"I've sent for Willoughby," he told Jesse quietly. "If you don't want your current state of debilitation reported back to your mother, I suggest you vacate the premises immediately."

"I'm not leaving Charlotte," Jesse said stoutly. "I'm responsible for her."

"Your loyalty is admirable but misguided. This attack was directed at me, and rest assured, I will handle it. You may return in the morning to visit Charlotte."

Jesse swayed on his feet but remained where he was, a stubborn look on his face. "I will have your word that you won't allow her to leave this suite," he demanded. "If she returns to the Green Light, I fear she won't survive another night."

Michael nodded. "I'm in agreement. She will be safe here. I will post my bodyguards outside her room."

After several more minutes of reassurances, Michael was able to convince Canby to leave by the back stairs. He returned to pace the suite while he awaited the physician's arrival.

Garrett had crossed the line when he recklessly committed murder, but this attack was far more reprehensible. Harming a defenseless young woman . . . Michael simply couldn't stomach it.

He'd given little thought to the possibility that Garrett might use Charlotte to exact retribution. In truth, he hadn't believed Garrett possessed the finesse required to come up with such a strategy. And it would have been far more effective to attack Michael directly, or to inflict some form of damage on the *Henrietta Dale*.

Clearly, Michael had underestimated Garrett's propensity to commit evil acts.

He wouldn't make that mistake again.

Chapter 16

So Garrett attacked Charlotte because you cut him out of your smuggling business?" Jordan asked.

"Yes," Seavey answered. He glanced at Hattie, as if to gauge her reaction, then continued. "Garrett had become far too great a liability to remain in my organization. In an earlier meeting, he'd alluded to the fact that he knew Charlotte was Hattie's sister. I admit that I dismissed his comment, paying no further heed to it." He sent an apologetic glance to Charlotte. "I will always regret that I caused you pain."

"I never blamed you, Michael," Charlotte said. "Indeed, you paid for my physician and kept me safe for as long as you were able." She turned to Hattie and Jordan. "My injuries, though painful, turned out to be not as severe as Michael had assumed." She closed her eyes, trembling for a moment before continuing. "Although if Jesse hadn't summoned Mona's bodyguards, I quite believe Garrett would have killed me."

"Possibly," Jordan agreed. "I've talked to the man, and

he clearly enjoys violence in all its forms." She looked at Seavey. "So you kept Charlotte at the hotel while she recovered?"

"Yes, for the next forty-eight hours. Then I felt it wise, since I was leaving town for a full day, that she travel with me." He paused, then shook his head. "It was the best I could do, and I see now that it wasn't enough."

"You can't be blamed, Michael, for what happened after you died," Hattie said softly.

From behind them, Frank made a disgusted sound. "On the contrary. His actions directly caused Charlotte's injuries. Clearly, Garrett planned to use Charlotte as leverage. When one engages in a lifetime of risky and illegal business activities, these types of violent acts are far too commonly the by-product."

Seavey flinched.

"Garrett was the one to beat me, so he is to blame," Charlotte stated with vehemence. "Michael was the one who tried to save me!"

Jordan held up her hand. "Can we move on?" Though the events Seavey had related were revealing in terms of Garrett's character, she still wasn't any closer to discovering a connection between Garrett and Holt's killer. "What happened after Jesse brought Charlotte to you?" she asked Seavey.

He shrugged. "I fear I don't have much more to tell you. I did, of course, make certain that Garrett received a 'message' designed to impress upon him that he should refrain from such reprehensible actions in the future."

"You avenged my attack?" Charlotte smiled tremulously

at him, placing a hand on his sleeve. "You are such an *honorable* man."

Jordan thought Seavey might have looked slightly abashed at her reaction.

He cleared his throat. "As I was saying, Jesse delivered Charlotte to my hotel suite two days before the maiden voyage of the *Henrietta Dale*. While I continued to oversee last-minute details regarding the seaworthiness of the ship and the accommodations for my passengers, I paid Willoughby handsomely to see to the treatment of her injuries. Accordingly, we set sail early on the morning of August 5 for Victoria, with a return trip planned for that evening."

"Whoa, wait," Jordan said, startled. "You said a minute ago that you kept Charlotte in the hotel until you left on a trip, at which time you took her with you. Are you telling me that Charlotte was aboard the *Henrietta Dale* when she ran aground?"

"That's precisely what I am telling you," Seavey said. "Charlotte served as chef for the opium smokers in my great cabin. It worked out well for all concerned, in my opinion. I needed a beautiful and charming chef to help my passengers enjoy their experiences with my pipes, and Charlotte needed a place away from the waterfront to heal."

Hattie gasped, her hands flying up to cover her mouth, her expression stricken. "*What?*"

"Oh, dear," Charlotte murmured, looking apprehensive.

Seavey frowned. "You needn't be worried, my dear, that Charlotte was in any way treated poorly. Indeed, she was working in luxurious surroundings, handling beautifully designed cloisonné enamel boxes, intricately carved jade pipes ... and, of course, serving a number of Port Chatham's societal elite."

"But to expose her to such wanton activities ..." Hattie's voice trailed away.

"Truly, I thought you knew, my dear. Charlotte came under my protection from the time she was beaten until the shipwreck. I had no expectation that Garrett would heed my threats to leave her alone; therefore, the only logical method of concealing her and keeping her away from him was to bring her on board."

"You thought the further ruination of an innocent such as Charlotte by introducing her to an opium den was *preferable* to leaving her under guard in your hotel?" Frank asked, his expression incredulous.

"My bodyguards accompany me at all times," Michael snapped, losing patience. "Forgive me, but I didn't trust any of my other men to keep her safe. Would you have had me put her at further risk? All because of the possibility that she would be exposed to a few upper-crust guests who smoked a drug that was, may I remind you, legal at that time? In luxurious surroundings, rather than in the squalor of a common opium den? Good God, man! It's not as if I forced her to smoke the stuff!"

"Frank, please," Charlotte chided softly. She fidgeted in her chair. "The decision was not Michael's alone—I asked to come along. I knew Jesse would be on board, and I ... well, I felt *comforted* by that knowledge. Jesse had become a dear friend, and I was petrified that Garrett would make another attempt on me the minute Jesse and Michael left town."

"Well, I'm confused," Jordan said. "I have a list of the survivors of the shipwreck, and, Charlotte, your name wasn't on it. I thought you didn't die until a year or two *after* the shipwreck."

"That's correct," Charlotte replied. "I was murdered on the waterfront approximately a year later, in an unrelated incident." She shook her head, folding her hands in her lap and refusing to meet Hattie's eyes. "You must understand. By the time I was rescued, I knew that Jesse was dead, and I had no idea what had happened to Michael or his bodyguards. I *had* to protect myself from Garrett, and the only way I knew how was to make him think I had gone down with the ship as well. When I saw Eleanor's reporters lurking about . . ." She looked at Jordan. "The reason you didn't see my name among the survivors is that I gave the authorities a false name."

"Dear God, Charlotte." Hattie wrung her hands, her expression distraught. "Why haven't you told us about this before now?"

"Because I didn't want you to think any less of me than you already do," her sister admitted softly. "I knew you disapproved of smoking opium, and that you didn't want to hear that I might have been pulled into that culture by Jesse. And to have been a chef for Michael . . . Well, I thought you'd blame him even more than you already did."

"So let me get this straight," Jordan interposed, before the conversation devolved any further. "Charlotte, you're telling me that you were on board the night the *Henrietta Dale* ran aground, and that you witnessed the entire incident, including the attempted rescue and the sinking of the ship?"

"Yes." Charlotte was silent, her gaze turning inward as she appeared to remember that night. "I was scraping out one of the pipes—the one carved from redwood, do you remember, Michael? It was so beautiful . . ."

"Yes, I recall it quite clearly," he replied gently.

"Michael spared no expense, you know, to provide his customers with an experience worthy of royalty. I was quite honored to be asked to serve as his chef," she assured Hattie.

Hattie frowned, saying nothing.

"Go on," Jordan urged.

Charlotte was trembling. "I was in the process of slicing a small wedge from a cake of chandu, to place in the pipe for Jesse, when we felt the most terrible jolt . . ."

The Rescue

FLUNG against the wall, Charlotte dropped the silver scraper and the pipe. Her cabin mates, reclined on velvet settees, were thrown to the floor.

She heard a sharp *crack* from overhead. A huge wooden mast plunged through the skylight, shattering it. Shards of glass rained down on her. The floor dropped from under her. Water rushed into the great cabin, soaking her satin slippers and the hem of her gown.

Someone scrambled past her, yelling, running for the door. Jesse was no longer beside her. Dropping to her knees, she attempted to shove debris aside. She strained to see through the gloom and layers of opium smoke. Where was Jesse? Where were the others?

"Someone, please help!" she cried, her voice a high, thin wail, but no one answered.

The floor shifted again beneath her, water sloshing against the velvet settee. At the other end of the room, she glimpsed a body floating in the debris-filled seawater. She struggled to her feet and waded toward it.

The floor canted sharply, throwing her against the mirrored wall. She heard terrified shouts from above as something crashed onto the deck. Her knees suddenly felt cold, and looking down, she realized the chilly water had risen to her thighs.

"Ahoy, down there!" a voice shouted.

"Help!" she screamed.

A head poked through the skylight, barely discernible. "Miss? Are you hurt?"

"No, but I fear the others are. There's someone just over there . . ." She tried to wade through the water, to no avail. "You must help us!"

He angled his head, staring silently for a brief moment in the direction she pointed. "Come, miss," he finally said, his tone quieter. "There's nothing we can do to help him."

"*No!* He's just unconscious. He'll be fine once we get him out from under the mast—"

"We don't have much time, and you must save yourself."

"No!" she sobbed. "It might be my friend! I won't leave him."

"Miss." The voice held patience as well as understanding. "This ship is precariously balanced in the surf—it could break further apart any second now. The waves are gaining height, and they will soon suck the ship deep into the sands. You must come with me now, or I'll be forced to leave you behind."

"Oh God, *please!* Can't you do something?"

"I'm afraid he's already gone." The man reached down to her. "Give me your hand, and I'll lift you out."

She stared over at the body, uncomprehending.

The floor shifted once again beneath her, throwing her off balance, and she screamed.

"Make haste, miss. I beg of you!"

Pushing away from the wall, she reluctantly reached up to grasp his hand. The man pulled her off her feet and out of the water, urging her to give him her other hand. In moments, she stood on a badly listing deck.

Destruction surrounded her. What had once been a ship possessing immense beauty and grace now seemed to be no more than piles of rubble. Canvas and rigging lay as it had fallen. Stacked taller than the height of a large man, it jumbled together with splintered pieces of wood that had once been yardarms.

In front of her, the bow of the ship had been forced up and onto the sand and driftwood. Behind her, the stern still lay in the water. Waves crashed against the hull.

Her rescuer kept a tight grasp on her elbow, holding her steady whenever she felt her balance give way. They picked their way around bodies and over snarls of rope and sails, their progress greatly hampered by the weight of Charlotte's drenched gown.

As they reached the ship's bow, she could hear faint shouts from the mist below. Her rescuer sliced quickly through a section of rope and used it to tie around her waist.

"I'm going to lower you down, miss," he explained as he secured the rope to the railing. "Someone below will guide you onto the beach."

"But what about the others?" she asked.

"They're gone," he replied in a gentle tone.

Dear God. *Jesse.* "No! I'm certain that if you just search the lower cabins . . ." Her voice trailed off on a hiccuping sob.

"Go on now, miss—I'll be right behind you."

Clinging to the rope, her heart pounding in her chest, she was lowered past bodies hanging in midair, tangled in the rigging. Mist swirled around her, adding to the chill of her soaked clothing and making it hard for her to see what lay below. Gradually, the faint light of a lantern beckoned through the darkness. Hands grasped her ankles, then her legs. She dropped onto the sand.

A woman worked briskly to untie the rope about her waist, then gave it a sharp yank as a signal to pull it up. She handed Charlotte a coarse wool blanket. "Sit, miss, and try to keep yourself warm. It will be some time before boats arrive to take you back to town."

Shivering, Charlotte glanced overhead. The hull of the *Henrietta Dale* towered over them. Just aft of the bow, she could see a massive log sticking out of the hull where the ship had rammed onto the sand. The stern sat lower in the water than usual, and the entire ship was canted at an angle so acute as to appear as if it would fall any moment, crushing them. The woman stood by Charlotte, her head angled so that she could watch overhead, her expression tense. Two other men sprawled on the beach only a few yards away, unconscious and injured. One, the town councilman she recognized from the great cabin, had blood darkening the side of his face.

"Are we the only survivors?" she asked the woman in a hushed voice.

"No," the woman replied, not pulling her gaze away.

"By the time my husband and I arrived, a few of the crew had already managed to climb down with one injured man. They left to hike back along the spit to the headland and summon more help from nearby farms. Until we can get a message back to Port Chatham, no one will know to bring their boats out here to help with the rescue."

"What about Michael Seavey?" Charlotte asked. "Have you seen him? And what of Jesse Canby?" she added, her voice breaking.

"Unless one of them is the man who was carried ashore a bit ago, or one of those two lying just over there, I'm afraid they didn't make it."

Chapter 17

I continued to ask throughout the night, but there was no indication that Jesse had survived," Charlotte told them, swiping at tears. "The first mate and another member of his crew walked the five miles back to a farm on the headlands, to notify the authorities of the shipwreck. It took until almost dawn, but more help did eventually arrive." Her expression reflected the rigors of that long, freezing night spent on the beach. "And along with help, of course, came the press."

"Eleanor Canby was there?" Jordan asked. "She must have been devastated by the news of her son's death."

"No, her reporters were at the scene of the wreck, but Eleanor didn't learn of Jesse's death until around dawn, when we were all brought back to Port Chatham. Until we were all gathered together on Union Wharf, even I wasn't willing to accept that Jesse hadn't made it out alive." Charlotte pressed her lips together for a moment before continuing. "I've never seen Eleanor so hysterical. She was raging at anyone who came close to her. When she saw you being lifted off the rescue boat, Michael, she became incoherent, ranting about how it was all your fault, that you were the reason her son was dead."

"She must have loved him very much," Hattie mused, "even though she professed to have disowned him."

"So perhaps you were the unconscious man the crew first carried to the beach," Jordan told Seavey.

He shrugged. "Obviously, I have no recollection of the event."

Jordan turned back to Charlotte. "Think, Charlotte. Can you tell me exactly who you saw on the beach that night?"

"There were so many people rushing around, what with the reporters trying to get us to tell our stories, the local farmers trying to help the injured, and others arriving in boats to transport us back to Port Chatham. Captain Williams wanted to go back on board, to see if he could find more survivors, but the rescuers felt the ship was too unstable. All I remember is being horribly cold, and feeling a terrible sadness. I didn't want to believe that Jesse might truly be gone."

"You cared a great deal for him." Hattie said it very softly.

"Yes. Though Jesse struggled with his own demons, he was a true friend to me during that time. I'll always remember him with great fondness."

Hattie hugged her, saying, "I'm just glad you survived."

"So pardon me for being the one to point out the obvious," Jordan said, "but we still don't know who murdered Michael, and I still don't have the information I need about Sam Garrett."

Frank roused himself from where he had been standing throughout Charlotte's story. "Indeed, I doubt anyone truly cared whether Seavey lived or died, or even the manner in which he died."

"Frank!" Hattie exclaimed, scandalized. "Michael is right here, you know."

"His insults fail to disturb me," Seavey replied mildly. "And as I've indicated, I've no wish to know the exact circumstances surrounding my death."

"Well, I do," Charlotte insisted. "And so does Hattie. You were kind to me, Michael, when I needed the help."

"That's a wonderful sentiment," Jordan remarked, "but unless someone can give me a clue how to go about this, we may be at a dead end."

"Good God, woman," Frank protested. "Your humor leaves much to be desired!"

"Pardon?"

"Even I wouldn't make fun of a man's death by indicating that he had arrived at a *dead* end!"

Jordan closed her eyes and prayed for patience. "What I meant," she explained, very carefully, "is that I may have run out of leads to investigate, to determine how Michael really died."

Charlotte jumped up, hissing, and began to fly around the room.

"Oh, for . . ." Jordan began, exasperated.

"He's *back*!" she screamed.

"What?"

"*Danger! Danger!*"

She meant the burglar, Jordan suddenly realized.

Giving the others a hand signal to stay put and remain

quiet, she rose from her chair and crept over to the door that opened onto the hall and listened.

"Another human has broken into your house?" Seavey inquired from right beside her, causing her to jump out of her skin, swallowing the scream that bubbled up.

"*Don't* scare me like that!" she whispered.

From down the hall, she heard a distinctive thump and a muttered oath.

Unbelievable. She pulled her cellphone from her pocket and hit speed dial. "The son of a bitch is back," she said to Darcy, sotto voce.

"What?" Darcy sounded alert, even given the lateness of the hour. It must be a talent developed by all law enforcement, Jordan reflected. "Who? Your intruder?"

"Yeah."

"Where are you?" she asked, all business.

"Kitchen."

"*Shit.* Go out the back door, *now.* I'm on my way. And hang up and dial Jase. He should be home by now. *For once, do not argue with me. Just do it.*"

"I'm already halfway out the door," Jordan assured, tiptoeing over to hold the door open while the ghosts floated through. She softly whistled for Malachi, who woke up instantly and trotted outside. Belatedly, he caught the sounds of more movement in the library and turned to let out a growl. Jordan shushed him and dragged him outside by the collar, which earned her a look of total canine outrage.

Ignoring him, she called Jase and quickly explained the situation. He hung up without bothering to reply, but not before she heard him running. Turning to peer through the darkness at Amanda's tent, she saw nothing stirring inside. No help from that front.

"You should confront this person," Seavey said beside her. "Never back down when facing your enemy. It merely encourages them to act more boldly the next time."

"You're absolutely right." She was sick and tired of people breaking into her home and threatening her. Threatening her *family*.

A baseball bat landed at her feet, with Charlotte zooming up to hover above it. "Use this, Jordan."

Hefting it in her left hand, Jordan stalked around the side of the house toward the scaffolding. She heard swearing coming from just above her. Looking up, she saw feet dangling from the hole above the French doors. The bastard was trying to crawl through.

Scrambling onto the first level of the scaffolding, she leaned over the metal pipe railing and swung the bat with both hands so hard her feet momentarily left the platform. It connected with a loud crack.

The intruder screamed, teetering for an instant on the header over the French doors. Then he fell backward. Grabbing for the metal crossbars holding up the scaffolding, he missed and fell to the ground below Jordan, arms and legs flailing. He hit the pile of siding, glancing off and toppling with it. Landing with a thud on the rock pavers, shingles falling around him, he let out a howl of pain, holding his ankle.

Malachi planted both paws on his chest, growling. The man went silent midshriek just as Jase skidded to a halt next to him.

Peering over the railing with bat still in hand, Jordan got her first good look at her burglar.

"Good Christ!" Michael Seavey said from the patio's edge. "It's that obnoxious little man who makes such a nuisance of himself in my hotel."

Chapter 18

You broke my ankle, you *bitch*!" Clive Walters screeched.

"Shut up." Jase pulled a still-snarling Malachi to the side and flipped Walters over on his stomach. Unconcerned with his injured foot, Jase rammed a knee into the middle of his back.

"Ow, ow, ow!"

Darcy, who was now walking across the yard toward them, tossed Jase her handcuffs.

"Bravo!" Seavey applauded, hovering at the height of the scaffolding and bowing to Jordan.

"Yes!" Hattie smiled up at her from below. "Well done, Jordan."

Charlotte made enthusiastic clapping motions, glaring at Frank until he followed suit.

"I assume you're okay?" Jase asked Jordan, craning his neck to glance up at the bat she still gripped.

"I'm fine. Really, really pissed, but fine." She climbed down to the ground and walked over to Walters, who was whimpering in pain. "What gives you the right to break into my home and terrorize me, you asshole?"

"And terrorize *us*," Charlotte reminded Jordan stoutly.

"Arrest her!" Walters screamed at Darcy. "She assaulted me. And get me an ambulance right now! I need to go to the hospital."

"He certainly is a distressingly unappealing man, is he not?" Hattie asked.

"Yes, my dear, he is," Seavey replied gently. "He gives respectable criminals everywhere a bad name."

Jase got to his feet and yanked Walters upright by his arms, which set him to wailing again when he landed on his ankle.

"Get her away from me!" he yelled, eyeing Jordan wildly while he held his injured foot in the air. "She's going to *kill* me!"

Jordan looked at the baseball bat, seriously contemplating his suggestion. Then, with a sigh, she dropped it on the ground.

"Shut the hell up," Jase told Walters, "or *I'll* kill you."

"Did you hear that?" Walters asked Darcy. "He threatened me! I don't have to take that!"

Darcy rolled her eyes.

"How many times do I have to tell you," Jordan snapped, "I didn't steal your goddamn papers!"

"You did, too! You and Stilwell both thought you could make money off items that belong to *me*."

Jordan gaped. "Why in the world would you think *that*? I didn't even know what was happening until I found Holt's body."

"You and Holt were in on it together from the very beginning!"

"What '*it*'?" she asked. "You're making no sense at all."

"You planned to steal the papers, then find and sell off the items listed in them."

"Do you even know what is in the papers?"

"Things that belong to *me*, that's what!" Walters snarled.

"I beg to differ—items from the Cosmopolitan Hotel belong to me," Seavey interjected. "This ill-mannered *squatter* has absolutely no claim to them."

"Let's not go there," Jordan told Seavey.

"Go where?" He looked confused.

"*Why not go there?*" Walters retorted. "There's no honor among thieves. You stole the papers from Stilwell, then killed him."

"Okay, that's it, you are officially insane. I had absolutely no *reason* . . ." Her voice trailed off as the clothing Walters was wearing—a dark hoodie and jeans—finally registered. "You broke into Holt's house looking for the papers, didn't you? And when I arrived, you shoved me down the steps, because you didn't want me to know you were looking for them."

Jase yanked Walters's arms higher into the small of his back, causing him to yelp. "You shoved Jordan down *concrete steps?*" he asked in a deceptively soft tone.

"Jase," Darcy warned quietly. "Give him to me."

"Give me five minutes alone with him," Jase growled.

"No."

Jase held on to Walters a moment longer, then with a sound of disgust shoved him at Darcy.

"I did *nothing* wrong," Walters sniveled. "I'm entitled to take back and protect what's mine."

"That refrain is getting old," Hattie observed. "Can't you encourage your friends to escort him off our property?"

"I'm working on it," Jordan replied grimly.

"Working on getting away with murder, and blaming *me* for it!" Walters whined.

Before Jordan could point out the sheer idiocy of that statement, another patrol car and an ambulance pulled up, lights flashing. They were attracting a crowd—several neighbors had emerged from their houses, looking bewildered.

"I glimpsed a gun lying on the floor of the conservatory," Frank told Jordan. "He must have dropped it when you hit him with the bat. I suspect it may be .22 caliber."

"I'll go get it!" Charlotte volunteered, sounding excited.

"*No!*" Jordan said hastily, envisioning a gun going off randomly. "Leave it alone; I'll get it."

"Get what?" Darcy asked, confused.

"He left a gun in the conservatory," Jordan explained.

"I did not!" Walters yelled. "It's *hers*, I'm telling you! How would she know it was there unless it was hers?"

Darcy sighed. "Leave the gun where it is. I'll have one of my deputies bag it for evidence. We can test it to see if his fingerprints are on it."

"I don't own a gun, and I didn't bring one with me!"

"We'll see if it matches the bullet we pulled from Holt," Darcy informed him.

"You know, I just don't get it," Jordan said. "Why are you so hell-bent to find those papers?"

"Oh, come *on*," Walters sneered. "Everyone knows you and Stilwell were looking into the murder of his ancestor. And that you'll do just about anything to solve murders for the ghosts in this town. But it's bad for business, don't you see? I *need* Seavey's ghost to hang around—he brings in more than half my bookings! I couldn't have either of you figuring out what happened, so that Seavey would have crossed over permanently, now could I?"

Jordan gaped at him. "You're shitting me."

"Good Christ!" Seavey remarked. "Does he *really* think I would cross over and leave *my* hotel in *his* hands, to be run into the ground? The man is truly delusional."

Darcy rolled her eyes. "Well, congratulations, Clive. You just got yourself arrested for attempted armed robbery. *And* provided an excellent motive for why you killed Holt. You're going away for a very long time, which means you won't be around to worry about the bookings in your hotel after all."

"Thank goodness," Hattie said. "I certainly wouldn't wish his continued presence on Michael."

"It's not robbery if I'm retrieving what *she* stole in the first place." Walters's tone was sullen.

"That's not how it works, pal. I have two witnesses who can testify that you attempted to break into Jordan's house, armed with a handgun."

"She has *six* witnesses!" Charlotte corrected.

"You can't testify in a court of law," Jordan pointed out.

"Sure I can—why couldn't I?" Jase asked, then clued in. "Oh, got it."

"Got what?" Walters asked suspiciously. "You can't talk like that in front of me. That's entrapment!"

Darcy closed her eyes, obviously reaching for patience. "Why don't you save us all a lot of time, Clive, and just admit that you killed Holt?"

"*She* killed Holt, I'm telling you!" he raged, spittle flying.

Darcy motioned to a deputy, handing Walters over to him. "Go with him to the hospital," she told the deputy crisply. "After they set his ankle, move him downtown to a holding cell. I'll be in tomorrow morning to take down his confession. Oh, and don't forget to read him his rights. The good news, Clive, is that you'll have plenty of time in jail to read law books and figure out how clueless you are about the justice system."

"I'm not confessing to anything!" he snapped. "I want a lawyer."

"In *that* regard, it appears that he is *most* knowledgeable," Frank observed.

Chapter 19

AFTER her first good night's sleep in two days, Jordan woke early and decided to take Malachi out to breakfast. Darcy had promised to call her as soon as she heard whether the ballistics for Clive Walters's gun matched the bullet pulled from Holt's corpse. If so, she hoped Walters would simply confess. Jordan didn't have anything pressing until she was due at the marina at nine for the telephone interview with Bob's historian friend regarding her sighting of the ghost ship. That left her with a couple of hours of rare peace and quiet in which to gather her thoughts and gain some perspective.

She shook her head while she hunted for Malachi's leash. What a crackpot Walters had turned out to be. Who in his right mind *murdered* to keep a ghost on the premises to haunt a business, because it was good for the bottom line? Then again, maybe Walters's reasoning wasn't all that different from others who had killed for money.

For some reason, though, she felt bugged by the whole

situation. All of the recent events—Holt's discovering historic documents in the wall of the hotel suite, diving to retrieve sunken treasure off the *Henrietta Dale*, his murder, Walters's subsequent frantic hunt for those documents—hinged on the events in 1893 leading up to Michael Seavey's murder. And she still didn't have a handle on everything that had happened back then. In fact, given how thin the historical sources were for that particular time frame, she might *never* know.

What had happened to the survivors of the shipwreck? Had Seavey been transported alive back to Port Chatham? If so, and if he had been murdered afterward, why didn't he remember the time between his rescue and when he was killed? And why did Sam Garrett feel the need to protect the identity of the man he saw shoot Holt?

She yanked open drawers and stopped to peer into cupboards, trying to remember where she'd last stashed the leash. "Where's your leash?" she asked Malachi.

He gave her The Look. "Roooo."

"Helpful," she said, then resumed her hunt.

If Walters *was* the killer, it seemed to her that her first order of business was to confirm some kind of connection between him and Garrett. She'd found no evidence that Walters could actually see ghosts. As far as she knew, Garrett had nothing to do with the Cosmopolitan Hotel. Which meant Jase might be correct that the connection could be familial. As he'd pointed out, even murderers had families.

She shoved the last drawer shut and straightened to stare at the kitchen while she mulled over that possibility.

Both men undoubtedly suffered from mental instability, though in actuality, their formal diagnoses would be quite different: Garrett was clearly a sociopath, while Walters exhibited symptoms of extreme paranoia. Still, a history of inherited mental instability *could* be indicative of a family connection.

She also needed to see if she could find any further mention of Seavey's murder. All of which meant she should keep reading through the historical documents she'd filched from the Historical Society.

Finally spying Malachi's leash on top of the stove—how the hell had it gotten *there?*—she tucked Eleanor's memoir and the pages from Captain Williams's diary under one arm, whistled for Malachi, then headed out the back door.

Though high clouds provided a pale gray cover, the temperature was mild, making for a pleasant walk to their favorite French restaurant. The prospect of a sinfully rich and filling breakfast, *caffé breve*, and a relaxed perusal of *The New York Times* struck her as the definition of pure bliss. She owed it to herself, she rationalized, to spend at least *some* time on those pleasurable pursuits before she cracked open Eleanor's memoir, which she felt certain would make her want to pull her hair out.

They walked to the corner of her block, passing Jase's house, which immediately had her feeling guilty that she hadn't yet thanked him for the roses. He was taking the day off to work with Bill and Tom on the library wall, and therefore certain to be in and out of Longren House. This gave her even more reason to vacate the premises, since she still hadn't a clue what she wanted to do about him. The man definitely rang all her bells.

Marietta, the plump, fiftyish café owner, who always made certain she had a special treat for Malachi, seated Jordan in the outside courtyard. "The usual on the espresso?" she asked Jordan cheerfully as she handed her a menu and the newspaper.

"That would be marvelous," Jordan replied with a grateful smile.

Despite the early hour, a number of locals came and went, most stopping in to pick up coffee and one of the restaurant's fabulous baked goods for their commute. A few lingered, however, taking the time to eat a leisurely breakfast.

When Marietta returned with Jordan's *caffé breve*, she ordered an omelet, then settled back in her chair, opening *The New York Times* to the national news page. Surely some politician's imbroglio with his mistress would take her mind off whatever was bugging her about the night of the *Henrietta Dale*'s shipwreck. Something was nagging at her, something she'd originally read, or that Michael Seavey had told her . . .

Six minutes later, after reading the same headline three times, she tossed down the paper in disgust. Until she figured out what was driving her crazy, she wouldn't be able to concentrate on anything else. Well, except the subjects she wanted to deny, such as the house remodel, the sexy guy currently remodeling it and revving her hormones . . .

She blew out a breath, picked up Captain Williams's diary pages, and started skimming. But other than a brief mention of his retirement the first week of September

1893, she found nothing of use. Resigned, she opened Eleanor's memoir and prepared to read chapter after strident chapter of preachy text, to see if she could find even a hint of something useful.

A third of the way into the small, leather-bound book, she *did* find a reference to opium smuggling. Jordan was certain it was a rehashing of her editorials, but she forced herself to read the passage.

> *In hopes of convincing my fellow citizens of the inherent dangers of opium, I decided to one day visit such a den of iniquity, so that I might describe my experience to my readers, thus giving them a real sense of the depravity of the drug's purveyors. However, even I was unprepared for what awaited me . . .*
>
> *In the middle of a bright, sunny day, I traveled down to the seedier section of Port Chatham's waterfront, where houses of ill repute vie for space with Chinese "laundries" and saloons. Choosing a laundry at random, I entered and proceeded directly to the room in the back, where I felt certain I would discover an opium den.*
>
> *Immediately upon entering the room, I was assaulted by layer after layer of thick smoke undulating in strata, like waves in the ocean, its pungent odor intensifying as I walked to the center of the room. Though small lamps had been placed throughout the*

room for illumination, they did little to permeate the gloom.

The room was lined with wooden bunks—pallets really—which were covered with the barest minimum of padding and small, filthy linens stuffed with straw, presumably functioning as a sort of crude pillow upon which the smoker could lay his head once he succumbed to the heinous effects of the drug.

Although many have told me that the atmosphere of an opium den has its own alluring and sensuous qualities, I found the place to be utterly depraved. Men and women with sunken, bruised eyes, dressed in soiled clothing, emaciated from the pernicious effects of the drug, had lit pipes and were passing them amongst one another . . .

"One omelet, plus an extra stack of whole-wheat toast to share with Malachi, as ordered," Marietta announced brightly, placing a plate stacked high with food in front of Jordan, forcing her to set aside Eleanor's memoir.

"Looks fabulous," she assured the owner, leaning over to breathe in the aroma of grilled veggies, farm-fresh eggs, and homemade hash browns. Forget dieting. She needed her strength to deal with the challenges of the next few days, right? She picked up a fork and dug in.

The woman reached down and picked up the small book, studying it for a moment. "Heavy stuff," she commented.

Jordan couldn't argue with her assessment. "I'm reading it to see if I can find more information about the 1893 wreck of the *Henrietta Dale*," she explained.

"Oh, that's right! I heard a rumor yesterday that you had seen the ghost ship." The woman cocked her head. "That must be *quite* the experience."

"Understatement of the year," Jordan muttered.

"Well, I'm sure you'll put your new, expanded powers to good use for our community."

After she left, Jordan gave Malachi a slice of toast, took a moment to moan in appreciation over a forkful of potatoes, then picked up Eleanor's memoir once more. She supposed she should be worried about getting food stains on it, but really, the world would be a better place if no one else ever had to read Eleanor's drivel again.

Rather than continuing to slog through the paragraphs about the waterfront opium dens, she flipped through pages, looking for something that would tie Eleanor to the rescue effort on August 5. She found what she was looking for in a chapter toward the end of the volume:

> *Events of recent days, which have taken a terrible toll on my family and others in our beloved Port Chatham, have now brought to light the horrifying truth of plans that could have wrecked the entire social fabric of our town.*
>
> *My only son, Jesse, was lost to me long before the night he was crushed by a falling mast when the ship he was a passenger on, the <u>Henrietta Dale</u>, ran aground on Dungeness Spit. Though I tried in vain to rid Jesse*

of his addiction to the pestilent drug, opium, he continued to seek out the company of those who suffered from the same addiction.

Many died the night that the <u>Henrietta Dale</u> *ran aground, but I can only say, in retrospect, that someone was looking over us all. For if the notorious Michael Seavey had been able to put in place his plans to use the ship to import opium and provide a floating opium den for his customers, more of our citizens would have fallen prey to his greed.*

I hold Michael Seavey directly responsible for the death of my beloved son, but I can only be relieved by Seavey's violent death just days later. Port Chatham remains an enviable place to live, based on that blessed turn of events.

May Michael Seavey rot in hell for all eternity.

Malachi whined, and without looking up from the page, Jordan held out another slice of toast. When he failed to take it from her hand, she dragged her attention back to the present.

Sam Garrett pulled out the chair across from her and sat down.

She dropped the toast and stumbled to her feet.

"Sit down," he said mildly, "before you draw attention to yourself."

She did as he ordered, taking a moment to glance around the small patio. No one seemed to notice her distress. Which, dammit, pissed her off. Garrett was interrupting what could have been a wonderfully peaceful, Zen-like breakfast. Well, aside from the garbage she was reading. But really, she was getting damn tired of being threatened, harassed . . .

He leaned over to sniff her plate. "'Tis a pity ghosts can't eat real food—I really miss it." He sighed. "At least if I try hard enough, I can manage a faint whiff of the intoxicating aromas."

"What do you want?" she asked coldly.

He raised an eyebrow. "I don't believe you will find it wise to take such a tone with me. I can reduce your mutt to a lifeless pile of fur in mere moments, should I become sufficiently displeased."

Jordan felt the blood drain from her face. "No!" she said quickly. Malachi growled, and she shushed him, placing a protective arm around his neck and keeping it there. "Please don't hurt him—he's just a dog."

Malachi gave her The Look, and she sent him a silent apology.

"That's better," Garrett said, leaning back with a humorless smile. "Now, pray tell, why haven't you told Seavey that I didn't murder him?"

"Things have been a little chaotic lately, and I just haven't found the time—"

"I'm not interested in hearing your excuses. I want it done. Today."

"Sure. Fine." She nodded emphatically. "But . . ." she hesitated, then plunged ahead, hoping she didn't increase his ire. "The thing is, I don't actually know who killed Seavey. And until I do—"

324 • P. J. ALDERMAN

Garrett waved a hand. "That is neither here nor there. The only fact that is of import is that *I* didn't murder him. Take all the time you want to discover the identity of the real killer—I have no interest in what you do with respect to your little investigation. But I want it immediately communicated to Seavey that I had no part in his death."

"So you'll swear to me that you weren't even in Port Chatham at the time Seavey was murdered?" she asked, not without some trepidation, tightening her hold on Malachi.

"For what it's worth, certainly. I was otherwise engaged."

"Doing what?"

He shrugged. "I don't see that it can hurt to divulge that part of my past life. The good Captain Williams and I were busy salvaging the opium from inside the hull of the *Henrietta Dale.*"

Jordan gaped at him. "So the captain was in on it all along?"

"Of course not. Think, woman! How could I have lured the ship onto the beach if Williams had known of my intentions? He approached me two days after the grounding and told me the story of how he'd discovered that Seavey had had secret compartments built into the hull for the transport of opium. He said that if I were to agree to assist him in retrieving the contraband, we could sell it and split the profits."

Jordan suddenly realized that *this* was what had been bugging her—the captain's original account of the ship-wreck that night, followed so closely by his retirement. He simply couldn't have been that broken up over the loss of a ship he'd sailed for just a few hours. So the only explanation that made sense was the one Garrett had just given her, that Williams immediately realized that no one would be the wiser if he came back a few days later to retrieve the *Henrietta Dale*'s valuable cargo. Such a cargo would have also given him the funds he needed to retire.

"Ah," Garrett said now, accurately reading her expression. "I see that you realized the import of Williams's behavior immediately following the shipwreck and, indeed, during the investigation of the cause of the grounding. By the time of the hearings into the grounding, Williams had carefully concealed enough money to retire comfortably, based on our salvage efforts. All he had to do was act broken up over the loss of his ship, making it look as if he were too grief-stricken to take the helm of another vessel any time in the near future." Garrett smiled, his expression reminiscent. "I must say, the chap was a consummate actor."

"But I don't understand," Jordan said. "If you retrieved the opium within days of when the ship went down, what was Holt diving for?"

"Unfortunately, Williams didn't have knowledge of all the secret compartments. And a portion of the hull had sunk in deeper waters, making the effort to dive and break open the compartments far more difficult."

That made sense. After all, divers then wouldn't have had the modern gear available today. She remembered now that the dive suit she'd seen Garrett wear that day on the spit had been odd looking. It probably represented what he knew of the dive suits from his own time on earth.

"Okay, I believe you," she said.

"I'm greatly relieved." His tone was wry. "However, I must insist that you make a point of notifying Seavey at once, and informing him of what you have learned. I grow weary from the inconvenience of avoiding him on the waterfront."

She suspected it was more than that, but she didn't want to push him any more than she had. "All right. You have my word that I will inform him sometime later today."

Garrett shook his head. "Unfortunately, I don't believe your word is sufficient. You see, I've always found that when threatened, people will do or say whatever they need to, to remain alive." He stood, then placed his hands on the table, leaning over her. "You have twenty-four hours to do as I bid, or I will return to eliminate those you consider your friends, including this mutt. Do you understand?"

She swallowed. "Yes, I understand."

He straightened, nodding. "Good. If you do as I request, this will be the last you see of me."

"Thank God for that," she muttered as he turned to fade away. With shaking hands, she picked up her bill and pulled out money to cover it.

"You're as white as a sheet!" Marietta exclaimed as she came over to remove the plates. "Are you all right? My food didn't give you indigestion, did it?"

"No." Jordan mustered a thin smile. "Your food was delicious as always. It was just something I read—it made me lose my appetite."

But as she walked back to Longren House, stopping frequently to kneel and hug Malachi, she suddenly realized her distress was partially caused by something she *had* read. Something that was even more shocking and horrifying than what she'd just endured.

She had a strong hunch she knew who had killed Michael Seavey after all.

Chapter 20

AFTER leaving Malachi in the care of Jase and Tom, she got into the Prius and headed for the marina. She needed to find Charlotte and ask her some pointed questions, but they would have to wait—she was running late for her appointment with Bob.

On the drive down, she was so distracted by her thoughts that she failed to take in any of the scenery. She *did* manage to avoid plowing through a couple of coach-and-fours, but otherwise, her mind was still focused on what she'd read and learned from Garrett over breakfast.

Michael Seavey had, in all likelihood, been the unconscious man the crew had taken off the *Henrietta Dale* in the first moments after the ship's grounding. So it stood to reason that he'd been transported back to Port Chatham for medical treatment, *and* that he wouldn't have remembered the trip. It also followed that if he had suffered from any sort of concussion, he could have remained unconscious for days. But she didn't believe he'd survived that long.

Before leaving the house, she'd double-checked the date of the newspaper article in the library that Hattie had shown her that first night, the one recounting Seavey's murder. The article had been dated just two days *after* the shipwreck, which in reality worked out to be little more than thirty-six hours after Seavey would have been brought back to town.

The *Henrietta Dale* had run aground late on the night of August 5, 1893, which meant that by the time Seavey reached Port Chatham for treatment, it had to have been the morning of the sixth. Which, in turn, meant that the murderer could have killed Seavey and dumped his body amid the chaos. It wasn't a stretch to believe that his body wouldn't have been noticed until the morning of August 7. The timeline worked.

And it would have been relatively simple to murder him, after all. The killer merely needed to be someone whose presence the rescue workers wouldn't have questioned, who made it a point of being in charge of transporting the unconscious Seavey to a doctor's infirmary. Once he had Seavey out of sight, it would have been easy to shoot him and dump his body under the wharf. All under the cover of darkness, if the killer had waited until that evening.

She pulled up in front of the Wooden Boat Society headquarters and killed the engine. Following a chattering group of tourists inside, she waited impatiently for them to move aside so that she could walk into Bob's office. The sooner she got this call over with, the sooner she could go home and verify her suspicions with Charlotte.

"Sorry I'm late," she said to Bob. "Has your friend called yet?"

"Nope." He looked up from what appeared to be a mock-up of a brochure about the upcoming boat festival. "You're good. When you didn't arrive right on time, I sent him a brief email, asking him to delay his call by fifteen minutes, just in case."

Jordan sat down across from him at the desk. "How do you want this to work? Do you want to put him on speaker, so that we can both talk to him?"

"Why don't we see what his preference is?" Bob replied. "I hear you had another visitor at your house last night."

"Yeah, Clive Walters." She gave him a brief recap. "Darcy and I think he might have murdered Holt and broke into my house looking for the documents, because he was trying to keep Seavey around as a ghost to improve business."

Bob leaned back in his chair, raising both brows. "Really? That's pretty crazy."

"Yeah, I thought so. We won't know for certain until Darcy—" Her cellphone rang, cutting her off. "That's probably her right now. Excuse me."

She stood up and walked a few feet away, pressing the screen with her thumb to answer the call. "Tell me he's our guy," she said without preamble.

"I don't know whether he is or not," Darcy said, sounding tired and exasperated.

"You're kidding me."

"No. The ballistics on the gun match, but he's lawyered up and not talking. Several guests also swear he never left the winetasting event that evening, and they would have no reason to lie for him. So if he slipped out, I can't figure out how or when. And he's definitely *not* confessing to the murder—only to wanting to stop you from getting hold of the documents you needed to solve Seavey's murder. He's claiming I'm protecting you and that *you* killed Holt."

Jordan stared out the window at the neat rows of expensive power boats and yachts in the marina. "So other than the sheer *insanity* of his faulty mental processing," she said slowly, thinking it through, "that means someone else might have planted the gun."

"Tragically, yes. I freaking *hate* this case. As of now, I'm concentrating on Sally as a Person of Interest, because she has the strongest motive. That could evaporate, though, if her ISP verifies that she was using email at the time of Holt's murder." Darcy sighed. "I don't suppose you remember the last time you were in the library?"

"No, not really . . . maybe that morning? I was gone all that afternoon and evening. And the house was wide-open. Anyone could have put the gun there."

"Yeah, you wouldn't want to lock your doors when you leave," Darcy said sarcastically.

"Hey."

"Sorry, I'm a little testy." Jordan heard her fiddle with some papers on her desk. "I can't believe I'm asking this, but can you question the ghosts and see if any of them know anything or saw anything? We could use the information to point us to the right person."

"I can ask, though they disappear with alarming regularity," Jordan replied. "One of these days I'm going to ask them where they go. Not, mind you, that I'm sure I really want to know."

"Well, get back to me as soon as you can, will you? I'm booking Walters on the attempted robbery, but a lawyer will have him back on the streets within hours."

"I'll call you as soon as I know anything." She ended the call. "Sorry about that," she said, turning. "That was Darcy, as I suspected."

"Yes, I heard," Bob said.

She froze midturn.

He held a very, very scary-looking, really, really *big* black gun in his hand. And it was pointed at her.

"But what about the conference call?" she asked stupidly, staring at the hole in the end of the barrel.

"I'm afraid I felt compelled to mislead you," Bob replied gently.

Chapter 21

Fuck." Jordan bent over, trying to control the roaring in her ears. With the thumb of her left hand, she surreptitiously speed-dialed Darcy. "I'm going to pee my pants."

"That's disgusting," Bob said. "Suck it up."

"*You* try having a b-big gun pointed at you," she retorted, feeling both nauseous and faint.

"Shut up." He followed her sidelong glance toward the other room. "And unless you want me to kill all those nice, innocent tourists as well, you won't try to get their attention."

Which was exactly what she'd been thinking. *Shit.* Where was a damn ghost when she needed one? Even Charlotte could have caused some kind of commotion with all the crap lying around his office, and the distraction would have given her a chance to run for it. The front door wasn't that far away.

She straightened gingerly. And focused on the hole in the end of the gun barrel. Again. "Why?"

"Why what?" He kept the gun trained on her as he

leaned over to pick up the wastebasket beside the desk. "You mean, why did I kill Holt? That's simple—he was going to expose my family background."

"But everyone already knows about your great-great-grandfather MacDonough."

"Not *that* ancestor. Sam Garrett."

"*You're* related to Garrett?" She stared at him, utterly confused.

"Good ole Grady married Garrett's sister not too long after Seavey's death. And I knew once you started looking at the marriage records, you'd figure it out. I couldn't have that. Cellphone, in here, now." He gestured with the wastebasket. "I can't have you trying to contact anyone."

Shit, shit, shit. She reached into her back jeans pocket and slowly withdrew it. Hopefully, Darcy was hearing all of this.

"I still don't understand," she said, trying to buy herself time. "What difference does it make if you're related to Sam Garrett? I would think that kind of notoriety would bring people in by the droves to the Wooden Boat Festival."

Bob snorted. "Being the descendant of a master ship's carpenter is *prestigious*. Being related to a mass murderer? Not so much. In case you haven't noticed, there's an economic recession, and people aren't making charitable contributions like they used to. One *whiff* of my being related to a mass murderer, and the contributions to the Wooden Boat Society would have dried up. Not to mention that the festival would have bombed this year. And Holt had plans to hold a *press conference*, the fool."

"You sent out a call?" Michael Seavey asked, materializing beside her. "Why does this man have a gun pointed at you? What have you done now?"

Her knees almost gave out in relief. She splayed a hand out at her side, hoping he understood the signal.

Seavey raised a brow. "Indeed, I never willingly engage in physical violence unless there is sufficient provocation."

"Have you 'called' the others?" she asked, sotto voce.

"I don't recommend calling anyone, unless you want me to shoot you right here and now." Bob gestured with the gun. "Come on, I'm losing patience with your juvenile stall tactics. Give me the damn phone."

She palmed it so that he couldn't see the lit screen and dropped it into the plastic basket. "The least you could do is have a nice hardwood wastebasket," she prattled. "Plastic is so, well, low class—"

"Oh, that's excellent," Seavey said, his eyes rolling around in their sockets. "Increase the ire of the person holding the gun. I'm amazed you've managed to remain alive this long, given your lack of survival instinct."

He had a point.

"I'm not stupid enough to spend money on a goddamn wastebasket, when that money would otherwise go straight into my bank account," Bob said impatiently. Setting down the wastebasket, he said in a more pleasant tone, "Okay, here's what we're going to do: You'll come around behind the desk, and then we'll quietly leave by the back door. If you make any noise, I'll drop you right here with a bullet through your spine. If you try to get anyone's attention, I'll kill you, then shoot them. Got it?"

"Oh, dear. This indeed might be more serious than I first believed," Seavey murmured.

"You think?" Jordan asked.

"I think what?" Bob knit his brow.

"Never mind. Where are you taking me?" She was afraid she already knew the answer.

"You and I are going on a little boat ride. Bodies are much harder to find if they're dumped out in the Inlet."

"He's quite correct in that regard," Seavey said.

"No shit," Jordan snapped. "Are you going to do something, or not?"

"What would you have me do? Try to knock the gun out of his hand? These are very close quarters—you might inadvertently be shot. I believe our best opportunity will occur once we are outside."

"Jesus," Bob snapped. "I just *told* you what I'm going to do. You're fucking crazy! I have a *fucking gun*, and *I'm* calling the shots. Now, *move*."

She rubbed trembling hands against her jeans, then walked around the desk. If she let him put her on the boat, she knew she was a goner.

Taking her upper arm in a painful grip, Bob snugged the gun barrel against her back. "Okay, let's go. Look like we're having a pleasant walk and chat, or you'll be responsible for the deaths of others as well as your own."

He pushed her toward the back door, told her to open it, and then they were outside on the docks. Seavey floated along next to them. Turning her toward a long line of boat slips, Bob said, "Keep going, but not too fast."

"Believe me," she retorted, her mind racing to come up with some sort of strategy, "I'm in no hurry."

"A sense of humor," he replied with a chuckle. "I like

that. In fact, I like *you*, Jordan. It's a damn shame I can't keep you around."

He actually sounded as if he regretted what he was about to do. "So why don't you give it some thought?" she bargained. "I'm willing to keep everything quiet. We can make a deal."

"No, you aren't," he replied, sounding amused. "This whole goddamn town listens to you now. They all think you talk to ghosts, which I know is a bunch of crap. You're just making this stuff up as you go."

Seavey puffed up threateningly. "He believes you are *lying* about us?"

"Call the others," Jordan murmured. "The more chaos, the better."

Seavey shook his head. "I don't want to put Hattie at risk. Or Charlotte, for that matter."

"How would they be at risk? He can't see you." Jordan added for incentive, "He murdered your nephew, you know."

Seavey's expression darkened.

"Oh, that's cute, Jordan." Bob chuckled again, this time digging the gun hard into her side and making her yelp. "Do you really think pretending to talk to ghosts is going to convince me they exist? I'm not that gullible. You must really need a lot of attention to feel good, babe, that's all I can say."

"But what about all that stuff you said about me seeing ghost ships?" she asked.

"I needed to keep tabs on you, that's all."

Unbelievable. She glanced over her shoulder in sheer astonishment. The man was *way* deep into transference, thinking she was vying for the limelight when *he* was the one going to such great lengths to do exactly that. The freaking bane of every psychologist's existence: the client's emotional drive to accuse his therapist of the psychological problems *he* suffered from. And she wasn't even getting paid to deal with this drivel.

But she'd be damned if she'd stand for him accusing her of *making this crap up.* She dug in her heels, slowing them down. "Okay, first of all, I really *do* see ghosts and ghost ships, you asshole. And second, why would I have the need to make any of it up?"

He shoved her to keep her moving forward. "How the hell do I know? Maybe you're new in town and feeling lonely. Maybe you think if you're quirky, Jase will take you to bed sooner. The bottom line? I don't really give a damn. The end result is that your lies and stories convinced enough idiots in this town that you really do talk to ghosts and can solve old murders. So Holt was going to ask you to look into Seavey's murder. And that meant you'd figure out the family connection to Garrett."

"You know," she said crankily, "if you'd just chosen denial over transference, none of this would have happened. You could've ignored the fallout from Holt's press conference, because it was just too horrible to contemplate actually having to murder someone. And really, denial is wonderfully effective. You could have claimed the historical data were wrong—that you weren't actually related to Garrett. People might never have even cared."

"You really *are* a pain in the ass, you know that? I have no clue what the hell you're talking about. Maybe killing you *will* be a pleasure."

"Fits with your family heritage," she snapped.

"I can confirm *that*," Seavey agreed. "Garrett took far too much pleasure from the violence he engaged in."

"You can jump in anytime now," Jordan told him, feeling more than a little desperate to get Bob's gun pointed in a different direction.

"Shut up," Bob growled.

"And I was right," she persisted. "Holt really *did* care more about family than he let on, if he was going to ask me to solve Seavey's murder."

"Yeah, he cared about the extra money he would make if he had a really good story to tell about those old opium tins," Bob scoffed. "Otherwise, they were just rusted crap he'd brought up from some old wreck. I tossed him and the tins back into the water." He jammed the gun into her ribs a second time. "Now *move it*. I've had enough of your stalling."

"Drop the gun, Bob." Darcy moved out from behind the bow on a large sailboat, her gun leveled at him.

Relief rushed through Jordan, and her knees buckled.

But as she crumpled, Bob wrapped an arm around her neck, yanking her against him and pressing the gun barrel against the side of her head. "Stand up, bitch!"

She gasped for air and locked her knees to ease the pressure against her throat.

"Keep your distance, Chief, or she gets it right here."

In her peripheral vision, Jordan saw Charlotte and Hattie materialize.

"He's got a *gun!*" Charlotte screamed, zipping in and out of the moored boats. "Do something, Michael!"

"If I make the wrong move, she could get shot," Michael explained. "We must wait for the right opportunity—"

"And if you don't take action soon," Frank said from behind Jordan and Bob, "she'll die regardless."

"Then I suggest *you* come up with a plan," Seavey retorted mildly. "I don't want Jordan's death or serious injury on my conscience."

"On that we agree," Frank replied. "The current living arrangements are adequate; I don't want them disrupted."

"This is not the time for an argument over the best strategy," Hattie pointed out.

Charlotte hissed, her zipping motions becoming ever more erratic.

"Would someone please just *do* something?" Jordan pleaded.

Bob's laugh sounded ugly. "No one can save you, not your imagined ghosts, not even your cop buddy here. We're getting on that boat."

"*Imagined?*" Hattie asked, her expression turning irritated. "He believes we don't exist?"

"The nerve!" Charlotte hissed.

"Can we focus on what's important here?" Jordan croaked as Bob's arm tightened.

"Yes, why don't we?" Darcy said calmly, her gun never wavering, her expression coldly professional. "This is a death-penalty state, Bob. It's iffy whether the DA will ask for it in Holt's case, but if you kill Jordan, that's seriously premeditated murder *and* kidnapping. Virtually guarantees a lethal injection."

"You've got three seconds to drop *your* gun, Chief." Bob didn't sound the least concerned, which really, really terrified Jordan. "If you don't, your girlfriend dies. And I know how much you like her."

"I can take her or leave her, to tell the truth," Darcy replied mildly. "She's a bit of a hassle."

"Hey," Jordan croaked.

"Well, you are," Darcy replied. "Every time I turn around, I'm getting you out of trouble. Frankly, I'm tired of it." She locked gazes with Jordan for a second and cocked her head slightly to her right, as if she were considering whether she really *was* worth saving.

Jordan slid her eyes to her left and spied Jase and Tom moving in silently from a dock that intersected theirs, keeping low to the ground. She pushed, trying to angle Bob more to her right, to keep them out of sight.

He tightened his arm, cutting off her air. Stars sparked in her peripheral vision. "Quit it." He jammed the barrel harder against her temple, splitting the skin. She felt blood trickle down the side of her face.

"He's hurting her!" Charlotte cried out and zipped around. "*Do* something, Michael!"

Jordan felt Bob stiffen and closed her eyes, realizing she'd just made the possibly fatal mistake of alerting him.

"Join the party, boys," Bob called. "Come on over here, hands raised, unless you want to watch your girlfriend get it."

Jase and Tom straightened, their expressions resigned. Jase sent her a look filled with chagrin, then settled his gaze on Bob with cold determination.

"Real smooth," Darcy told her. "Remind me never to bring you to a shoot-out again."

"Sorry," Jordan croaked.

Bob motioned for the men to join Darcy. "Over there, where I can see you."

"I always knew you were a prick, Bob," Jase said mildly.

"And you're a self-righteous asshole," Bob told him.

"Boys, boys," Darcy scolded, sounding bored, her eyes anything but. "No need to trade insults."

"Really, Jordan," Seavey reproved. "Are any of these humans of use to you at the moment?"

"They might be if you cause enough of a commotion," Jordan retorted. "What good is it to have ghosts around if all you're going to do is comment on the proceedings?"

Jase exchanged looks with Bob and Darcy, it dawning on them that they weren't alone.

"So I'm going to count to three, Chief." Bob sounded surprisingly genial. "And you're going to drop your weapon. One . . . two—"

"Okay, okay, fine." Darcy held her gun up, then lowered it slowly to the dock, never taking her eyes off him.

"Oh, great," Frank said, disgusted. "Law enforcement today must receive little or no training."

"Excellent," Bob told Darcy. "Now, your backup. The one in your left ankle holster?"

"Sure, no problem." Darcy kept both hands outstretched, then reached down with one and hitched up the leg of her jeans. She pulled a small gun out of a hidden holster and placed it next to the other one.

"Kick them into the water," he ordered.

"Good Christ!" Seavey exclaimed "Order her not to comply, Jordan!"

Darcy hesitated, then sighed. "Those guns cost good money, Bob. I don't exactly have the department budget to replace them."

"Shut up. I'm not going to ask you again."

Darcy gave him another quiet look for a couple of beats, then did as she was told.

Jordan closed her eyes. *Think, dammit.* She had to do something that would distract him, that would give the others the opening they needed. But what?

"The marine charts," she said suddenly, opening her eyes.

Everyone looked at her as if she'd lost her mind.

"Who gives a shit about the marine charts?" Bob asked.

"I do," Jordan insisted. "You didn't go out to Holt's to retrieve marine charts—you went out there to try to find the documents Holt had discovered at the hotel. Right?"

"Who the fuck cares?" Bob started dragging her backward down the docks, his gun trained on the others.

"I care, dammit," she gasped, bringing both her hands up to claw his arm where it pressed against her windpipe. "If I'm going to die, I want my friends to make certain Hattie and Michael Seavey know the truth about the shipwreck."

"You found out something important?" Hattie asked.

"Not now, my dear," Seavey said.

Charlotte hissed and flew over Bob's head, missing by mere inches.

Jase's expression had turned more frantic. Tom was looking from Jordan to Darcy, waiting for some kind of signal.

"No one cares about your lies, got it, Jordan?" Bob grunted. "Christ. If I didn't need you to get me off this dock right now, I'd shoot you and dump you into the water. *Normal* people freeze in terror and behave. But no, you can't quit mouthing off—"

Jordan took as deep a breath as she dared, then closing her eyes and praying, she let her knees fall out from under her, throwing her weight to the side.

Bob started swearing. Charlotte swooped down, knocking the gun partially out of his hand.

A loud *boom* echoed right next to Jordan's ear, and Darcy started to fall. Seavey closed in, grasping the gun and struggling with Bob, who started screaming, not understanding what was happening.

Darcy fired as she went down. The bullet went through Seavey, hitting Bob, who fell on Jordan, pancaking her against the wooden timbers, his weight squashing the air out of her lungs. She wheezed, her vision blurring, her fingernails scrabbling for purchase on the wood as she struggled to crawl out from under him.

Bob's weight was suddenly gone and Jase was holding her tight, his arms banded in a vise around her. "Don't you know *any* self-defense moves?" he growled into her hair.

"No," she said, holding onto him just as tightly, "but I'll let you teach me some."

"A little warning would have been nice," Darcy groused, holding her arm, blood flowing freely between her fingers.

Tom dropped to the dock beside her. "How bad is it?" he asked urgently, pulling her fingers away from her arm. "Let me see."

"I don't fucking believe it!" Darcy snarled, ignoring Tom and keeping the gun pointed at Bob, who was lying facedown on the dock, moaning and gurgling oddly. "You got me shot *two times in one month?*"

"I think that was Charlotte," Jordan sniffed, reluctant to leave Jase's arms.

Charlotte huffed. "I *saved* you!"

"You certainly did," Jordan agreed, giving her a weak smile over his shoulder.

"Well done, Seavey," Frank said grudgingly, having pulled Hattie to safety.

Seavey made an elaborate show of dusting off his suit coat. "A life of crime *can* come in handy at times, can it not?"

Jase pulled Jordan well away from Bob, then retrieved Darcy's cuffs. He walked back over to Bob, kicking his gun into the water, then knelt to flip him over and cuff him. Tom was on the phone, calling 911.

"You carry *three* guns?" Jordan asked, faintly incredulous.

"Middle of my back," Darcy replied, standing as two more patrol cars and an ambulance drove into the marina parking lot, sirens blaring. "Son of a bitch is still alive, more's the pity. You complaining about me being armed to the teeth?"

"No." Jordan shuddered.

"Don't *ever* do this again," Jase said fiercely, coming back to hold her. "My heart fucking *stopped*."

"But I didn't do anything," she protested, her voice muffled against his chest. She was fairly certain she didn't want to quit holding onto him, either. Any time this millennium. "I had an appointment for a conference call. I had no idea."

"Fine. Just don't 'not do anything' ever again. Got it?"

"Shook us up real good, babe," Tom said from beside Darcy. "When Jase got your call..." He paused and shrugged. "I've never seen such a laid-back guy move so fast."

"So I called *you*?" Jordan asked, finally easing back. "I thought I called Darcy."

"When you didn't respond and I heard Bob's voice in the background," Jase explained, moving her out of the way of the medics who needed to get to Bob, "I borrowed Tom's cell and called Darcy."

"How'd you find me?" Jordan asked. "GPS tracking of the cell signal?"

Darcy rolled her eyes. "You've *really* got to quit watching crime shows. Small towns don't have that kind of capability. I knew about your meeting with Bob this morning and put it together. My guys were at an accident out on Highway 20, so I told Jase and Tom to back me up."

She turned to the medics, who were starting to work on Bob. "He's got a sucking chest wound. You two would be doing the world a favor if you didn't try all that hard to revive him."

"Tsk tsk." One of the medics winked at her without pausing. "So bloodthirsty. I had no idea, and I don't mind telling you, I find that pretty hot."

Jordan let her head fall against Jase's shoulder and waved a limp hand. "I really *do* need to pee now."

Chapter 22

JASE drove Jordan's Prius home because she was shaking too badly to be trusted behind the wheel. At her insistence, he and Tom then left her in the care of the ghosts and went back to nailing siding onto the library wall. Amanda had hip-hop blaring on a boom box in the backyard while she weeded. Occasionally, Tom fired up what Jordan assumed from the deafening, grinding roar could only be the sawsall. The cacophony sounded eerily, blessedly normal.

She sat in the kitchen with everyone around her—Hattie and Charlotte at the table, Frank in his usual place, leaning against the counter behind her, and Michael Seavey standing nearby. Malachi lay at her feet where she could reach down and rub his stomach while she sipped the chamomile tea Charlotte had made for her.

Seavey brought out a cigar, preparing to light it. She glared at him, and to her surprise, he slid it back into his suit coat pocket.

"Pray, explain to us once again the ludicrous reason this man tried to kill you," he ordered.

"He thought I was going to expose a part of his past—the fact that he was related to Sam Garrett," she said. "He had a reputation to uphold as the president of the Wooden Boat Society, and he was desperately afraid unsavory details would come out that would cost him his position or harm the charitable contributions to the society. Evidently, the board of governors gets together once a year and determines his salary based on his fund-raising efforts."

"And Garrett refused to tell you who he had seen shoot this great-great-nephew of mine, because the man was a family member of his?" Seavey asked.

"That's my supposition, yes." Jordan took a sip of tea, which felt wonderfully soothing on her sore throat. She'd have marks where Bob's arm had pressed against her neck for days to come, a fact that had put a grim look in Jase's eyes.

"Charlotte, I need to ask you more questions about the night of the shipwreck, if you don't mind."

"Are we back to that?" Frank asked, exasperated.

"Yes," Jordan replied, determined. "By doing some more reading, and from having another chat with Garrett, I've figured out that Garrett was the one who lured the *Henrietta Dale* onto the beach that night. Captain Williams then contacted him, I believe, on the seventh, and told him about the hidden compartments and the opium. The two of them returned to the ship to salvage as much as they could."

She turned to Seavey. "I was always bothered by

Williams's claim that he was so devastated by losing the *Henrietta Dale* that he retired from service. After all, he'd only sailed her for a few hours when she went down. I know now that it was a smoke screen. He didn't want anyone figuring out what he and Garrett were up to, and he also didn't want anyone suspicious about where he got the funds to retire."

Seavey scowled. "I hired Williams because I knew he had the . . . traits, shall we say, to do whatever I asked of him. Nevertheless, I am surprised he turned against me so quickly."

"I suspect he transferred any loyalties he had for you once he found out about your murder—he probably approached Garrett *after* Eleanor's article appeared in the newspaper. What continued to puzzle me, though, was that Garrett swore that he didn't murder you." Jordan shifted in her chair, uneasy at the thought that Garrett might still be lurking somewhere nearby. "In fact, he's been threatening me to make certain I told you so."

Seavey scowled. "That's unacceptable—I will look into it."

"No!" Jordan and Hattie said it at the same time.

"I don't think it's necessary," Jordan added. "He said he'd leave me alone as long as I did as he wished."

"And I don't like you taking any chances, Michael," Hattie said. "Unless, of course, there's simply no other way to ensure Jordan's safety."

"I don't believe I'm in any danger at this point," Jordan assured her.

Charlotte spoke up. "I don't understand. If Garrett didn't kill Michael, who did?"

"Eleanor Canby," Jordan said.

Charlotte and Hattie both gasped, but Seavey nodded thoughtfully. "Of course. Because of Jesse's death on board the *Henrietta Dale*."

"The only other possibility would have been the Customs inspector, Yardley. But unless he found the bodies of his men, he wouldn't have had any real proof. Whereas Eleanor had the reality of her son's death," Jordan explained.

"I read portions of her memoir this morning, and she clearly held Michael personally responsible for Jesse's death." Jordan looked at Charlotte. "Didn't you tell me that her reporters were milling around during the rescue that night?" At Charlotte's nod, she continued, "Do you remember *who* was transporting the stretchers of the three wounded men to Willoughby's clinic? And I'm assuming they *were* sent to Willoughby's?"

Charlotte frowned. "Now that you say that, I believe only two stretchers were loaded onto the wagon and sent to Dr. Willoughby's. Eleanor was directing that effort, because of her close connection to the doctor."

"And it would have been easy to simply have Seavey's stretcher carried farther down the waterfront, to a location where someone wouldn't pay it any heed."

"Dear God, *yes*." Charlotte sent Seavey a chagrined look. "I was so upset, I simply wasn't paying any attention."

"No one would have expected you to," Seavey replied gently.

"On that part of the waterfront during those years, all kinds of crimes were commonplace," Jordan pointed out.

"If, under the cover of darkness, Eleanor had paid some-one to put a bullet in you and dump you under the wharf, no one would have intervened or come forward to talk to the authorities about what they saw. You were just an-other unsolved murder on the waterfront.

"Eleanor would've felt she needed to report on your murder, because to *not* do so would have raised suspicion. But there were no follow-up newspaper articles, because there was no investigation. The police had nothing to go on. Your body was discovered the next morning, when one of her reporters wrote and submitted the story, which Eleanor probably reviewed and edited, just to make cer-tain it said what she needed it to say."

"I had no idea that Eleanor was capable of such vio-lence," Hattie said quietly.

"She probably wasn't until Jesse's death pushed her over the edge," Jordan told her. "Charlotte, you said Eleanor was hysterical on the docks when she discovered that Jesse wasn't among the survivors, correct?"

"Yes, she was inconsolable," Charlotte said, her expres-sion distant as she remembered. "Two of her reporters had to drag her aside at one point, because she was screaming at Captain Williams, demanding to know why he hadn't done more to save his passengers."

"I suspect she slipped into a sort of fugue state at that point, then ordered that one of her reporters get rid of Seavey," Jordan surmised. "My bet is that if you asked her a week later about it, she would have no memory of the incident. I could try to hunt down personal papers or memoirs by her staff, to try to verify my speculations—"

"There's no need," Seavey interrupted. "Indeed, I find it perfectly plausible that Eleanor murdered me."

"All of this—both present and past—is a result of the actions you took back then," Frank told him.

"Frank!" Hattie gasped. "That's not fair!"

He shrugged. "Perhaps not. But Seavey was engaged in illegal activities that drew Port Chatham's less desirable elements. His decision to hire Garrett as his partner, in particular, was fateful."

Michael frowned pensively, then sighed. "I'm afraid I can't argue with that reasoning."

Jordan studied his demeanor, growing concerned. "I think we all make decisions during our lives that lead to unintended consequences," she pointed out. "I doubt you had any reason to believe that Garrett would be so callous. He was part of a fire crew aboard a steamer when you met him, right?" When he reluctantly nodded, she continued. "Therefore, you would have had no reason to believe that he was a cold-blooded murderer."

Seavey's expression remained troubled. "Still, my judgment was faulty."

Jordan shivered. "Believe me, there seems to be a lot of that going around."

Chapter 23

LATE that afternoon, Jordan sat on her porch swing, drinking a glass of wine and reading escapist fiction. For the moment, she'd had all the memoirs, diaries, murder, and mayhem she could take. The guys had left for the day, a peaceful silence descending in their wake. She was debating whether she could handle going to the pub, given that everyone would want a full explanation of the day's events. For now, she was enjoying her solitude.

"Thought I'd find you hiding out here." Darcy's voice pulled her out of a particularly racy sex scene that had her remembering what it had felt like to be held by Jase.

Darcy's right arm was bandaged and in a sling. Jordan had called the hospital earlier to check on her and had been told she'd suffered a flesh wound and would be released after treatment. Looking more than a little worn around the edges, Darcy climbed onto the porch and sat down next to her.

Jordan handed Darcy her wineglass, which she accepted

gratefully, draining half of it in one gulp before handing it back. "You doing okay?" she asked.

Jordan nodded. "Feels a little unreal, if you want to know the truth. Like it happened to someone else. But then I get pulled into the story I'm reading, and I relax, and a flash of what it felt like to have the gun held to my head takes me by surprise."

Darcy stretched out her legs. "Flashbacks. You're going to have those for a while." She let out a huge yawn. "Bob's out of surgery. He'll be transported to a prison hospital as soon as he can be moved. I got him to admit he offered to take Holt out to the spit, then murdered him. My guys are executing search warrants on Bob's house and boat. And as I predicted, Clive is out on bail, awaiting trial on the attempted robbery charge." She gave Jordan an apologetic look. "Unless you decide to file assault charges for him shoving you down the steps at Holt's place, he's probably going to get probation."

Jordan frowned. "Michael Seavey won't be happy about that—he thought he was rid of him."

Darcy grinned again, then sobered. "You came damn close today."

"I'm choosing to be in denial over that for a while longer. I don't think I'm ready to face it quite yet." Jordan turned, bracing herself in the corner of the swing so she could face Darcy. "Get this: The jerk thought I was making up all the stuff abut the ghosts. That I was telling stories and using historical documents to embellish them, in a bid to gain attention, and to convince Jase to take me to bed. Unbelievable!"

Darcy grinned. "So since some asshole murderer accuses you of dreaming up the ghosts, you're finally willing to admit to yourself that they are real? I like it—it's just twisted enough thinking to really appeal. We cops are rather fond of dark humor."

"Oh, shut up," Jordan grumbled.

"The whole bit about Jase, though—that's just crazy," Darcy continued. "All you have to do is go knock on his door, and he'll be glad to drag you off to bed. He would've done that weeks ago, if you'd been ready."

Jordan gave her an exasperated look.

"He took tonight off," Darcy offered. "So he'll be home."

Jordan glared.

"Go over there and jump his bones," her friend ordered. "Don't force me to deliver you to his doorstep at gunpoint."

Jordan sighed. "He *is* pretty damn wonderful, isn't he?"

"You even have to ask?"

* * *

IT took her an hour to shower and dry her hair, then convince Hattie and Charlotte that she could dress for the occasion on her own. Charlotte was adamant, of course, that she had no clue how to present herself to a beau. Jordan pointed out that if she did anything out of the ordinary, Jase would see right through it—that he expected her to simply be who she was.

Which was an outfit of stylish jeans, light makeup, and a comfortable pale blue cotton sweater that was reasonably flattering to her figure. Still, as she stood on his porch, staring at the doorbell, she realized she was nervous.

Rubbing damp palms against her jeans, she ignored the bell and raised a fist to pound on the solid wood door. And dropped her fist back to her side. Then raised it again.

The door swung open, and Jase stood in front of her, backlit by the chandelier in his front hall. He wore a faded blue Henley, jeans so old they were white at the pressure points, and his feet were bare. His eyes, for the first time since she'd met him, held shadows.

In that instant, she knew she was making the right decision. She smiled, feeling the trembling of her lips.

He studied her face silently for a long moment, and then a look of utter peace came into his eyes that she'd never seen up until now.

Opening the door wide, he held out his hand.